D0069266

BE
MINE
FOREVER

BOOKS BY D.K. HOOD

D.K. HOOD

BE MINE FOREVER

bookouture

Published by Bookouture in 2021

An imprint of Storyfire Ltd.
Carmelite House
50 Victoria Embankment
London EC4Y 0DZ

www.bookouture.com

ISBN: 978-1-83888-855-8
eBook ISBN: 978-1-83888-854-1

This book is dedicated to all the people who work tirelessly through troubled times to keep us safe.

PROLOGUE

Black Rock Falls

Saturday

Fear gripped Laurie Turner in a rush of panic, and wrapping her coat around her, she hastened her step along Stanton Road. Night dropped like a curtain, plunging her into darkness in the middle of nowhere. A storm rumbled in the distance and the first splashes of rain brushed her cheeks. As thunder rolled across the midnight sky, the forest, so beautiful during the day, had become a threatening menace. Within the intermittent flashes of lightning, shadows moved through the trees like faceless men in long black coats.

She dashed on into the night stumbling on the uneven sidewalk. The cut-through to Ravens Way was only a few more yards away. As the ground shook and lightning zig-zagged the sky, she glanced over one shoulder at the empty street. Not a soul was out in the storm, not a single vehicle rode the blacktop. But was she alone? Consumed by the creepy second sense that someone was behind her, she turned into the dark alleyway and hustled along. With each step, tree branches reached out with long witch-like fingers to drag her into the murky depths. An unfamiliar noise came close by and she stopped mid-stride to listen but the only sound came from the wind rushing down the alleyway. A gust whipped up the fall leaves and they swirled around her, mixed with twigs and dirt.

Ahead, she made out the dim glow of streetlights and hurried on. Panic had her by the throat as footsteps sounded on the gravel. Was someone behind her, hidden in the dark? Heart pounding, she took off at a run, burst onto the sidewalk, and headed in the direction of her home. She slowed at the corner and glanced behind her once more at the empty road. As she turned back, the headlights of a vehicle blinded her as it rounded the corner and slowed beside her. Nerves at breaking point, she grasped her backpack to use as a weapon and then sighed with relief at the sight of a familiar face.

"Wanna ride?"

Looking all around, she fumbled with the door handle and then climbed inside. "I'm sure glad to see you. My car wouldn't start and I dropped my phone so I had to walk." She fastened her seatbelt and leaned back, closing her eyes. "It's kinda spooky tonight with the storm and all."

"Uh-huh." He turned up a tune on the radio and accelerated at speed.

As he flew past her turn, and headed back to Stanton, she swallowed hard. Where was he taking her? Unease crawled up her spine. "I live out of Ravens Way."

"Uh-huh." His eyes remained fixed on the road. "I saw a deer in the forest a ways back, I wanna go see if it's dead." He stopped the vehicle and pointed into the trees. "Over there."

As thunder rolled and rain splattered the windshield, she turned to stare into the dark forest. "I can't see anything."

"Surprise." A singsong voice came from the back seat.

The next instant, a band slid around Laurie's neck and tightened with force, dragging her up and back in the seat. Pinned by the seatbelt and helpless, Laurie grabbed at her throat, and fighting for one precious breath of air, opened her mouth in a silent scream. A wad of cloth hit her tongue and filled her mouth with a rancid taste and then someone dragged her hands away; she couldn't fight.

Heart bursting, pain shot through her head and as her sight moved in and out of focus, she heard a deranged giggle. As the next flash of lightning filled the interior, she stared into the contorted grinning face of pure evil.

CHAPTER ONE

Sunday

"He's perfect—maybe too perfect." Sheriff Jenna Alton had been scrolling through the applications for a new deputy and had finally found someone suitable. "Well, I asked you all to help me find a suitable deputy and out of the six applicants, this one sure looks interesting. Who found Zac Rio?"

"I asked him to apply." Shane Wolfe smiled at her. "I'm glad he did."

Jenna lifted her gaze to her good friend and Black Rock Falls Medical Examiner, Shane Wolfe. "How did you find him?"

She eyed her friend across the outdoor table she'd set up for a Sunday cookout with her friends. It was a beautiful fall day and they'd spent a relaxing time enjoying each other's company. Dr. Shane Wolfe was a man wearing many hats. As handler for Deputy Dave Kane an off the grid special forces sniper, he had contacts that went to the Oval Office. The proud Texan, who resembled a Viking marauder, was a widower father of three girls. His daughters and his role of medical examiner over three counties in Montana kept him busy.

"Well, it was Julie." Wolfe was referring to his daughter. "She met a couple of new kids at the school who mentioned their brother was a LAPD detective. He's been working as a teacher's aide at the high school. Hardly a fitting occupation for a man with his skill set. I checked him out, introduced myself, and asked him if he'd be interested in applying." Wolfe smiled at her and sipped his beer.

"He'd fit in your team just fine and you have that big house with separate accommodation for a housekeeper or nanny sitting empty."

Jenna peered at the image of the young man, Zac Rio: twenty-five, six-three, dark curly hair and with skills far beyond what she required in a deputy. She shook her head. "I'm not sure. He has a ton of degrees. How did he do all that by twenty-five?" She handed the iPad to Dave Kane, her second in command and close friend. "What do you think, Dave? He sounds too good to be true and he's overqualified for the job. Why would someone like that want to live in Black Rock Falls?"

"The background check on him revealed a few more details." Kane shrugged. "He's the genuine article. Maybe he wants to rest his mind. I can't imagine what it would be like to have a memory like his or his IQ. He would have been a child prodigy if someone had recognized his intelligence. He finished a law degree but didn't sit the bar exam because of problems at home but by that time he had a few other degrees under his belt. He joined the LAPD and made detective but after his parents died in a plane crash, things went downhill fast family wise. So, he decided to care for the sixteen-year-old twins, one of each by the names of Cade, and Piper. They were pretty wild and he needed to get them settled in a different environment." He scratched his cheek and then met Jenna's eyes. "A contender for my job, huh? He's also a sharpshooter."

"Never." Jenna laughed. "His hobbies are everything and anything to do with media. He'd be an asset at crime scenes and be able to handle the dreaded media releases."

"That doesn't explain why he wanted to leave the sunshine and come here. California is a big state, with plenty of room to move around." Deputy Jake Rowley handed his wife Sandy a plate of food from the grill and dropped into a chair.

"The kids were staying with their grandma." Wolfe leaned back and crossed his legs at the ankles. "Well, step-grandma and they'd never gotten along with her. They started getting into trouble at school." He frowned. "It often happens after a tragedy; kids feel lost and take their aggression out on everyone. Zac tried keeping them in the big smoke but it didn't work out. He figured a complete break and a new start in a backwoods town would straighten them out. He's been here a month now."

"In Black Rock Falls?" Kane pressed two fingers to his forehead. "Does he know about this town's reputation?"

"He does now." Wolfe shrugged. "I've spoken to him and he'd welcome the challenge. He figures he can keep his siblings safe."

"We've had an influx of twins of late." Sandy, Rowley's wife, passed a bowl of salad to her husband. "This will make three sets of new twins in town, all around the same age and all fraternal. Susie Hartwig at Aunt Betty's mentioned it yesterday."

"Rio sounds interesting." Suddenly starving, Jenna piled food on her plate. "Do you think he'll cope? It's nothing like Los Angeles."

"Yeah, I do. He'll prefer the slower pace and there's plenty for him to do around here on his downtime. We have great schools and he can get involved with the local drama society. I hear he writes plays and directs as well." Wolfe glanced around as his daughters emerged from Jenna's ranch house.

Surprised, Jenna stared at him. "So, he's a man of many talents? I like that he has a cultured background."

"Are you saying we're not cultured?" Kane grinned at her and raised a glass of pinot noir in a toast. "I figure we're doing okay. Look at Julie, she's had her artwork displayed in the town hall. Can't get more cultured than that."

Jenna chuckled. "I didn't mean to suggest y'all aren't cultured. Now getting back to discussing a new deputy, I want this to be a team decision, and if you all agree, then we'll take him."

"We need the help and he's solid." Kane helped himself to a steak and added the trimmings. "And we do have a spare SUV cruiser just sitting in the parking lot."

"It's a yes, from me." Rowley grinned. "I'll be glad to show him around."

"Great. I'll contact him later." Jenna looked up as Emily, Wolfe's eldest and a fine ME in the making, sat down at the table along with sixteen-year-old Julie and Anna, the baby of the family. She looked at the girls. "Grab some food before it gets cold."

She'd barely finished her meal when the 911 ringtone sounded on her phone. She pushed to her feet and walked away from the table, heading to the house to take notes if necessary. As she climbed the steps, she accepted the call. "911, what is your emergency?"

"My daughter is missing." The man sounded frantic and his voice quivered as he spoke. *"She went to cheerleader practice last night and wasn't in her bed this morning. I figured she'd left early and I'd missed her but she's not answering her phone."*

Jenna walked inside the house and heard footsteps behind her, Kane had followed her and dashed past her to the kitchen, his boots clattering on the wooden floor. As she walked through the door, he had a pen and notebook waiting for her on the table. She put the phone on speaker. "Okay, I'll need to take down some details. Who am I speaking to?"

"Dr. Bob Turner out of Ravens Way." His breath was coming fast as if he'd been running. *"My daughter is Laurie, Laurie Turner."*

Jenna sat down and placed the phone on the table. "Okay Dr. Turner, you're speaking with Sheriff Alton. I'll need your full details and Laurie's. How old is she?"

"Sixteen." Turner gave his details. *"I've been calling her friends and nobody has seen her since she left practice at the school gym last night."*

The all too familiar shiver of uneasiness slipped down Jenna's spine and she exchanged a meaningful look with Kane. "Okay, and what time was this?"

"Around nine, nine-thirty last night." Turner heaved a long sigh. *"I didn't notice her missing until this morning. I called her phone and it's not responding. I went out to hunt her down this morning in case she'd slipped out before I woke. I went to Aunt Betty's Café and then I checked around town again but I couldn't find her."*

With her mind running down her list of the necessary procedures in a missing person's case, Jenna stared into space for a beat. "Does she own a vehicle?"

"Yeah, but that's not here either." Dr. Turner sounded frantic. *"No one has seen it and it's distinctive, it's a 1950 Ford pickup, and painted fire-engine-red."*

Jenna made notes. "Okay, we can put out a BOLO for the truck. Does she have a boyfriend she might be with?"

"Nope, she broke up with a boy by the name of Wyatt Cooper a couple of weeks ago. I called him and he hasn't spoken with her since."

It had been such a relaxing Sunday. Jenna stared at Kane and his face was grim. She gave herself a mental shake. "Okay, Dr. Turner. I'm on my way." She disconnected and pushed the phone into her pocket.

"I'll go grab my jacket and weapon." Kane hurried from the house.

"What's happened?" Wolfe came into the room loaded up with dirty plates.

Jenna explained. "We'll head out now. Sorry to ruin the cookout."

"We all had a relaxing afternoon. It was great!" Wolfe smiled at her. "Don't worry about anything. I'll explain what's happened to the others and get these in the dishwasher. I'll be sure to set the alarm before we leave."

Relieved, Jenna smiled at him. "Thanks, Shane. I'd appreciate it."

"I'll tend the horses to save you time when you get home." Rowley appeared at the kitchen door, carrying plates of food. "Sandy will store the leftovers in the refrigerator."

Grateful for such wonderful friends, Jenna squeezed his arm. "Thanks, Jake."

She rushed to her room to collect her duty belt and sheriff's department jacket. Giving her friends a wave, she hurried out the door as Kane drove up in his black unmarked truck, affectionately known as the Beast. Climbing inside, she fastened her seatbelt and entered the address into the GPS. A thought came to her. "Just how many glasses of wine have you had, Dave?"

"One." Kane gave her a long stare. "Have you ever known me to drink more than two glasses of wine, like ever?"

Jenna shook her head as they headed out the gate and hit the blacktop. "No, can't say that I have. Why is that?"

"Living in Black Rock Falls is a delight as well as a curse." Kane flicked her a glance. "I'm never sure what's going to happen in any given hour, and I like to be clear-headed and ready for anything."

CHAPTER TWO

Still damp after a late storm the previous night, the lowlands and mountain vistas surrounding Jenna's ranch appeared to have received a new coat of paint. Dressed in an artist's palette of fall colors, they sparkled under the late afternoon sun and gave off a fresh aroma. It had been good to see rain after a dry spell had muted the lush green landscape, although the storm had been loud. She had discovered apart from the fear of the vet and baths, Duke, Kane's bloodhound, had added loud storms to his repertoire of fear. Her enjoyable Saturday evening with Kane watching movies had been disturbed by howls loud enough to wake the dead. The noise had sent her black cat, Pumpkin, climbing the drapes and hissing like a leaky furnace. When Kane, finding it amusing, had howled along with his dog, it had taken her forever to untangle Pumpkin and calm her down.

Such were the changes in personality happening to Dave Kane of late. After his wife had died in a car bombing, he'd withdrawn into himself but as the years slipped by, he'd slowly come to terms with his loss. He was still the same, lean, mean fighting machine, ex-special forces sniper, who'd arrived in town some years ago but somehow now, he laughed more and seemed to be living his life to the full. It was as if a great weight had been lifted from his shoulders and seeing him happy made her smile. They'd taken the first tentative steps toward a relationship but the decision to keep it strictly private had been unanimous. Being sheriff had responsibilities and if things didn't work out between them, they'd remain friends and no one would be the wiser.

They headed into the town of Black Rock Falls, Jenna's gaze moved over the crowd of people making repairs to the rain-soaked Fall Festival banners. As Kane slowed the Beast to negotiate the people spilling onto Main, Jenna waved back at the cheery greetings of the townsfolk, who'd voted for her to protect them for an extended five-year term. The festival ran from Tuesday through Saturday and was a much-anticipated tourist attraction. Apart from the popular white-water rapids, and hiking or riding in the forest, this year the town was hosting the chainsaw wood carving championships at the showgrounds, an art competition in the town hall, and a farmer's market in the parklands. All this along with the normal street vendors and performers who swarmed to the festivals throughout the year, left Jenna hoping the violent crime side of her profession would slip into obscurity.

She glanced at Kane. "I'll call the media as soon as we've spoken to Dr. Turner. I'm going to need people to man the hotline phones."

"Yeah, Maggie and Walters might be able to do the first shift." Kane looked over at her. "We could have the calls diverted to our phones for the night shift and sort out better arrangements for the morning?"

Jenna considered asking their secretary, Magnolia Brewster, or Maggie, as everyone called her, and the semi-retired deputy Walters to do a Sunday shift and sighed. "Yeah, Rowley's had a few beers, he'll be okay for the morning. I'm glad Sandy can drive him home. Although, the way she's expanding, she won't be able to fit behind the wheel for much longer. She is what? Only five months or so by now?"

"She might be having twins." Kane shrugged. "Although, they went for an ultrasound last week and Rowley hasn't mentioned anything."

Jenna smiled. "Yes, Sandy is playing her cards close to the vest. Most new moms can't wait to show off the images."

"I guess they want to keep things private." Kane winked at her. "Sometimes it's for the best."

"Oh, absolutely." Jenna scanned the GPS. "Ravens Way lies parallel to Stanton. I call this the creepy part of town. I wouldn't go near those alleyways after dark. I wonder why there are no streetlights on this stretch of Stanton?"

"I guess the town council hasn't caught up with the growth of the town." Kane turned right and then instructed by the GPS, took the first left. "There are streetlights here. It's a newer area." He pulled up outside a brick house with a white picket fence. "This must be the place."

Jenna led the way through the gate and along the driveway. She knocked on the door and it flew open straight away. She stared at the disheveled man, his eyes wild and with his comb over hair hanging over one ear. "Dr. Turner?"

"Yes, that's me." Turner scowled at her, obviously agitated. "What took you so long?"

Ignoring the smell of alcohol on his breath, Jenna lowered her voice and used a calming tone. "My ranch is out on the other side of town and I had visitors. I left the moment you called. May we come inside and talk to you?"

"I guess." Turner eyed Kane suspiciously.

Jenna followed his gaze. She had to admit, dressed all in black, with his Stetson pulled down low over his eyes and wearing his weapon on one hip like a gunslinger, Kane at six-five and over two hundred and fifty pounds of muscle, didn't resemble a law officer. "Ah, this is Deputy Kane."

"Okay, come in but you should be out looking for Laurie." Turner walked down a short passageway and into a family room. "Someone might have kidnapped her."

"Why would someone want to kidnap her? Has anyone contacted you?" Kane pulled out a notebook and pen.

"No, no one has called." Turner's eyes flashed with anger. "I'd tell you if they had."

"Is there any chance she just ran away? Have you had any arguments lately?" Kane was pushing the man hard.

"Only the usual things." Turner sat on a sofa and held his head in his hands, staring at the floral carpet. "She's only had her driver's license for a few months and she drives way too fast. I should never have given her the Ford for her birthday. She could be lying in a ditch somewhere."

The poor man was beside himself with worry and Jenna exchanged a look and a shake of the head with Kane to make him back off a little. "Do you have a photograph of Laurie we could use?"

"Yeah." Turner stood and took a framed picture of a girl standing beside an old red Ford pickup from the mantle. He looked at it for a beat and then handed it to Jenna. "I took this on her birthday."

Jenna took out her phone and used her camera to capture the image. "Is this her vehicle? Was she driving last night?"

"Yeah." Turner sighed. "It's not a long drive to the school from here." He attempted to correct his hair, running his fingers through the oily strands. "As there was no game on this week, the cheerleaders decided to practice. They use the school gym and usually finish around eight-thirty or nine at the latest."

"How come you didn't notice she hadn't come home?" Kane lifted his head from his notes. "She should have been here by at least ten."

"I fell asleep in front of the TV." Turner couldn't sit still and rocked back and forth. "I've fallen asleep before and she usually leaves me here. I'm bad-tempered when woken sudden."

"I see." Kane dropped his gaze back to the notebook. "Do you like a few drinks before bedtime?"

"Yeah, I've taken to drinking more than I should since my wife left me." Turner avoided meeting Jenna's eyes. "But I'm stone cold sober now."

"Okay." Jenna leaned forward. "So, what time did you notice she was missing?" She frowned. "It was a little after three when you called me."

"I figured she'd gone out before I came down for breakfast." Turner looked at her, his eyes red-rimmed. "I called her to bring home milk and she didn't pick up. I've been calling all day. Then I called her friends."

"What time was this?" Kane sat, pen raised, looking at him.

"Around eleven." Turner picked up a cushion and held it to his chest, squeezing it. "When I called her friends, no one had seen her since she left the school. One of the girls mentioned she sometimes hangs out at Aunt Betty's Café so I went there and asked the manager if she'd seen her. The nice woman took me to the back room to show me the CCTV footage and there was no sign of Laurie. It's as if she's vanished."

"It would be hard to hide a 1950 red Ford pickup." Kane raised both eyebrows. "Maybe she went to visit her mom?"

"We don't know where she is living." Turner clasped his hands in front of him. "I came home from work and Jeanette was gone, no note. She cleaned out our bank account and vanished. That was six years ago. I obtained full custody of Laurie and since then, we haven't heard a word from her."

"You didn't report her as a missing person?" Kane's gaze hardened. "Aren't you worried about her safety?"

"No! She's not missing." Turner became agitated. "She told me if I didn't quit drinking, she'd leave me and never contact me again. She took her clothes, her car, and our money." He glared at Kane. "I'd say she's just fine."

"Did you hit her?" Kane's face showed no sign of emotion. "Or your daughter?"

"I don't remember much when I drink." Turner started to rock again. "But she was always complaining I did this or that."

"I see." Kane gave him a long, considering stare. "Is there anything you need to tell us about, Dr. Turner? You're a psychologist and still practicing, so I assume your wife never had you charged with abuse?"

"She wouldn't dare." Dr. Turner gave a smug smile. "The court ruled her as an unfit mother and if anything happened to me, Laurie would be placed in foster care. She wouldn't want that, now would she?"

"I guess we'll have to find her and ask her." Kane turned his attention to Jenna. "Laurie could have broken down along the highway. Maybe we should head out to the high school and retrace her steps?"

"Yeah." Jenna nodded. "Would you mind if we take a look at her room? Does she have a laptop?"

"Okay but her bed hasn't been slept in." Turner stood. "She changed the linen yesterday and it's in the wash. Her room is as neat as a pin."

How convenient. Jenna frowned. "So, the laptop then, it gives us a better idea of who she's in contact with on social media." She forced her lips into a small, calming smile. "You sit down and direct me to her room."

"Up the stairs, first on the left." Turner dropped onto the chair. "Take whatever you want."

Jenna stood. "Thank you. I'll need permission from you in writing to check her phone records as well. Deputy Kane will give you some paperwork to sign. I'll need you to complete a missing person's report and sign a brief statement about your circumstances. Including the fact you don't have contact with your wife or know her whereabouts."

"Is all this necessary, Sheriff?"

Jenna wanted to roll her eyes at his lack of cooperation. "What information you give us now, means we can concentrate on finding Laurie rather than chasing down people who are no longer involved in her life."

"Oh, very well." Dr. Turner's nostrils flared with a snort of anger. "Give me the paperwork."

She headed up the stairs and found the room. It was spotless. She checked through the bedside drawers and found photographs of cheerleaders, with Laurie front and center, but no journal. She slid the laptop into an evidence bag and was heading back down the stairs when she noticed the bolt on the inside of the door. Taking out her phone, she took a few images of the door and room before hurrying downstairs.

As she walked into the family room, she tucked the laptop under one arm and turned to Dr. Turner. "Before we go, I'll need the contact details of her ex-boyfriend and does she have a best friend? If so, I'll need her details as well." She looked at the distraught man and handed him her card. "If you hear from her call me. I'll be contacting the media and putting out a BOLO on the pickup. As soon as we have any news, I'll call you. Just sit tight, Dr. Turner. We'll do our very best to locate your daughter."

They climbed into the Beast, and Jenna looked at Kane. "This is going to go two ways, if we can't find the truck, I figure she's run away or heard from her mom and went to see her. If the truck shows up then something has happened to her because from the look in her eyes in that picture, the truck means one hell of a lot to her. She wouldn't leave it behind."

"My gut tells me something's not right." Kane stared at the house.

Jenna held out her phone toward him to show him the image of the bedroom. "She has a heavy-duty bolt on her bedroom door."

"If he was violent, I'm not surprised." Kane snorted. "I can't tolerate men who hit women."

Jenna clicked in her seatbelt. "What's your take on him? His mood changed from distraught to angry like flipping a switch and it's always a red flag when a person won't look you in the eyes, right?"

"Yeah and I'm seeing a ton of reasons why a kid would want to get out of a situation like that. Her father drinks and beats on his wife and maybe her as well." Kane rubbed his chin thoughtfully. "Giving a decked-out hotrod to a sixteen-year-old, when he just admitted his wife cleaned him out, seems a little overindulgent." He sighed. "Most parents start out with a safe but less expensive choice. It seems like a pay-off to me. Nothing he said is sitting well with me right now."

Concerned, Jenna turned in her seat toward him. "I figure he might be involved but if so, why call us and report her missing?"

"It's not unusual for someone involved in a crime to try to insert himself into an investigation, it's all part of the thrill. They usually believe they have an iron-clad alibi. He's already pulled the blackout card as an excuse for his behavior." Kane started the engine. "Say he fell asleep in front of the TV at ten, he'd be sober in the morning and it would be unlikely she wouldn't wake him on her way out. That pickup would be loud when it started." He turned onto Stanton and headed toward the high school. "If he did do something to her last night, he's had all night to hide her body and make the necessary calls. Contacting us could just be part of his plan."

CHAPTER THREE

In normal circumstances, Jenna would have search and rescue out as soon as a missing person's report was filed, especially in the case of a sixteen-year-old, but something wasn't sitting right with her. Before they organized a search party, she had to confirm the girl was missing. Establishing a timeline and identifying the last person to see Laurie, was following procedure. They would need to know where to concentrate the search. Of course, once the media release hit the news, townsfolk would come forward and with the help of the forest wardens, and search and rescue, they'd be scouring the forest and surrounds in well-organized teams.

Jenna contacted Maggie and Walters to take the hotline calls. With everything set, she could focus on the investigation. She leaned back in her seat and looked at Kane. "I'll hold off with a search until we check with the boyfriend and best friend. If things weren't so good at home, Laurie's friends might be covering for her. We should split the questioning; the girlfriend is more likely to confide in me and the boyfriend in you."

"Maybe." Kane drove into the high school parking lot. "Well, look what we have here."

Jenna couldn't miss the fire-engine-red hotrod pickup sparkling as if it had just emerged from the carwash. "Oh, it's going to be a shame to dust that for prints."

She peered inside as Kane pulled up beside it, then slid out and took a better look. "Empty. How do you get into this thing, there's no lock on this side?"

"They open on the passenger side. Why is it here?" Kane climbed out his truck and walked to her side, snapping on surgical gloves. "The doors are locked, and she must have the keys, so what happened to prevent her driving it home?" He went to the hood and pushed his fingers inside the grill. "Ah, got it." The hood popped and he lifted it and peered inside. "Sabotaged." He pointed into the engine. "Someone pulled off the battery cable."

Jenna walked around the pickup. "So, she'd slide out the passenger side and then lock the door?"

"Yeah." Kane smiled at her. "Way back then, having to unlock your door with the traffic flying past was a safety issue, so they slid across the bench seat and out the passenger side. The roads were narrower those days as well."

Something crunched under Jenna's boots and she bent down. "There are pieces of a phone down here and the battery is by the back tire. I'd say she dropped her phone and it smashed." She straightened and walked back and forth. "Nothing else, she must have taken the case with her."

"Not something she'd do if she was in trouble." Kane stood, hands on hips, staring at the pickup. "So, we can assume she got a ride with a friend or walked. It's only a mile or so from here to her home." He headed back to the Beast and collected a forensics kit. "I'll dust for prints."

Jenna watched, not really surprised when the vehicle came up clean. "Hmm, that's not good. The car was disabled and wiped clean." She frowned. "So, she was set up; we need to know who delayed her so she couldn't get help from one of the other cheerleaders."

"This isn't looking good, Jenna." Kane removed his gloves. "There could be any number of girls and boys in a cheerleading squad and then you can add parents, friends, family members. This is getting out of hand already." He looked out over the parking lot. "She's been missing for hours. If she'd smashed her phone, it would be normal for her to go home or failing that to a friend's house to stay overnight. As none of her friends have seen her and we don't know if she's in contact with her mom, we have to assume she's in trouble."

Jenna thought for a few seconds. "Okay, we go see the girlfriend and find out what she knows. She'll be able to tell us the name of the captain of the cheerleading squad. Next we go see her and ask her to contact everyone who she can remember was at practice and ask them to return to the gym at six." She pulled out her phone. "I'll contact the principal and ask him to open up the hall." She made the call as she walked back to the Beast.

"That sounds like a plan." Kane climbed behind the wheel and added the coordinates into the GPS. "The girlfriend lives five minutes from here."

Vicky Perez lived in a very picturesque wooden ranch house at the end of a long driveway on Pine. Jenna inhaled the scent of flowers and admired the overflowing garden beds on each side of the porch. The neat, well cared for home was nestled among pine trees and seemed to blend in with its surroundings. She went alone to the front door and knocked. When a middle-aged woman opened the door and stared at her with one hand over her mouth, Jenna moved quickly to reassure her. "Mrs. Perez? There's nothing for you to worry about, I've come to speak to Vicky about Laurie Turner."

"Bob called this morning looking for Laurie, has something happened to her?" Mrs. Perez waved Jenna inside. "Come in, I'll get Vicky for you."

Jenna followed her into a clean kitchen. "We're trying to locate Laurie. She didn't go home last night."

"Oh, that's not good." Mrs. Perez went out and stood at the bottom of the stairs. "Vicky, come down to the kitchen now, the sheriff wants to speak to you about Laurie."

A girl appeared at once and came down the stairs at speed. She was dark-haired and exceptionally beautiful. Jenna smiled at her. "Do you recall what happened last night after practice?"

"Yeah, we collected our stuff and left as usual." Vicky frowned. "I went over this before with Laurie's dad. You do know he's the school counselor, don't you? He grilled me like I'd done something wrong."

Taken aback, Jenna blinked. "Really? He didn't mention anything to me at all. Can you just think back to when you last saw Laurie, what she was wearing, who she was with, and what she was doing?"

"We wear our old uniforms for practice. A whole bunch of us walked out to the parking lot and she went to her pickup." Vicky twirled a strand of hair around her fingers. "There was this almighty clap of thunder and someone bumped into her and she dropped her phone. It smashed."

Wanting to know who had delayed Laurie, Jenna raised both eyebrows in question. "Who bumped into her?"

"I didn't see, there was a crowd of us all walking together. One of the girls I think but I'm not sure. Laurie was really upset her dad would find out and then Becky suggested she take it to Cory, he's the maintenance guy and cleans the gym after practice. He's real good at fixing things, especially phones. So, she went off to speak to him. Becky went to chase after Wyatt Cooper and then we all went home."

Jenna took out her notebook and pen and took down the names. "So, what's Becky's last name and Cory's too?"

"Becky Powell and Cory Hughes." Vicky's eyebrows met in a frown again. "Becky shouldn't be chasing after Laurie's boyfriend, they only just had a fight, I don't think it's over. He was there watching her at practice like always." She sighed. "Although, everyone knows she likes Cory, she's always drooling over him."

Ignoring the statement, Jenna nodded. "Did you see her talking at length with anyone else at all that night?"

"Yeah a few people." Vicky thought for a few minutes. "We went to the refreshments kiosk for a drink, and she chatted to Dale. He was working behind the counter. He's on the football team but his aunt owns the kiosk and opens it for us during practice. Marlene was there too, Marlene Moore, she's on the cheerleading squad. She is always hanging around Dale. He's the quarterback, so everyone wants to be his date at the prom."

Jenna was having a hard time keeping up with the teenager's personal life. "Including Laurie?"

"Including everyone." Vicky grinned. "But he plays it real cool."

"I see." Jenna wanted to roll her eyes. "Can you tell me the name of the captain of the cheerleading squad?"

"I am." Vicky smiled.

Jenna heaved a sigh of relief, at least this part of the investigation was easy. "I'll need you to call the squad and everyone you can remember was at practice last night. Tell them the sheriff wants them at the gym at six tonight. Laurie is missing and we need to find out her movements. We found her pickup in the school parking lot so she must have taken a ride with someone."

"She wouldn't take a ride with someone she didn't know." Vicky lifted her chin. "She's smart, not stupid. I've been calling everyone all day and no one has seen her since last night. Are you sure her father hasn't locked her in the cellar? He threatens her all the time. He tells everyone he doesn't know where her mom is but she's still working at the beauty parlor in town. He told her if she tries to take Laurie away from him again, he'll kill her."

Jenna stared at the girl. "You heard him threaten her?"

"No, but everyone says so." Vicky's brown eyes widened. "What if he's killed Laurie?"

"Don't talk nonsense. He's a fine student counselor and I've never heard a bad word against him." Mrs. Perez shook her finger at her daughter. "You can't believe everything you hear."

Jenna held up her hand to prevent an argument. "Do you happen to know Mrs. Turner's phone number or where we can find her?"

"Yes. I know her number by heart, we were at school together." Mrs. Perez rattled off the number.

Jenna entered it into her phone. "Has anyone called her?"

"Not that I'm aware." Mrs. Perez frowned. "It would be too far for Laurie to walk alone at night. She lives in town."

Jenna punched in the number. "I'll call her now." She walked down the hallway and went outside.

The phone rang several times before a woman answered. "This is Sheriff Alton, am I speaking with Jeanette Turner?"

"Yes, this is she."

Not wanting to alarm the woman, Jenna kept her questions general. "Could you tell me when you last spoke to Laurie?"

"She called me last Thursday to chat about the Fall Festival, they're having a parade and she wants me to come by. Why? Is she in trouble? It's that damn pickup, isn't it? Has she had an accident?"

Taking a deep breath, Jenna kept her voice calm and professional. "Not that I'm aware. I'm trying to locate her is all, she didn't go home last night. She isn't in trouble with the law, Mrs. Turner. If she calls or drops by could you let me know please?"

"Yes, I'll call her, she always answers my calls."

Concern for Laurie washed over Jenna. This wasn't the news she needed right now. "Thank you." She disconnected and walked back into the house and made her way to the kitchen. "Jeanette hasn't heard from her either."

"Okay. Vicky, pick up your phone and we'll split the list and get everyone back to the gym." Mrs. Perez grabbed the landline and looked at Jenna. "We're used to calling everyone to make plans. I'll make sure they're all there."

Relieved, Jenna smiled at her. "I really appreciate your help, thank you." She handed her a card. "Here are my contact details, call me if you hear anything, anything at all no matter how insignificant."

"Okay." Mrs. Perez pulled out a notebook from a kitchen drawer. "Come on, Vicky, start dialing."

Jenna headed for the door. "I'll see myself out."

She moved swiftly along the hallway and outside to Kane's truck. After explaining, she leaned back in her seat. "The boyfriend may still be in the picture. We'll go see him next and I'll get out a media release and see if anyone has seen Laurie."

"It would be unusual for a girl of her age with so many friends, on foot, not to contact someone. I mean, she could have dropped by here and called her mom, they are obviously on good terms. Even if she didn't want to go home one of the friends from her inner circle would have seen her." Kane turned the truck around and headed back to Stanton. "I guess we should speak to the boyfriend but I have a very bad feeling about this, Jenna. If she was attacked on the street, the chances of finding her alive are slim. I figure we conduct a search along Stanton, like you said no streetlights. Anyone could have dragged her into the forest and no one would've heard or seen a thing."

CHAPTER FOUR

"You'll never amount to anything." His ma's voice shattered his thoughts. "You're a waste of my time. The sooner you leave school and go work with your pa the better. I'll be glad to see the back of you."

"I'm sorry I don't earn more, Ma." He looked at her curled lip. "I'm doing the best I can. Dad doesn't have a position for me yet. When he does, I'll move out."

"And leave me here with nothing to live on?" His ma shook her finger at him. "You're just like him, he don't care if I live or die."

He couldn't win. Nothing he said pleased her. "I'll still look after you, Ma, but right now I have to go do something before dark." He turned to leave.

"That's right, leave me alone again." She moved toward him, fists clenched. "If you were still little, I'd lock you in the closet to teach you some respect."

He backed away from her, remembering the terror of the dark smelly hole in the wall. He'd learned enough "respect" to last a lifetime. "I do respect you, Ma. I'll be back soon and we'll watch TV."

"Liar! You're going to see her again, aren't you?" She spat at him. "You're just like your father, a no good, useless SOB."

It was pointless arguing with her. When she looked at him, she saw a replica of the man who'd cheated on her and set up house with a bottle blonde. He headed for the door, he hated living here. The day his pa had walked out he'd made it clear he had no room for him in his new life but he'd promised him a position in his business even though he'd be expected to start at the bottom and work his way up. Of late, he'd started helping his pa, driving over on Sundays to do yard work, and dropping by each morning at his business to show his enthusiasm. He had to get away. Anything would be better than living with his ma.

He walked through the trees and along a track that led to the old barn and smiled at the sight of a friendly face. She was his everything and they had plans to move in together but first they needed to find a place for Laurie Turner. He walked to her and they kissed. "I've been looking forward to coming here all day."

"Yeah, me too." She linked her arm through his. "It was fun last night. I want to do it again."

They strolled together to the old barn and he pulled out a key for the padlock. "Me too."

It had been a rush watching her strangle Laurie and bringing the girl here to their secret place. Sitting her up to watch them make out had stirred something feral inside him. It was like a hunger he couldn't satisfy and he wanted more. "We'll take her out and dump her, I know a ton of places to hide her."

The smell of death greeted him as he opened the barn door wide. Propped up against the wall, Laurie's expressionless eyes stared at them in the gloom. Her skin was blue and her legs stuck out from beneath her, the flesh bruised as if she'd been sitting in blood. Beside him he felt a tremble go through his girl. "She don't look so pretty now, huh?"

"Seeing her here in our special place makes me mad." His girlfriend scowled at him. "She'll stink up the trunk."

He shook his head. "No, she won't. Remember last summer I painted the kitchen for Ma? I took a box of plastic sheets from outside the general store. I have tons more stashed in here. We'll wrap her up and dump her."

"Look what I have." She grinned and opened her purse to reveal a pile of surgical gloves. "We'll take everything, her clothes and shoes, and when we're done dumping her, we'll burn them and the plastic sheet. We don't want anyone tracing her back to us because I'm not done yet." She walked into the barn and stared at Laurie's body. "I'm not done with her either. Look at the way she's looking at me—she thinks she's all that." She turned and a determined look crossed her face. "I want to do a whole set of them. We'll go down in history as the Cheerleader Killers." She snorted with a sudden burst of laughter and then stopped and frowned. "We'll need to be smart because I'm not planning on going to jail."

"Don't worry your pretty head about that." He slid his arm around her shoulder and admired their first kill. "We're way too smart for the cops to pin it on us. We'll dump her backpack in the forest and they'll never look for her out at the mines." He squeezed her. "There'll be nothing left of her here, I have the perfect place to burn everything."

CHAPTER FIVE

Jenna and Kane drove slowly along Stanton from the high school to the alleyway, in the direction Laurie would have taken on foot. Jenna peered into the forest. She'd buzzed the windows wide open to pick up any smells. With Duke sitting in the back seat, any scent of death usually caused a reaction and the bloodhound had sat motionless the entire time. "We'll need a search party for this to work."

"If Laurie was the victim of a thrill kill, it's unlikely the killer would have dragged her very deep into the forest." Kane flicked her a glance. "He'd have attacked, made her walk into the forest, killed her, and then walked away. So, if she's dead, I figure her body will be on the edge somewhere."

Jenna pushed the hair from her eyes. "Yeah, unless she got a ride with someone." She threw her hands into the air. "Why is it that as soon as we have a festival in town something happens?" She stared at the blacktop. "If someone's harmed this girl, we have a thousand tourists to consider as well. It will be like searching for a needle in a haystack."

"Let's hope she's just holed up at a friend's house and we can go home and eat leftovers." Kane flashed her a smile. "Or we'll have to be forced to stop by Aunt Betty's for supper before we head out to the meeting. As Rowley tended the horses and I have food in the truck for Duke, there's no reason to go home before the meeting."

Jenna snorted. "How come you always find an excuse to drop by Aunt Betty's Café? No matter in the middle of a murder case or after an autopsy, it's the same."

"A man has to eat to keep up his strength." Kane chuckled. "So, we can go out hunting and fishing to feed our families."

"That's what stores are for." Jenna yawned. "I often wonder how you'd survive without Aunt Betty's Café."

"Oh, I'd survive." Kane accelerated along Stanton. "Have you seen the size of the steaks at Antlers Tavern?"

As they drove to Wyatt Cooper's house, Jenna called Rowley to bring him up to speed and followed it with a quick call to Wolfe. As a team, she liked to keep everyone in the loop. When the Beast stopped beside a small cabin-style home, she checked the address and shrugged. "This is the place. I hope Wyatt Cooper is at home. You take the lead and I'll hang back." She slipped from the seat and headed up the garden path. "He might talk to you man to man." The rank smell of burning came in a cloud of smoke from the backyard.

"I doubt it." Kane's nostrils flared. "To him I'm still a cop."

Jenna knocked on the door and a man in his fifties, wearing a plaid shirt and jeans, stared at them open-mouthed. "Sheriff? Anything wrong? Is it about the smoke?"

"Nah." Kane tipped his hat. "Mr. Cooper? We'd like a word with Wyatt."

"Sure, sure, come in." Mr. Cooper turned and walked inside. "He's out back burning trash. I'll go get him." He headed through the house. "Wait here."

Jenna hung back as a lean muscular young man of about sixteen came walking into the hallway smelling of smoke. He ignored her completely and looked up at Kane.

"Where did you play football, man?" Wyatt grinned at Kane.

"College is all." Kane smiled back and took a relaxed pose; being non-threatening gave him an advantage. "I figure you know why we're here?"

Jenna bit back a smile. A typical ploy to make a person believe they knew he was involved in something. She waited expectantly for Wyatt to speak.

"Nope, I have no idea why you or the sheriff are here." Wyatt looked at her. "Ma'am— and why do you want to speak to me on a Sunday afternoon?"

"I hear you broke up with Laurie?" Kane's voice lowered as he leaned conspiratorially toward him. "Did you have a fight?"

"Ah, I know what this is all about." Wyatt jerked his head back. "Her father called asking me if I'd seen her last night. I told him, yeah, I'd seen her break her phone but she'd hightailed it inside to speak to Cory before I could say anything. I told her dad just that and he hung up on me."

"So, you knew she was upset and didn't wait for her in the parking lot?" Kane kept his voice at the same level. "With everyone gone, didn't you worry about her out there all alone at night?"

"Look, man, she's been hanging around Cory since he started working at the school." Wyatt sighed. "He's a loser, smokes dope, and is way too old for her. I made a stand, you know, him or me. She just ignored me and walked away. So, why would I hang out waiting for her in the parking lot? I went to Aunt Betty's, grabbed a burger, and came home."

"What time was that?" Kane had adopted his bored expression.

"He was here at ten." Mr. Cooper poked his head out of a door. "My wife had gone to bed and I waited up for him. We watched the news together. Why do you need to know?"

"Laurie didn't make it home last night." Kane straightened. "Any idea where she might be?"

"Nope. Her dad didn't mention anything about her not getting home." Wyatt dragged a hand through his hair and stared into space.

"He should have called last night and me and the boys would've gone out looking for her. Her truck is hard to miss."

"Her truck is still in the parking lot." Kane was regarding him closely.

"Holy shit!" Wyatt moved around restlessly, eyes darting in every direction. "Have you called Vicky? She isn't that far away and Laurie would walk there if she'd had car trouble."

"Yeah, we've spoken to Vicky." Kane folded his arms across his chest. "What makes you think she had car trouble?"

"Well, it makes sense, if her precious pickup is in the parking lot then she must have walked home. She couldn't call anyone for help, could she?" Wyatt shrugged. "I doubt she'd wait back for Cory to finish work and get a ride with him either. His sister hates her and there'd be hell to pay if she discovered Cory gave Laurie a ride."

"His sister?" Kane took out his notebook and pen. "No one mentioned he had a sister."

"Yeah, she's on the cheerleader squad. Her name is Verna, Verna Hughes." Wyatt rubbed the back of his neck. "Cory has to clean up and lock the gym after the practice sessions but his sister doesn't hang around, she grabs a ride or drives her ma's vehicle."

"Who else was there watching?" Kane made notes.

"The usual crowd, some of the football team, Cory of course, Stan Williams the photographer guy, and Dale Collins was running the kiosk as usual." Wyatt dashed a hand through his hair. "Darn, I can't remember everyone."

The phone in the house rang and moments later, Mr. Cooper came into the hallway.

"Ah, excuse me, folks, but that was Vicky, she wants everyone who was at the gym last night to return at six." Mr. Cooper's eyebrows met in a frown. "Something about Laurie going missing. You're to call any friends you can remember being there."

"Sure thing, Dad." Wyatt looked back at Kane. "I'd better go. You'll be at the gym tonight?"

"Yeah." Kane folded his notebook and pushed it into his pocket. "We'll see you there."

Jenna turned and headed out the door. As they reached the Beast, she peered at Kane over the hood. "Do you think he's involved?"

"Hard to tell." Kane opened the door and slid behind the wheel.

Jenna climbed in, rubbed Duke's ears, and settled in her seat. "He seemed a little jumpy to me."

"Yeah, well he obviously still has feelings for Laurie and being interviewed by law enforcement is upsetting for most people." Kane started the engine. "He did seem concerned for her wellbeing, which is a plus but if we find her murdered then all bets are off."

Jenna pulled out her phone. "I guess it's time for a media release. She seems to have vanished without a trace."

CHAPTER SIX

The news about Laurie's disappearance hit the media and although no calls came in about Laurie's whereabouts, as usual the townsfolk stepped up to join the search parties. For now, the local search and rescue had taken charge until Jenna had the time to get her people organized. As daylight was fading, any treks into the forest would be postponed at nightfall and resumed at daybreak. Kane sat opposite Jenna in Aunt Betty's Café as she organized a command center and called in deputies from surrounding counties to assist in a door-to-door search of the area from the school to Laurie's home. She worked with confidence, as unfortunately organizing searches had become a fact of life in Black Rock Falls. Being part of a forest had its advantages: they could always rely on the forest wardens for assistance and of course, their close friend Native American Atohi Blackhawk had already called to offer his help.

Kane glanced at his watch. They had an hour before they had to head to the meeting at the school gym and he'd insisted on eating before a long night of investigating ahead of them. He'd noticed how Jenna skipped meals during a crisis, something that seemed trivial but with the pressure of work and long hours, grabbing a meal was as important as breathing. No one could concentrate or make important decisions without eating. This was why he appreciated Aunt Betty's Café, it served great food, was open from six in the morning to way past eleven at night, and was rarely without a stream of customers but members of the sheriff's department could dash in for takeout or a meal and be served without delay.

He took in Jenna's strained expression as she made the calls. His fingers itched to reach across the table, squeeze her hand, and take her worries away. He smiled when she placed her phone on the table. "I don't have to ask if everything is organized. You have this."

"I'm just glad Webber is still a badge-holding deputy. He offered to man the command post this evening. Rowley will take over in the morning. We'll be directing the boots on the ground first thing until the new shift of deputies arrive." Jenna rubbed her temples. "Cory Hughes is going to be opening the gym tonight. If he has Laurie's phone, I want it. He might have been the last person to have seen her alive."

"Or have her holed up somewhere." Kane sipped his coffee. "It was a great idea to get all the potential witnesses together in one place. It will save a ton of grunt work."

"We need more deputies." Jenna let out a long sigh. "I'm always calling in assistance from Blackwater."

"It was lucky Webber was available." Kane leaned back in his chair. "He usually goes fishing on Sundays."

Colt Webber had interned for Wolfe at the ME's office but had recently become his forensics assistant. He was still on the payroll as a deputy and stood in for them in times of need. Kane nodded. "Ah, the food is on its way." He scanned her face. "Please eat something. I worry about you."

The food arrived and they thanked the server and Kane caught Jenna giving him a puzzled look. "What?"

"Why are you coming over all protective again?" Jenna nibbled on one of her fries. "Part of me likes knowing you care but then I worry it will become a problem when we're on the job—like when you first arrived." She raised her gaze to him. "Or next thing, you'll be calling me ma'am again."

Trying hard not to react by grinning, Kane cut into the prime ribeye and sighed. "I'll always have your back, Jenna. That won't ever change." He looked up at her. "Would I take a bullet for you? You betcha." He chuckled. "That's not being overprotective, that's just doing my job."

"Okay. You win." Jenna sighed wearily. "Time is ticking by, let's eat."

After finishing their meal, Kane dropped a pile of bills on the table and then followed Jenna from the café. They would be at the gym early and it would give them time to get organized. They'd stopped by the office and collected a ton of business cards to hand out and had copies of Laurie's image to show around. When they arrived at the school, the parking lot was surprisingly full and he parked outside the front of the gym. "It looks like we have a big turnout. I guess they watched the news."

"Yeah." Jenna gathered her things. "I hope someone has information or this is a complete waste of time." She glanced around. "She could be out there somewhere alone and hurt."

Kane turned to her. "You've had people searching for her from the moment we confirmed she was missing. There's not much more we could have done. It would have helped if her father had notified us early this morning rather than waiting until three before calling. You know as well as I do, if someone has abducted her, the chances of finding her alive after so long are slim. It's close to twenty-four hours now since anyone has seen her."

"Yeah, every hour that goes by makes it less likely we'll find her alive." Jenna climbed out and collected a pile of notebooks from the back seat. "Although at sixteen, she could be holed up somewhere so there's still hope."

Kane slid out from behind the wheel and unclipped Duke's harness. He made sure he always secured his dog in his vehicle. He often drove at speed and in an accident if a dog weighing one hundred pounds went flying through a windshield it could be lethal for both his loved pet and anyone unfortunate enough to collide with him. Clipping Duke's harness into the seat restraint took no time at all. He hated seeing dogs standing unrestrained in the back of pickups, as if their owners had no care about their pets or others using the highways. He rubbed the dog's ears. "I know it's been a long day, but we'll be heading home soon."

"At least he can sleep when he wants to, we're not so lucky." Jenna handed him a pile of handouts. "We'll need to get the names of everyone here tonight."

"Sure." Kane took the papers and they headed inside.

The brightly lit hall was filled with people all sitting on lines of plastic chairs as if waiting for a town meeting. The place had the usual school gym smell, slightly sour with a touch of eau de old socks, and books. He had expected a crowd milling around but to his surprise, Emily greeted him at the door and Shane Wolfe and his daughter Julie were close by. "Hi, Emily, did you organize all this?"

"Me?" Emily chuckled. "I helped but it was Dad's idea. He even convinced them to open the kiosk for refreshments when you've finished talking to them. As soon as people started arriving, he had them pulling out chairs from the storeroom and setting them out in lines. Julie helped me take down the details of everyone coming through the door. We thought it would save time?" She handed Jenna two notebooks. "I'll wait by the door in case anyone else comes by."

"I can't thank you enough." Jenna gave her a hug. "The place is crowded, surely not everyone here is from the cheerleader practice?"

"I'm afraid not." Emily indicated to a news crew. "They did a live broadcast from outside the hall and showed Laurie's red pickup.

After that tons of people arrived. We've divided the ones who were here to the right of the hall, the sightseers to the left." She shrugged. "That was Julie's idea, so you could ask questions directly to them."

Kane looked at Jenna and raised one eyebrow. "So, if everyone's here, who is out searching?"

"I have it under control. Search and rescue have over one hundred volunteers out looking for her." Jenna straightened. "This is where we'll find the answer to what happened to her and be able to focus the search in the right direction." She glanced at him. "I hate standing up in front of a crowd, it's worse than during my last election." She headed toward the podium.

Kane fell into step beside her. "These are your people. They're waiting for instructions— you'll be fine."

CHAPTER SEVEN

After wrapping Laurie Turner in plastic, they'd heaved her into the back seat, and covered her with a blanket. She'd been heavier than he'd expected and sweat beaded on his brow and trickled down his back from the exertion. His girl had fashioned aprons from the plastic sheets and they'd wrapped them around their bodies. He'd seen enough cop shows to know about leaving evidence behind. All set, they'd driven through town far away from the search parties and headed out to the old mines. As long shadows crept in around them, he drove slowly to the place they'd chosen to dump Laurie's body. The excitement he'd had when his girl had strangled her had ebbed. This part of the plan wasn't thrilling at all. "We have to make it fast. Did you see the news? The sheriff expects everyone who was at the cheerleading practice to be at the gym by six."

"I know. You look bored." She curled a strand of hair around her finger and one hand rested on his thigh. "You figure once they're dead they're no fun anymore?"

He pulled up beside an old mine entrance and as he turned his vehicle around, the headlights picked up the cloud of dust they'd left in their wake. "Kinda." He shrugged.

"Help me drag her out." She climbed out, looking strange in the blue surgical gloves with a plastic sheet wrapped around her jeans.

An awful smell seeped out of the bundle as they dragged Laurie to the mine entrance. Inside, the passageway to the shaft was dark and foreboding. A "keep out" sign blocked the way. They dropped her on the ground and pulled at the plastic to unwrap her, spilling her naked body onto the barren soil. He swallowed hard. Laurie looked up at him with a blank expression, deathly white. Blue had replaced her once pink lips and her healthy glow had turned into a mask. He needed to get away.

"Look at her. She's still staring at me." His girl aimed a kick at the body. "Stop looking at me, Laurie. You can't have him, he's mine."

"Hey." He tried to comfort her. "She's dead. Let's go."

Without warning, his girl pulled a screwdriver from her boot and threw herself on the body. He turned away unable to look at her. Seeing her kill had been exciting, thrilling but this made him sick to his stomach. *What is wrong with me?*

"Why isn't she bleeding?" His girlfriend looked over her shoulder at him breathing heavily. "I want to see her bleed."

He took her arm and eased her to her feet, unwrapped her fingers from the screwdriver, and tossed it down the mineshaft. "She's dead. She can't bleed when her heart's not beating. Help me clean up here and we'll head to the school before we're missed. We'll need to stop by the park and get washed up."

After collecting the plastic and wrapping their aprons and gloves into a big ball, they carried it to the trunk. He'd burn everything later. He drove the vehicle fifty yards from the body and they ran back. They dragged dead branches over the ground to remove footprints and tire marks. By the time they reached their ride, his girl had calmed down some but she still had a sour expression.

As he drove back to town, he glanced at her. "What's wrong? It felt good killing her, didn't it? You taught her a lesson."

"I don't feel anything. It wasn't good enough. The next one, I'm gonna mess up real bad." She folded her arms across her chest. "You know I love you, right? So, maybe you can take her to a house I found in town, like a date and then 'surprise', I'll be there waiting for her. I want her to know that I'm better than she is and that you chose me over her. I want her alive and suffering, so the last thing she sees is me with you. Strangling Laurie was too fast, it didn't last long enough."

The wild look in her eyes and the way she talked aroused him. His heart raced. Excitement tingled through him, he wet his lips. Watching her kill Laurie had turned his girl into a superhero. He worshiped her. She had said she loved him and it made him feel wanted. Not even his ma had done that. If it made his girl happy, he would walk through fire to see her kill again. He slid one arm over her shoulder and pulled her closer. She smelled like Laurie, slightly putrid, but the memory of her strangling her for him made him smile. "Yeah, make her suffer." He rubbed his chin on her hair. "They all deserve to suffer."

CHAPTER EIGHT

The hall fell silent as Jenna moved in front of the lectern. She noticed the media jump into action and suddenly felt exposed. Her life as DEA Agent Avril Parker was long gone, but the vulnerability that even plastic surgery couldn't erase, surfaced the moment she stood in front of a camera. Two things she couldn't change were her voice and her eyes, and the idea of being discovered hiding in plain sight in Black Rock Falls was never far from her mind. The Cartel she'd messed with, even though all had been reported dead, had fingers that stretched out in all directions.

It would be the same for Dave; although he was officially dead and had remained off the grid, his past life had come back to haunt him. It would seem no matter how hard they tried to remain hidden, the threat was a constant nagging ache. She glanced at him standing straight beside her, her rock, and then cleared her throat. "It's good to see everyone here. First, I need to know if anything unusual happened to Laurie during practice. Did she argue with anyone?" No hands went up. "Okay, next I need to know who was with Laurie Turner in the parking lot after practice."

A show of hands shot up. "Okay. I want you to stand against the wall. Deputy Kane will take statements from you but before you go—did any of you return to the gym with her after she dropped her phone?"

She waited but no one raised their hands. "Okay. Did anyone speak to Laurie when she returned to the hall?"

"Yeah." A man wearing jeans and a faded T-shirt pushed to his feet. "I spoke to her."

A buzz of conversation went around the hall. Jenna nodded. The man had to be Cory Hughes, the school maintenance man and cleaner who Vicky had mentioned earlier.

"Okay, I'll need to speak to you as soon as I've finished here." She looked back at the people in the hall. "Was there anyone hanging around or touching Laurie's pickup when you left the parking lot?"

Not one person put up their hand but people had already started to stare suspiciously at Hughes. Jenna waited for people to stop talking and looked over the crowd. People were still filtering in the door and Emily was taking names. "Okay, did anyone see Laurie between nine and nine-thirty last night?'

"I did." An elderly woman wearing spectacles gave Jenna a wave.

Jenna smiled at her to encourage her. "Will you come and speak to me, please?" She looked around the room. "Anyone else see her or hear anything unusual in the vicinity of Stanton Road between the school and Ravens Hill?"

No one stepped forward. Disappointed, Jenna heaved a sigh. "Okay, I'm looking for volunteers for search parties starting at daybreak and going through until we find her. Please report to the command center outside the sheriff's department. The search parties will need to be changed during the day, so we'll be starting at staggered times, six and twelve. Anyone willing to help with getting out supplies to the volunteers during the day, coffee, water, sandwiches, and the like, it will be greatly appreciated."

A group of young men waved at her and she pointed to one of them. "Yes?"

"We have trail bikes and can help get supplies out to the search parties." He smiled. "I'm Levi Jones. Who do I see?"

"Come see me." Susie Hartwig from Aunt Betty's Café pushed to her feet. "I'll see you get what you need."

To Jenna's surprise, Mayor Petersham stepped out from the back of the hall. He nodded to Jenna. "Evening, Sheriff. The town council will pick up the tab for supplies. Just send the bill to my office, Susie."

"At cost then." Susie frowned. "I'm not planning on making a profit over someone's misfortune."

"We all know how much Aunt Betty's Café contributes to the community." Mayor Petersham smiled broadly. "Don't we, folks?"

After the applause had died down, Jenna nodded toward the kiosk. "The kiosk is now open for refreshments. Thank you for coming. I'll see some of you at first light."

As Jenna stepped down to speak to Cory Hughes, a skinny woman with a cameraman right behind her burst into Jenna's personal space and stuck a microphone in her face. Surprised, she took a step back and looked at her without saying a word.

"Deni Crawford, *Blackwater News*. Tell me, Sheriff Alton, how did you win another term as sheriff?" Crawford leaned in, spewing bad breath like rotting fish. "You don't seem to be coping with the crime in Black Rock Falls, it's like murder central over here."

Wanting to cover her nose, Jenna moved back again but the woman followed her, relentless and rude. She straightened. "I'm not sure what you mean. We have a missing girl, not a murder. In fact, the last murder to occur in Black Rock Falls was almost a year ago. If I recall three murders occurred over summer in Blackwater, not here. That's your town, not mine. My county covers many thousands of miles and yes, we do have criminals using our vast forests to hide off the grid but, my goodness, how would you cope in the big city? Just a minute." She scrolled through her phone. "As an example, twenty-five people were shot and twelve killed in one day in Chicago this week. Hmm, it makes Black Rock Falls kind of tame don't you think?" She held up her phone to show the news report.

"Ma'am." Kane came to her side. "Ah, there's someone you need to talk to."

Jenna nodded, glad to get away. She looked at the woman. "I'll be happy to give out media updates on the search for Laurie Turner but I don't have time to discuss statistics with you."

"Okay guys, cut." Crawford looked at Kane. "How come you're always there to rescue the sheriff? Don't you believe she is capable of doing her job?" She gave him a smile, wafting her bad breath all over Jenna. "Or is there a little romance going on between you and you're being overprotective? You live on the same ranch. How about a little inside story on what happens behind the scenes when you're off-duty?" She touched his arm. "It would make a great weekend supplement, all glossy color pages."

"The woman in yellow over there, Sheriff." Kane ignored Crawford completely and pointed to the back of the hall. "I'll get back to the others." He turned his back and walked away.

Jenna nodded. "I'll be right there as soon as I've spoken to a witness." She moved her attention reluctantly back to Crawford. "You said you wanted a scoop? I have one for you."

"Great, go ahead." Crawford pulled out her notebook.

Jenna wrinkled her nose. "There's a special on mouthwash at the general store." She walked away, heading in the direction of Cory Hughes.

"Hey." Kane caught up with her. "What was that all about?"

"I have no idea." Jenna shrugged. "Someone with delusions of grandeur, I guess. She's right off the mark if she believes our private life is a hot topic of conversation. Townsfolk have better things to do with their time."

"I'm not sure I liked her inferring you can't do your job without me." Kane frowned. "For a reporter, she is very uninformed."

Jenna stared at him. "Trust me, I don't care what she thinks. We have enough egocentric people to deal with, forget about it and keep your mind on the case."

"Sure." Kane's mouth twitched into a smile. "Just give me a wave if you need protecting." He walked away.

Taking Cory Hughes into a quiet corner, Jenna pulled out her notebook and pen. He was tall and lean, about twenty, with collar-length hair that hung over one eye. "Thank you for coming forward. Can you tell me about seeing Laurie in here after the practice session?"

"Sure." Hughes leaned against the wall. "I was sweeping up and she came running in the door in a real panic. She'd dropped her phone. It was in pieces, the screen smashed and the battery missing. She asked me to fix it."

Jenna nodded. "Did you?"

"Nah, it was too far gone and I told her." Hughes scratched his cheek. "She was close to tears, said her pa would be angry. I told her I'd go see if any unclaimed phones had turned up in lost and found. Maybe she could use her SIM card in one of them."

Hopeful he still had the remains of the phone, she continued making notes. "And where is the phone now?"

"In my office, well, if you could call the closet where I keep my stuff an office." He gave her a slow smile. "I haven't had time to check the lost and found as yet."

"Great!" Jenna smiled. "Can you get it for me? I have someone who can repair it if necessary and I found the battery."

"Sure." Hughes straightened. "I'll go get it."

"Before you go…" Jenna moved in front of him. "Then what happened?" She regarded him closely, waiting for any change in body language.

"Nothing, I put the bits of phone into a plastic bag and stuck it on a shelf in my office." He shrugged. "I locked the front door behind her and went home."

"Did you see her truck in the parking lot?" Jenna folded her notebook and placed it into her pocket and then pulled out a card and handed it to him.

"Nope." He stared at the card, turning it over in his hand. "I turn out the lights before I leave and my truck is out back. I drove straight past and onto the road. I didn't look to see if anyone was hanging around, all I wanted to do was to get out of there."

Jenna chewed on her pen. "So, she would've had to walk back to her truck in the dark?"

"It's not that far and she had time to get there before I closed up." Hughes shrugged. "It was getting late, and when I turn out the lights it makes the kids hurry on home. I'm not their nursemaid and they're not babies."

Slightly uneasy, Jenna frowned. "Did you see another vehicle on the road?"

"Yeah, I passed an eighteen-wheeler heading out of town but nothing else until I drove down Main." He shook his head. "I don't really take much notice of the vehicles I drive past unless they do something stupid."

"Do you live with anyone?" Jenna lifted her chin. "Anyone who can verify what time you arrived home?"

"I live with my ma and my sister. My pa walked out on us recently." He frowned. "But by ten Ma was in bed and Verna didn't come home until later. You'll just have to take my word for it, Sheriff."

Jenna nodded. "Okay thanks, go grab the phone and if you think of anything else or hear anyone mentioning Laurie, please call me."

"Sure." Hughes walked into the crowd.

"Ah-hem." The sound came from behind Jenna.

She turned to see an elderly woman in a yellow dress peering at her over her spectacles. "Ah, sorry to keep you waiting. You saw Laurie last night?"

"Yes, I did indeed." The woman fiddled with her purse. "She was wearing her cheerleader outfit and carrying a backpack. Imagine a young woman walking out in the middle of the night dressed like that? Then I see a vehicle slow down beside her, just like you see the men chasing after streetwalkers on TV shows. She jumped straight in and the car drove away in the other direction toward Stanton. Now I know Laurie lives out of Ravens Way, I can't figure why she'd climb into a car when she was so close to home."

Heart pounding, Jenna took out her notebook again. "Your name, ma'am, and address?"

"Mrs. York." She rattled off her details.

A breakthrough and so early in the case would be incredible. Jenna needed all the details. She waved Kane over, as he seemed to be able to identify every vehicle on the planet. "What time was this, do you recall?"

"Close to nine-thirty." Mrs. York nodded as if to herself. "There was a storm coming, so I gave my dog a run in the yard and was heading back inside when she came running out of the alleyway."

Holding up a hand, Jenna stared at her. "Running? Was someone chasing her?"

"Not that I could see. I was looking through tree branches but I know it was Laurie." Mrs. York turned her attention to Kane and then moved it back to Jenna. "She moved under the streetlight, looked behind her, and then hurried along the sidewalk. Next minute, headlights came round the corner and the vehicle stopped, she jumped in. They drove off and I went back inside. It was none of my business what she was doing."

Jenna pushed on. "Did you see who was driving or notice anyone else in the vehicle?"

"No, I'm afraid not." Mrs. York screwed up her eyes. "No, just a dark shape is all I remember. You see, Laurie was bending over looking in the window. She obscured my view."

"This is Deputy Kane." Jenna indicated to Kane. "Can you describe the vehicle to him for me please?"

"I can. It wasn't one of those trucks the young people usually drive, it was a Chrysler sedan, maybe green or gray." Mrs. York smiled up at Kane. "I know it was a Chrysler because we have one and it was similar."

"I'll find some images." Kane pulled out his phone. "We'll see if one of them looks familiar."

Jenna returned to the lectern. "Could I have your attention, please?" She waited for the buzz of conversation to die down. "Does anyone here know anyone who drives a Chrysler sedan, green or gray?"

The silence was deafening. "Okay, there is a stack of my cards on the table beside the entrance. Please take one, and if you see anyone driving a similar vehicle, take down the plate number and call the hotline on my card. Thank you."

Jenna scanned the hall. Hughes was heading her way carrying a plastic bag. She stepped down from the lectern and went to Kane's side. "Excuse me, Dave. Did you get the statements from the people who spoke to Laurie in the parking lot?"

"Wolfe took over, so I could rescue you from the reporters." Kane gave her a lopsided smile. "He's almost through by the look of things."

"Okay." Jenna handed Mrs. York her card. "I'll leave you with Deputy Kane. If you think of anything else, call me. Anything at all." She glanced at Kane. "Finish up here. I'll talk to Hughes again and do the rounds of the hall. We'll drop by the command center and then we'll head home. We have an early start in the morning."

CHAPTER NINE

Monday

Mist still curled through the lowlands when Jenna and Kane arrived at the control center at daybreak. The fall morning had a crispness in the air with the distinct tangy, earthy smell that came from dead leaves. In the distance the snowcapped mountains dominated the landscape. It had been a cold night and if Laurie was out there alone and injured, her chances of survival would be minimal. The search parties had insisted on going long into the night before it became too dangerous to be moving around the forest. As they rounded the building Jenna stared at the crowd. People had gathered at the back of the sheriff's department and spilled onto the sidewalk. She recognized some of the deputies from Louan and Blackwater but not the man standing beside Rowley. She eased her way through the crowd toward him. It seemed Rowley had completed the organization at some ungodly hour and groups were leaving with forest wardens and deputies all carrying maps.

"Morning." Rowley nodded in her direction and handed a deputy a pile of maps. "No sightings of Laurie at all overnight but we're doing a grid search of the forest two miles alongside Stanton. Atohi will be back by noon. He worked until late into the night with his team, checking all the trails wide enough to drive a vehicle. I'll move the command center to the front desk now everyone is organized."

"So, you have everything under control?" Jenna smiled at him.

"Yes, ma'am." Rowley collected his things. "Maggie will be in at nine and same with Walters to give me a break so I can go have breakfast."

"I can watch the desk." Emily Wolfe was leaning against her silver Colorado and straightened to come toward them. "I don't have classes today. You go eat."

"Thanks." Rowley looked tired. "I won't take long."

Jenna frowned. "Take your time, you look exhausted. We'll manage just fine."

She took in the young man beside him. Dressed in a Black Rock Falls deputy uniform, he could only be Zac Rio. Tall, slim, and muscular, with dark curly hair and standing around six-three, he had a friendly intelligent expression. She offered him her hand. "You must be Zac Rio? I'm Jenna Alton and this is Dave Kane." His handshake was firm but brief.

"Welcome to crime central." Kane shook his hand.

"Oh, I don't think so." Rio shook his head. "What's happened here in the last few years is a weekend's work elsewhere. This is a massive county. I'm not surprised people come here to disappear."

Jenna liked him already. "Come inside, we'll show you around."

"Thank you." Rio looked around. "I arrived just in time by the look of things. How do you manage with only two full-time deputies?"

"We call in help from the other counties." Jenna took the steps. "We currently have a teenage girl missing. I'll bring you up to speed."

"No need." Rio flicked her a glance. "Wolfe walked me through the case last night." He gave Duke's head a scratch. "I know all about Duke as well and Wolfe gave me the run down on every new forensics technique he's used over the last month or so."

"Yeah he tends to do that but loses me halfway through." Jenna grimaced. "Although, Wolfe never ceases to amaze me. He puts in the hours and is amazing at his profession." She led the way to the front of the building and walked inside. "He and his girls helped out at the school gym last night. We'd have been there until way past midnight without their help."

They moved inside the office and she sank into her chair behind the desk. Kane sat down and Rio stood. Jenna smiled at him. "Take a seat. You'll be working in the main office with Kane and Rowley. If necessary, we have a communications room we can use. My office will be getting upgraded in the next few weeks. As you can see by the work going on outside, we've had substantial additions made to the building." She thought for a beat. "Then there's the house. It's fully furnished and has room for a housekeeper. It's owned by this office so no rent to pay. I've replaced all the mattresses and linen. It's good to go. You can move in when you're ready."

"Yes, Wolfe mentioned that as well." Rio smiled. "I'm paid up until the end of next week, so we'll make the move then. I'll need time to pack."

"Good." Jenna leaned on the desk, and clasped her hands. "I'd like to know about your experience with missing persons and murder cases."

"I've handled many of both and solved all but one." Rio removed his Stetson and placed it on her desk. "I'm very interested in criminal behavior and because I was gifted or cursed with an incredible memory, I retain everything I read or see. My problem is, I'm not a behavioral analyst. I appreciate Deputy Kane is a profiler and Wolfe informed me you have the ear of Jo Wells, the FBI's top behavioral analyst. I can provide you with case studies on the fly as comparisons, which would be of some help." He clasped his hands together. "I'm studying Montana law, as between states the differences are considerable as I'm sure you both know. You're not from around these parts, are you?" He shrugged. "That's another annoying feature, I seem to be able to pinpoint accents with accuracy, although Kane here has me baffled."

"Do I?" Kane gave Jenna a knowing look. "I figured I'd started to blend in fine."

"You're a mixture, so I'd say you moved around as a kid." Rio snapped his fingers. "Army brat?"

"Yeah, we moved around some." Kane smiled. "Have you lived in California all your life?"

"Yeah, but this is our home now." Rio frowned. "I lost my folks in a plane crash a year ago. I left my brother and sister with my step-grandma and they didn't settle. It was a nightmare. They ran away and it took me weeks to find them." He pushed a hand through his hair. "Having fifteen-year-olds living with me in a one-bedroom apartment wasn't going to work, so we moved here. I took any job I could find and got the kids into school. They've settled down well but I missed law enforcement. When Wolfe hunted me down and told me about the available position here, I had to apply."

Jenna nodded. "It's not the same as having a detective's shield, we all work together according to our strengths."

"Yeah, Wolfe explained." Rio glanced at Kane. "A good leader plays to their strengths and from what I see nobody is complaining."

"Your application mentioned an interest in media." Kane stood and went to the counter and filled Jenna's coffee pot with water from the sink. "Does this mean you'll be able to handle the dreaded press releases?"

"Sure." Rio smiled. "I can capture crime scenes and take any images you require as well. I have a trunk load of equipment at your disposal."

Jenna grinned. "Sweet. I figure we're all going to get along just fine." She stood, picked up her notebook, and grabbed the pen for the whiteboard. "Now, I'll get down some notes on what we know about Laurie Turner's disappearance."

"If you'll allow me to make things easier for you, Sheriff?" Rio smiled. "I could handle the whiteboard. I don't need notes, it's all in here." He tapped his head.

"Well, that would save me a ton of time." She handed him the whiteboard marker. "Go right ahead."

"If and when necessary I can distinguish behavioral patterns as well, so can give you an idea of where a killer might strike next." Rio cleared his throat. "Well, in a place this size an approximation at least."

"Yeah." Kane collected cups and added the fixings to Jenna's desk. "We discussed 'comfort zones' with Jo during our last case. It's good to know you can recognize a pattern at the get-go, it will save time."

Jenna leaned back in her chair and stared at them. "Right now, we have a missing girl. So, get your heads around the evidence to date. The vehicle is significant and the woman who noticed Laurie, said she was carrying a backpack."

"Yeah, could she have planned to run off with someone, a boyfriend perhaps?" Rio paused from adding notes to the whiteboard and opened his hands wide. "Girls of Laurie's age do it all the time."

"You have experience with cases involving sixteen-year-olds?" Kane filled three cups and returned the pot to the heat and then sat down.

"Happens I do." Rio sat back down, ignored the fixings, and blew on the hot brew. "My brother and sister are twins, they just turned sixteen. I don't remember life being so complicated at that age. It's as if they're at war with the world." He glanced at Jenna. "They just took off and I found them at a soup kitchen three days later."

"Did they have a problem with their grandma?" Kane added cream and sugar to a cup and stirred slowly.

"Yeah, she has a tendency to run down my folks and believes everyone is useless." Rio sighed. "That's water under the bridge now.

They are happy at Black Rock Falls High School and have settled in well. I was expecting it to take longer but I figure they appreciate the chance to start fresh."

"That's good to know." Jenna smiled as Kane pushed the cup toward her and then tended to his own. "But this girl broke up with her boyfriend, we've spoken to him and the other guy she apparently liked was—"

"Cory Hughes." Rio waved a hand at the board. "He had her phone but wasn't the last person to see her alive."

"Yeah and he doesn't drive a Chrysler sedan, his ride is a GMC pickup." Kane thumbed through statements Wolfe had taken the previous evening. "He was very cooperative. Wolfe has the phone, and he'll be able to check the phone records and we'll have a list of her contacts."

"Hmm." Rio looked at Kane. "So. Someone unknown bumped into her, she dropped her phone, took it to Hughes and when she came out someone had tampered with her car." He narrowed his gaze. "I know zip about engines. How long would it have taken someone to disable her truck?"

"If the person knew how to lift the hood, no time at all, but how many people would know the technique? I only know because I worked on one as a boy." Kane looked thoughtful. "Assuming people were still leaving when Laurie returned to the gym, no one noticed anyone tampering with her pickup."

Jenna's mind was working overtime, and she'd replayed the scene in her head repeatedly. "I figure Laurie's abduction was planned." She looked from one deputy to the other. "The tampering happened during the training session. Her friend Vicky stated that someone in the crowd bumped into Laurie and knocked the phone out of her hand. That could've been a set-up. It was common knowledge she had the hots for Hughes, so who else would she go to for help? They all said he fixes everything including phones."

"Yeah that makes sense." Kane sipped his coffee.

Jenna could see it as clear as day. "Laurie goes to speak to Hughes. He can't fix her phone so she heads back to her pickup. During this time Hughes leaves so when Laurie realizes her vehicle won't start, she's stuck. Hughes has gone, she has no phone so she heads home on foot. Whoever picked her up must have followed her and then driven up and offered her a ride home." She stood and added notes to the whiteboard. "She knows the person driving the Chrysler and climbed in without fear. What we need to find out, is what happened next."

A knock came on her door. It was Emily. "We have a body!"

CHAPTER TEN

A sinking feeling dropped over Jenna and she stared at Emily in disbelief. "Female?"

"Yeah. A linesman found her out at the old mine. She's naked and cut up some from what the man said. Here are the coordinates. The guy is still on scene. His name is Al Watson." Emily's face showed no emotion as she passed Jenna a slip of paper. She had mastered the concealment an ME must have to cover their inner emotions. "I'll call Dad." She turned in a toss of her long blonde hair and vanished down the hallway.

"Is she the trainee medical examiner?" Rio looked after Emily with obvious interest. "She doesn't seem old enough."

"Well, like you, she's some years ahead of her time." Kane smiled. "She still has years of study ahead of her, but with Wolfe to guide her, she'll make a fine medical examiner." Kane swallowed his coffee and stood. "I'll call Rowley and let him know we'll be locking the office." He strolled out the door with Duke on his heels.

Jenna stood. "Sure, thanks." She looked at Rio. "Do you have your cameras with you?"

"Yeah they're always in my truck." Rio smiled at her. "It's a hobby."

Jenna nodded. "Great, then follow us to the location. You'll be recording the scene."

"Sure, but what about Rowley?" Rio looked genuinely concerned. "He's my superior and I don't want to be treading on anyone's toes."

Astonished by his concern, Jenna met his gaze. "I'm your superior, Kane is deputy sheriff but we work as a team. I need Rowley here to hold the fort while we are recovering the body and I'll need you to record the scene." She smiled. "It's horses for courses, Zac, and that's how we roll around here."

"Okay." Rio finished his coffee and smoothed down his hair before pushing his Stetson on his head. "I figure I'm going to enjoy working here."

They headed out in a convoy, moving through town trying hard not to attract too much attention. The last thing Jenna needed was the media destroying evidence at a crime scene. As the media's attention was on the search parties, by the time they left town and headed for the industrial lowlands that spread out between Black Rock Falls and Blackwater they'd left the media vans far behind. The GPS led them along an old uneven road. Mounds of dirt and rocks long covered by weeds dotted the surrounding grasslands. Cabins long deserted had plants growing from the gutters and sat in general disarray. The exhausted gold mines had recently been sold to a mining company, who'd returned favorable assays and planned to reopen the lucrative industry. New mines meant prosperity for the town and work for a ton of people. A good source of energy was vital and new electricity lines had been erected over the last six months.

The white paint of a vehicle sparkled under the morning sun and Jenna made out the lineman's truck parked beside one of the new electricity posts. "That must be our guy."

"If he's working alone it would have been a shock finding a body way out here." Kane pulled up beside the truck. "I wonder what he was doing over by the mine shaft, it looks like it's some ways from here?"

After scanning the area, Jenna unclipped her seatbelt. "I guess we're going to find out."

Behind her, Rio slowed his vehicle and stopped but like Wolfe, he remained inside. Jenna smiled to herself. It was a sign of a good detective to wait and not enter the crime scene before invited. Once they approached the body, Wolfe would take the lead. An ME's investigation took priority at the crime scene and she valued his knowledge. She opened the door and her boots hit the hard soil. By the time she rounded the hood, Kane had coaxed the man out of the cabin of his truck. She walked up to him. "Al Watson?" She made the introductions. "Where did you find the body?"

"Over there." Watson pointed to the right. "I was making repairs to the connection and seen something so I drove over to look."

Jenna nodded. "Did you get out the truck or touch anything?"

"No, ma'am." Watson's faced paled. "I turned right around and hightailed it back here and called 911."

"You did the right thing." Relieved, Jenna glanced at Kane and he went to speak to Wolfe. She turned back to Watson. "Did you see anyone hanging around or driving by this morning?"

"Nope, not a soul." Watson ran both hands down his face. "It was a shock seeing a young girl like that."

Jenna understood the feeling. "Will you be okay?"

"I guess." Watson swallowed and his Adam's apple bobbed up and down. He was sheet-white. "Is she the missing girl that's been all over the news?"

"I have no idea at this time." Jenna had to keep him from informing the press. "I must insist you tell no one about this until we establish who it is and notify next of kin. The press will be all over it and it would be a terrible shock to the family if they hear about it on the news. Plus, crucial evidence could be destroyed if they come here and stamp all over the crime scene. Do you understand, Mr. Watson?"

"Sure." Watson's gaze drifted over to Wolfe's van. "I'll call in sick and go home. I'm done here for now."

"That would be for the best." Jenna walked him to his truck. "We have your details and will contact you if we need any more information." She handed him her card. "Call me if you think of anything else."

"I will, thank you." Watson climbed into his truck and drove away.

Jenna walked back to the Beast and climbed inside. "He spotted the body from up the pole and went to look."

"I was hoping we'd find Laurie Turner alive but after discovering someone disabled her truck, I wasn't optimistic." Kane drove to Wolfe's van and parked in a patch of long dry grass.

As she picked her way with care around Wolfe's van, she caught the smell of decay. She pulled out a couple of facemasks and handed Kane one. "From the smell, she's been dead since Saturday night."

"What have we got?" Kane stood beside her on the perimeter of the scene as Wolfe processed the body.

"Female approximately the same height, age, and hair color as Laurie Turner but her face is too damaged to make a visual ID." Wolfe peered at them over his facemask. "I'll let Rio finish capturing the scene and then Webber will take the stills before I examine the body but I know the killer inflicted the stab wounds post-mortem by the lack of blood loss. She wasn't killed here. The livor mortis, the bluish-purple discoloration under the skin of the legs and buttocks due to gravitation of blood after death, indicates she was in a sitting position for hours before being moved."

A solid weight settled in Jenna's stomach at the sight of the body. The girl had welts around her neck and multiple stab wounds over her face and chest. It didn't take too much insight to see the rage behind the attack. Multiple stab wounds and to the face was very personal. Whoever did this, hated this girl. She turned to look for

Kane, and found him checking all around the scene, walking back and forth. As he came back to her phone in hand, she went to his side. "Find something?"

"Yeah." Kane indicated behind him. "Someone sure went to the trouble of covering up any tracks, they swept the area."

A prickle went down Jenna's spine. "Show me."

"Someone dragged those dead bushes over there and pulled them over their tracks. The bushes are heavy, which means they're strong, so I'd say male with muscle bulk." He snapped on a clean pair of surgical gloves. "I tried pulling them together and it wasn't easy."

"Hmm. Interesting." Rio came to her side. "I've captured the scene. I've used a grid filter on the images so it's easier to identify evidence when we leave the scene." He frowned. "That woman wasn't murdered here. Her body is clean, no defensive wounds that I can see, no blood. It's a dumping ground but there are scuff marks beside the body, something the unsub missed. It looks as if they kneeled beside the body to inflict the wounds. Small puncture wounds, like an icepick or similar."

"Unsub?" Jenna looked at him. "I heard Jo using that term, what does it mean?"

"Unknown subject." Rio regarded her with a surprised expression. "You've worked cases with the FBI. It's a term they commonly use now, I guess to soften the word 'killer' because, in truth that's who it usually refers to. It's common with law enforcement."

Impressed, Jenna regarded her new deputy with interest. *Have I been out of touch, that long?* "Okay. Go on."

"So, if the girl wasn't killed here, there's a primary crime scene out there somewhere." Rio glanced at Kane. "I noticed you checking the ground. It looks like the killer covered their tracks."

"Yeah, sure does." Kane regarded him closely. "What else did you get from the attack?"

"Hate." Rio's mouth turned down. "They wanted to make sure the victim was dead, which makes me believe the unsub is known to the victim."

"I figure that fact is well established by Mrs. York's description of Laurie getting into the Chrysler." Kane shook his head slowly. "From her account, Laurie appeared scared and was pleased to see the person in the vehicle."

The too familiar feeling of dread crept over Jenna, she hugged her chest and stared at the body. "This person is living among us. We must find the Chrysler sedan. Starting with the CCTV footage from town to see if it went by and when. From the high school to here they would've driven through town."

"Maybe." Kane rubbed his chin. "If he's local he'd know where the CCTV cameras are situated and take the backstreets. He seems a mite too careful to risk being caught on film."

CHAPTER ELEVEN

Wolfe examined the area around the victim. Even without blood loss, such a violent attack produced bodily fluids spatter and he kept everyone at a distance until he'd taken samples. The tin doorway to the shaft yielded a clear result, and he made sure Webber took shots of the pattern. From what he could see it was a frenzied attack with attention made to the face and eyes of the victim. It happened post-mortem, and might have been an afterthought to cover evidence or the killer had an underlying mental problem. He would discuss his findings with Kane and even call in Jo Wells, the FBI behavioral analyst, to look at the victim.

"Did you see this?" Kane indicated inside the roof of the mine entrance. "That's spatter from something being tossed and tumbling, throwing out a pinwheel pattern." He pulled out his Maglite and scanned the sandy bottom of the entrance. "No footprints or brush marks." He turned to Wolfe and smiled. "I figure he threw the murder weapon down the mine shaft."

Wolfe moved closer. "You don't say?" He examined the marks. "I concur but how far does this cave go before it drops into oblivion?"

"The main shaft would be covered." Kane edged inside keeping to the wall. "It's for safety reasons and they blocked them off, when the place was sold. With luck we'll find the weapon inside."

Intrigued, Wolfe followed close behind, searching the ground with the beam of his Maglite. "There's a fresh chip out of that beam, it must have ricochet off and be close to you."

"Found it." Kane crouched and shone his light over a screwdriver. "Do you want soil samples from in here as well?"

Wolfe slipped the screwdriver into an evidence bag, labeled it, and waited for Kane. "This is vital. I sure hope we find prints on it." He made his way back to the body. "Add it to the chain of custody book for me and there's a milk crate in the back of my van. Drop it in there with the soil samples."

"Sure." Kane took the evidence bags and strode out the mine.

Wolfe went back to the body to examine the wounds. He had little doubt they'd found the weapon. He leaned in closer and spotted something in the victim's mouth. He turned to Emily. "She has something thrust inside her mouth. I'll open her jaw for you to pull out the object." He looked at Webber. "Open an evidence bag, we don't want any contamination."

He opened the jaw and it moved easily—rigor had come and gone. Now he made out a ball of fabric and as Emily lifted it from the victim's mouth using tongs, he shook his head in disbelief. "Get that bag sealed." He turned to Jenna. "The victim has a pair of men's briefs in her mouth. This means something to the killer. It's significant."

"What do you think, Kane?" Jenna turned and stared at him.

"I agree." Kane moved closer. "This entire scene is weird. I'm not speculating until Wolfe has her on the table. I see strangulation marks as well. Nothing makes sense here."

"Weird is right." Rio shook his head. "I'd like to know what was going on inside the head of this killer."

Wolfe looked at Jenna. "We'll need Dr. Turner's DNA for comparison but mitochondrial DNA would be better. Can you contact her mother? When you speak to either of them, I would advise they not view the body and leave the identification up to me."

"Her mother works at the beauty salon in town." Jenna's expression was troubled. "I really won't enjoy giving her the bad news. I know we can't confirm anything but we all know this is Laurie Turner. I've seen enough here. I'll go by the salon and see if we can find her mother. Will you be conducting the post this afternoon?"

Intrigued by what he was seeing before him, Wolfe nodded. "Yeah. There is so much here to process. I'll be starting on the preliminary examination as soon as we return to the morgue." He frowned. "She's well into decomposition. I'll be able to get a TOD for you when I get her back to the lab but I'd say from her temperature and state of rigor she died around the time she climbed into the vehicle."

"So maybe strangulation?" Jenna rubbed her temples.

Exasperated, Wolfe raised his eyebrows. "You know darn well I can't give you a cause of death until I've completed the autopsy. It's obvious she received some type of restriction to her neck from the bruising but from the lack of it as well, it appears to be what I'd usually see from a cord tightened from behind."

"Sorry, I shouldn't jump to conclusions." Jenna kicked a clump of grass and looked at Kane. "It's just that, she was in the vehicle and from what I'm seeing is bruising way up under the neck, as if someone was in the back seat and strangled her from behind."

"Yeah." Kane moved in closer. "Or more likely attacked her from behind when she climbed out of the vehicle. Mrs. York has a pretty good recollection of the event. She doesn't mention Laurie looking in the back seat, and people usually acknowledge another person in a vehicle. Why would the second person be in the back seat? It's a sedan, most friends would ride shotgun."

Wolfe looked from one to the other. "Until I determine the cause of death, this discussion is a waste of time." He nodded toward Rio. "Are you coming to the autopsy as well?"

"Sure, if I'm not needed elsewhere." Rio glanced at Jenna. "Would you like me to relieve Rowley?"

"You'll need to familiarize yourself with the running of the office before I let you do that." Jenna cleared her throat. "The locals will be suspicious of you at first. With Rowley, when he gives them advice, they take it."

"Good to know." Rio moved away to speak to Emily, who was bagging the victim's hands.

Wolfe stood back and waited for Emily to finish and then turned to Jenna. "I'm done here. We'll bag her up and get her into the morgue. Autopsy is at two but I need the DNA sample from Mrs. Turner yesterday."

"I'm on it." Jenna nodded and looked at Rio. "Head back to the office and get the images and footage uploaded, Rowley will give you the passwords and make sure Wolfe has all the data first. We'll be back soon." At his nod, she turned to Kane. "Let's go hunt down Mrs. Turner."

Wolfe stared after her. Jenna was wearing her detached facade again. It was just as well; informing a mother her daughter might have been murdered was gut-wrenching but worst of all was having to insist they refrain from viewing the body. Some would always insist and then the image of their mutilated child remained with them forever.

CHAPTER TWELVE

Pushing down the emotion of seeing a brutally murdered young woman dumped like garbage, Jenna walked away, took a few deep breaths to clear her mind, and removed her facemask and gloves. She balled them up and shoved them into a paper bag Kane was holding out for her. As he rolled up the top of the bag and stowed it on the floor of the back seat of his truck, she looked at him closely. His eyelashes covered his expression but she knew that his brain was working overtime. During her time at Quantico, she'd become close friends with a writer and often he'd go quiet and stare into the distance or just sit and do nothing. Kane did the same and she often wondered what was going through his mind. Her friend told her it was a writer's trance, the time when the magic would happen and a story would drop into a creative mind but with Kane maybe he was weighing up the evidence. As he gave Duke a rub around the ears, she heard him whisper something to the dog that made him bark. The loud noise inside the cab of Kane's truck startled her. "What's wrong with him?"

"He's fine." Kane smiled at her. "I just told him we'd be heading to Aunt Betty's Café soon and as it's Monday, Susie will have some leftovers from the Sunday special for him. She always puts something by for Duke."

Jenna waited for him to slip behind the wheel. "Susie is always so nice to everyone. I wonder why she isn't married? You'd think she'd meet everyone eligible in town working at Aunt Betty's. They do say a way to a man's heart and all that."

"Hmm." Kane rubbed his chin and thought for a beat and then gave her a wink. "Nah. Nice as she is, I wouldn't trade her bacon and eggs for your toast." He grinned. "I think it's cute the way you try to cover up the burned bits with extra butter."

Jenna chuckled. It was good to break the horror of the morning with a little light teasing. "Aw shucks, Dave, now I'm blushing." She fluttered her eyelashes and pressed one hand to her heart.

"That doesn't mean I expect you to cook me breakfast." Kane's smile flashed white. "I'm happy to take my turn. You know that, right?"

"Yeah, Dave, I do." Jenna sighed. "I hate to break this mood but we have a job to do and a very unpleasant one. This will be the second time I've had to give bad news to someone in the beauty parlor, they'll be refusing me entry soon."

"I know what you mean. This part of the job stinks." Kane turned the Beast around and they headed for the highway. "I'm hoping this is a one-off but if this guy hits again, I figure we need to search for a killing ground. A barn or perhaps a garage."

Jenna stared at a vista of wheatgrass. As the wind moved over it, creating ripples, the lowlands turned into a golden ocean, and she wished she was far away on a beach somewhere. She had to drag her mind away from the idea of splashing through waves and feeling sand between her bare toes and listen to him. She nodded. "Yeah, the screwdriver was a strange weapon of choice. With so many people carrying hunting knifes, it seems strange to bring a screwdriver out here." She blinked at Kane as an image flashed across her mind. "I've often seen carpenters or handymen carrying screwdrivers in back pockets or hanging from a utility belt." She thought back. "In fact, I'm sure I saw the handle of one poking out of the top pocket of Cory Hughes' work shirt."

"We'll check it out after the autopsy." Kane shrugged. "Wolfe might have found prints or trace evidence."

"I hope so, but Hughes doesn't drive a Chrysler sedan. So, I guess he's off the list." Jenna leaned back trying to compose the words in her mind she needed to say to Laurie's mother.

It took tact and a calm demeanor to deliver devastating news. She thought it through and satisfied, she glanced at Kane. "First impressions on Rio?"

"Smart and up to date." Kane turned onto Stanton and headed toward town. "He's somewhere between Rowley and Ty Carter, I figure. Ty has experience and can take in the whole picture at a crime scene as if he's reliving it in his head. That comes from working across many crimes. Rowley is still a little green. He's good but needs direction—but he doesn't need to prove anything to me, he is solid."

Jenna took out her notebook and flicked through the pages. "It will be interesting to see if Rio's memory is as good as he says. I've read about people like him and instant recall is amazing. He does seem on the ball and I liked his take on the crime scene. He is right, this attack on Laurie Turner seemed very personal. It has to be someone she knows."

"Yeah it seems so." Kane pulled up outside the beauty parlor and stared at her. "You gonna be okay? You've gone sheet-white."

Jenna unclipped her seatbelt and moistened her lips. "Yeah, I'll be fine but come in with me. You have a calming influence in most situations and you can catch her if she faints."

"There goes my reputation again." Kane removed his Stetson and ran a hand through his hair before replacing it. "Now all the guys in town will think I have a stylist cut my hair. I'll never live it down."

Knowing Kane was trying to make light of an awful job, she squeezed his arm and then slid out the truck. She found Mrs. Turner in the break room sipping coffee. A slim woman, with red lips and fingernails, and her long hair tied up in an elaborate weave, lifted her head from a magazine to stare at her as if she'd grown two heads. "We're here about your daughter, Laurie."

"Did you locate her?" Mrs. Turner stubbed out a cigarette in an ashtray on the table and looked at Jenna.

Jenna shook her head. "We're not sure. We found the body of a female earlier today. It could be Laurie. She hasn't been identified."

"A body? What happened to her?" Mrs. Turner's voice rose to a panicked shriek. "Take me to her. I want to see her."

"We haven't determined the cause of death." Kane moved into the room and closed the door behind him. "She is with the medical examiner. I'm afraid you won't be able to view the body."

"Then how will you know if it's my Laurie?" Mrs. Turner's eyes filled with tears that spilled down her cheeks. "This can't be happening."

Jenna sat beside her. "I need a DNA sample from you. A swab from inside your cheek is all. I'll know in less than an hour."

"Okay." Mrs. Turner dragged in a shuddering breath. "It's his fault. Her father refused to allow her to move in with me. He said if I made a fuss, he'd have me declared as an unfit mother. He tells people I'm dead, you know." She shook her head. "He's violent. I couldn't live with him a moment longer. I tried to take Laurie and run with her but he obtained a court order and dragged her back. I've had no visitation rights. I've had to sneak time with her." She opened her mouth for Jenna to take the swab.

Jenna placed the sample inside the tube and sealed the bag. She stood. "You did the right thing leaving an abusive relationship. His position as a school counselor would have made him believable to the courts, I'm afraid. Not so much now. We support victims of spousal abuse in Black Rock Falls. If this had happened now, you could have come to me for help."

"Thank you and yes, I've seen the flyers." Mrs. Turner stood and collected her purse from a bench. "I can't stay here doing nothing, I'm going to the ME's office. I'll wait there for the result."

"Do you have someone we can call to go with you?" Kane had removed his Stetson and was rolling the edge with his fingers. "A minister? Close friend?"

"Yeah, Father Derry." Mrs. Turner pulled a bunch of tissues from a box and wiped her eyes. "He's been very helpful through all my troubles with Bob."

Jenna pulled out a card and handed it to her. "I'll call him. Here are my details if you need to contact me." She looked at Mrs. Turner and the poor woman's grief surrounded her like a heavy weight. "Wait a while before you go, it will take a couple of hours before the ME has the results. Do you want me to ask Father Derry to meet you here? I don't think you should be driving."

"Okay." Mrs. Turner sniffed. "Have you informed Bob?"

Jenna shook her head. "Not yet. We'll speak to him as soon as we have the results of the test."

"Why can't I see my little girl?" Mrs. Turner sat down heavily and peered at her through tears. "What happened to her?"

"I'm not able to give you any information, I'm truly sorry. At this stage we don't know for sure it's Laurie." Jenna squeezed the woman's arm. "Dr. Wolfe, the medical examiner, will explain everything once he has the results of the test."

"Okay." Mrs. Turner pulled a pack of cigarettes from her pocket and lit up using a silver lighter. She blew out smoke in a stream. "I'll wait here for Father Derry."

"Sure." Jenna stood and headed out the door, pausing at the front counter. "Mrs. Turner has had some bad news. Father Derry will be by soon, can you show him to the break room?"

"Okay." The girl behind the counter nodded like a bobblehead.

As they headed for the truck, Jenna looked at Kane. "She's in a bad way."

"Yeah, breathing in fumes all day from the salon and smoking as well, it's a wonder she can breathe at all." He climbed into his truck and started the engine. "Wolfe's and then Aunt Betty's for lunch?"

"Yeah." Jenna pulled out her phone to call Father Derry. "If the DNA results are back by then, we'll go and inform Bob Turner about Laurie. I guess then it will be time for the autopsy. Can this day get any worse?"

CHAPTER THIRTEEN

In the school hallway, she paced up and down chewing her fingernails. She'd taken too many sneers and smart remarks from the cheerleading squad to last her a lifetime. Yeah, they'd dropped her to the B team but not for her performance. They'd cut her for one of their friends, a daughter of the local bank manager. She understood the truth now. How the girls on the team manipulated people, using the money or position of their parents to move up in the world. The flirting with her boyfriend and his response had made her mad. He'd been flattered and wouldn't stop talking about how this one or that one had hit on him. Her fingers trembled at the thought of any of them as much as looking at him. She'd won his heart but since they'd cut her from the squad, she'd noticed his eyes wandering to some of the other girls. She had to put a stop to it and lied to him. Turning the tables on the way the guys thought about cheerleaders hadn't been difficult. His ego was his downfall and making him believe they had devised a plan to steal him from her then publicly humiliate him had been easy. Her plan had worked.

He was incredibly vain and so good looking the girls at school idolized him. He walked with a swagger but she controlled him now. The idea of stealing the player's soiled briefs from the locker room when the team were busy in the showers had been pure genius but convincing him to take them had been difficult. As he walked toward her at morning break, she dragged him into a quiet corner and kissed him. "Did you get them?"

"Yeah." His brow furrowed into a frown. "You know if they catch me doing this, they're going to think I'm kinky or something. Why do we need sweaty shorts and how long do you figure we can get away with this before someone starts complaining their clothes are missing?"

She took the plastic bag he handed her and thrust it into her backpack. "You didn't touch them, did you? You picked them up with the bag?"

"Yeah, I did like the last time." He brushed the hair away from her face and kissed her again. "Tell me, why you need another pair, it goes way past people thinking Laurie was a slut, doesn't it?"

"It's the same reason we wrapped her in plastic and wore gloves." She ran her hand through his hair. "DNA. This way the cops will believe someone else killed her."

"That doesn't seem fair, blaming someone else." He looked worried.

"That's why I needed another pair. I need to kill another one." She smiled at him. "I watched your face when I strangled Laurie. You loved it and I've picked out the next one. We'll stuff the briefs in her mouth to throw off the cops. Two different sets of DNA found with the bodies will confuse them." She looked at him and giggled. "I'll take out a few of the squad and they'll be begging me to come back." She touched his cheek. "Now go and be nice to Becky. Not too nice now. It's the parade tomorrow and everyone will be occupied. We'll need a plan to get her somewhere secluded. There's an empty house in town, I was walking by and saw the last owner leave the key above the front door. We'll go there. All the blinds are down, it will be dark inside, and I can hide real easy. Take her upstairs and I'll be inside waiting. I'll leave the backdoor open and have everything ready. Becky deserves this, I've heard her talking and she really wants to make you look like a jerk, so she'll be putty in your hands."

"What do you want me to say to her?"

"Hmm, let me see." She twirled her hair around her fingers and thought for a beat. "Say you're trying to avoid me, that I follow you, something like that. We'll need a nice quiet place to get her into your vehicle." She tapped her lip. "I know. Ask her to meet you in the library. It's open on Tuesdays until ten. If she shows, make her believe I'm there, stalking you and then sneak out to the parking lot. Say you'll give her a ride someplace you can make out with her, without me knowing."

"What you gonna do to her?" He trembled with excitement against her. "Last time, you kinda changed like in a good way. Watching you made my heart race and after when we made out, with her dead eyes watching us, it was incredible."

"It will be a surprise." She kissed him hard. After she'd killed two or three more cheerleaders, he'd never dream of leaving her. She smiled, enjoying the power she had over him, and this was just the start.

CHAPTER FOURTEEN

As Jenna and Kane headed back to the office, Wolfe called with the results of the DNA sample. The dead girl was Laurie Turner. Jenna called off the search at once and headed to Dr. Bob Turner's residence. They parked outside and then walked to the door. Her knocking was answered after a few minutes and Dr. Turner glared at her. Jenna met his gaze. "We have some news about Laurie."

"She's dead, isn't she? My wife called me and told me you'd found a body." Turner's eyes flashed with anger.

Jenna glanced at Kane. "I'm afraid she is, yes."

"I gathered as much as you went to my ex-wife to obtain a DNA sample. It would have been more professional to have contacted me first." Dr. Turner's voice became like granite. "It's amazing how fast you found Laurie's mother, I've been looking for Jeanette for years. She'll blame me for Laurie's death but then she blames me for everything. That woman was always a bad influence on Laurie." He cleared his throat. "Now can you leave, Sheriff? I don't want your condolences; I have funeral arrangements to make." He slammed the door in her face.

Jenna exchanged an amazed look with Kane. "Is that the same Dr. Turner who called 911. Wow! That's some change around in behavior."

"People react differently to bad news." Kane raised an eyebrow. "It's not your fault."

Jenna chewed on her fingers. "I guess we should've told him we'd found a body at least."

"We couldn't ask either parent to physically identify the victim." Kane shrugged. "We identified the victim through DNA to prevent the parents being distressed. We didn't know for sure it was Laurie Turner."

Jenna sighed. "It's done now." She climbed inside the truck. "I sure could do with a strong cup of coffee."

"Sure." Kane headed back to town.

Inside Aunt Betty's Café, the wonderful aroma of fresh pie and coffee closed around Jenna like a warm hug. There was something special about the café, the name said it all really. The décor and homely atmosphere brought back memories of her childhood sitting on her grandma's lap and eating cookies fresh from the oven. Kane was right to bring her here after a grueling morning. Yeah, they could've collected takeout and eaten in her office but she needed a timeout to get her head right before another stressful afternoon. After finishing her meal, she sipped her coffee and allowed her mind to wander.

Dr. Turner had taken the news without blinking an eye and talked about arrangements for Laurie's funeral, which was a little strange considering how he'd acted the first time they'd met. It had been like speaking to two different people. If he suffered mood swings, he would be the last person she'd consider capable of advising troubled kids. As soon as Kane had placed his empty cup on the table, Jenna pushed to her feet. "Let's go. I need to drop by the office."

As they drove through town, she scanned her notes on the investigation. When she returned to the office, she'd need to set her deputies to work. They had to go through Laurie's laptop and she'd be interested to know if Wolfe had had time to check out her phone. She glanced up as Kane slowed to avoid a group of people spilling onto the road. When he hit his siren, a woman clutching a baby to her chest burst through the crowd and ran toward them. "What now?"

"Help me, please." The woman's long blonde hair was a mess, tears had tracked mascara down her cheeks. In her arms a baby screamed. The woman hammered on Kane's door. "Don't let him hit me again."

"I won't let him near you." Kane turned to Jenna. "Orders?"

Jenna assessed the situation. "Take care of her. I'll go see what this bunch of cowards are doing, standing by and watching a woman being assaulted. Call for backup."

"Jenna—" Kane stared at her.

"Don't say a word. The townsfolk need to know I can deal with trouble alone. I know you care about my safety." Jenna glared at him. "My town, my problem. Let me do my job, Dave."

"Okay." He held up both hands in surrender. "Go do your job but just remember, people like to see a strong leader, not one who is trying to prove they can knock a guy off his feet." He smiled at her. "Even if you can." He waved a hand toward the group of men cheering the offender on. "Then you have the crowd. If they step in, I'm there and nothing you say will stop me. That's what I'm paid to do, Jenna."

"Your first priority is the woman and her baby." Jenna climbed out the truck and pushed her way through the group of men spilling from Antlers, the new tavern in town. She didn't recognize any of them as locals and as they all had the same club jackets—clearly, they belonged to a group of men on a hunting trip or similar. She raised her voice. "What's going on here?"

"Nothin' for you to be lookin' at, Sheriff." A man with a smug expression stepped away from his friends. "It's a private matter." He wiped blood from his knuckles onto his jeans. "Ain't it, boys?"

After murmuring their agreement, all eyes turned to her. Many of the men had grins from ear to ear. Indignant, Jenna straightened. "Assaulting people in my town is an offense."

"She hit me first." The man rubbed his cheek. "I was just showing the boys here how I deal with a wife who just won't listen. I told her I'd be away this week and she goes and follows me here. Then she takes offense to me chatting with the girl behind the bar. I mean—" he opened his hands out wide and flashed her a lop-sided smile "—what woman wouldn't want a piece of this?" He looked around as his friends laughed. "I gave her a baby to keep her quiet but she don't stay quiet. Followin' me here, checking up on me. That makes me look weak."

Jenna shook her head. "I'm taking you downtown for a little chat. The townsfolk hereabouts don't like men who beat on their wives. I'll get my deputies to speak to the witnesses."

"She ain't gonna press charges against me." He glared at Jenna. "And do you figure you're strong enough to cuff me?" He pointed to her sidearm. "Oh, that's right, you'll hold a gun to my head." He looked around at his friends and grinned. "Get out your phones, boys, police brutality coming my way." His gaze shifted back to Jenna. "I'll have your badge, lady. You don't know who you're dealing with."

People had collected on the sidewalk. To one side, she made out Kane getting the woman and her baby inside his truck. He looked over the top of the Beast and raised both eyebrows. Jenna gave him a slight shake of her head, unbelted her duty belt, and handed it to the local gun store owner. "Okay, now it's just you and me." She shrugged. "What's your name?"

"John Law and I ain't going nowhere." He stood his ground, hands on hips, grinning at her. "It's easy for you hiding behind a badge. If I make the wrong move, you'll have me for resisting arrest."

Noticing Rowley pushing through the crowd, she smiled at him. "Here, hold these for me please." She peeled off her jacket and handed Rowley her badge. "There, that makes us even."

"Even?" Law laughed at her. "The badge and coat don't make you a sheriff, the town makes you the sheriff. Whatever. Stay out of my business." He turned to walk toward a pickup.

Jenna charged after him and grabbed one arm. "I'm arresting you for assaulting your wife." She pulled his arm up behind him and reached for the other, cuffs in hand.

In an instant, he'd twisted around. The slap caught her across the cheek like a whip and she tasted blood. She ducked his second blow and caught the rage on his face. He planned to strike her again and that was not going to happen. The years of training she'd done with Kane in the early hours of the morning had prepared her for men like Law. They liked to dominate and control. Rather than get mad, everything around her went into slow motion. Out of the corner of her eye she could see Kane restraining Rowley. She ducked the next slap and Law, red in the face, came at her like a raging bull, his fists clenched.

Perfect. Kane had taught her how to disable by aiming in just the right place. She spun and kicked hitting Law's kneecap with the heel of her boot. One strike and he fell into a pile of pain. She turned and looked at Rowley and Kane. "Cuff him." She read him his rights. "When you get him in a cell call Doc Brown but I want him charged with assaulting a law officer, resisting arrest, and spousal abuse."

"Yes, ma'am." Rowley cuffed Law and dragged him limping to his cruiser.

"You broke my leg. I'm going to sue you. This is police brutality." Law's face contorted. "You're dead, lady. My friends have everything on film."

Jenna collected her things and buckled on her duty belt. "That's good and so do many of the local townsfolk. The judge will see you resisting arrest and striking me." She touched her cheek and ran her tongue over the split inside her mouth. "You came at me first, Law, a defenseless woman. I just defended myself." She turned to Rowley. "Get him out of my sight."

"Do you want me to collect the phone footage?" Rio was at her side.

Jenna shook her head and scanned the crowd. "No, I'll do that. I know many of the people who filmed it. Take Mrs. Law and her baby to Her Broken Wings. It's a refuge for battered women. Two streets up on the left. Get her statement. Explain, we'll need her to testify in court or he'll walk." She turned to the crowd and raised her voice. "I'll need the footage."

As people came forward, her heart sank at the sight of Deni Crawford, the impossibly rude *Blackwater News* reporter heading her way with a satisfied smile. Talk about being in the right place at the right time, the busybody reporter had caught the entire episode on film. She turned to face her. "No comment."

"Oh, come on, Sheriff." Crawford held out the microphone. "You must have something to say to the people of Black Rock Falls?" She smiled at the camera. "It's not every day we see a sheriff in action, while her deputies stand by and do nothing."

Refusing to rise to the bait, Jenna looked straight into the camera. "In Black Rock Falls we don't tolerate spousal abuse or bullying so please donate to Her Broken Wings Foundation and help those in need. Thank you." She turned her back on Crawford and addressed the crowd. "Okay who filmed the incident?" She took out her cards. "Email a copy to me please."

As she moved between the people, she noticed Kane coming out of Antlers carrying something. He stopped at his truck and leaned against the door watching her. With all the footage emailed to her and names taken of witnesses, she made her way back to the Beast. She looked at Kane's stern expression but he said nothing and just handed her a towel filled with ice. She took it from him and pressed it against her throbbing cheek. Now the adrenalin had worn off, her face ached. She looked at him. "How is Mrs. Law?"

"Frightened and hurting." Kane frowned. "Her husband has been beating on her for some time. I wanted to tend her injuries but she wanted to feed the baby and told me to leave her alone."

Jenna watched as Rio escorted the woman to his cruiser. "Let's go before that news reporter films anything else, I'm doing." She climbed into the Beast and waited for Kane to get behind the wheel and start the engine. "I saw you holding Rowley back. Thanks for letting me deal with the situation but I wasn't expecting it to be all over the news tonight."

"You made it perfectly clear you had a point to prove." Kane was staring straight ahead. "The big loud mouth bully who beat up on his wife needed taking down a peg. Being knocked off his feet by a woman your size in front of his friends will take a long time to live down, especially when it makes the news. It's just as well his wife is leaving him. He'd take it out on her for sure." He pulled into his space outside the sheriff's department and turned to look at her. "It's difficult, Jenna." He pointed to his chest. "In here, seeing Law put his hands on you made me want to tear him apart, but in here—" he pointed to his head "—I knew you could take care of yourself but when you gave up your weapon—*Jesus,* Jenna." He shook his head. "I had palpitations."

Jenna smiled at him. "You re-trained me well, and I'm at my peak but I have to admit, knowing you were there watching my back made it a whole lot easier."

CHAPTER FIFTEEN

Head throbbing, Jenna walked into the sheriff's department to find Atohi Blackhawk waiting for her. Maggie had supplied him with coffee and sandwiches. Her friend looked weary and she smiled at him. "Thank you so much for searching all night. We found a body out at the old mines and Wolfe has just confirmed it's Laurie Turner."

"That's some way from where I found her backpack. It belongs to Laurie. It has a tag with her name on it." Blackhawk lifted a large evidence bag from beside his chair and handed it to her. "I decided to ride my trailbike through the forest and it was on the trail we searched yesterday about half a mile from Stanton. I marked the place with tape and have the coordinates." He held up his phone. "I took shots of the trail and all around but whoever dropped it there didn't leave a trace. I'll forward them to everyone now."

Jenna stared at the backpack. She'd take it to Wolfe when they went to the autopsy. "We're looking for a primary crime scene and it may be close to where you found this, we'll go and check it out. Did you touch it or go through it?"

"Nah." Blackhawk shook his head. "I had a pocket full of gloves and evidence bags with me, in case we found anything during the search." He sipped his coffee and regarded her with interest. "What happened to your face?"

Jenna closed the door and sat in her office chair. "Some crazy wife beater. He's in the cells and will be on his way to the county jail as soon as he's charged."

"How did your deputies allow this to happen?" His brown eyes flashed with anger. "Men who beat on women are contemptible."

Surprised by his concern, she smiled. "I'm fine. I wanted to handle him myself but it was a little difficult. I ordered Kane and Rowley to stand down." She stood and filled a coffee cup and then searched the drawer for Tylenol. "Rio is taking her to Her Broken Wings, they'll make sure she gets the best of care and assistance." She took her coffee back to the desk. "Have you met Zac Rio yet?"

"I have." Blackhawk nodded slowly. "He seems efficient but I'd say you have another overqualified deputy in your team. He's ambitious. Have you considered he might go against you in the next election? I know that's years away but by that time he'll be well established in town."

Jenna tossed the towel and ice into the sink and looked at him. "That's way too far into the future for me to worry about and my head is filled with this case." She indicated to the whiteboard. "We've gone from missing girl to murder victim in the last few hours. As soon as Rio gets back, he can handle the press because as soon as they get wind that I called off the search they'll know we've found a body."

"Do you know how she died?" Blackhawk turned his hat around in his hands and looked at her. "I didn't see any blood spatter, nothing at all around her backpack. I did a good recon of the area."

Having been with Blackhawk on a search in the forest many a time, she had seen his skills firsthand. A superb tracker, he was an asset and gave his time freely, refusing payment as if it was an insult. She valued his friendship on all levels, she'd trust him with her life. Jenna nodded. "We won't know until the autopsy. This one is difficult, maybe strangulation with post-mortem wounds. The autopsy is at two, I'll know more then."

A brief knock came on her door and Kane walked inside with Duke at his heels and nodded at Blackhawk. "I've checked out Laurie's laptop, it wasn't password-protected. There's nothing there at all unusual. The friends we've spoken to already make up the social media contacts. Her emails are very general. Even her search history is based on her assignments. No clues there at all. Not even a nasty comment."

Jenna stood and added information to the whiteboard and then turned to Kane. "Atohi found her backpack. We'll take it to Wolfe to examine."

"Yeah, I read the file." Kane went to the counter and poured himself a cup of coffee. "You sure you weren't a cop in a past life?"

"Me?" Blackhawk chuckled. "Who really knows which way their spirit guide has led them? Although, I don't like putting men in cages, so perhaps not." He shrugged. "But if I saw a rabid dog, I'd take it down without a second thought." He grinned at Kane. "Don't look so concerned, Eagle Eye, I have no plans to start murdering people. It is not in my nature and I find digging holes too much of a chore."

Jenna looked up as Rowley and Rio arrived at her office door. She waved them in. "What do you have for me?"

"Mrs. Law is in safe hands at Her Broken Wings. She lives out at Louan and they've arranged for her to go and collect her belongings while her husband is in custody." Rio handed her a document. "She gave me a statement and will press charges for assault. The social workers at the shelter have everything under control, they've even arranged a pro bono lawyer to represent her if necessary."

"Yeah, we took the charge sheet and evidence to date to the DA along with Mrs. Law's statement and ours; we had enough to obtain an arrest warrant." Rowley looked pleased with himself. "The DA wants statements from you and Kane and any witnesses willing to come forward to support his case. Law will be held in county waiting for a bail hearing. They are on their way to collect him."

Glad she had such efficient deputies, Jenna smiled. "Good to know. We'll get the statements before we leave for the autopsy and you can drop them into the DA's office. I'm happy Mrs. Law and her baby are being cared for in Black Rock Falls. She'll have a fresh start here." She clasped her hands around her coffee cup. "We're due to attend an autopsy at two. Rowley, I need you to start chasing down the witnesses in the Law case. The contact details are in the files. It would be easier if you could call them and ask them to come in to make a statement and then you'll be here for the transfer of our prisoner." She glanced at Rio. "Rio is attending the autopsy but he'll be back to relieve you as soon as possible."

"Rather him than me." Rowley ran a hand through his unruly hair. "The smell of that place makes me sick to my stomach." He swiped at the end of his nose. "I'll get at it." He headed for the door.

"I'll need you to sign off on the media release please, Sheriff." Rio placed a sheet of paper on her desk.

Jenna read through it and was impressed by the presentation, which gave the barest details, and none of the evidence found at the scene. "I can see you've written a few of these in your time. Great job. Ask Maggie for our media contact details and call it in." She signed the bottom of the page and handed it back to him.

Taking a few seconds to put her thoughts in order, Jenna waited for Blackhawk to finish his coffee and then smiled at him. "I really appreciate your help. The backpack might give up valuable evidence."

"Any time." Blackhawk looked at Jenna and stood. "I'm only a call away if you need me." He yawned. "I'm heading home to get some rest. I don't envy your next job, Jenna. I hope Shane can give you a clue to finding this killer." He pushed his hat on his head and followed Rio out the door.

Jenna stared after them. "That's one drawback about being sheriff." She grimaced. "I don't have an excuse to avoid an autopsy." She met Kane's combat face. He was already zoning out his emotions. "Although, this case is intriguing." She sighed. "In its own horrific way."

CHAPTER SIXTEEN

Steeling herself for the gruesome task ahead, Jenna tried to ignore the smell of the morgue and the cold that seeped through her clothes. She heard Kane clear his throat and Rio's boots click on the tile as they walked in a procession, her in the lead, to the examination room with the glowing red light outside. Her deputies' faces were grim as they shed their jackets and suited up for the autopsy. The air filled with mentholated salve and gloves snapped into place. Once everyone was ready, she scanned her card at the door and they all stepped inside. As usual, Wolfe had completed the preliminary examination before they arrived. Screens held X-ray images and an assortment of results from various tests he'd already conducted in their absence.

They walked to stand a little to the side of Wolfe, Emily, and Colt Webber, to peer at the victim's body on a gurney under the bright light. As they turned to look at them, she held up the evidence bag. "Atohi found Laurie's backpack, where do you want it?"

"Emily and Colt will go through it in another room." Wolfe waved them away. "I want this room as clean as possible."

Jenna handed Webber the plastic bag and smiled at Emily behind her mask. "Last semester, you must be excited. What's next?"

"Tons. I'm planning on completing an accelerated medical degree, then I'll have at least two years of residency before I can apply to be certified. There's a ton more studying to do if I want to specialize in forensic pathology. Right now, I'm more concerned about the postgrad finals." Emily shrugged. "I'm usually confident going into examinations but this means so much to me, I'm a little nervous."

"Sometimes that's a good thing." Kane wiggled his eyebrows. "Overconfidence can be a curse."

"You always say something to make me feel better." Emily squeezed his arm and then hurried after Webber.

"Before we start…" Wolfe moved his attention to Jenna. "The last text Laurie made was at five on Saturday evening. I went through everything going back a month, it is all general chat. The only interesting text between her and Wyatt Cooper, the boyfriend, was about him being annoyed about the attention Cory Hughes, the maintenance man, was giving her. It was then they broke up. Laurie told him she didn't like jealousy and blocked his calls."

"That's motive." Jenna considered the information. "Cooper was at the practice and could've followed her. If she needed a ride, she'd likely get in his vehicle." She looked at Kane. "We'll need to see what he drives." She turned back to Wolfe. "What else do you have for me?"

"We have some trace evidence." Wolfe indicated to the screen. "The men's briefs are a generic brand and untraceable but they held significant amounts of DNA. We also found a trace of foreign saliva on the screwdriver and extracted a good DNA sample." He moved to the screen. "The samples are unrelated to the victim and each other." He puffed out a long sigh. "Both of course are useless unless we find a match. As Cooper and Hughes had some involvement with Laurie, I'd start there but it will be a huge task. I'd suggest you call in Jo Wells and ask if Bobby Kalo can run the samples through the FBI databases."

"It's a bit early to call in the FBI." Kane frowned. "We'll get those samples and hunt down a few suspects before we contact them so we don't look like complete jerks."

"It's your call." Wolfe went back to staring at the results. "This case is complicated and I'd have thought you'd appreciate some input from Jo. She's a friend, she won't pull the FBI card if you don't specifically ask her to intervene in the case."

"Fine." Kane didn't look amused. "I'll call her if I can't figure out this guy."

Excited by the evidence, Jenna stared at the screen. "So, we may have two suspects?"

"Yeah, there's a chance." Wolfe's gray eyes flicked to her.

"I figure the saliva was an error and the briefs a message." Rio examined the results. "He looked at Kane. "What do you think?"

"I'll be listening to what Wolfe has to say before making any decisions or running to the FBI for help." Kane shrugged. "Seems to me the killers went to extreme measures not to leave any trace evidence."

Jenna lifted her gaze to the images on the screen. Wolfe had photographed both sides of the body. She looked at him. "We're interrupting you, please go on."

"Okay." Wolfe used a remote to bring up another set of X-rays. "There's no sign of blunt force trauma outside the perimeter of the stab wounds. As you can see of the twenty-two stab wounds on the face, eyes, and torso, in ten, we have evidence of damage to the underlying bone. The hyoid bone is fractured but the larynx isn't crushed." He turned to look at them. "I took samples of blood and I'm running a tox screen as routine but I tested specifically for a variety of sedatives to rule out the date rape scenario. I found no trace of any sedative in her system and I found no latent prints on her body."

Jenna examined the body. Apart from the stab wounds and neck bruising, the body only had a few superficial bruises. There were no defensive wounds. "Any sign of sexual activity?"

"No." Wolfe walked to the body. "I have already mentioned the livor mortis but as you can see from the extent in the lower regions of the body, she was in a sitting position for some time, perhaps eight hours or more before being relocated. I found something notable as well." He looked at Kane. "If you could help me turn her over?"

"Sure." Kane moved the body with great care and gentleness.

The unease drained away from Jenna as the need to know what happened to Laurie Turner took precedence and she moved closer. "Oh, I see it. There's a crease on her back."

"I took swabs as decomposing skin collects trace elements like a magnet. There were dust particles, nothing special but I found traces of polyethylene. In my opinion she was wrapped in plastic or was at least lying on plastic. The plastic sheet was creased and caused the mark on her back. This would account for the clean crime scene and the light coating of sandy soil on the body at the scene."

Jenna nodded, seeing the scene unfold in her head. "The killer wrapped her in plastic and took her to the mines, where he stabbed her post-mortem as you've established. That would account for the bodily fluids spatter and then after tossing the screwdriver down the mineshaft, he rolled her out of the plastic, covered his tracks, and headed for the hills."

"Hey, wind it back some." Kane was examining the back of Laurie's neck. He'd lifted the hair and was peering at the crossed over mark on the neck. "She was sitting for some time on plastic, but who just sits on a plastic sheet and waits to be strangled." He glanced at Wolfe. "I've seen this before, it's a classic attack from behind." He followed the mark to under the jawbone. "It's under the chin. I figure we've two people involved, one driver and the killer in the back seat, perhaps hiding. Laurie climbs in and the driver pulls away. The second drops a cord around her neck and crosses it over, pulling her up and over the seat. Maybe she had her seatbelt on and was pinned." He lifted his attention back to Wolfe. "Did you find any trace under her nails?"

"No, and she'd have blacked out in about ten seconds." Wolfe motioned for Kane to assist him rolling her onto her back. "The stab wounds are all inflicted by the same instrument. They differ in depth, which would indicate the attack continued until they tired. The main concentration is to the face and breast areas."

"I've seen something similar." Rio was standing arms folded over his chest and leaning against a counter. "It was a case where a guy's wife murdered his girlfriend but she used a kitchen knife. The same attack pattern, face and chest."

Jenna nodded. "That's good to know, so we could be looking at a spurned lover perhaps?" She stared at Kane. "Although, she seems too young to be involved in a love triangle."

"We could be looking at a female killer." Kane narrowed his gaze. "A very jealous woman."

Milling over the situation Jenna nodded. "Maybe two female suspects." She stared at Kane. "She'd more likely take the offer of a ride from a woman or even two."

"More like she knew the driver." Kane shrugged. "That's the impression of the witness and from her clear descriptions of everything else, I'd say she doesn't miss much."

"Getting back to the autopsy…" Wolfe pulled down the mic to record his findings. "We have the body of Laurie Turner, age sixteen years and two months. Caucasian, brown eyes and hair. She is average height and weight for her age. The injuries to the upper torso and face number twenty-two and are consistent in size and shape of a screwdriver found at the scene. Trace evidence on the screwdriver is a match for Laurie Turner and foreign DNA was located in an overlay suggesting it arrived after the cessation of the attack." He turned off the mic and looked at Jenna and her team. "I'll pause for questions but I need to keep the audio record undisturbed as I'll need to make an exact copy of my findings for the report."

Jenna took a step back as the examination of the body followed. This was the part that usually caused even the most experienced law enforcement officers to buckle. Organs removed, examined, weighed, and samples of stomach contents taken made her glance away a few times to catch her breath. She didn't have to worry about Kane, he seemed to take everything in his stride and was assisting Wolfe, but her interest wandered to Rio. He had surprised her so far. On the job, his input was intelligent and he knew his stuff. It was no different in the morgue. His gaze hadn't shifted from the autopsy, as if he was mentally filing every detail, and perhaps he was. He showed a keen interest in his eyes and was listening intently to Wolfe's every word. For a young man, he had knowledge beyond his years and as a person she liked him. He'd fit into the team just fine and for her to make that judgment on his first day was remarkable. Her attention snapped back to Wolfe the moment he started talking again.

"Stab wounds vary in depth and angle. The depth is from two and a half inches to half an inch on the chest and there are two four-inch incisions on the lower torso." Wolfe glanced up at Jenna. "I count ten wounds to the chest and lower torso and twelve wounds to the face." He turned off the mic as Emily and Webber came back into the room. "Ah good. Emily, take over and complete the sutures." He turned on the mic. "My conclusion is that cause of death is homicide by asphyxiation due to strangulation by an unknown subject. All other injuries were inflicted post-mortem by person or persons unknown at this time." He turned off the mic and looked at Jenna. "All my findings will be in my full report."

Jenna turned to Emily. "Was there anything of interest in the backpack?"

"Not inside, no. Just the usual things a girl would need at practice but her pompoms were missing. They usually have their own for practice. We found quite a few different sets of prints on the backpack and some fibers that could be from the interior carpet of a vehicle. They look too fine to be from a rug or similar. We've entered all the information on file and the samples are waiting for processing."

Jenna looked at Kane. "We'd have to print everyone at the practice, all her friends, and her father, to use for elimination."

"It's a waste of time." Kane shook his head. "If they took so much care to cover trace evidence, they wouldn't handle the backpack without gloves. They dropped it miles away from her body to put us off their trail."

"I'd be looking more closely at the fibers." Rio moved closer. "She would drop her backpack on the floor between her legs, when she got into the vehicle. If the backpack has picked up some fibers, we could trace them to the vehicle. We know the make and once we know the model and year, it would be easier to narrow down the owner."

"Leave it with me." Wolfe pulled down his facemask and headed for the door. "I'll get to it immediately."

Jenna turned to Kane and Rio. "Let's go." She followed Wolfe out the door. "There are so many databases we need to search. Bringing in the FBI computer whizz kid Bobby Kalo would make life so much easier. "I'm calling Jo the moment we get back to the office. Are you okay with that?"

"Sure." Kane dragged off his mask and smiled at her. "This case is going to need all the boots on the ground we can muster."

CHAPTER SEVENTEEN

Outside the ME's office, Jenna sucked in gulps of fresh mountain air but the smell of death lingered in her nostrils as if it had taken up permanent residence. She followed Kane to his truck and leaned against the door just breathing. At the end of the road, she could see people milling around Main. The preparations were in full swing for the Fall Festival parade the following day. The theme this year was sport and local teams would present their players on floats. A band followed by cheerleading squads would march down Main and the mayor would officially open the festival. The rest of the week would be filled with excitement and although at times the tourists could be a problem, she looked forward to the bunting, smiling faces, balloons, and cotton candy. All festivals brought a myriad of aromas, from the fried onions, barbecued ribs, and the famous pulled pork to the cake and candy stalls. She almost wanted to roll in it with delight.

"There goes our dance at the Fall Festival." Kane slid an arm around her shoulder and gave her a squeeze. "I was looking forward to having my toes crushed again this year." He grinned at her. "For someone who can learn hand-to-hand combat moves so easily, I can't understand why you can't dance." He winced when she dug him in the ribs. "Although, you're getting better."

Jenna snorted. "Have you thought it might be you?" She poked him again. "I didn't step on Ty's feet when we danced at Antlers."

"Yeah, but Carter was holding you way out here." Kane spread his arms. "He has a keen eye, and probably noticed the scuffs on my boots."

Jenna rolled her eyes. "Thanks, Dave, I feel so much better now." She ducked away and headed around the hood. "I guess we'd better get back to the office."

"I figure we should hunt down Cory Hughes first, he should be at the school at this time." Kane opened his door. "If he's innocent, he'll give up a DNA sample but we'll have to obtain permission from Wyatt Cooper's parents to test him."

Jenna nodded. "Sure, and we need the samples yesterday. Let's go."

She stared out the window, wanting to be part of the organizing happening in town. She often helped out here or there, her deputies saving some of the older townsfolk from the heavy lifting, but she only got a glimpse of Main, as Kane took the backroads. After a few turns they sped along Stanton toward the school. The parking lot was empty but they passed a few kids walking home in groups. "From what Hughes said he parks round back."

"Okay.' Kane drove around the main building and parked behind a white pickup.

Jenna wrinkled her nose at the smell coming from the line of dumpsters and buzzed up her window. She scanned the area. "The backdoor is open. Maybe he's working close by."

"I hope so. We've been away from the office for hours." Kane climbed out and went to the back of his truck. "I'll grab a DNA test kit."

Jenna stared at him. "If you're worrying about Duke, don't. Maggie will be feeding him snacks and he'll probably be sleeping them off."

"Maybe but he doesn't know Rio." Kane pushed surgical gloves into his pocket and shrugged. "With him working next to me, he might think I've been replaced. He doesn't like strangers." He looked at her. "I figure if he gets worried, he'll head back to the res. You should see him there, Jenna, he gets so excited. I didn't think that dogs remembered their mothers but he does. I often wonder if I should have given him to Atohi?"

Jenna ignored the stink of garbage and stared at him in disbelief. "Are you joking? When you spent time in the hospital, he howled at the door and insisted I take him to every room in the cottage to look for you. He slept under the Beast for weeks and refused to eat. I had to drag him out and then give him one of your dirty shirts to sleep on and hand feed him in his basket. He might be excited to see his mom but you are his world." She looked at him uncomprehending. "You must know that, right?"

"You never told me that before." Kane's brow wrinkled into a frown.

Jenna shook her head. "No, because you weren't you when you came home from the hospital. You didn't remember me let alone Duke."

"I did remember Duke." Kane removed his hat and rubbed the scar on his head. "Selective memory." He cupped her cheek. "Sorry, I remember everything just fine now. You saved my life and I abandoned you."

Jenna moved closer. "You came home." She smiled at him. "Even with no memory, you came home with me. You're with me now. That's all that matters."

"I'm a lucky man." Kane brushed a kiss over her lips and then stiffened and looked over her shoulder and dropped his hand. "I think it was just a bug in your hair, Sheriff."

What? Jenna noticed Cory Hughes leaning against the doorframe, grinning like a baboon. It was obvious Kane was trying to conceal a tender moment from prying eyes. She cleared her throat. "What's so funny, Mr. Hughes?"

"Well, it's not often I see the sheriff and one of her deputies making out with the trash." Hughes chuckled. "I'll leave you two love birds alone."

Annoyed, Jenna marched toward him. The last thing they needed was Hughes spreading rumors all over town. "If asking someone to pull a bug out of my hair is your idea of making out, I think you need professional help." She followed him inside. "Don't go anywhere, I'm here to see you."

"I gave my statement and I have nothing more to add." He led the way inside the school.

"We are eliminating the last people to see Laurie Turner alive from our investigation." Kane moved to her side. "We'll need a DNA swab from inside your mouth. It's painless and if you're not involved in her murder, you have no need to be concerned."

"Murder?" Hughes paled. "Last I heard she went missing. She's dead? How? What happened to her?" He looked at her wide-eyed.

Either Hughes was in shock or he was great at play acting. She'd witnessed psychopaths act remorseful when they had no empathy whatsoever and usually went by her gut feeling during interviews. "The cause of death is under investigation. There was DNA found on her body and we're collecting samples from all her friends. We're not accusing you of anything, this way if you had nothing to do with her death, it takes suspicion away from you."

"I'd never hurt Laurie." Hughes rubbed both hands down his face. "I knew she liked me but getting involved with a sixteen-year-old would cost me my job. I told her to go make up with Wyatt when she broke her phone." He dashed a hand through his hair. "She kissed me on the cheek and ran out the door giggling."

"Did you follow her?" Kane's voice was so low, Jenna could hardly hear him. "Sweet young thing like her, no one would know, right?"

Jenna understood Kane's unsavory comment about Laurie as an interviewing technique used by FBI profilers during questioning. It made the suspect believe the interviewer was of like mind and often prompted a response. Perpetrators often enjoyed talking about their exploits to likeminded people.

"No, I didn't follow her." Hughes straightened. "I went home like I told you." His eyes flashed with anger. "I'd never hurt Laurie. I'll give a DNA sample to prove it."

Easily said from a killer who knew he'd covered his tracks. Jenna nodded. "Thank you. I didn't realize she was a close friend. I'm sorry for your loss." She motioned toward Kane. "Deputy Kane will take the sample."

Jenna noticed a screwdriver, in his top pocket. It was a different color to the one they'd found at the crime scene. "Do you always carry that particular screwdriver?"

"Yeah." Hughes looked puzzled. "This one is the right size to fit just about everything in the school, so I keep it handy."

"Does anyone in your household own a Chrysler sedan?" Kane was gloving up and his voice had become almost conversational.

"Yeah. My mom has one, it's an old one, she don't drive it much." Hughes opened his mouth for Kane to swab.

"Thanks." Kane sealed the sample and asked Hughes to sign the form. "Is it green by any chance?"

"Yeah, why?" Hughes wiped his mouth with the back of his hand. "She run a red light or something?"

"Not that I'm aware." Kane sealed the evidence bag. "Does your sister drive the vehicle?"

"Sometimes." Hughes frowned and shifted from one foot to the other. "But she's not long gotten her license."

Jenna took in the change of demeanor. "Why didn't you inform me about the vehicle at the meeting at the gym? I did ask if anyone knew someone with a green Chrysler sedan. It was right after we spoke about the phone."

"I guess I didn't hear you." Hughes scratched his head. "I'd gone to get Laurie's phone for you, remember?"

His excuse was plausible and he'd cooperated so far. Jenna nodded. "Yeah, that's right, you left before I made the announcement." She thought for a beat and changed tact. "Did Verna get along with Laurie? Verna was on the same cheerleading squad as her, wasn't she?"

"Yeah they were but they didn't get along." Hughes looked defensive. "Now don't you go thinking anything nasty about Verna. She's had a bad life. My parents fostered her for a year and then adopted her. People don't understand her is all."

"Do you get along?" Kane's voice had dropped to a whisper. "It would be strange having a teenager move in. I'm not sure I'd like to share my parents with a stranger."

"It's not like that at all." Hughes shook his head. "Darn it, she's my best friend. I'm glad she's one of the family now." He frowned. "I'm glad she's there. Since Pa walked out, Ma has become a pain and blames me for everything. Like it's my fault he left her?"

"It's hard for everyone when folks break up." Kane grimaced. "We have everything we need, thank you for your time."

As they climbed back into the Beast, Jenna turned to Kane. "Did you get a vibe from him?"

"He wasn't acting like a guy who thought Laurie was too young for him, and someone who might cause him to lose his job if he became involved with her. I would expect his reaction from a longtime lover. His words said one thing and his actions another." Kane started the engine and backed out. "That was overkill. If his mom owns a Chrysler sedan, we only have his word he was driving his truck on Saturday night. If he parks in the same place, it would've been out of sight—or Verna was driving it."

The possible scenario dropped into Jenna's mind. She could see where Kane was going. "He was working here on Saturday night and could have easily disabled Laurie's pickup." She frowned. "But how did he make her drop her phone?"

"Verna." Kane turned back onto Stanton. "From what everyone was saying there was quite a crowd in the parking lot that night. They were all excited about the festival, making plans and such. Maybe she followed her outside and bumped into her. All the girls of her age are always carrying their phones and talking. They live in their own worlds. Most never know what's happening around them."

Jenna thought for a while. "I'm not so sure. It seems to me he could have had Laurie, she fancied him and the attack on her looks too much like something a jealous woman would do and he admitted Verna didn't like her." She shook her head. "We might be looking at this the wrong way. The killer might be Verna."

"Maybe but it would be difficult to murder her and then move her body alone, and men attack women's faces as well." Kane grimaced. "I need to speak to Jo. I've read something about a killer who attacked the eyes of his victims. In that case, he knew all of them. It might be a trait. If they can't look at him, he's not responsible. I'll need to dig deeper."

CHAPTER EIGHTEEN

After leaving the school, Kane headed to the home of Wyatt Cooper. There would be a chance he'd be home by now and maybe one of his parents would be there to sign the consent form. As they pulled up outside the rambling ranch-style home, he glanced at Jenna. "Fingers crossed we get this done today. We need answers."

"I'm just hoping Laurie's death is the result of a bad argument and not the first in a line of cheerleader murders." Jenna pushed open her door. "I feel like the clock is ticking and we're getting closer to finding another corpse." She looked at him as she rounded the hood. "I figure we'll need Verna's DNA as well. I'm still not discounting her involvement or Hughes in this case."

After gathering another test kit, Kane followed her to the front of the house. After Jenna pressed the bell, a woman in her late thirties opened the door, and stood staring at them with an astonished expression. He nodded to her. "Mrs. Cooper?"

"Yes." Mrs. Cooper stood as if guarding the doorway, both hands clutching the doorframe. "Is something wrong?"

"Not at all." Jenna smiled at the woman. "We're collecting DNA samples and fingerprints to eliminate suspects in Laurie Turner's murder. We'd like to get a sample from Wyatt if he's home."

"We just heard on the news about her death." Mrs. Cooper pressed a hand to her chest. "She was such a sweet girl. Wyatt is heartbroken." She shook her head. "I guess you'd better come inside. I'll go and get him."

Kane followed Jenna through the door and they waited in the hallway at the foot of the stairs. The scent of lavender furniture polish filled the house and exploded a wave of memories for him. His mother had always made her own polish using beeswax and lavender oil. He recalled her telling him how it made everything shine, even his boots. Upstairs they could hear mumbled conversations and Wyatt Cooper appeared at the top of the steps.

"Have you found out who killed her?" Wyatt shook his head slowly. "If only I'd waited, she would've been okay. I was too pig-headed and figured she'd get jealous seeing me talking to Becky."

"We wouldn't be here chasing down DNA samples if we'd found her killer." Jenna was regarding him closely. "You can't blame yourself, Wyatt. It's the killer's fault, not yours, and we'll find out who did this to her. You have my word."

"Thanks." Wyatt looked at Kane. "I can't believe the mayor is going ahead with the festival with Laurie dead and all. It doesn't seem right. We're expected to show too, like nothing happened."

The show must go on. Kane nodded. "When something like this happens, it's sometimes best to allow life to go on as normal. It's a traumatic event and normality is the best cure." He met the young man's troubled gaze. "We need DNA—"

"Yeah, Mom just told me." Wyatt frowned. "Do you need to take blood?"

"No just a swab." Jenna smiled at him. "Open your mouth." She took the sample. "There you go, that was easy."

After pulling the fingerprint scanner device from his pocket, Kane moved closer. This is painless too. He guided Wyatt through the process. "Thank you for your cooperation."

"That's okay." Wyatt rubbed the back of his neck. "I hope you find who killed Laurie."

Kane waited for Mrs. Cooper to join them. "I have some paper-work for you to sign." He rested the documents on a side table and explained the contents. "Thank you." He sighed. "We'll get going. We have to get this sample back to the lab."

"I'm so sorry for your loss." Jenna headed for the door.

As they drove away, Kane turned to her. "Now that was genuine grief. Blaming himself is normal, he felt responsible for her and wanted her back. I don't see him as jealous."

"He seems like a normal healthy teenager to me." Jenna shook her head. "But then Ted Bundy was regarded as a really nice guy too and he murdered thirty-six women. He makes the psychopaths we've had to deal with in Black Rock Falls look like amateurs."

After dropping by the ME's office to give the samples to Wolfe, Kane took the backroads back to the office to avoid the crowds. They arrived a little before five to see Duke's nose pressed against the door. From the marks spread across the glass, he'd been there for some time. As Kane stepped inside, a bark of excitement greeted him followed by a happy dance of epic proportions. He was used to having an excited dog weighing a little over one hundred pounds charging at him but it was only by his quick reflexes he managed to catch Jenna before she headbutted the front counter. As she hung over his arm, Duke was licking her face with enthusiasm. "Hey, settle down, Duke. We're happy to see you too but Jenna doesn't need a bath."

Oh, he'd said the "B" word and Duke stopped moving and hightailed it under Maggie's desk. Kane straightened and tried not to laugh at the saliva dripping from Jenna's chin. "Sorry. He was just being loving."

"Yuk." She shuddered. "I told you he'd be frantic." She headed for the bathroom. "I need to wash up."

"There's someone here to see you." Maggie was grinning from ear to ear. "Those FBI agents and their dogs." She glanced down beside her. "But best you settle Duke. He's shaking so much, if I put my feet on him, I'd get a foot massage."

Kane nodded. "Sure." He smiled and pulled a bag of cookies from his jacket pocket. "Duke, I have cookies." He coaxed him out and rubbed his ears. "I'm sorry we took so long. We'll go by Aunt Betty's on the way home. Okay?"

It seemed the cure for all that ailed Duke was covered by cookies and the mention of Aunt Betty's Café. Kane leaned on the counter. "Any idea why Jo and Carter are here?"

"They didn't say." Maggie shrugged. "They arrived about five minutes ago and they're not wearing their FBI jackets."

Kane nodded. "Where are Rowley and Rio?"

"In the communications room." She smiled. "They work well together. They had people lining up to give statements in the Law case and had them all filed in no time at all. The county picked up Law and now they're searching through CCTV footage for the vehicle you're trying to hunt down."

"Thanks." He glanced up as Jenna came through the main office and headed his way. "Jo and Carter are waiting in your office, Rowley and Rio are scanning CCTV files."

"Okay." Jenna headed for her office door. "I wonder what they want?" She bent to rub Duke's ears. "He seems fine now."

Kane chuckled. "Yeah, he's much like me. Give him a cookie and he'll forgive anything."

"I'll try and remember that jewel of information." Jenna laughed and pushed the door open to her office.

CHAPTER NINETEEN

"Jo, Ty. How good to see you again and who is this beautiful young lady?" Jenna smiled at the young girl clutching a Boston Terrier on her lap.

"This is Jaime and Beau." Jo smiled warmly at Jenna. "We're staying at The Cattleman's Hotel for the Fall Festival."

"Nice to meet you, Jaime. I'm Jenna and this is Dave Kane." Jenna smiled at the little girl. "I've been looking forward to meeting you. Did you come in the chopper? I bet that was fun."

"I liked it fine but Beau was shaking all over." Jaime frowned. "He seems okay now. What happened to your face?"

Jenna touched her sore cheek. "Oh, I just bumped it is all."

"When I hurt myself, Mommy kisses it better for me, but adults don't do that, do they?" Jaime gave her a wide-eyed stare.

"Well, Kane's dog gave my face a good lick before so I'm good to go now." Jenna glanced at Ty Carter sprawled in a chair, his trusty Doberman, Zorro, sitting beside him. The pair of them were a complete contrast: Carter gave the impression of a lazy cowboy, chewing on a toothpick, untidy blond hair at his collar, wearing cowboy boots and a battered Stetson, while his dog sat upright, ears pricked, coat glossy, and ready for action. "Ty, nice to see you. Are you all here for the festival?"

"Nope, I'm here for some recreational pursuits: eating, playing cards, or pool and drinking. I might find time to go fishing as well." He looked at Kane. "Do you have any vacation time due? I'd appreciate your company."

"Unfortunately, we have a homicide to investigate." Kane shrugged. "We had planned to call you."

"Ah, no way." Carter held up his hands. "I'm off-duty but Kalo is in the office if you need him to hunt down anything for you."

"I'll be happy to help." Jo leaned back in her chair. "But I promised Jaime she could watch the parade."

Jenna went to the counter and filled the coffee machine. "We'll have time to run a few things past you later when Jaime is asleep."

"Sure." Jo smiled. "I was hoping to introduce Jaime to Shane's daughters. I think she'd get along with Anna but I guess he'll be busy too?"

Jenna pulled out cups and the fixings. "He will but Julie will be taking Anna to the festival. She's very responsible and they have a housekeeper who never misses a parade. Maybe you can tag along with them?"

"I'll call and ask Shane later." Jo looked at Kane. "Was it something in my field of expertise you needed to discuss?"

"Yeah, it's complicated." Kane dropped into a seat and removed his hat. "Like most things that happen around here."

"Well…" Carter straightened and tossed the toothpick into the trash. He looked at Jaime. "I have a hankering for a slice of Aunt Betty's peach pie. She has every flavor of ice cream. If your mom says it's okay, would you like to come with me and try some?"

"Can I, Mommy?" Jaime grinned. "Please, please, please?"

"Sure, but don't be too long." Jo turned to Carter. "You'd better grab a slice of that pie for me as well." She looked at Jenna. "It's the best in town, right?

Jenna laughed. "It sure is."

"Let's go." Carter offered his hand to the little girl. "We'll walk, it's not far and the dogs need a run." They headed out the door.

"Okay." Jo leaned forward in her seat. "What's happened?"

Jenna poured three cups of coffee and placed them on the table. She sat down and brought Jo up to speed with the Laurie Turner case. "Like Kane said, it's complicated."

"Hmm." Jo drummed her fingertips on the desk. "The cause of death confuses things, strangulation from behind isn't upfront and personal, which appears to contradict the post-mortem stabbing."

"Then we have the delay." Kane indicated to the whiteboard, which had been brought up to date by Rio in their absence. "She was strangled and left in a sitting position for some hours, wrapped in plastic, and moved to the lowlands. We know she was stabbed in that location by the spatter pattern over the metal door to the old mine."

Jenna chewed on her bottom lip. "It doesn't fit any crime of passion I've seen before."

"That's because it's not." Jo sipped her coffee and thought for a beat. "I'm wondering if this is a White Knight murder."

"In what context?" Kane looked puzzled.

"This type is the next step up from a man coming to a woman's need. This subject is really a subordinate to a dominant personality. He would see her as a goddess, someone he admires. He craves her favor and will do anything to please her including being an accessory or committing murder for her. So, we could have two killers working together. I have no doubt it's two people involved, likely a male and female but it could be two females. It's not unusual for two jealous females to hunt down women they hate." Jo stood and stared at the whiteboard. "So, are you assuming she was strangled by the subordinate and stabbed by the dominant?"

Jenna nodded. "Yes, I think it's possible. We have a witness to say she took a ride in a car, and we're assuming from the time of death it happened sometime after that. Kane believes she was strangled inside the vehicle but we can't ignore the fact she may have been attacked leaving the vehicle by a taller person. From the position of the marks on her neck either is possible so I can't discount the subordinate male."

"I'd say inside the vehicle but I disagree with the idea the subordinate strangled her." Jo stared at the autopsy photographs. "If a person isn't a killer and is ordered to take a life, the first kill would be clumsy. It takes four minutes to strangle someone to death, sustained pressure is required or the victim regains consciousness. In that time, someone in this category would reduce the pressure, the cord would slip as they tried again. This isn't evident here." She looked at Kane. "You've seen this before, surely?"

"Yeah, sometimes the victim wakes up and they have to strangle them again." Kane was on his feet staring at the images. "The marks on Laurie's neck are from sustained pressure, so this was the dominant of the two and I figure the attack was committed by the same person."

"Exactly." Jo stared at the post-mortem wounds and nodded slowly. "This is a frenzied attack but what triggered it?" She stared at the board. "Any clues at the scene?"

"Nothing." Kane sighed. "As you can see the entire area was swept clean."

"Okay. Let's wind it back to the actual murder." Jo turned to look at them. "So, why take her from the vehicle and sit her on a plastic sheet. Why sit her up? It would have been easier to lie her down. They obviously planned to move her and a sitting body in rigor would have been difficult to move."

"Maybe that's why they waited overnight." Kane pointed to the images of the scene at the mine. "They left very little trace evidence. They must know about forensics to some degree."

"You're missing my point." Jo leaned one hip against the desk. "Why sit her up in the first place?"

A chill ran down Jenna's back as she contemplated the gruesome scene. "Oh Lord, they wanted her to watch them."

"That's my take on it and the men's briefs pushed in her mouth is telling the world she's easy." Jo looked at Jenna. "Okay, so fast forward to the morning they dumped her at the mine, what would trigger an attack to the face and eyes?"

Jenna rubbed her temples. She felt like she was back at Quantico again. "It's jealousy, she wanted to destroy her looks, and make her ugly."

"Not just that." Kane turned away from the board. "The dominant killer believed Laurie was still looking at them or looking at her subordinate. It was the trigger."

"That's what I believe too." Jo sat down and reached for her coffee. "Classic dominant with psychopathic tendencies, subordinate follower with a White Knight complex."

"I'd profile him with a dominating mother, or grandmother in his life, who runs him down all the time and he sees the killer as a hero, someone who cares enough to kill for him." Kane dropped into his seat. "Now all we have to do is find them."

"Remember the technique we discussed during interviews, Dave." Jo frowned. "These types of criminals don't respect the people they hurt. You have to get down to their level, no matter how dirty it makes you feel." She sighed. "It's sometimes the only way to get them to talk about what they've done. If they think you're of the same opinion they'll often open up and boast about what they've done."

"It makes me feel like a pervert speaking that way." Kane flicked her a glance. "But it's a tried and true technique."

Jenna squeezed his arm. "After listening to psychopaths boasting about their kills nothing you say in an interview will worry me, Dave. We use what works and like Jo said, it's a recognized interviewing technique, and not indicative of your thoughts."

The phone buzzed and Jenna reached for it. "Hi, Shane, what have you got for me?" She put the phone on speaker.

"We have a DNA match. The briefs belong to Wyatt Cooper. No match on the saliva as yet." Wolfe cleared his throat. *"This seems very suspicious to me, too darn obvious when every care was taken to leave the body clean."*

Jenna nodded. "Yeah, it does. Jo is here on vacation. We're getting her take on the case now. Do you want to listen in?"

"Hi, Jo. I'll call you later. I'm snowed under here at the moment." Wolfe sighed. *"Jenna, I'm finishing up my report and checking results. I'll have them to you soon."*

"Okay, thanks, chat soon." Jenna disconnected. She looked at Kane. "What do you think?"

"It seems too much of a coincidence the DNA is a match to Cooper." Kane rubbed the back of his neck. "If he'd been involved, why would he make sure there's no trace evidence and then leave a calling card behind? No one is that stupid."

"I have to agree." Jo nodded. "It's as if they're trying to shift the blame to someone else."

Jenna tapped her bottom lip, thinking. "Cooper was jealous of Hughes, he admitted it but nothing else fits."

"All this—" Jo waved a hand toward the whiteboard "—was triggered by jealousy. So, you have a few options. I believe this is a female dominant and a male subordinate but there is always a chance it could be one killer but from what I'm seeing here, it's not likely for these reasons: If Cooper was pushed to a jealous rage when Laurie went to Hughes instead of him for help, in my experience, a killer of this type would use rape as a punishment, rather than stuffing his briefs down her throat."

"And the killers have been so careful not to leave evidence." Jenna shrugged. "It doesn't fit." She looked at Jo. "What do you suggest?"

"You'll need to hunt down any guys Laurie was attracted to because one of them might be the subordinate and his girlfriend the killer. Alternatively, you need to discover if there was anything else to trigger an attack. Maybe something going on at school between the girls. Laurie was on the cheerleading squad, did she take another girl's place for instance, was there a rivalry there?" She shook her head. "Failing all of the above, we could have an opportunistic thrill killer who likes to keep corpses overnight and then mutilate them. In this case, the murderer would be male for sure, but as there was no sexual contact, it would be unusual—but then unusual is usual in Black Rock Falls."

CHAPTER TWENTY

By the time, Jo and Carter had taken Jaime back to The Cattleman's Hotel, it was getting late. Jenna and Kane went over the case files making notes until Rowley and Rio emerged from the communications room. Both looked tired after reviewing the CCTV footage. Jenna looked up at them. "How did you go?"

"We found a similar vehicle traveling through town at nine on Saturday night. The feed is too distorted to make out a plate number or who was driving." Rowley sighed. "The camera lens is dirty or we have a wasp's nest in there. It was that bad. Nothing visible from the bank cameras, Miller's Garage, or the gun store."

Jenna nodded. "Well, that's a shame." She glanced at her notes. "Did you get all the paperwork for the Law case over to the DA?"

"Yeah." Rio nodded. "The escort arrived at three to collect Law. He's safely locked away in the county jail until his bail hearing. I followed up on Mrs. Law and her baby. She has collected her things from the family home and has settled into one of the safe apartments run by the Her Broken Wings Foundation. She will remain there for as long as necessary but won't be returning to Blackwater."

Relieved, Jenna smiled. "That's good to know."

"How is your face?" Rowley frowned at her. "You're going to have a shiner."

Jenna touched her cheek. "I'm fine, thank you." She cleared her throat and brought them up to date with their interviews and Wolfe's results. "As you go past the Hughes' house on the way home, I was wondering if you could try and persuade Mrs. Hughes to allow you to take a DNA sample from Verna?"

"I can try." Rowley looked a little uncomfortable. "I'm convinced Mrs. Hughes is a conspiracy theorist. Sandy has had a few run-ins with her, she isn't a pleasant woman and hates law enforcement. She may not allow me through the gate. Her place is posted but I can try."

Concerned over Rowley's safety, she shook her head. "Don't worry. If she's posted 'no trespassing' signs, she's within her rights to defend her property. Going there at night without backup is out of the question. I doubt Verna is going anywhere, I'll drop by with Kane in the morning." She smiled at her deputies. "There's overtime on offer, for the festival. I'm calling in some help from Blackwater but I'd like one of us to be on duty here until ten, ten-thirty tomorrow and Wednesday. Walters has volunteered to take the rest of the week. He'll be taking over at six."

"I'll do tomorrow." Rowley shrugged. "I'll be in town anyway. Sandy wants to finish up at the house in town and make it nice for when Zac moves in." He chuckled. "I can't stop her. Her mom says she's nesting—whatever that means. She's not happy at the moment unless she's cleaning or setting up rooms and she ran out of things to do at the ranch last weekend."

Jenna looked at Rio's puzzled expression. "Sandy is Rowley's wife and they're expecting. She gave up work last week and has been keeping herself busy is all."

"Ah, I see." Rio smiled.

Jenna waved him away. "Okay, head off home. Maggie has already left for the day. We'll lock up. See you in the morning." She smiled at Rowley. "Give my best to Sandy."

"I will." Rowley touched his hat and headed for the door.

Jenna shook her head. "I hope Sandy doesn't overdo things, with the baby and all."

"I'm sure Doc Brown is keeping a close eye on her." Kane took his hat from the desk and ran his fingers down the center crease. "You ever thought about having kids?"

Although taken aback by his question, Jenna didn't hesitate. "Yeah, and I'm aware the clock is ticking. Why?"

"Just asking." Kane seemed consumed by a fleck of cotton on his black Stetson. "It's been great sharing everyone's kids but it's not the same as having your own."

Jenna tidied her desk. "I couldn't agree with you more."

"That's good to know." Kane pushed the hat on his head and then bent to rub Duke's ears.

A low rumble filled the room and Jenna's attention moved back to Kane. "Do you mind if we drop by Aunt Betty's for dinner? It's been a long day and I'm famished. We still have to feed the horses and I don't feel like cooking tonight."

"Sure." Kane collected his things and closed his laptop. "I'll finish up filing my reports at home. Let's go."

Jenna inhaled the instant she stepped into Aunt Betty's Café. Its sinfully delightful aromas of dishes that were guaranteed to go straight to her hips made her glance at Kane, suddenly understanding his need to buy takeout to keep in his freezer. Living the long hours during cases, it was good to have something to pop into the microwave when they arrived home. The problem was, apart from a freezer filled with steak, Jenna didn't really have anything she didn't have to make from scratch.

Aunt Betty's was busier than usual with the tourists in town. As she edged around tables filled with people and made her way to their seats, she heard a bark. She turned to see Duke sitting in front of the counter. She looked at Kane. "Won't you look at that, he's ordering his dinner."

"He jumped the line as well." Kane grinned and sat down at their reserved table and picked up the menu. "I could eat just about everything on here tonight. Pulled pork, honey glazed potatoes, and peach pie for me tonight."

Jenna removed her jacket and hung it over the back of the chair. "I think I'll have the same but I'll take the small portion." She laughed at his expression. "I do get hungry too, you know."

After Suzie arrived to take their order and placed a filled bowl for Duke on the floor, she smiled at them. "What will you have tonight?"

After giving Suzie their order, Jenna sipped a glass of water and leaned back in her chair. "Mind if we talk about the case?"

"Nope." Kane stood, removed his jacket and hat, and then sat down closer to her. "We'd better keep it generic. We don't know who might be listening."

With their backs to the wall and in the corner, the hum of conversation would cover any discussion. Jenna lowered her voice. "I'm not sure about Wyatt Cooper, I know you figure he's not involved but I still reckon we should talk to him about where he might have lost his underwear. I mean, could anyone have been in the vicinity of his laundry basket?"

"That's a good point." Kane was leaning close listening intently. "There wouldn't be many places he'd be changing his shorts." He stared into space for a few seconds. "A swimming hole maybe, but he wouldn't take spares, most would jump in the water and head home wet."

Nothing came to Jenna. She'd had no experience with teenage boys. She thought back to the first time they'd spoken to Wyatt. "He asked if you'd played football. He is on the team." Her face grew hot and she looked away. "Never mind."

"Out with it." Kane bumped her shoulder. "That's the first time I've seen you blush. Come on, ask me, I know you want to."

Jenna huffed out a breath. "It's not something I really need to know but it's a theory." She could feel her cheeks burning. "When you practiced or whatever, I guess you sweated a lot, is it usual to shower and change clothes after training?"

"It depends, on how much gear you're wearing and the temperature, but yeah I used to sweat right through. We practiced before classes, so we showered and changed. Before you ask yeah, I changed my shorts. I figure most guys would." Kane smiled at her. "I know the high school team practices before classes. Do you figure someone took his dirty laundry from his locker?" He pushed a hand through his hair. "Thinking back, most guys just stripped off and left their clothes in a pile on the bench. So, if your assumption is correct, we could be looking at someone who is either on the team or works with the team."

Jenna nodded. "I think we should ask him." She glanced at him. "Although, it's pretty embarrassing asking a sixteen-year-old about his underwear."

"Not if they were found stuffed in the mouth of his murdered ex-girlfriend." Kane shook his head. "He has motive. He was jealous. He's admitted it and didn't like her talking to Hughes. The problem is it's just too darn obvious that he's the killer unless I've read him all wrong."

"Well, Jo agrees with you." Jenna rubbed her temples. "Personally, I figure divulging where we found his briefs will be giving away vital evidence. Something only the killer would know and I don't believe Cooper is stupid enough to leave a calling card."

"We need to inform him we found his shorts at the crime scene and watch his reaction." Kane shrugged. "Although, Jo did offer a variety of scenarios, I agree with you, and I'm leaning more toward Hughes and his sister. I have a gut instinct about a dominant woman being involved, and if Verna is as tough as they say, she fits the profile."

"Yeah, we'll need to see for ourselves. Sometimes people's reputations are unfounded. We'll head out first thing in the morning and catch her before she leaves for the parade." Jenna pulled out her phone and searched her files. "Taking the possible football link into consideration there's another name, well two names that Vicky Perez mentioned, we should follow up. The quarterback, Dale Collins, runs the refreshments kiosk for his aunt on training days, and both he and a cheerleader by the name of Marlene Moore were seen chatting to Laurie before she disappeared. They might have some information. I'd like to know what they talked about that night."

"We don't have a link between them." Kane peered at her notes. "Vicky just said Marlene is always hanging around Collins. That would be normal for a quarterback, they usually have a fan club."

"I'm thinking out of the box, Dave. We'll hunt them down after we've spoken to Verna." Jenna smiled as the food arrived. "Oh, this looks good."

"Thank you." Susie beamed. "Enjoy, I'll send someone back with a pot of coffee."

"Do you figure she'll give you her recipes?" Kane grinned at her. "Nah, don't ask."

Jenna frowned. "Why? Is it because I'm hopeless at cooking?"

"Nope. I think they'd be locked away in a vault." Kane chuckled. "And by the way, I happen to like your little idiosyncrasies. They make you special."

CHAPTER TWENTY-ONE

Tuesday

The internal clock inside Kane's head woke him at five. He pulled on his workout gear, a sweater, and sweat pants and then headed out into the misty morning to do his chores. As usual Duke tagged along and Pumpkin, Jenna's black cat, was sitting on a haybale waiting for them to arrive. He took the horses out to the corral and stood for a second to admire the view and enjoy the horses. He placed one boot on the new gate he'd purchased from the Crazy Iron Forge out of Blackwater and relaxed, allowing the murder case filling his mind to seep into oblivion for a few minutes. The need to complete his chores and head into work tugged at him and with a sigh, he turned to walk back to the barn. He paused mid-stride at a sound coming from inside. Both the dog and cat were around his feet and the ranch was like Fort Knox, no one crossed the boundaries without setting off an alarm. He heard the scrape, whine, plop again and edged alongside the wall before turkey peeking around the door. He barked out a laugh at the sight of Jenna, mucking out one of the stalls. "Morning."

"Hey." Jenna leaned on a pitchfork and smiled at him. "It's cold this morning and I figured I needed to loosen up before we worked out." She glanced at her watch. "I want to be leaving here by six-thirty to be sure we catch the Hughes family at home."

Kane picked up a shovel and scooped and tossed manure into the wheel barrow. "Have you decided anything about the saliva sample found at the crime scene?"

"Yeah." Jenna had moved onto the third stall. "I sent it to Bobby Kalo to run through the DNA databases last night but unless our suspect has been in trouble with the law, or served in the military, we won't find a match."

Kane kept up a steady pace and didn't stop to look at her. "They have access to all the DNA databases, including the ones people use to discover their family tree. We might not get a direct hit but we might get a close relative."

"I hope so." Jenna broke open a bale of straw and shook it out inside the stall before repeating the process in the next one along. "We need something to go on and it seems to me, whoever stabbed Laurie with the screwdriver left the saliva. They were in a rage and could have been shouting obscenities for all we know. Spittle can fly out all over when someone is angry."

Kane rolled the wheelbarrow out to the compost pile behind the barn to empty it and then followed Jenna to her ranch house. It was their normal routine, they washed up and then completed a brutal workout before showering and eating breakfast. Their uniform had changed a little since their stint as FBI consultants. The need for unencumbered movement had become clearer with each arrest they made. They both now preferred regular jeans, a T-shirt, and a sheriff's department jacket. Jenna would wear blue jeans, an open neck blouse, and had swapped her duty belt for a less cumbersome holster and a jacket with more pockets. He preferred black, and wore his Glock in a hip holster, with his badge displayed on his belt. The change hadn't as much as raised an eyebrow with the townsfolk and although Rowley had asked the question, Jenna had informed him as sheriff and deputy sheriff, they could wear what they pleased.

They rolled through town at close to seven and arrived at the Hughes home a little after. Kane gave his siren a blast and went up the driveway with his wig-wag lights flashing. He turned to Jenna. "I don't want them taking pot shots at us."

"If they have nothing to hide, they shouldn't be so worried." She turned to him. "They must have had regular visits when they were in the foster system."

Kane approached the house, doing a visual scan of the area, windows, and doors for any sign of a shotgun pointed in their direction. A dusty old Chrysler sedan was parked under the trees out front. "Yeah but that was some time ago, when Verna was a kid, things have changed around these parts since then."

The door opened, Cory stepped out, and the screen door slapped shut behind him. Kane buzzed down his window. "Is it okay with your ma if we have a chat?"

"Sure?" Cory's brow wrinkled into a frown. "What's up?"

Kane climbed out and waited for Jenna to join him. He followed her onto the porch step. "Can we come inside?"

"Ma, the sheriff is here." Cory turned away from the door. "Can they come in to speak to you?" He turned back and stood to one side. "Straight ahead, she's in the kitchen. Verna is cooking breakfast. She has the parade this morning and can't be late."

"We won't keep you long." Jenna tucked a DNA test kit under one arm and followed Cory down the hallway.

The house smelled like a chicken coop and Kane had to maneuver his way around piles of junk. The adoption would never have been approved if the house had been in this state. He assumed since the adoption had gone through and her husband had walked, Mrs. Hughes had become a hoarder. He stepped over empty bean cans and piles of newspapers. the mounds of trash showed evidence of rodents, the place was a mess. He eased inside the kitchen. Here it seemed the kids had made a space to cook and eat but it was minimal. Kane waited in the doorway and batted away the flies.

"I guess you know, we took a sample of Cory's DNA to eliminate him from the investigation into Laurie Turner's death?" Jenna waved a test kit. "We weren't aware Verna was adopted, so we're here to ask if we can get a sample from her as well. We're testing all of Laurie's friends."

"I was never Laurie's friend." Verna scowled at them over one shoulder. "She used her family's money and her pa's position to get on the cheerleading squad. The rest of us had to earn our place."

"I see but all the same, we'd like a test if it's okay with your ma?" Jenna looked hopefully at the woman seated at the table with a cigarette held between her fingers.

"Nope, I won't give my permission." Mrs. Hughes shook her head. "You got no right to take my boy's DNA. Now he'll be on the FBI's database for life."

Kane cleared his throat. "He's old enough to give permission, Ma'am, and the sample would only be a problem if he's planning a life of crime and from what I'm seeing, he's hardworking and good at his job."

"He's a janitor." Mrs. Hughes rolled her eyes. "He cleans up trash."

"Maintenance is a very respectable profession." Jenna looked horrified. "He is responsible for all the auxiliary staff working at the school. He does a great job."

"He's a no-account just like his father." Mrs. Hughes waved a hand around the house. "He don't like it here. He wants to find his own place and leave me to fend for myself. He figures I'll just stand by and let him take Verna with him." She took a long drag on her cigarette. "It just ain't gonna happen."

"Okay." Jenna exchanged a meaningful glance with Kane. "Before I go, have you seen anyone hanging around the school, or the cheerleaders. Someone who isn't on staff?"

"There is one guy." Cory buttered a slice of toast and stood leaning against the counter to eat it. "The girls call him Stalker Stan. Stan Williams. He hangs around some, takes photos and asks them for dates." He shrugged. "I mentioned him to Mr. Turner being as he's a shrink and all and asked him if I should report him… Stalker Stan, I mean. He figured he was harmless enough."

Kane frowned. "Does he get too friendly at all?"

"Not that I'm aware." Cory chewed slowly. "No one mentioned anything."

"Any idea where we can find Mr. Williams?" Jenna took out her notebook and pen. "How old would you say he is?"

"Dunno, thirty maybe." Cory pushed more bread into the toaster. "He lives in a room over the general store, acts as their security overnight, and drives the school bus."

"When was the last time anyone drove the old Chrysler sedan?" Kane looked around the faces in the room.

"I drove it last Saturday night to practice and once to go to the store." Verna shrugged. "Ma don't go out much."

Kane looked at her. "Did you give Laurie a ride on Saturday night?"

"No, I had to pick up a cherry pie from Aunt Betty's for Ma." Verna glared at him. "I'm not allowed to give people rides in Ma's car."

"I'm waiting to eat here." Mrs. Hughes stubbed out her cigarette in an overflowing ashtray on the table and glared at them. "Enough with the questions."

"Sure, thank you for your time. We'll see ourselves out." Jenna turned and waved him away.

Outside, Kane took a few deep breaths and turned to her. "How do people live like that?"

"It's a fire hazard and now I feel like I have cooties." Jenna pulled out a packet of wipes from her pocket and washed her face and hands.

She thrust them at him. "Here, don't get in the truck until you wash your hands. That place needs to be condemned." She stared at him. "Is there anything we can do?"

Kane shook his head. "Nope, if they had garbage piled up outside, the council could order them to clean it up but inside, they have the right to live in squalor if they choose to." He wiped his hands and face before slipping behind the wheel. "It's a shame we can't eliminate Verna. Now I've met her and seeing the circumstances she's living in, the pair of them make a very interesting couple. She's strong and dominant and Cory is constantly belittled by his mom. We can't discount them as suspects."

"You have echoed my thoughts." Jenna shuddered. "But brother and sister?"

Kane turned the Beast around and headed back to the highway. "They both know they're not related and he admires her. It's possible."

"Let's see if we can hunt down Williams." Jenna was checking the databases on the mobile digital terminal. "I can't find anything apart from his background checks to become a school bus driver. He looks clean." She checked out a few things and then leaned back in her seat. "The kids have a school free day for the parade today, so no school bus. He might be at home."

"It's worth a try." Kane shook his head. "I'm not happy with a thirty-year-old guy hanging around sixteen-year-olds and asking them on dates. He sounds like a creep to me."

"I'm surprised the parents haven't complained." Jenna huffed out a sigh. "I guess as he's been cleared to drive the bus, he's not a danger."

Astonished, Kane shot her a glance. "The background check would have been basic, maybe this state, maybe just this county. He could have committed offenses elsewhere or he's just not been caught yet." He crawled along Main and finally parked a short distance from the general store. "I'd like to know what his interest is in young girls.

Usually men aren't quite so brazen. They'll go watch the football to sneak a peek at the cheerleaders but showing up at the practice? He's up to something, I can feel it in my bones."

"So, do you want to take the lead in the questioning and lean on him a bit?" Jenna pushed on her hat and smoothed her hair behind her ears. "You might make him talk."

"Yeah." Kane smiled at her. "I'd like that."

CHAPTER TWENTY-TWO

It was busy in town, with everyone getting organized for the parade. People milled around, setting up tables to sell a variety of goods, from flags to cookies. Excitement hummed through the excited chatter. The Fall Parade was a big event for Black Rock Falls and like Jenna, the day for everyone had started at dawn. She walked beside Kane to the general store and they went round back. The store was very old and one of the first buildings to be constructed in town, the apartment, once the residence of the owner was accessed by a long wooden staircase. As she climbed the creaky steps, brown paint flaked off the handrail like confetti, she stepped with care. "I hope this staircase will take your weight."

"It's not rotting, it's just old is all." Kane examined the handrail. "A lick of paint and a few nails and it would be fine." He touched her shoulder. "If this guy is remotely involved, I might have to get down to his level, same as I did with Hughes and talk dirty to make him believe I'm just like him."

"Yeah, I agree. Getting a suspect on side and making them believe you are of like mind lulls them into a false state of security. Get at it and say what you must to get the information we need." Jenna reached the landing and thumped on the door. "Mr. Williams? Sheriff's Department."

The door opened and a handsome man wearing jeans and a sweatshirt peered at Jenna with a half-smile. His brown hair hung over one of his dark brown eyes and he gave her the once over before straightening at the sight of Kane. Jenna cleared her throat. "Mr. Williams?"

"Yeah that's me, Stan Williams." He frowned. "Is there a problem, Sheriff?"

"We're investigating the murder of Laurie Turner." Kane spoke over Jenna's shoulder. "May we come inside?"

"Sure." Williams stepped back allowing the aroma of freshly brewed coffee to flow outside. "The place is a mess. There's not much room up here for me and my hobby."

Jenna peered around the surprisingly light room. It was clean and tidy but one wall was crammed with photographs of cheerleaders. A bench held photography paraphernalia and a light screen was set up in one corner. "You have a photography studio up here?"

"It's a passion." Williams smiled. "I'd love to capture you. You have remarkable skin, the camera will love you."

Noticing the hard line of Kane's mouth as he examined the images of young women on the wall, she shook her head. "Ah, thanks but no thanks. I hate having my photograph taken. I don't like looking back and realizing how old I look now. Photography isn't my thing. You need to talk to Kane, he's always taking shots." She turned to stare out the window to give Kane the chance to take the lead. "What a great view of the mountains."

"Do you invite the cheerleaders here to have their photographs taken?" Kane turned to look at him, with his back to the window.

"Yeah, sometimes." Williams stared at the images as if entranced. "There's so many memories here, I can't take any of them down."

"I bet." Kane dropped his voice into a confidential tone and led Williams to the far corner. He pointed to an image. "She's pretty. How did you get her up here alone?"

"They're comfortable with me. I'm part of the furniture." Williams leaned closer to Kane and chuckled. "You should see the ones without the uniform."

"Interesting. Maybe you could show me sometime, when I'm not with the boss?" Kane moved along the wall staring at the images.

"Sure, I'm free after six most nights." Williams smiled. "I never believed that people of like mind would be in law enforcement but I have friends from all walks of life, lawyers, judges, and doctors, would you believe?"

"Yeah, the job doesn't reflect taste, does it?" Kane smiled. "Look at me, you'd figure me for a beer man and yet I prefer a glass of pinot noir."

"I learned long ago not to judge a book by its cover." Williams chuckled. "But we still have to watch our backs."

"Yeah, we sure do." Kane raised his eyebrows. "Did you photograph Laurie Turner?"

"Laurie?" Williams smiled. "Yeah but not here. I take photographs of the squad at the gym and at games but her father would cause trouble if I asked her to come here." He winked at Kane. "He doesn't understand."

"So are the photos for your own pleasure or do you have a group of like-minded enthusiasts?" Kane moved slowly along the wall, leaning in to examine the images. "Great action shots. They're very professional, no wonder the girls want you to take their photographs."

"Oh, I supply images for the year book and local newspaper plus any promotions the school wants to do. I offer them free of charge of course." Williams ran a finger over the face of one of the girls. "So many favorites. I could never choose just one, could you?"

"They do say variety is the spice of life." Kane looked at him. "Tell me about Saturday night. You were at the gym taking pictures of the cheerleaders. Did you talk to anyone in particular?"

"I talk to everyone." Williams went to his computer. "I got some great shots."

"Do you capture everything? The spectators for instance?"

"I sure do." Williams laughed. "Some of them are in my private collection."

"As we're of like mind, can I have a copy of the file?" Kane pulled a thumb drive from his pocket. "I'd like to see who was there." He handed him the stick.

"I guess." Williams looked taken aback. "I haven't had time to edit the file. What about the sheriff? I don't want this getting into the wrong hands."

"That's okay." Kane smiled at him. "The sheriff is only looking for crowd shots, to verify who was watching the practice." He leaned in close. "Unless you have anything else to share?"

Jenna stared in amazement as Williams obediently pushed the drive into his laptop and transferred the files. She moved away from the window and walked slowly toward them. "Where did you go after the practice?"

"I came home." Williams indicated to his laptop. "I downloaded my files and send a few emails. Around ten I walked down to Aunt Betty's for pie and coffee. It's busy in town on Saturday night and I like to be with people."

Jenna nodded. "Did you speak to anyone in particular?"

"I spoke to strangers mostly, tourists, I guess." Williams smiled at her. "I'm a sociable guy."

"What's your ride?" Kane looked at him. "Is it one of the trucks parked out back?"

"Yeah, the GMC." Williams checked his watch. "Is that all? I want to grab breakfast at Aunt Betty's before the parade."

Jenna headed for the door. "Thank you for your time."

"Do you have a card?" Kane wasn't following her. "I'd like to drop by sometime."

"Sure." Williams pulled one from his wallet and handed it to him. "I'll look forward to it."

Jenna headed down the steps and walked to the truck in silence. She climbed in and waited for Kane to slide behind the wheel. "Don't tell me, we came here to investigate a suspect in a murder and stumbled over another darn pedophile ring?" She thumped her fist on the seat. "In my town? Again?"

"Maybe, maybe not. He still had time to commit murder, although he doesn't drive a Chrysler sedan." Kane pulled the truck out of the space and they crawled up main to the office. "We'll see what's on the file and if he's sending out underage images to a bunch of friends over the internet, including law enforcement, judges, and lawyers. It may just be talk but if it isn't, we'll turn it over to the FBI."

Jenna leaned over the back seat and rubbed Duke's ears, he had been fast asleep and yawned explosively. "Okay but that means you'll have to drop by his place and sit there while he shows you disgusting images."

"If there's anything suspicious on the file he gave me, I'll go with Carter, then we have the FBI in at the get-go." Kane shrugged. "He can turn it over to the sex crimes unit, then it will be Josh Martin's problem."

"Okay." Jenna rubbed her temples. "I'll need to write this up and plan our next move. At least all the cheerleaders will be together for the rest of the day. They have the parade and then there's a photoshoot with the football team. So, they'll be occupied as a group until at least midday." She glanced at her notes. "I'd like to have a chat to Dale Collins and Marlene Moore to see if they recall anything from their conversation with Laurie on Saturday night at the gym."

"The best time to find them will be before they get organized, after the parade they'll split up and go see the attractions around town." Kane stared out the window. "Some of the parents will be here as well, if we need statements. Almost everyone has a day off today apart from us. Even the bank is closed."

Jenna pushed open the door. "I feel as if I've done a day's work already." She checked her watch. "It's only ten-thirty."

"You go ahead." Kane stared down Main. "I'm going to grab something from the cake stall before everything is sold." He hurried away with Duke bounding behind him.

Shaking her head, Jenna walked up the steps, through the glass doors and went to greet Maggie on the counter. "Anything for me this morning?"

"Nothing new, no, but Rowley and Rio have organized the Blackwater deputies in your absence." She wrinkled her brow. "We have four from Blackwater and two of Crenshaw's boys coming in from Louan for the duration. Rowley reserved rooms at the motel for them some time ago, and some of them are willing to work double shifts if you feed them right and give them a bed for the night."

Relieved, Jenna smiled. "The mayor insisted I get all the help I needed for the festival, to free us up for the Turner investigation, so agree to anything they need and send the accounts to his office."

The front door opened and Sandy walked in, smiling broadly. "Hey, Jenna, Maggie."

"I'm afraid Rowley isn't here. He's out organizing deputies." Jenna waved her toward her office. "I'm just about to brew a pot of coffee, are you allowed to drink coffee?"

"Yeah sure." Sandy rubbed her swollen belly. "We're doing just fine." She smiled. "I didn't want to miss the parade and I'll be going to see my mom later, but while Jake is on duty here, I'm going to finish up at the old house."

Jenna filled the coffee pot, collected cups and the fixings, and set them on her desk. "You sound like you're missing work."

"Me?" Sandy shook her head. "Not at all. The ranch keeps me busy, now we have chickens and horses to tend. It is remote though and I'm a town girl but I have the dog to keep me company. Dave was saying he's going to help Jake beef up the security. The house is safe enough but with the baby and all, I'd like a perimeter fence alert as well."

Jenna nodded. "Well, once we've solved this case, Kane's your man and I'm sure if Shane's not busy, he'll be over to help as well."

"That would be good." Sandy took the cup Jenna offered. "Thanks. I hope I'm not holding you back from working?"

Jenna sat down and shook her head. "No, we're just taking a few minutes to regroup and it's been a long time since breakfast for Kane. He'll be here soon with armfuls of cakes to keep himself going." She grinned. "I had no idea men ate so much food."

"Yeah, since Jake built the gym out at the ranch and with his visits to the dojo, he is always hungry as well." Sandy chuckled. "But he sure looks good." She sipped her coffee.

"Who looks good?" Kane came into the office and dumped bags onto Jenna's desk. "Hmm coffee." He went straight to the counter to pour a cup and then dropped into a chair.

Jenna pushed the cream and sugar toward him. "Girl talk." She winked at Sandy. "What did you buy?"

"Everything." Kane pulled a bag toward him. "You can have anything you like but the banana cream pie is mine."

"I hear Jake's voice out in the hallway." Sandy finished her coffee. "I'll have a quick word with him and be on my way. Thanks for the coffee." She gave them a wave and hurried out the door.

"Jake has everything under control here." Kane dug into his pie with a plastic spoon and sighed in delight. "The cheerleaders are in a group in the park and waiting for the football team to arrive. We can catch them before they start the parade. It doesn't begin until twelve. They'd planned for eleven-thirty but they have some problems with the sound system at the podium set up for the mayor, so we have plenty of time."

"Good." Jenna scanned her notes. "I want Rowley and Rio checking the MVD for green Chrysler sedans in the area."

Jenna stared at the mound of food on the table. It smelled wonderful but, she wasn't hungry. She peered into a bag containing individual caramel pecan pies. *Maybe just the one.*

CHAPTER TWENTY-THREE

He found his girl in the crowd of people heading into town and pulled her into an alleyway. "Are you sure you want to do this? Becky seems like a nice girl."

"A nice girl, huh?" His girl's mouth turned down and her eyes flashed with anger. "Of course, they're nice to your face but she wants to make you look a jerk. She's probably asked one of her friends to follow you to take pictures to plaster all over her Facebook page to prove a bet or something. You're a trophy to them, nothing more, all you guys are. They don't care about your feelings they just want to bring you down. They're just like your ma." She leaned into him. "I'm the only one you can trust. We have secrets between us and they bind us together. I'll never treat you bad but if you love me like you say you do then you'd care that they're mean to me. My life would be better without them. I can't kill them without you."

A shiver of excitement curled in his belly. It was like dropping down real fast on a rollercoaster. She always made him feel the same rush, as if he'd been strapped to the front of a freight train. "Okay. Are you sure no one will be at home? I don't see any for sale signs outside, are you sure it's empty?"

"I'm sure. I've been by a few times and its empty. The people that lived there leave the key in the same place each time. I figure it's for the handyman or someone to get in to fix up the place." She grinned at him. "I've been inside. It's perfect. There are new mattresses on all the beds still wrapped in plastic. There's cleaning products in the laundry, we can clean up real good before we leave."

He nodded trying to show enthusiasm but he liked Becky, she didn't seem at all nasty and he'd gotten on well with her. Becky had been very enthusiastic about a date with him and had kissed him passionately under the bleachers. He hadn't dared mention the kiss. His girl would go crazy and stab Becky a hundred times. He could handle watching the girls being strangled but the stabbing made him sick to his stomach. He lifted his girl's chin and looked at her to convince himself he couldn't live without her. "I'm worried, killing someone in the middle of town with so many people around, that someone will see us leaving."

"We'll leave by the backdoor, it's surrounded by trees and I already have a key. They left two hanging in the lock and I just took one. I'll put it back later and I left the other one on a nail beside the door. I'll kill the power when I go inside so bring a flashlight. Take Becky upstairs, there's a bedroom on the left at the top, it has a big closet and I'll hide in there. Get her with her back to the closet and I'll do the rest." She giggled. "Then we can strip her off and make her sit and watch us. We'll clean up, I'll return the key, and we'll slip out the backdoor. You can burn her things like before and no one will know a thing. She can stay there until they sell the house and by the time they find her, we'll be hunting down Vicky Perez."

He wiped the back of his hand over his mouth and shuffled his feet. "The sheriff has been talking to everyone who was at the gym on Saturday night. Do you figure she suspects us?"

"Us?" She barked a laugh. "No, of course not. We are just as sweet as pie and much smarter than they think. They'll be looking for an old man, a pervert, a sex offender. Everyone knows Laurie was easy and so are the others, so it will show up they were playing around." She grinned. "In any case they'll be hunting down the guy who owns the briefs and blame him." She ran a finger down his cheek. "Don't forget, we need more of them, so select carefully. By the time we've finished, the sheriff will have so many suspects she won't know what to do." She pouted at him. "I want to stay here with you but we have to go, or we'll be missed. I'll walk around the back of the building and come out behind the bank. We can't be seen together." She went on tiptoes to kiss him. "I'll see you tonight." She scampered away down the alleyway turning out of sight.

He stared after her, a mixture of excitement and dread crawling over him like an ants' nest. He pushed all doubt from his mind and imagined Becky propped up against a wall, naked, eyes staring into nothingness watching him with his girl. All of a sudden, sunset couldn't come fast enough.

CHAPTER TWENTY-FOUR

Jenna looked at Kane over her desk. "Hand over the thumb drive, we might as well scan the images while we're taking a break."

"We won't have time." Kane collected the remaining purchases and took them to the small refrigerator in Jenna's office. "We'll have to walk to the park if we want to speak to Collins and Moore. Main is closed off for the parade as of five minutes ago."

"Okay, I'll upload them to our files and we can look at them later." Jenna finished her coffee and sighed. "My cruiser's parked around back, we could take the backroads?"

"It would be quicker to walk." Kane washed up the cups and turned them upside down on the sink.

"Hey." Carter knocked on the door. "You planning on eating tonight?"

Jenna smiled at him. "Yeah but we have to head home and tend the horses plus we have an ongoing murder case."

"Well, you have to eat and I'm inviting you both to join me, Jo, and Jaime at The Cattleman's Hotel Restaurant for dinner at seven." Carter shook his finger at Jenna. "Don't tell me you have nothing to wear, I know you both keep numerous changes of clothes here at the office."

"It's lovely of you to ask but we can't." Jenna shook her head. "We're still hunting down suspects. We just don't have the time to go back to the ranch and then to eat out at The Cattleman's Hotel, it takes an hour to get a meal there."

"Yeah you do." Carter rested one hip on the edge of her desk. "I'll go tend your horses. If you let me take your cruiser, I'll be able to get through the security and be back here in time to shower and change for dinner." He glanced down at Duke. "I'll even let Duke into your backyard. He likes me, he'll come no worries."

Jenna raised an eyebrow in question at Kane and he shrugged. She looked at Carter and nodded. "Well, I guess we do have to eat and it means we'll be in town if we're needed." She took the cruiser keys out of her desk drawer and tossed them to him. "We'll see you at seven."

"You sure will." Carter looked at Kane. "I'll drop by and collect Duke around five, that should give me plenty of time."

"I'll leave him with Maggie." Kane smiled. "He doesn't like the fireworks, so will be more than happy to be at home tonight." He looked at Jenna. "We need to go."

Jenna stood and pulled on her jacket. "I'm right behind you." She followed Kane and Carter out the office.

Main had transformed into a promenade filled with people, kids with balloons and cotton candy. Brightly colored bunting hung across the road and from every store front in town. The sidewalk was packed with stalls selling everything imaginable and townsfolk and tourists moved from place to place in swarms like bees attracted to the bright colors. Loud music blared over speakers attached to streetlights interspersed with announcements from the festival committee. They walked by a hastily built podium for the mayor to address the crowds and passed the vans used by local media stations.

She kept close behind Kane. His size was an advantage in a crowd and people parted to let him by as he strode along. If she kept directly behind him, she had a clear path. Sheriff or not, her small frame was lost in a sea of people. She sidestepped a mother with kids trailing behind her holding hands, their mouths ringed with the unmistakable red of a toffee apple. One small girl had the stick from her cotton candy stuck in her hair. Excitement thrummed through the town and everyone had a smile for her as she walked by.

They finally reached the park and Jenna stared in amazement. Football teams stood at one end waiting to head to their float. A marching band was warming up with an awful assortment of sounds and the cheerleaders fussed over their uniforms and pompoms, some practicing moves or doing pointing and giggling. Inside the perimeter of the park, it was easier to move and Jenna pulled out her phone and located the images of Collins and Moore. She showed the screen to Kane. "Normally I'd say split up but I'll get lost in the crowd. I think it's best we stay together."

"The cheerleader squads are close, so we'll see if Marlene Moore is with them." Kane peered over the top of his sunglasses and narrowed his gaze. "Darn, they all look the same."

Jenna headed in the squad's direction. "Then we'll ask, the girls will know her." She walked up to the first girl she came to and held out her phone. "Have you seen Marlene today?"

"Yeah, she's over there with Vicky." The girl pointed. "Standing next to Becky."

Jenna thanked her and led the way around the group of girls. As they approached, Becky and Marlene stopped talking and nudged Vicky in the ribs. Jenna pasted a smile on her face and pulled out her notebook and pen. "Marlene Moore, may I have a word with you?"

"Sure." Marlene shrugged and followed her out of earshot of the others.

"I believe you were at the gym on Saturday night speaking with Dale Collins and Laurie Turner. Can you remember what you were talking about?"

"Maybe." Marlene stood with her pompoms on her hips. "I don't want to speak ill of the dead but Laurie was a flirt. She had been talking about seeing Wyatt watching her in the crowd, so she dragged me over to speak to Dale. He only opens the kiosk for us during practice and I figure he gets tired of girls hitting on him all the time." She looked away with a bored expression. "His aunt usually runs the kiosk but she doesn't think it's worth her time to open it for a couple of hours for us, so Dale opens it."

"Really?" Kane gave her a quizzical stare. "Don't all the members of the football team have admirers?"

"Yeah, but they only go with cheerleaders." Marlene touched her hair. "Is that all?"

Jenna shook her head. "Can you recall anything at all that was said? Did Dale make a date with Laurie, or plan to meet her?"

"No, he hasn't asked anyone to the Fall Festival Ball as yet." Marlene rolled her eyes. "He likes to keep his minions waiting, I guess."

Jenna smiled. "So, he's not your type?"

"Dale?" Marlene laughed and looked up at Kane. "I prefer tall, dark, and handsome." She pointed in the direction of a tall blond teenager. "As you can see, Dale is the opposite."

"Okay." Jenna folded her notebook. "Thank you for your time." She handed her a card. "If you can think of anything else, call me."

"Sure." Marlene walked away and Jenna saw the card flutter to the ground.

"The football team is getting ready to head to the float." Kane hustled through the cheerleaders.

Jenna ran behind him and they reached the football team as they congregated at the far end of the park, in the dog walking enclosure. She made out Dale Collins' blond hair and headed in his direction. As she made her way through the team, Kane moved ahead of her and led him over to the fence. She smiled at the confused look on the young man's face. "You're not in any trouble. We want to know if you can remember speaking with Laurie Turner last Saturday night in the gym."

"Yeah, sure I do." Collins frowned. "It's terrible about Laurie. Have you found who killed her yet?"

Jenna shook her head. "Not yet. What did you talk about?"

"The specials." Collins stared at his shoes. "I asked her how her truck was going. I teased her a bit about it being a guy's ride. She laughed. The next thing Marlene came over and told her Wyatt was spying on her again, and Laurie went back to sit with the squad." He lifted his gaze to Jenna. "I didn't see her after that, I have to clean the kiosk after the break. I count the money and lock it up. I went home soon after."

"So, you don't hang back to chat to the cheerleaders after practice?" Kane was watching him closely.

"Nah." Collins grinned. "After the game is the best time, when everyone is all pumped up and wanting to celebrate. I try and keep as far away from them as possible during the week. I need to keep my grades up and they're a distraction." He glanced over his shoulder as the decked-out float pulled up at the curb. "I gotta go." He turned and jogged away.

Jenna looked up at Kane. "I wanted to have a chat with Wyatt Cooper as well."

"That will have to wait for later." Kane was peering over the heads of the crowd. "As soon as the mayor does his speech, the floats head down Main and do a turnaround at the showgrounds before coming back. We'll catch him then."

As they headed back to the sidewalk, the crowd squashed in around Jenna. A sensation of claustrophobia gripped her and she pulled on Kane's arm to stop him disappearing into the throng. "Dave, I'm getting swamped back here."

"Hang onto my belt, we'll cross Main before the parade starts and take the backroad to the office." Kane turned and grinned at her. "Unless you want a piggy back?"

Rolling her eyes, Jenna twirled her fingers to make him turn around. "The belt will be fine." She gripped his belt and they moved through the crowd and the next thing she found herself inside Aunt Betty's Café. "What are we doing here? You have enough cakes to feed an army at the office."

"Yeah but as we were passing, I thought I'd drop in while everyone is outside watching the parade." He grinned at her. "We can work anywhere, and it's a nice quiet place to sit and go through the image files. We can access them on our phones and I know you don't like eating cake for lunch, so you'll be able to get something here."

Jenna sniffed the air. "And you smelled the aroma of chili wafting down the sidewalk." She shook her head. "Okay, you win." She waved him to a table.

CHAPTER TWENTY-FIVE

They spent the next couple of hours going through a ton of images of cheerleaders. Jenna had to admit, some of the photographs bordered on unsavory but then some people would look at them as action shots of a cheerleading squad's routine. It was all in the eye of the beholder. She looked up wearily from her phone. "Find anything suggesting Williams is a pedophile?"

"Nope but if I had a daughter and I thought men were sharing some of these shots, I wouldn't be too happy. The routines happen in a split second and are innocent enough but Williams somehow makes them indecent." Kane rubbed his chin thoughtfully. "I'm still not convinced there's not more to him than meets the eye. He is obsessed with cheerleaders and it could easily lead to murder." He opened his hands. "Thinking out of the box here. If he lured one to his apartment and she refused his advances, strangling her to keep her quiet is something that I've seen before."

Jenna closed the files and looked at him. "That will be hard to prove. I did notice he had a set of pompoms on his desk but assumed they were props for his photographs but now we know Laurie's are missing from her backpack it throws suspicion on him."

"We'll need to get closer to Stan Williams and see how he ticks." Kane leaned back in his chair. "I'll call Carter and convince him to come with me to pay Williams a visit tonight after dinner. You'll be wanting to chat with Jo, I'm sure."

Jenna nodded. "It's going to be the only time we have free. If Rio and Rowley find any Chrysler sedans in town similar to the one that gave Laurie a ride, we'll be spending the rest of the week hunting down their owners." She stretched and glanced at her watch. "We'll go find Wyatt Cooper and then head back to the office. I guess you'd better grab something for Duke as Ty is going to take him home soon."

"See, you do care about my dog." Kane tucked his phone inside his pocket and stood. "I knew he'd grow on you eventually."

Laughing, Jenna stood. "I've always liked Duke. I mean who wouldn't love those sad brown eyes? I've just never been in a position to have pets. It's a responsibility I couldn't risk taking, like marriage and kids. Life is different now. Yeah, we still face dangers but we have reliable people around us who care. I'd never had that before. For me friendship and loyalty came at a price."

"Yeah, well that's all behind us now." Kane smiled at her. "All I have to worry about is murdering psychopaths."

Jenna dropped a pile of bills on the table and headed to the door. "Look, the football team float is pulling up at the end of the park. Let's have a little chat with Wyatt Cooper. If we can make it through the crowds, we'll be able to catch him before he heads off."

Although the crowds had eased a little, the football team had scattered leaving only a few of the players in small groups chatting. Jenna spotted Dale Collins with a small group of friends and headed in his direction. She noticed his smile vanish as she approached. "Sorry to bother you again. Does anyone know where we can locate Wyatt Cooper?"

"He took off." Collins shrugged. "He said he had something to do later. He sure don't seem too upset about Laurie." He frowned. "At least, the rest of the team will be at her funeral, to pay our respects."

"What do you mean by that remark?" Kane's eyes narrowed. "There's no plans for a funeral at this stage. Did he say something?"

"Yeah, he told us he wouldn't be going to her funeral." Collins straightened. "He didn't give a reason. Why don't you ask him yourself?"

"I'll be sure to." Kane's gaze moved over the others watching the interaction. "We have a team of deputies from other counties here for the festival, so don't try to buy liquor at the showgrounds again this year. We don't want to find any of you boys locked up in the cells come morning."

"We'll be sure to remember that, Deputy." Collins turned his back and walked toward another group of players.

Annoyed by Collins' arrogance, Jenna stared after him. "That went well."

"I figure we have someone flying under the radar." Kane rubbed the back of his neck. "The problem is none of the people we've spoken to have raised any red flags, with the exception of Williams." He waved a hand at the marching band following the cheerleaders into the park. "Someone here knows something. One of these kids knocked Laurie's phone out of her hand and I'm convinced whoever did it, is involved with her murder."

Seeing the way the students gathered together in groups gave Jenna pause to consider what Kane had said. She shrugged and followed him from the park. "Maybe not." She thought back to her time at school and turned to him. "Say one of them disliked Laurie and was part of a prank to have her walk home? There may have been a small group of them involved, one of the guys disables her truck and one of the girls bumps into her. Look around you, everyone is chatting in groups. I remember this happening when I was at school, in the parking lot, on the way home, waiting for the bus, we'd chat for ages."

"Yeah, I remember." Kane removed his hat and scratched his head before replacing it. "Why?"

"If I recall, when we spoke to Hughes, he knew just about straight away that Laurie's phone was toast and he just placed it in a plastic bag and he locked up and went home."

"Yeah, that's what I remember." Kane stopped walking and turned to look at her. "Where's this leading, Jenna?"

Like a jigsaw puzzle slipping into place, Jenna smiled at him. "Well, he said he didn't see anyone in the parking lot. He said it was empty and dark when he drove by. Where was everyone? Why weren't there some kids still hanging around when Laurie couldn't start her truck and decided to walk home?"

"Maybe because Laurie was inside longer than he remembered." Kane shook his head slowly. "There's no way a group of kids could commit a murder like that. Do you think they're all involved? No way. One of them would flip out with the stress."

Unconvinced, Jenna stared at him. "Look back in history. Cult figures influenced people to do terrible things, even commit suicide. Right now, I'm open to any suggestions. We have a young girl brutally murdered in the morgue and practically no evidence and what we do have was probably planted."

When they arrived at the office, Jenna found Rowley at the front counter and Rio updating files on the computer. As Kane headed into her office to call Carter about visiting Williams later, she checked her watch and then leaned on the counter. "Bring me up to date and then go home and take a break before your next shift."

"Sure." Rowley turned his iPad around to show her. "These are the seven green or gray Chrysler sedans of around the same model in town. We know about the one that Mrs. Hughes owns and tracked down five. Three of these are in use and two are in barns and haven't been driven for years. The last one is in the used car yard here in town, it's been there for about three months." He pointed to the three names on his list. "We visited all three of the owners and all have an alibi for Saturday night. They were all at home with family members and all three owners are in their late sixties. No one else drives their vehicles."

Jenna nodded. "Good work." She lifted her chin and sighed. "So that really leaves the Hughes' vehicle." She slapped the table. "You'd better get along home but I'll be in town for a while tonight so you don't have to be back until six-thirty. I'll be at The Cattleman's Hotel while Kane talks to a suspect with Carter."

"Thanks." Rowley smiled. "I'll have time to drop Sandy at the old house before I come back."

"That's good." Jenna sighed. "Now, I'll try and figure out a way I can get a search warrant to seize the Hughes' vehicle to see if Wolfe can find any of Laurie Turner's DNA inside."

"I might have that sorted." Rio walked to her side. "Verna has admitted to driving the vehicle on Saturday night, she didn't like Laurie, and her brother was one of the last people to see her alive. Add to this, we believe the killer had an accomplice who knocked the phone from Laurie's hand and Cory had plenty of time to disable her truck during the practice. I figure we have probable cause."

Impressed, Jenna smiled at him. "Write it up and see if you can catch a judge to issue a warrant. I'll be in town tonight, so you can get on home too, once you get back."

"Jenna." Kane walked out her office and went to her side. "Carter had Kalo run Stan Williams through the sex offenders' database and his name came up in a sealed FBI juvie document. We can't use it against him but it was a heads up. Seems that as a fifteen-year-old, Williams was caught molesting five-year-old girls at a birthday party."

CHAPTER TWENTY-SIX

Sandy Rowley gave Jake a kiss goodbye as he left their old home in town. "Go, I'll be fine. I have my Thermos and cookies if I get hungry. When I'm done here, I'll watch the fireworks from the front window."

"Stay inside and call me, if you need me." Rowley touched her cheek. "I'll be at the office."

She gave him a little shove. "Go, Jenna will be waiting for you. I'll see you soon."

"Close the door behind me." Rowley moved down the stairs, turning to watch her before he hurried to his SUV.

He'd insisted on checking all the rooms before he left. Since she'd found out she was carrying their child, he'd been super overprotective but she didn't mind. Having such a kind, loving husband was a wonderful gift she valued greatly. She glanced around the house. It was as neat as a pin but the delivery guys had left papers and footprints everywhere. The house belonged to the sheriff's department, willed to them by a deputy killed on duty some years ago. To make the inside nice, Jenna had replaced the three mattresses, bed linen, and drapes. Jake had painted the interior during a six-month slow period after the melt and now it was ready for the new occupants to arrive. Zac Rio and his twin siblings would be moving in the following weekend.

She moved from room to room, making sure everything was spick and span. The hectic day, watching the parade, and visiting her mother had exhausted her. The house had an empty, cold feel about it since they'd removed all their possessions. A radio would have been nice to break the silence as hearing the creeks and whines of the old house was putting her nerves on edge. She finished her chores, stowed away the cleaning utensils, and leaned against the kitchen counter deciding what to do to pass the time. She checked her watch willing the time to go by faster. Jake wouldn't be by to collect her until at least eleven, he said his shift finished at ten-thirty but he'd spend time chatting with whoever took over the next shift and by the time he arrived home, he was usually about an hour later than expected. She poured a cup of hot chocolate from her Thermos and went upstairs to the back bedroom. Her favorite stuffed leather chair was set in front of the window, she could watch the comings and goings in town. She curled up, finished her hot chocolate, and must have dozed off to sleep. Something woke her and disoriented in the darkness, she glanced around for some moments to get her bearings before staring at her watch. The digital readout told her it was a little before nine. The lights in the hallway had been on when she came into the room but she'd sat in darkness to best observe the view outside the window.

Perhaps a bulb was out. She stood to turn on the light. She flicked the switch off and on. Nothing. A wave of panic surged through her at an unusual sound from downstairs. She'd lived in this house for over six months before moving to the ranch and she could identify just about every noise in the old house. Heart pounding, she slid back into the room and pressed her back against the wall. The creak came again and a slight jingle like the sound of keys. If it had been Jake or even Jenna dropping by, they'd have called out and turned on lights, not crept around. Someone was in the house.

The sound of footsteps came again, like boots on the polished floor. In blind panic, Sandy searched her pockets for her phone. She could see it in her mind's eye inside her purse on the counter beside the Thermos. How had someone gotten inside? Jake had insisted she take the key to the front door with her rather than return it to its place above the door. She placed one hand on her swollen belly. If the intruder moved into a room, she could slip down the stairs and go for help. Footsteps moved through the kitchen. Cabinet doors opened and closed. Terrified, Sandy's breathing came so fast, she feared someone would hear her.

The noise came again and then a familiar sound, a snap like someone pulling on surgical gloves. Cold shivers ran down her spine as the footsteps came closer. Each step precise, and taking the stairs in a controlled pace with no rush. *They know I'm here and they're coming to hurt me.*

Without a weapon, Sandy had nothing to use to defend herself. She moved deeper into the shadows and held her breath. She recognized the squeaky hinge of the door to the first bedroom at the top of the stairs and the sound of someone sliding open the closet door. Now was her chance. She slipped out the room and with her pulse thundering in her ears, crept along the hallway. Just as she reached the open door to the first bedroom, the old grandfather clock in the hallway downstairs struck nine. Terror had her by the throat and sweat beaded on her brow as she dashed toward the stairs. Footsteps thundered behind her and out of the darkness, someone grabbed her hair tearing her scalp. The next instant, pain shot through her face as her head slammed into the doorframe. Blood ran into her eye and she staggered back the way she'd come, feeling along the wall, trying to get away. A loud clang broke the silence and rang through her head in a wave of suffering. She fell to her knees, and rolled into a ball and played dead to protect her unborn child.

Only heavy breathing came and then someone took her by the feet and dragged her inside a room. A boot scraped past her and she squeezed her eyes shut tight. She could sense someone leaning over her and held her breath. Lungs bursting, she waited for them to leave the room. The door slammed shut as they ran back down the hallway. Sandy swiped at her eyes, nauseous and dizzy. Alone in the dark, the sky outside the window lit up in a streak of green. The firework display danced across her vision before everything went black.

CHAPTER TWENTY-SEVEN

Nervous excitement thrummed through Becky Powell as she stepped inside the library to meet her date. She spotted him at once, leaning casually against a bookcase, flicking through pages of a book. He raised both eyebrows at her and walked out into the hallway. She followed him down the back stairs and he waited for her at the fire door. She smiled at him. "Has she followed you again?"

"Yeah, but she didn't see me leave." He pulled her close to him. "I've found a place we can go. It's nice and private. Did you bring your pompoms?"

Becky grinned. "Yeah, they're in my backpack. I'm guessing you want me to do a routine for you… a real private routine?"

"Something like that." He cupped her chin and kissed her. "We'd better slip away before she notices I'm missing. Leave your ride here, I have a truck out back. Keep to the shadows and when you get inside, duck down so she can't see you if she happens to look out the window when I drive by."

When his hand closed around her fingers she nodded in silent agreement.

"Nice and quiet." He pushed open the fire door and led her outside.

Heart thumping with anticipation, Becky followed him into the cool night. She hadn't had too much luck dating anyone of late and stealing him from under the nose of one of his admirers made it all the sweeter. She couldn't stop grinning as she hurried around the edge of the building and climbed into his truck. As she hunkered down, he took off slowly and she could see the streetlights on Main blink past above her. "Where are we going?"

"Not far but we'll have to sneak into this place." He glanced down at her. "It's an empty house, but they've left all the furniture. It will be real comfortable for us to get to know each other."

Becky giggled. "Oh, I can't wait. I've never been on a date like this before. Are you sure no one is going to come by?"

"Certain." He slowed the truck and pulled in under a tree. "Remember, not a sound and we stick to the shadows. I don't want the neighbors to see us or they'll call the cops. I came by earlier and unlocked the backdoor, so we're gonna sneak in there." He handed her a small lantern from the back seat. "Once we're inside, I'll use my flashlight to get upstairs but when I close the drapes, we can turn on the lantern. It will be real cozy."

Becky's heart raced as she followed him through the long shadows up a driveway and down a small pathway to a door. They moved inside and she smothered a giggle. The house smelled of furniture polish, and clean air as if it had been well aired. Following the flashlight beam they headed upstairs and as they climbed higher, the hand holding hers became damp. She liked that he was nervous being with her and sneaking into an empty house with him in secret made it so special.

At the top of the stairs, he turned into a bedroom and quickly closed the thick drapes. The flashlight blinded her for a few seconds as he aimed it at her. "Hey, drop the light and I'll turn on the lantern."

"Give it to me." He took the lantern from her and set it on the nightstand but didn't take the light from her eyes. "Show me your pompoms."

Blinking, Becky slipped her backpack from her shoulder and unzipped it. She pulled out her pompoms and setting her backpack at her feet, waved them at him. "Now will you lower the light?"

"Nah, you promised me a special routine." He indicated to the bed. "I wouldn't want your clothes to get all messed up. Your folks will know we've been making out. Why don't you slip out of them for me?"

Becky's face grew hot. "You first."

"I'd love to—" he chuckled "—but then I'd have to put down the flashlight. "We'll take turns. Come on now, wriggle out of the skirt and top before I lose interest and take you home." He tilted his head and looked her up and down. "I went to a ton of trouble to organize this just for you, Becky. I figured we wanted the same thing? I thought you were special."

"You think I'm special?" Becky dropped her pompoms and removed her top and skirt. "Better?"

"Much." He trained the flashlight on her. "Kneel on the floor and fold up your clothes, I don't want them getting messed up. When you're done you can watch me."

Confused, Becky stared at him. "You're starting to creep me out."

"Did you think I'd just jump your bones? I don't treat my girls like that, Becky." He shook his head. "I like things slow and easy. I'd like to be your last boyfriend so let's make our first date one to remember."

He seemed so sincere. Could he be asking her to go steady on their first date? She couldn't believe her luck. She fell to her knees and quickly folded her clothes. A swishing sound came from behind her. Like a whisper of a breeze but she ignored it, engrossed in looking at him. "I worry about the girl in the library causing trouble. Are you sure she didn't follow us?"

"I'm sure, I'm only interested in you right now." He shrugged. "If she bothers us, I'll deal with her."

Becky smiled up at him. "What will you say to her?"

"I'll tell her I love her more than life."

The flashlight blinded her. Surprised by his reply, she squinted at him through the glare. "What did you say?"

The floorboards creaked behind her and something dropped over her face to settle on her neck and tightened. Slammed down with a knee in her back, and her face pressed hard against the wooden floor, she fought for air. "Help me."

As she opened her mouth gasping, he stepped forward and bound her hands with tape. Bewildered, she gaped at him. "Why are you doing this?"

"Because I like you." He grabbed her chin. "And it makes my girl angry."

Cloth hit her tongue. She gagged, shaking her head to dislodge his grip but he wound tape around her head covering her mouth and then stood back, aiming the flashlight into her eyes. She gaped in disbelief as he leaned casually against the nightstand as if enjoying the show. Using her last ounce of strength, she rolled, trying to unseat the person behind her. The cord slackened and she flipped to her feet. She'd done the move a hundred times as a cheerleader. She sprinted for the door and ran down the stairs, tripping over and rolling to the bottom. Battered and heart pounding with fear, she staggered to her feet and bolted for the backdoor. Light spilled through the kitchen windows like a beacon to show her the way.

She could hear them behind her. Footsteps ran in all directions hunting the hallways. She reached the backdoor and turned around, using her bound hands to search for the handle. Fingers slipping, she turned the knob and the door swung open. Cold air hit her bare flesh as she dived outside narrowly missing a hand trying to grab her. In terror, she ducked away and dashed along the narrow path heading back along the way they'd entered the house. She'd seen lights in nearby homes and increased her pace. The person behind her was gaining, she could hear heavy breathing and footsteps on the gravel. The edge of the building loomed, highlighted by a streetlamp. In a few more paces, she'd be out on the road and sprinting toward another house, people, and safety. She rounded the side of the house at speed and a figure stepped out of the shadows. Strong hands grabbed her and spun her around. The person who'd chased her moved into the light and she recognized her at once. She wanted to scream but the gag was filling her throat and making it hard to breathe through her nose.

"Take her back upstairs." The young woman's lip curled. "I haven't finished with her yet."

Terrified of what was to come, Becky aimed a knee at her dream date's groin but he sidestepped and hoisted her over one shoulder and then headed back inside. Blood rushed to her head as he carried her up the stairs but when he dropped her on the floor, she kicked out. She wanted to inflict as much damage as possible. He flipped her over as if she weighed nothing, dragged her back to her knees, and an instant later the horror began again.

Terror gripped her as the cord slipped around her neck sliding into already painful grooves. Her tormentor pulled her head back and the cord cut deeper into her flesh. From behind her she could hear the young woman's heavy breathing and in front of her, her dream date had dropped to his knees to watch her intently. What had she done to make them so angry?

"Kiss her." The female's voice rasped from behind her. "Take her last breath. Do it!"

"I can't." He looked past Becky to the person strangling her. "She's turning blue." He wiped his mouth with the back of his hand. "Why is it taking so long?"

"Because I want her to suffer." The young woman behind her giggled. "Kiss her and I'll end it."

Unable to breathe and losing consciousness, Becky pushed back hard and managed to drag in one precious breath. She tried to fight but the girl behind her was strong. In panic, she rolled again. She had to get free.

"Do something." The female tightened the cord again and pressed a knee harder into her spine. "Or I'm leaving you to deal with this mess."

Fighting for her life, Becky stared at him, willing him to take pity on her but the flashlight didn't move from her face. God help her, he was enjoying seeing her suffer. Terror had her in its grip but she'd never give up. A beam of light moved across the room. Maybe he'd changed his mind or this was just a prank but the next instant, agony seared through her temple. Oh Lord, he'd hit her. Dizzy, she slumped to the floor. Head splitting, she glanced up to see him in a shaft of moonlight, his eyes wild as he raised the flashlight above his head, and then the room folded in on itself.

CHAPTER TWENTY-EIGHT

After finishing a steak so big the sides came on different plates, eating a wedge of chocolate cake, and then relaxing to a hum of conversation, Kane leaned back pleasantly satisfied. He sipped his one glass of wine and waited for Jenna, Jo, and Jaime to head up to Jo's room at The Cattleman's Hotel before pulling out his phone to call Stan Williams. He hadn't planned to give the man a head's up of his arrival but didn't want to spook him by turning up with Carter unannounced. "Hi, Stan, it's Dave Kane, will you be home tonight?"

"Yeah sure, I'm not home just now, so make it after ten-thirty. I have a ton of cold beer to go with the photographs and some videos I've taped as well." Williams sounded enthusiastic.

Kane nodded to Ty Carter. "Great, I'm bringing a friend. We're out at The Cattleman's so we'll keep ourselves entertained."

"Catch you later." Williams disconnected.

"You do know this isn't my department?" Carter took a toothpick from his top pocket and tossed it into his mouth. "We'll need to be careful or he'll be shouting entrapment."

Kane had given it some thought. "Not if we don't arrest him." He smiled. "If we find anything suspicious, we'll turn it over to the FBI's Child Exploitation and Human Trafficking Task Force. They have the resources to follow up and make the arrests. I've found these crimes can be widespread and they use undercover units to break pedophile rings."

"Yeah." Carter leaned back in his chair clearly amused. "You're preaching to the choir here." He pointed a finger at Kane. "I can't quite figure you out. I picked you as military first day we met but my gut feeling is never wrong. Heck, I've solved cases on gut feeling alone." He shook his head in a frustrated manner. "I've worked beside you, seen how you move, shoot, and prioritize. You have inside knowledge you shouldn't have access to and the guys upstairs cleared you and Jenna in minutes. Shane had no hesitation in recommending you for the last case." He scratched his cheek and looked at him, his green eyes intent. "Look man, I'm not prying and I don't want to know the details but you know what I figure?"

Kane rolled his eyes in a dramatic gesture to show his amusement, although deep down inside the old warning bells were blasting like air-raid sirens. "What do you figure?"

"I'll lay my cards on the table but I'll expect you to say nothing." Carter leaned forward and dropped his voice to just above a whisper. "You, my friend, are an off the grid black ops operator sent here undercover to unravel some mystery." He watched his reaction closely. "No? Then the powers that be are hiding you here in plain sight. I also figure Jenna is aware of what you are and Shane is your handler."

Amazed but not surprised by his insight, Kane barked a laugh. "Okay, well if that were true, you've just compromised my mission and I'd have to kill you." He gave him a look to stop any further conversation. "That's the way it goes, right?"

"Yeah and you'd do it too but I'm a Seal. Killing me might not be so easy." Carter observed him solemnly. "I know snipers, and you're not the first one I've worked with. You can flip the switch any time you choose, can't you? Drop into the zone, make your heart slow and take out a target without a second thought. From what Jo says, Jenna refers to it as your combat face. You disturb her, you know? Sometimes she doesn't know what side of you to expect."

Astonished by the revelation that Jenna had spoken to Jo about him, Kane finished his wine and stared at him. "Like you, the military trained me to kill. They gave me the skills and I use them lawfully and I'm always in complete control. To say Jenna is in any way concerned about me is a darn right lie. We spend all our downtime together and she wouldn't do that if she thought I might hurt her."

"I saw you man, the night we discussed the car bombing out of DC. I watched her and she was frightened by your reaction." Carter sipped his beer. "You turned to stone and walked out in the middle of a discussion. What was that all about?"

Kane fell into the lie in his records about a life he'd never lived. "If you know so much about me, you'd know my sister was killed in a car wreck. The images brought back memories is all." He heaved an exaggerated sigh. "The woman in the photographs looked just like her." He narrowed his gaze. "End of conversation." He waved at the waiter. "We have to go. I'll get this."

"No, you won't." Carter pulled out his credit card. "We've both been consulting with you, so the bureau pays. We haven't made a small dent in our budget this year. The one thing Jo did negotiate for coming here was a massive allowance to cover cases. Let's face it we have to travel far and wide from Snakeskin Gully—when we get an assignment."

With the hairs on the back of his neck still prickling from their conversation, Kane smiled to break the tension. "If you insist."

"Tell me more about this guy." Ty leaned back in his chair and stared at him. "What waved a red flag when you interviewed him?"

"You mean apart from a shrine to underage cheerleaders?" Kane raised both eyebrows. "You're not the only person with a gut feeling."

*

Behind the general store Kane pulled into the parking space beside Williams' truck and they made their way up the creaking back stairs. The porch light was on, spilling a weak yellowish glow over the steps. High above, the night's final fireworks display shot into the sky, sending the darkness into a parade of bright sparkling colors, and filling the pristine air with the stink of gunpowder.

He knocked and heard footsteps as Stan Williams came to the door. It opened and Williams looked past Kane to Carter with a worried expression that eased as Carter moved into the light. "Stan, this is Ty, a friend of mine from Snakeskin Gully here for the festival."

"Come inside." Williams held out a hand to Carter. "Nice to meet you. It's good to find two men in town of like mind. Many don't understand my passion for cheerleaders."

"Oh, I like cheerleaders just fine." Carter moved the toothpick across his mouth and smiled with it clenched between his teeth. "I've dated my fair share, well more than my fair share. Being the quarterback in high school helped some."

"Yeah, the problem is, people find it unusual that I prefer the cheerleaders from high school, they don't understand that as they get older the allure isn't there anymore." Sweat coated Williams' brow and he carried the odor of bleach. Kane said nothing but walked straight to the wall of images and turned back to Carter. "See, he's captured them in every pose?"

"Yeah." Carter moved along the bench. "You collect pompoms too?" He chuckled. "Like trophies? How many pairs do you have?"

"A few." Williams wiped the sweat from his brow on his sleeve. "You've seen my latest shots, is there anything else you want to see?" He shrugged. "I do have to work in the morning."

Kane smiled, noticing the additional pompoms from the last time he'd been inside Williams' home. "What about the images of the girls you take here, in the studio. Can you share them with us?"

"There are quite a few but I'll show you some of my favorites." Williams went to his computer and scrolled through a page of image files and then opened one and stood back. "This is Shirley, she worked on Saturdays in the store downstairs and she'd drop by to model for me."

"Did you pay her?" Carter leaned on the desk peering at the screen. "For modeling?"

"Yeah, she needed the cash." Williams opened a file of a young woman holding the pompoms and wearing just her underwear. "She was real cute."

"Was?" Kane looked at him. "What happened to her?"

"Her family moved away and I read somewhere she'd gone missing." Williams frowned. "It was five years or so ago. I'm not sure."

Kane ground his teeth as the images and explanations went on for half an hour. He'd seen enough and now had other concerns he had to discuss with Jenna. He straightened. "We'd better let you get some rest. Did you at least have a good time at the festival today? The fireworks were spectacular. I missed the ones just before but we caught the earlier ones from the window at The Cattleman's."

"Fireworks? Oh, they put on quite a show, don't they? I spent my time taking photographs as usual but I had something else to do tonight." Williams didn't meet Kane's eyes, shifting his gaze to the pompoms on the bench. He swallowed and his Adam's apple bobbed. "It was good of you both to drop by. Maybe we can spend some time one weekend, when you're back again, Ty, or I can send you some of my shots? Do you have any we could swap?"

"I'm sure I'll be able to find something to share. I'll be in touch. Dave has your details." Carter removed his hat, ran a hand through his shaggy blond hair, and headed for the door. "We'll see you later." He disappeared down the stairs.

Kane hurried after him and once inside the Beast he looked at Carter. "I thought he was a predator but now I'm seriously considering he may be a possible suspect in Laurie Turner's murder."

"How so?" Carter pushed on his Stetson.

Kane started the engine. "Pompoms."

CHAPTER TWENTY-NINE

Jake Rowley disconnected a call from Jenna. She was still at The Cattleman's Hotel and in Jo's room, waiting for Kane and Agent Carter to get back from speaking to Stan Williams. Although he'd checked Williams out and had found nothing suspicious, and no complaints made against him, apparently Bobby Kalo out of the FBI office in Snakeskin Gully had unearthed something in his past. They'd found zip on the search warrant for the green Chrysler sedan admittedly driven by Verna Hughes. The judge ruled it was hearsay and not probable cause. Rowley tidied the front desk and pulled on his jacket. The deputy assigned to take over for the next few hours had already arrived and he'd explained everything he needed to know. It was just a precaution to have the sheriff's department open until all the revelers in town had headed home. The day had gone fine, with only the usual disturbances and arguments that happened when a crowd of people descended on the town. It had been a long day and he looked forward to crawling into bed. He yawned and called Sandy. She'd be glad to know he was on his way to collect her.

The phone rang and rang with no reply. He checked the number and tried again. A knot of worry curled in his stomach and then he took a few deep breaths. She'd mentioned going upstairs to watch the fireworks and drink hot chocolate in her favorite chair and had probably fallen asleep. Of late, she'd been sleeping like the dead. She'd missed the old stuffed leather chair and wanted to take it to the ranch. He'd even asked Jenna if he could buy it for her and was confused at her refusal but the surprise came the day they'd finished the nursery. A delivery truck had arrived at the gate carrying a fine leather chair, made especially for nursing mothers. It rocked and was complete with footrest. It was a gift from Jenna and Dave. He could still hear Sandy's woops of joy. She would treasure it always.

Rowley climbed into his SUV and drove the short distance to the old house, surprised to find it in darkness. Sandy wasn't afraid of the dark but when they'd lived here, he'd never arrived home without seeing the porch light blazing a welcome and at least the hall light on downstairs. He parked and rushed to the front door, using his key to gain entrance. The house stunk of bleach as if someone had emptied and entire bottle on the floor. "Sandy?"

He flicked on lights. Nothing. Concern knotted his gut as he pulled out his Maglite and searched each room, looking for her. Nothing seemed disturbed. He walked into the kitchen and as the Maglite flooded the room, he made out Sandy's purse and Thermos on the counter, same as when he'd left her. "Sandy, are you up there?"

Nothing.

Fear gripped him for her safety but his training clicked in to prevent him rushing up the stairs into unknown danger. If he heard a sound, he'd call for backup but likely Sandy was asleep in the bedroom. He eased his weapon from the holster and crept up the stairs avoiding the creaky steps he'd come to know so well. He reached the landing and keeping his back to the wall, aimed his Maglite down the barrel of his Glock. Sweeping the hallway, he moved slowly to the first bedroom at the top of the stairs. The door hung open and the stink of bleach was choking. With his back flat to the wall he aimed his flashlight inside the room and gaped in horror. A young woman, her blue lips stretched wide around something stuffed into her mouth and her skin a deathly shade of gray, sat against the wall, her eyes fixed in a death stare. Blood matted one side of her head and ligature marks crisscrossed her neck. His Maglite reflected in a pool of liquid surrounding her and as he moved the beam around the room, he noticed another wet patch on the plastic covered mattress was dripping onto the floor.

Heart threatening to tear through his ribs, he turned away and checked the second bedroom. It was empty and nothing had been disturbed. The door to the next bedroom, the room he had shared with Sandy, was shut. He holstered his weapon, gave himself a mental shake to ease the panic threatening to overtake him, and pulled a surgical glove from his pocket. He used it to open the door and then stood to one side to turkey peek inside. The streetlight he'd once thought annoying shed an orange glow through the room, across the polished wood and over the figure of Sandy, lying motionless on the floor, her face bloody. He rushed in and fell to his knees beside her feverishly feeling for a pulse on her neck. "Sandy, come on. Open your eyes."

Under his fingers he could feel blood pumping through her jugular, and pulled out his phone to call the paramedics. "This is Deputy Rowley. I need the paramedics, head injury, the patient is non-responsive, breathing, and five months pregnant. Yes, Sandy Rowley, my wife." He gave the details and went back to her. "Sandy." He brushed the hair from her face and felt the lump on her head. She was out cold.

He used his Maglite to check her, running one hand over her belly and waiting for what seemed like an eternity. His heart jumped with joy at the movement inside. As he cradled Sandy's head in his lap, he called it in. Jenna was still in town and Kane had just arrived at the hotel so they'd be only minutes away. Relieved, he stroked Sandy's face and her eyes fluttered. "Sandy, stay still now, you've hurt your head. Do you hurt anywhere? Is the baby okay?"

"Someone hit me with a flashlight." Sandy sounded groggy and she gripped his arm. "I can feel the baby moving, and nothing hurts but my head. I thought they might have kicked me again."

He looked down at her in horror. "Who kicked you?"

"I'm not sure, it was dark. The power was out." Sandy touched her face. "They kicked me under the chin and I blacked out."

Rowley helped her to sit up, stood, and then carried her to the old chair. He removed his jacket and draped it over her. "The paramedics are on their way and Jenna and Dave will be here soon." The image of the dead girl flashed across his mind. He didn't want Sandy to see a brutal murder. "I've checked the house, there's no one here. I'll go and see if the power has been turned off at the breaker box. Just wait here for a second."

He pulled out gloves and snapped them on as he walked down the hallway and closed the door to the first bedroom before he ran downstairs. He went into the laundry to flip the breaker and lights spilled through the house. He checked the backdoor and finding it unlocked, turned the key before running back up the stairs to Sandy. After checking her over again, he crouched beside her. "How are you feeling?"

"You mean apart for my head feeling as if it's been split in two? I'm okay." Sandy gripped his arm. "I'm dizzy and sick to my stomach but okay. Why? Do you need to go somewhere?"

"No, I'm not leaving you alone again, but this is a crime scene and Jenna won't want the paramedics destroying evidence. Will you be okay if I carry you downstairs? We'll wait in the family room for the paramedics. You'll need to go to the hospital; you have a nasty cut on your head. I'm coming with you. I'll follow right behind in my SUV, okay?"

"Sure." She reached out a hand and squeezed his arm. "Don't worry, I'm tougher than you think."

He stood and helped Sandy to her feet and then lifted her into his arms. Heart in his mouth, he descended the stairs. It might look good in the movies but negotiating the steps was hazardous with his precious cargo. Once he'd deposited her safely on the sofa, he sighed with relief. "They should be here soon."

"Can you grab my purse and the Thermos from the kitchen?" Sandy gripped his arm. "I'll need my purse at the hospital."

Rowley smiled at her. "Sure, I'll be right back."

After taking the purse and flask to Sandy, the unmistakable sound of Kane's siren blared outside and Rowley closed the door to the family room before he hustled to let them in. He needed to speak to them without Sandy overhearing. He opened the door to Jenna and Kane. Rio and Agent Carter followed them inside. He looked at their concerned faces. "Sandy is in the family room, she's conscious and doesn't know about upstairs. Can we keep it that way?"

"Sure." Jenna lowered her voice. "What's it look like?"

Rowley leaned in so only she could hear. "I figure it's another cheerleader murder."

CHAPTER THIRTY

Trembling with a confusing mixture of exhilaration and blind panic, he drove like a maniac in the direction of the old barn. His girl was giggling about how they'd come close to being discovered. The deputy's SUV had pulled up out front just as they reached the front door to leave. They had planned to lock the backdoor and leave by the front. The deputy had come inside, missing them by seconds. The backdoor had clicked shut behind them just as he'd entered the front door calling out a woman's name. "That was too darn close and who is the woman he was calling out for?"

"His wife, I figure." His girl grinned at him like a cat who'd just finished a plate of cream. "Some pregnant woman was upstairs when I was taking the cleaning stuff into the bedroom. I had to kill her."

Sickened, he turned to look at her, swerving on the road before she screamed at him to be careful. "You've killed a pregnant woman? How and why? What did she do to you to make you kill her?"

"She could have seen us and told the cops. I know her, she's married to one of the deputies, and now he'll be out for our blood." His girl shrugged. "She was easy to kill, I hit her with my flashlight and when she dropped, I kicked her in the face just to be sure."

Sweat trickled between his shoulder blades and the bile curdling in his stomach threatened to rush up his throat. He had to get away from her and find time to think. "I'll drop you home. I'll go and burn the clothes now. If you've killed a deputy's wife, they'll be hunting us down tonight. They'll have already found Becky. They'll find us, I know it."

"Not if we're careful. There was some blood when you killed Becky, so when you're done, wash your clothes, take a shower, and make sure you clean your boots with bleach. When they're dry polish them to get rid of the smell." She gripped his arm. "No evidence means they can't catch us."

Realization dawned on him. He'd. Killed. Becky. His girl had ordered him to hit her and he'd complied without question. There'd been no thrill and he'd seen the betrayal in Becky's eyes as he'd slammed the flashlight into her head. *I'm a murderer.* He glanced at his girl; things had changed and being with her unnerved him now. He couldn't trust her and didn't know what she might do next. "This was the last one. It's getting too hot out there. Did you see all the Blackwater deputies in town today? We came too close to being caught."

"We'll stop when I say and I have one more to kill. When she's dead, I'll be happy." She leaned against him. "You want to make me happy, don't you?"

He cleared his throat. Her touch suddenly made his skin crawl. "Sure I do, you know that, right?"

He had to make an excuse—anything not to kill again—but he'd seen her face and the thrill she'd gotten from killing. She'd never be satisfied. Now he'd killed Becky, he was in deep shit. If he tried to stop his girl, she'd turn on him and murder him in his sleep. He needed help, someone he could trust to give him advice, someone who couldn't tell the cops. As he drove, he ran the idea through his mind. A priest was out of the question, he wasn't Catholic, and old Doc Brown would find some excuse to tell the sheriff. He'd have to talk to someone before his girl chose her next victim.

CHAPTER THIRTY-ONE

Torn between giving reassurance to her friend and processing a crime scene, Jenna turned to Carter. "Call Shane for me please and then go upstairs with Rio to give Wolfe a rundown of what's happened. We'll need to preserve the crime scene. I'll speak to Sandy and be right there."

"Sure." Carter glanced at the forensics kit in Kane's hand. "We'll need gloves, a mask, and booties."

"Help yourself." Kane dropped the bag on the hall stand and flipped it open.

Jenna looked at them. "Not one word about the other victim to Sandy. She's been through enough already."

"I hear sirens in the distance, it must be the paramedics." Kane frowned. "If you want to speak to her, you'd better hurry."

"You know how to deal with trauma victims far better than I do. I'll be the support crew and take down notes. I can imagine the pain she's in, my head still aches from the slap from Mr. Law." Jenna opened the door to the family room and went inside with Kane close behind her. She smiled at Sandy. "We leave you alone for a few minutes and look what happens."

"Me? Look at you with a black eye." Sandy leaned back in the chair. "At least you fought back. I played possum and hoped they'd leave me alone."

"That was the best thing to do." Kane squeezed her shoulder. "It wasn't you they came here to hurt. We figure they were looking for someone else. What do you remember?"

"I'm sorry, I don't remember much at all." Sandy was holding a wad of tissues to her cheek in an attempt to slow the flow of blood. "I don't figure I can tell you anything."

"Yeah you can." Kane squatted beside her. "You'd be surprised what the mind sees even if we don't register it at first. Go back to when you arrived. Did you see any vehicles parked close by?"

"No, only the red pickup next door, and it's always there at night." Sandy looked at him. "Everything was normal. I cleaned up the papers and dirty footprints left by the delivery guys, poured a cup of hot chocolate from the Thermos, and came up here to rest and watch the first display of fireworks."

"Did you have the doors closed downstairs?" Kane pulled out more tissues from a box on the floor and handed them to her.

"I checked the backdoor when I arrived." Sandy dabbed at the cut on her head and winced. "It was locked then and the front door needs a key to open it."

"Then what happened?" Kane smiled at her. "You sat here and drank your chocolate. Did you fall asleep?"

"Yeah I did and then something woke me, a noise in the hallway." Sandy frowned. "It was dark and I'd left all the lights on for when Jake arrived."

"So, you heard a noise and then what happened?" Kane's face was filled with emotion.

Jenna leaned against the wall and looked at her battered friend and tried to quell her anger. Her gaze moved to Rowley balanced on the arm of the chair holding Sandy's hand. She'd never seen him so pale and he was trembling with rage.

"I went into the hallway and heard sounds and then someone came at me, I tried to run but they knocked me down. They hit me with a flashlight and when they kicked me—" Sandy blinked and then stared at Kane. "They were wearing cowboy boots, something flashed like a medallion or something on the boots. That's all I remember until Jake arrived."

"Did they say anything?" Kane regarded her closely. "Did you smell anything?"

"No, they didn't say anything." Sandy thought for a beat. "There was a smell, I'm not sure what it was, cologne perhaps?"

"One person or two?" Kane glanced at Jenna and then back at Sandy.

"One, it was only one." Sandy sighed and dabbed at her head again. "One set of footsteps came running behind me, I'm certain."

Jenna smiled at her. "You did really well." She headed for the door. "The paramedics are here. I'll come by the hospital and check on you later. No doubt, the doctors will want to run a ton of tests."

"They will." Sandy gripped Rowley's arm. "I'll be fine. Don't drive when you're angry. Wait awhile and call my folks, I'll need some things. Ask Mom, she'll know what to bring."

"Okay." Rowley kissed her. "I'll be right behind you."

The paramedics came in with their usual swift efficiency, checking Sandy and getting her onto a gurney before whisking her away. Jenna had expected Rowley to dash after her but he slumped against the wall and covered his face with both hands. She walked to his side. He always reacted well to orders and obviously needed some direction. "You have things to do. Contact her parents and then follow her to the hospital. You have a long night ahead of you, these things take hours. We'll be by as soon as we've processed the scene. Do you need me to get anything from the ranch for Sandy?"

"No." Rowley straightened and a strange calm had descended on him. "Sandy still has things at her parents' house. I'll call and ask her mom to bring the necessities. They'll keep her in the hospital for at least overnight, won't they?"

Jenna nodded. "Yeah, they'll want to make sure she and the baby are okay."

"Babies." Rowley's eyes filled with unshed tears. "Twins, one of each, we were keeping it a secret until my parents come back from vacation. God, I hope they're okay."

She hadn't seen Wolfe slip in the front door with Emily and Colt Webber at his side. She turned at his voice.

"Did she have any bleeding or contractions? Could you feel the babies moving?" Wolfe was staring at Rowley.

"She was only bleeding from her head injury. I felt the babies moving and no contractions." Rowley looked relieved to see Wolfe.

"Was Sandy lucid?" Wolfe was regarding Rowley intently.

"Yeah, not at first, but yes she was answering Kane's questions just fine." Rowley took the drink Emily thrust into his hands. "I don't have time to drink coffee, she'll need me at the hospital."

"Sit down and drink the coffee." Wolfe patted him on the shoulder. "Call her parents and get what she needs for a couple of days' observation. Trust me, the moment the paramedics wheel in the gurney, she'll be having scans and there will be doctors crawling all over her. You'll be stuck in the waiting room for hours. It's best you sit here for a while until the shock wears off a bit before you get behind the wheel."

"Okay." Rowley removed his Stetson and dropped into a chair. He looked up at Jenna. "For the first time in my life, I feel like killing someone. The monster who killed those girls laid hands on my wife." His hands shook around the cup. "It's obvious they'll stop at nothing."

Jenna waved everyone from the room. "Get suited up, folks, and get that crime scene processed. I'll be up in a moment." She waited for them to leave and looked at Rowley. "That's a perfectly normal reaction. I get mad when people are killed and when Dave was shot, I wanted to kill the man who did it." She crouched beside him. "You're a great deputy and you know we have the best team around, so I want you to trust me to catch this guy." She squeezed his arm. "I need to know the office is in capable hands while I'm working on this case. You'll need to step back now that Sandy is involved." She noticed his face stiffen and sighed. "Look, I know it's difficult to stand by when something like this happens but when we catch him, if his defense team believe there was any chance of a conflict of interest, he'll walk."

"Yeah, I understand." Rowley stared at the door. "Do you figure Agent Carter and Wells will stick around now?"

Jenna shrugged. "Maybe but they're always there if we need them. Drink your coffee and make the calls. I'll go and see what's happening upstairs."

She suited up and skirted past Colt Webber who was checking every inch of the staircase for hairs. "Find anything?"

"Yeah, a fiber that might be from a pompom." Webber held up an evidence bag. "It's the right color."

Jenna nodded and moved up the steps, following the voices into the first bedroom. "What have we got, Shane?"

"This one is different to the last one but the same in many ways." Wolfe pointed to the marks on the girl's neck. "Someone tried to strangle her and couldn't kill her so they bludgeoned her to death by the look of it. I'll know more from the post. So that's different, so is the tape, and I'm assuming the material poking out from under the tape are men's briefs. She isn't naked but her clothes are missing."

Jenna moved closer to the victim. "I know her, she's the vice-captain of the cheerleading squad. Her name is Becky something." She pulled out her phone and scrolled through her files. "Becky Powell." She thought for a beat. "We have a connection. She was chasing after Wyatt Cooper the night Laurie was murdered."

CHAPTER THIRTY-TWO

After seeing Rowley off with the promise of following as soon as possible, Jenna pulled Kane to one side. "I'll leave Rio to observe Wolfe. If he has a near perfect recall like he says, he'll be taking in the entire scene and can apply it to our investigation at will. I've seen all I need to see and Wolfe doesn't need our help. I figure we canvas the area while things are fresh in people's minds. The lights are on in many homes and I can see people watching us through windows."

"Okay." Kane followed her from the house. "I'll be interested to see what Wolfe finds in the autopsy. At first, I thought this might be a copycat killer but when Wolfe mentioned the briefs, well we've never mentioned that detail to the press, have we?"

"No, we haven't." Jenna stopped walking and turned to him. "Even with the blood and all, that's Becky Powell. I recognize her and as soon as we've finished here, we'll have to track down her parents and give them the bad news." She shook her head slowly. "They won't even know anything is wrong. If she was out on a date, they might not be worrying just yet."

"You know they'll want to rush to the morgue and see her tonight." Kane kneaded his shoulder and stared into the street. "It's as if they don't want them to be alone. It's heartbreaking to tell them they have to wait."

Jenna started to walk again. "Maybe but when they see her, she won't be covered in blood. That's not a memory any loved one should have to suffer."

"Trust me, I know." Kane pulled out a notebook and pen. "Let's get this over with."

They spoke to everyone along one side of the road and down the other and pulled blanks on the two homes opposite. Both families had just gotten home from the festival and had only seen the arrival of the paramedics. They crossed the road and went to the neighbor. Jenna rang the bell and the door opened at once. "Good evening, I'm Sheriff Alton and this is Deputy Kane, we're investigating an incident next door. Did you hear anything unusual or see any unfamiliar vehicles parked close by this evening?"

"Well it happens I did." A woman in her late sixties pointed at a tree opposite. "There was a silver GMC truck parked under that tree. It was there for about three hours and left just after Deputy Rowley arrived home." She looked at Jenna and lifted one shoulder. "Not that I'm a busybody, but I went outside to walk the dog and noticed the vehicle. Now I know the people across the road all went to the festival this evening, so the truck wasn't a visitor. I was suspicious and kept my eye on it to see if anyone was loading it up with stolen property."

Jenna exchanged a look with Kane and nodded. "That was very thoughtful of you. Did you see anyone or hear anything?"

"Well, I thought so, maybe someone running on the gravel pathway between my house and the one next door. I looked out but couldn't see anything with the trees and all." She paused a beat. "I watched out the window and just before eleven, Deputy Rowley arrived in his SUV. I know he'd moved out, so I thought that was strange. I heard him calling out for Sandy and figured she must be working inside so I didn't worry too much. It was just after that I noticed the GMC had gone. It crept away without a sound." She pulled a face. "That's all I can tell you. I didn't see anyone at all, I'm sorry."

"Are you sure it was a silver GMC truck?" Kane tilted his head to look at her.

"I sure am." She smiled at him. "My son has one and it's just the same but he lives in Blackwater."

"And he had no reason to be here in town tonight?" Jenna watched the woman's reaction. "Does he visit you often?"

"My son is an ER nurse and was working last night." She sighed. "He tries to get to see me but his work keeps him busy. He's either working or sleeping lately."

Jenna nodded. "Yes, they work very hard."

"What happened next door? I saw Sandy being taken away in an ambulance, is she going to be okay?"

"I hope so." Jenna pushed a hand through her hair. "We're trying to get to the bottom of what happened to her."

"I've written down what you've told us in a statement." Kane handed the woman his statement book. "Could you please read it through and sign it? Please print your name and contact details here." He pointed to the document.

The woman complied and Jenna smiled at her. "Thank you for your assistance." She handed her a card. "If you think of anything else, or that truck comes back, write down the license plate if you can but don't go near it, call me immediately."

"Sure." The woman looked at the card. "I'm glad I could help."

Dreading her next assignment, Jenna made her way back to the house and they both suited up again. Rio was doing a search of the ground floor and she went up to him. "Anything to report?"

"A few things, there are scuff marks on the floor in a number of places and Webber found traces of DNA at the bottom of the stairs and in the hallway outside the front bedroom. I figure they're from a struggle as I recall Rowley telling me Sandy had come here specifically to make sure the floors were spotless." He shrugged.

"I'm not sure why, my brother and sister will have them scuffed the moment they walk inside."

Taken aback, Jenna stared at him. "Do you still want to move in here, even after a murder?"

"Sure." Rio met her gaze. "People die in houses all the time. I know it's a crime scene but once you've released it and the cleaners have been inside, I don't have a problem." He raised both eyebrows. "I don't believe in ghosts and I gather the locked door from the kitchen leads to accommodation for a live-in housekeeper? That would be perfect, if I can find one to live here."

Jenna had thought she might have to sell the house and buy another to replace it. Rio's news was a relief. "Well then, that's fine and Maggie has a list of suitable housekeepers you can interview. By the way it's in your employment contract, that as this is the sheriff department's property, you'll only have to pay the utilities and there's provision made for a housekeeper."

"Why do you figure I took the job?" Rio smiled. "Trying to get by and care for the twins has been a nightmare."

Jenna checked her watch. "It's getting late. Once Wolfe has processed the crime scene you'd better get on home."

"You'll need an officer on duty to guard the scene." Rio looked concerned. "In case the killer comes back to contaminate the crime scene."

"We have four deputies from Blackwater and Louan cooling their heels at the motel." Kane pulled out his phone. "They can split the shifts but I doubt Wolfe will want to return again in the morning. He's usually thorough and I gather you've taken footage of everything?"

"I sure have." Rio waved a hand toward the stairs. "I took images of every step as well."

Jenna glanced at Kane. "Go make the calls." She turned back to Rio. "Okay, I'll speak to Wolfe and then we're heading out to inform next of kin."

She headed up the stairs and into the room. The body of Becky was on a gurney and Wolfe was making ready to leave. "I'm going to speak to her parents. What time tomorrow for a viewing?"

"Eleven." Wolfe turned to her. "Autopsy at two. Rowley must have been minutes away from saving this girl. She was still warm when we arrived, her body temperature hadn't fallen much at all, no onset of rigor. I figure she was killed not long before he arrived at the house." His eyebrows drew together. "She died while Sandy was unconscious in the other room. You'll need to keep that information from her. At least until she is over the shock of what happened."

"That's going to be difficult but I'll do my best." Jenna stood hands on hips and surveyed the room. "We'll come by after we've spoken to the victim's parents. Kane is organizing a patrol to watch the house overnight; Rio will need to head home when they arrive." She looked at Carter. "Are you staying or do you want a ride back to the hotel?"

"I'm staying." Carter was examining the ceiling. "Shane is not through here yet."

"I'd appreciate his help if you can spare him? We have a ton more areas to process and I haven't started on the other bedroom yet." Wolfe indicated to the floor. "The killers tipped bleach over the victim but where the body pressed against the wall, I found trace evidence. They rushed the cleanup and I'm going to check every inch of this room before we leave."

Jenna wrinkled her nose at the pungent smell of bleach. "We shouldn't be too long. I'll drop by Aunt Betty's Café, I'm sure we all need coffee to keep us going."

"Good idea, we'll use the family room. It's a clean area and no one went in there during the attack." Wolfe sighed. "Keep as quiet as possible, we won't be popular with the neighbors. Webber is going to be searching all the trash cans out front of the houses before we leave. The victim's clothes are missing and the killers could have dumped them before leaving."

Jenna nodded. "It only takes one mistake and we'll have them. That will be their downfall. Killers all believe they've committed the perfect murder. There's no such thing."

CHAPTER THIRTY-THREE

The wind was picking up, rustling the trees and making the fall leaves rain down across the blacktop. In the streetlight, it reminded Kane of a flock of butterflies. He leaned against the door of his truck waiting for Jenna. Concerned about Sandy and how Rowley was coping, he pulled out his phone to get an update. "Hi, Jake, it's Dave. Any news?"

"Some. They performed an ultrasound on the babies and assured me they're fine but Sandy is having a brain scan. She said her vision was blurry. Her folks are here and mine are on their way. It's going to be some time before they complete all the tests and stitch her up. I'll know more later."

Kane glanced up as Jenna walked to his side. "We'll drop by before we head home. Do you need a change of clothes or anything else I can get you?"

"Nope, my parents will grab what I need if I have to stay."

"Okay, we'll see you soon." Kane disconnected.

"Any news?" Jenna pulled open the door to the truck.

Kane slid in behind the wheel. "Babies are fine, nothing on Sandy yet." He backed out the parking space and headed into town. "The Powells' address is already in the GPS." He looked at Jenna. "I get a knot in my stomach every time we have to inform next of kin. It's something you can never get used to, is it?"

"Nope." Jenna leaned back in her seat. "I try and rehearse what to say in my head but when I get there I'm never prepared."

As they entered Main, Kane was surprised to see the clusters of people still milling around, most of them young people in small groups chatting or eating takeout. The hotdog cart was doing a fine business and seemed to have an endless supply. He smiled. "How do they keep that cart going, day and night?"

"They own the convenience store and with six grown sons, they can keep going around the clock." Jenna smiled. "They have more than one cart." She pointed at the people in a line outside Aunt Betty's. "Oh, I have to call Aunt Betty's. They're so busy tonight, I should order coffee for the team and we'll drop by on the way back. Wolfe said it's going to be ages before he's through. I'll order some food as well." She made the call.

Kane headed for the Powells' house and smiled to himself. She was using one of his tactics, to ease the stress of the night. A girl's brutal murder and the senseless attack on Sandy had shaken the team. He could feel the simmering anger from everyone with the exception of Rio. His introduction to Black Rock Falls had been tough but he'd handled himself with a professionalism he hadn't expected. He glanced at Jenna. "I figure Zac is going to be a real asset to our team. He didn't need any direction and just mucked in and got the job done."

"I agree but do you think he's what he seems?" Jenna cleared her throat. "I mean he acts like he's seen it all, no emotion. Most guys of his age would have puked at the sight of a girl bludgeoned to death but he took it in his stride."

Kane nodded. "He must have a built-in mechanism. Think about it. He can't forget anything he sees and as a detective in Los Angeles, he's seen his fair share of blood and gore. Not being able to forget is an incredible freak of nature. It's not classed as an eidetic memory. That's being able to recall an image for about a minute in detail and he hasn't got what's classed as a photographic memory either. What he has is a mixture of long-term memory and instant recall, something that hasn't really been labeled correctly yet. His IQ must be off the board but whatever the doctors decide to call it, he's had it forever. I guess he's learned to cope with it and turn off the emotion attached to the memory."

"You do that all the time." Jenna shrugged. "What's so different?"

"I don't have his memory." Kane kept his eyes on the road. "I do turn off emotion but it's part of my training and it's a technique I used to make the shot and kill the target. I don't forget the people I've killed but I've learned not to dwell on it. He must do the same. His memory is a gift and a curse." He slowed as the GPS indicated they'd reached their destination.

Outside the house, he removed his hat and turned to Jenna. "Here we go."

"The front porch light is on and they're probably waiting up for her." Jenna removed her hat, dropped it onto the seat, and opened the door.

They walked up to the front door, and Kane pressed the doorbell, hearing the chimes echo inside. Footsteps and then a woman wearing a dressing gown flung open the door.

"Mrs. Powell?" Jenna stepped closer.

"Yes, what can I do for you, Sheriff?" The woman gripped the front of her gown and her mouth hung open. "Oh, sweet Jesus, has Becky had an accident?"

"May we come inside?" Jenna lifted her chin.

"Yes, of course." She turned as a man walked from a side room. "Albie, something's happened to Becky."

Kane looked at the distraught man. "Is there somewhere we can sit down?"

"Yes, in here." The man waved them into the family room and stood in the middle staring at them.

"Mr. and Mrs. Powell, please sit down." Jenna waited for them to sit on the sofa. "I'm sorry to inform you, Becky is dead."

"How? She never drives fast." Mr. Powell looked up at them, his face drained of color. "What happened to our little girl?"

"I'm afraid that is yet to be determined." Jenna sat opposite. "She was found about an hour ago in a house on Stanton. I identified her on scene but we'll need you to make a formal ID."

"I need to go to her." Mrs. Powell was staring straight ahead obviously in shock. "She'll be all alone. She needs her mother."

Kane cleared his throat. "She's not alone, Dr. Shane Wolfe the medical examiner and his daughter Emily are with her. She's in good hands, safe hands."

"When then?" Mr. Powell seemed to shake himself and took his wife's hand.

"Tomorrow at ten at the medical examiner's office." Jenna looked from one to the other. "You mentioned Becky was driving tonight, what is the make and color of her vehicle?"

"It's a red Chevrolet Equinox SUV." Mr. Powell looked troubled. "She said she was going to meet friends at the library. She came home for dinner and then went back out. I told her not to be late because of school tomorrow. She promised to be home by nine-thirty. We were getting worried."

"Do you recall the names of any of the friends she was going to meet?" Jenna took out her notepad.

"Some boy, I think." Mrs. Powell looked at her husband. "She dressed real pretty and was so excited she hardly touched her meal."

Kane nodded. "So, no names you can recall? What was she wearing?"

"What do you mean by that?" Mr. Powell's eyes widened. "Are her clothes missing?"

"We need a list to make sure nothing is missing." Jenna flicked Kane a meaningful glance. "If you don't mind?"

"White top and a denim skirt, she was wearing her boots. Brown cowboy boots with fringes." Mrs. Powell's eyes filled with tears. "She took a backpack and her pompoms. I saw her putting them into her bag."

Kane nodded. "Is there anyone we can call, family or a minister?"

"No, we'll call the family." Mr. Powell ran both hands down his face. "It's better coming from us. I'll call her brothers, they're both away at college. And then the rest of the family." He pushed unsteadily to his feet. "Ten tomorrow at the medical examiner's office, you said?"

"Yes, that's right." Jenna stood and handed him her card. "If there's anything you need or can recall, please contact me, day or night."

Kane looked at the devastated couple. "We'll see ourselves out. I'm so sorry for your loss." He led the way outside and back to his truck.

"It will hit them soon." Jenna climbed into the seat and pushed on her hat. "After we drop by for takeout, swing past the library parking lot. We might locate Becky's vehicle." She let out an explosive sigh. "It's going to be a long night but we'll have to keep going. We'll need more evidence if we're going to catch the killer."

CHAPTER THIRTY-FOUR

Steam billowed as the hot shower spilled over her and washed every trace of Becky Powell from her hair and skin. The scent of roses filled the room, removing the smell of the dying girl and bleach. She'd shampooed twice and scrubbed her skin after sneaking into the house and undressing in the laundry. She'd dumped her clothes in the washing machine and cleaned her boots with bleach before creeping upstairs to the shower. Once she was done, she'd take her laundry downstairs and start the machine. Within the hour, she'd have everything in the dryer all spick and span.

Her mind replayed seeing Becky die. It was as if she could relive the moment, rewind, and fast forward at will. Her heart still pounded at the memory of the look in her boyfriend's eyes as he raised the flashlight. The evil in him had thrilled her. It wasn't the killing; it was making him do it for her. Power had surged through her. After they'd dragged Becky against the wall and turned her head to watch them, his kiss had been brutal. She'd pushed him away and enjoyed seeing him crushed at her rejection but there'd been no time to waste, they'd had to leave and he'd followed her orders like a pet dog. She controlled him now. He'd never leave her.

After drying her hair, she wrapped a towel around her and collected her things, creeping downstairs to the laundry, setting the machine, and slipping back unnoticed. She checked the time; of late, she timed everything. The washing machine cycle took thirty minutes on a small load and she could set the timer on the dryer and go to bed. Not that sleep beckoned her. She wondered if her boyfriend had added the pompoms to their collection in the old barn. They looked good side by side on the shelf. No one went there, it was their secret place. Since his pa had left, they were the only people to visit the old barn.

Her mind went to Vicky Perez. Planning out her demise exhilarated her. She enjoyed frightening people and after chasing down the pregnant woman at the house and hearing her beg for her life, she wanted more. An indescribable rush filled her at the expressions on their faces when they knew they were going to die. If she could make it last longer, it would feed her raging hunger for death.

CHAPTER THIRTY-FIVE

Jenna placed the box containing coffee and snacks for the team in the back of the Beast and covered it with a blanket. She jumped into the passenger seat and waved a hand at Kane. "Drive past the library parking lot." She buckled up. "We might be lucky for once and find her vehicle."

"If we do, I'll check it for prints but I doubt the killer would have set foot near it." Kane turned into the library parking lot. "He's too careful." The lights moved in an arc across the lot. "Well, we have a hit."

"Thank goodness." Jenna smiled at him, pulling back the urge to give him a high-five. "I'll run the plates. You go check for prints."

As the MDT worked through its program and confirmed the owner, she waited for Kane as he dusted and lifted fingerprints from the vehicle. In no time, he was back. "I've added them to the file and sent a copy to Wolfe for identification." He turned the truck around and headed back to Rowley's old house. "I hope the coffee will still be hot. It's gotten quite cold tonight."

Jenna nodded. "So do I." She turned in her seat to look at him. "The coffee is in Thermoses; we'll have to drop them back to Aunt Betty's in the morning but I'm sure Rowley will need something hot and the coffee at the hospital is disgusting."

"Yeah, I remember." Kane pulled a face. "I wonder how Sandy is doing?"

Jenna tucked her hair behind one ear and adjusted her hat. "Jake would have called if it had been bad news. I'm keeping my fingers crossed."

As they pulled up outside the house, Jenna spotted a Blackwater Sheriff's Department vehicle outside with a deputy on duty. She gave him a wave as Kane pulled up behind Rio's cruiser. It was Carter who greeted them at the door and Jenna nodded to him. "Anything happening I need to know about?"

"Tons." Carter indicated to Wolfe's van. "Wolfe has the victim in his van but he's waited for you before he leaves. There's something he needs to show you upstairs. The scene's been processed, you won't need booties just gloves."

"I'll take the coffee into the family room and be right behind you." Kane headed down the hallway.

"Sure." Jenna gloved up as she followed Carter upstairs. She entered the first bedroom and scanned the weary faces. "We've set up coffee in the family room if anyone needs a break." She looked at Wolfe. "What have you got for me, Shane?"

"Ah, I'm glad you're back." Wolfe turned to Emily. "Go and grab me a cup, I'm dead on my feet." He turned back to Jenna. "We've found a distinct difference to the blood spatter involved in both crimes." Wolfe turned as Kane bounded into the room. "If you look here…" He pointed to droplets of blood on the floor and above on the ceiling. "Look at the arc and the pattern of blood spatter. This is the transfer pattern from a blunt instrument after it hits the victim, and we're assuming from Sandy's statement it was a flashlight. The killer brought it up in an arc after striking the victim. The second blow picks up the victim's blood and centrifugal force flings it out in an arc."

Jenna stared at the blood spatter and nodded. "Yeah, this indicates the killer raised the weapon above their heads more than once."

"But there's more." Carter moved the toothpick across his lips and smiled at her. "Now look at where Sandy was attacked." He led the way down the hallway and into the front bedroom. "What do you see?"

Why did Carter make her feel like a rookie? Jenna sighed. "Yeah, it's the same thing here. Sandy told us how this occurred, what are you getting at, Carter?"

"It's the size of the arc made by the blood." Kane stepped beside her. "This proves we have two killers." He shrugged. "An arc is part of a circle, so by determining the size of the arc, we can obtain the killer's height. The killer's height with arm outstretched plus weapon—" he demonstrated with his arm "—is the diameter of the arc."

"That's interesting." Jenna stared at the blood spatter. "So, who do we need to make these calculations? Geometry was never a strong subject of mine."

"I already made the calculations." Rio shrugged. "Sandy's attacker was five-five and the victim's close to six feet." He handed Jenna his notebook with precise diagrams. "From the violence of the first victim and the many attempts to kill Becky, I would be looking at a man and a woman teaming up to murder."

"There is something else." Carter inclined his head. "The victim's backpack hadn't been touched by anyone but her, but it was open. I checked inside. Her clothes are missing like in the Laurie Turner case, and Webber found a part of a pompom on the stairs. We'll need to confirm it from her parents but I think she had her pompoms with her. I figure whoever did this took her clothes and her pompoms. Trophies perhaps?"

The last thing Jenna needed was another serial killer or killers in town. She pressed her lips together and thought for a beat. "Yeah, I'm of the same opinion and her parents mentioned she had taken her pompoms with her."

"Another thing." Wolfe narrowed his gaze. "When we do the autopsy on Becky, I'll have Sandy release her X-rays and scans to me for comparison. We'll be able to calculate the force used in each case." He looked at Jenna. "From this evidence, and the spatter we found at Laurie Turner's crime scene, we can assume the same person inflicted wounds on both Laurie and Sandy. They both came back as a person around five-five." He looked at Jenna. "This is all I need here. I'll wait for Webber to finish checking the trash bins and then get the body on ice. I'll bring the team over after the parents' viewing and we'll do a walk through in daylight and then, you can get the cleaners in."

Jenna nodded. "Okay great." She glanced at Rio. "Thanks for staying back."

"My pleasure but if the coffee is in a to-go cup, I'll grab one for the ride home." Rio stood to one side as Jenna headed downstairs.

"We'll be doing the same." Jenna looked over her shoulder at him. "We're heading for the hospital next to check on Sandy. I figure Rowley will need a decent cup of coffee as well."

After Webber returned with the news that he'd found nothing of interest in the garbage, Jenna returned the unused coffee and food to the box. She smiled to herself as Kane grabbed sandwiches from a bag and filled two, to-go cups of coffee from the Thermos. She took the coffee from him and followed Kane out to his truck. "Nothing spoils your appetite, does it?" She set the two to-go cups of coffee in the console and stared at him.

"Some things do." Kane pulled the plastic wrap off a pastrami on rye and bit into it with a sigh. "But when the job gets in the way of staying healthy it's time to quit. Eating when under stress is calming." He indicated toward the sandwich. "Eat, it's going to be a long night."

Jenna's phone chimed and she stared at the caller ID. It was Rowley. Her heart picked up a beat and she put the call on speaker. "Is Sandy okay?"

"Yeah, she'll be okay." Rowley sounded exhausted. *"The babies too. She has a concussion and needed six stitches in the wound on her head and three above her eye."* He let out a long sigh. *"I'm staying with her tonight. My folks brought me a change of clothes but I've sent them home now. Sandy can't have visitors. They want her to rest here for a couple of days."*

Jenna nodded. "Take all the time you need, Jake." She stared at the sandwich on her knee. "We'll drop by anyway. I have a Thermos of hot coffee and sandwiches from Aunt Betty's if you want them?"

"Oh, boy. I'm famished. Thank you. I'll come down and meet you out front. I'm sure you want to get on home."

Jenna glanced at Kane. "We're leaving now, head on down." She disconnected. "Thank God she's okay."

"Yeah." Kane licked his fingers and then started the truck. "It's just as well or we'd have had a vigilante deputy on our hands. I figure you'll need to keep Jake on a short leash. Us guys don't take too kindly to people hurting our womenfolk."

CHAPTER THIRTY-SIX

Wednesday

Sleeping in just happened to be the one thing that never happened to Jenna. She sat bolt upright when a scrape came on her bedroom door, followed by a thump on the bed and a good face washing by Duke. "Yuk, how did you get out?" She pushed him away but couldn't resist rubbing his ears before reaching for a packet of wipes on her bedside table and washing her face.

"You'll hurt his feelings." Kane's voice sounded muffled.

"Dave?" She blinked into the dim light. "Is something wrong?"

"Nope, I'm just checking on you is all?" Kane poked his head around the door. "When you didn't show for work by eight, I started to worry and let myself in. When I saw you were sound asleep, I put on a pot of coffee."

Bewildered, Jenna stared at the bedside clock. Her usual morning workout started at six with Kane after they'd tended the horses. By eight-ten, she should be heading for the office. "Oh, darn. I'm sorry, I never oversleep."

"It's all good, Rio is at the office with Maggie. They both figured we had something to do this morning and anyway, I needed some spare time to update the files. We're all squared away now." Kane carried two cups of coffee into the room and placed them on the bedside table. "I called Rowley. Sandy is doing okay. She's a bit battered and will be staying for a day or so. The doctor wants her to rest. Rowley's father has offered to tend the animals and will stay on the ranch until Sandy is home." He sighed. "I told Rowley to take all the time he needs. He can't be involved in the investigation and might as well be with Sandy when she needs him."

Relieved, Jenna nodded in agreement but her head hurt. "That's good news about Sandy." She patted the edge of the bed. "Sit down." She leaned back in the pillows. "Why did you let me sleep so long?"

"You fell asleep on the drive home, Jenna. You haven't recovered from the head injury. You've likely been walking around with concussion. Mr. Law belted you pretty hard." Kane sat beside her and gently touched the bruise under her eye. "The bruise on your face is purple and I know it hurts. An extra hour or so isn't going to make any difference to the investigation." He handed her a cup. "We're waiting on a formal ID on the last victim. Rio has already issued a media report—it's generic and I approved it—so it will make the news. He did mention we are looking for a silver GMC truck and has asked the owner to come forward."

Jenna sipped her coffee. "Good luck with that." She took his hand and squeezed. "Thanks for covering for me. I guess I did need the rest. My face does hurt and my head aches some but I don't feel concussed just exhausted. It's been a grueling week so far."

"With two murders to solve…" Kane smiled ruefully. "It's only going to get worse before it gets better."

"It seems Rio arrived just in time." Jenna finished her coffee. "I'll have him hunting down our suspects to discover where they were last night."

"Hmm, well most of them would have been at the festival." Kane sipped his coffee and stared at the wall thinking. "Wyatt Cooper seemed to vanish after the parade and I don't recall seeing him with any of the groups of people hanging around town. I figure we should pick up where we left off and see how he reacts to knowing his DNA was at Laurie's murder scene."

Reluctantly Jenna released his hand and sighed. "We can't tell him about the briefs, it's a part of the evidence I want suppressed. It's a signature. I don't want any potential copycat killers getting in on the act."

"So, we just tell him about his DNA and watch his reaction." Kane stood and looked down at her. "I'll cook, while you shower." He lingered at the door. "I'm leaving Duke home today as we have the autopsy this afternoon and some follow-up interviews. I figure he'd appreciate time with Pumpkin and the horses rather than being stuck in the office all day." He rubbed his shoulder and moved his arm around in circles as if it hurt. "Carter called earlier. He said Jo is taking Jaime out for the day and he's going fishing. I figure it was his way of reminding us they're on vacation."

Jenna frowned. "Is there something wrong with your arm?"

"Maybe." Kane thought for a beat as if deciding to tell her something. "I'll ask Wolfe to check it when we go for the autopsy." He stared at the ceiling as if contemplating what to say. "I'll go make breakfast."

Instead of leaving the room, he grabbed the notepad beside her bed and scribbled a note. A flash of annoyance moved over his face.

I'm sure I've been chipped and I figure it's moved. I cut one out when I returned after my last assignment. I figure when I was shot, they replaced it somewhere I couldn't reach it. The chips are not only used for location they can pick up every word. If it's there, I want it out. If they can't trust me by now, they never will.

Annoyed and astounded, Jenna swallowed hard and took the pen from his hands and wrote back.

If you have one, they don't trust me either. I'll ask Wolfe to check me too. How will he know?

Jenna passed the notepad back to Kane and rubbed her shoulder feeling all around for a lump.

Kane wrote fast.

He'll run a scanner over you. They'd have chipped you for sure when you went undercover. They'd need to know where you were in case you missed a contact.

Infuriated, Jenna nodded and mouthed "Okay" before heading silently to the bathroom.

After breakfast, Jenna stood for a few moments, inhaling the fresh air and allowing the perfumes of fall to center her. As a fragrant breeze lifted her hair, she stared across the lowlands and turned to enjoy the view of the mountains, the peace and serenity away from the craziness of her job. Her home had the best of both worlds and was the one reason she'd purchased the ranch. It had changed so much since Kane arrived. Apart from his skills as a crime fighter, he seemed to be able to turn his hand to just about anything. The ranch had been painted, the vast rooms and the cellar changed into a gym with hot tub. Changes had been made all around, the stables, the corrals. She'd have never been able to do everything on her own—it had been good to have a man around. She smiled at him and climbed into the truck. "You know, the day you walked into my life, I thought you'd been sent to kill me. Oh boy, my instincts were off that day. Things have been a rollercoaster between us over the years but I wouldn't change a thing."

"Well, I could have done without the injuries." Kane flashed her a white smile. "I'm glad I came here too, putting aside all the murders and danger, meeting you and the team has been like finding my family. This is my home. I'm not going anywhere, Jenna. I belong here."

Jenna leaned back and sighed. "I know, I do."

Fall leaves blew across the blacktop as they headed along the quiet roads toward town. Jenna was enjoying the view as Kane accelerated up the on-ramp to the highway. Without warning he slammed on the brakes, sending Jenna surging forward against her seatbelt. A speeding silver GMC truck fishtailed past them barely missing the front of the Beast. It hit the dirt alongside of the highway sending a shower of rocks and clouds of dust in its wake. She stared after the vehicle as it disappeared into the distance. "Jerk! He's an accident waiting to happen. If he goes through town at that speed, he's going to kill someone. Isn't that truck a match to the vehicle seen outside Rowley's house during the murder? Go get him, Dave."

"My pleasure." Kane flicked on lights and sirens and the truck lifted with a roar and shot off along the highway.

The blacktop turned into a black snake winding away through a sea of green, and other vehicles became flashes of color as they sped by. Torn between exhilaration and fear, Jenna gripped the seat. She tried to relax and enjoy the rush of speed but she preferred to be in control. Trusting Kane's driving had taken some time to get used to. Fearless came close but foolhardy he wasn't. They slowed to take a sweeping bend and then the powerful engine threw her back in her seat. The Beast had become an unstoppable missile.

It had been named the Beast for a reason. Tricked out didn't describe Kane's custom-built truck but the name, however went close to describing the power and protection it provided. Before Kane arrived in Black Rock Falls the specially designed truck had been made to protect him. Reinforced like a tank with bulletproof windows, its specially designed motor was updated yearly to keep the Beast running at premium performance. It was in fact a rocket on wheels and Kane could take it apart and reassemble it blindfold. He drove it as if it was an extension of himself, which taking into consideration the weight and power of the vehicle took skill. She'd driven it once or twice and it had been like wrestling a black panther. Terrified of damaging it, she'd driven like a teenager on their first driving lesson only to find out much later it was capable of withstanding a bomb.

As they flew passed eighteen-wheelers, Jenna gripped tighter but when they passed other vehicles with a *zip, zip, zip,* she chanced a glance at the speedo. They were hitting 150mph on the straight and ahead the silver truck was hammering for all it was worth. "Can we catch it?"

"Oh, yeah." Kane grinned. "We're running on nitro, if we went any faster, we'd be airborne." He chuckled. "Trust me, the upgrades I work on with Wolfe during the downtime make the vehicles in spy movies look like toys."

As they came level with the silver GMC, a man looked wildly out the window. Jenna gaped in disbelief. "That's Law. He must be out on bail. Why is he driving like a madman?"

"How is he driving?" Kane stared at the vehicle. "I figured you'd put him in the hospital, you sure kicked him hard."

"Clearly not hard enough." Jenna picked up the microphone. "Pull over now or we'll ram you. Do it now Mr. Law. You can't get away."

The trucked pulled up and bounced and skidded on the dirt alongside the blacktop. They stopped behind him and Jenna climbed down from the cab, drawing her weapon. People got one chance with her to be nice and as her face still hurt from the slap she'd received from this man she wasn't giving him a second chance. "Hands where I can see them." She moved closer to the door. "Are you carrying a weapon?"

The truck door flew open and Law came out like a tornado with his fists flying. She ducked away as his knuckles brushed over the top of her head. She turned and caught a flash in the sunlight as he drew a knife. She took aim but Kane had moved into her line of fire, placing himself between her and the blade. The next moment, Law was on him, waving the knife from side to side as if completely oblivious to the fact both of them were armed.

"You want some of this?" Law's eyes blazed with fury. "I'm gonna gut you from navel to neck."

In the next instant Kane had knocked the knife from Law's hand. A grunt and a scuffle was followed by the sound of a slap like a gunshot. Jenna kept her weapon trained on Law. The suddenly subdued man was bug-eyed and pressed against his truck holding his cheek.

"Hands behind your back, Law." Kane pulled Law's hands behind him and cuffed him.

Jenna stared at the hunting knife glinting on the blacktop and then back up at Law. He'd decided in a split second of madness to gut her and Kane, for a speeding fine.

"He hit me." Law glared at Kane with contempt and rubbed his reddened cheek on one shoulder. "You saw him. That's police brutality."

"I was within my rights to shoot you for pulling a knife on the sheriff but when you resisted arrest, I figured, nah, give this guy a taste of his own medicine." Kane smiled at him. "How does it feel to be slapped, huh? I treated you the same way as you treat your wife. Now you understand what it's like to be bullied and beaten by someone bigger than you. I'm sure you'll find out just how it feels to live in fear when you're in jail. Most in there don't take too kindly to men who beat on women."

Jenna read Law his rights. "I'll be charging you for reckless driving, armed attack on a law enforcement officer, and resisting arrest." She pulled out her phone and called Rio. "We're out on the highway about five miles south of town. Come and pick up a prisoner." She disconnected and looked at Kane. "Rio is on his way." She leaned into Law's truck and grabbed his keys. "Get in the back seat, Mr. Law. You can sit in there." She waited for him to climb inside and locked the truck.

"We could've taken him into town." Kane's eyes narrowed.

Jenna shook her head. "He'd likely have spat at us or tried to headbutt me from behind." She glanced at the man now subdued in the back of his vehicle. "He must be on something. No one is stupid enough to attack two armed officers."

"I'm wondering why the hurry." Kane stared at his boots. "He must have been given bail late yesterday and went home, why come back to Black Rock Falls? He'd have an order against him not to go near his wife."

Jenna shook her head. "We'll need to find out." She waited for him to meet her eyes. "Why did you block my line of fire and step between me and the knife?"

"You were on the back foot, after ducking from the first blow." Kane shrugged. "He'd have stabbed you before you had time to raise your weapon and aim. I was watching your back is all." He gave her a long look. "I used necessary force to subdue him. I sure as hell didn't want him dead. He deserves jail time in general population. I figure it will change his outlook on life and his attitude to women."

CHAPTER THIRTY-SEVEN

He'd tossed and turned all night, searched the internet for answers, and finally found what he needed on the school's website. It was a bio for Dr. Robert Turner, the shrink hired by the school to fix kids' heads and he just happened to be Laurie's pa. The post was directed to both parents and students, stating complete confidentiality on any matter of concern. Becky Powell's death had been all over the news, not her name but the fact a girl's body had been found in town. He couldn't eat his breakfast and went back to his room. He read and re-read the post about the doctor before heading to school and the moment he walked into the building, he went to the office. "I want to speak to Dr. Turner."

"You're not required to give a reason or your name… well, to me anyway." The woman behind the counter looked him over. "If it's an excuse to get out of failing your grades, he won't help you."

He rubbed the back of his neck and tried to come up with an excuse. "I've been having real bad dreams. I need to speak to someone about them is all."

"Oh, sure." She lifted the phone on her desk and spoke to someone in hushed tones and then looked up at him. "It must be your lucky day, he's free now. You can go straight in. Third door on the left. When you're done drop by and I'll issue you a hall pass."

He nodded and tried to squash the rolling in his stomach. Would speaking to the doctor about his fears betray his girl? Turner couldn't say anything to anyone, so he should be safe. No one would know he'd been to see him. He knocked on the door and stepped inside. Rather than a couch the doctor sat behind a desk and looked at him over his spectacles.

"You're having bad dreams?" Turner leaned forward and rested his clasped hands on the desk. "Sit down."

"No, I said that to come and see you." He sprawled in the chair. "Nothing I say here goes any further, right?"

"That's correct, patient-doctor confidentiality, but to afford you that, I'll need your name." Turner frowned. "What's on your mind?"

He gave his name and then chose his words carefully, making like he had these friends that he figured were a little crazy because they kept talking about killing girls. When the doctor asked questions, he told him what had been reported in the press but left out any other details. He said he was frightened for his life, that his friends might try and kill him if they knew he'd ratted on them.

"Well, unless you give me their names, you're not ratting on anyone but as my daughter Laurie was murdered, any assistance you can offer the sheriff will be dealt with in the strictest confidence." Turner looked nonplused as if discussing his murdered daughter happened every day. "She was a cheerleader like her mom. They'd practice together but I was glad when my wife left. I wanted Laurie to stop cheerleading. I refused to watch her flaunt herself in front of everyone like a common whore."

Stymied, he stared at Turner. "You saying, you figure she deserved to be murdered?"

"No of course not." Turner's fists clenched on the desk. "Let's say she attracted the wrong sort of attention. Football players are trouble and she knew the risks she was taking."

He rubbed his chin. This wasn't going as he'd expected and the doctor was no help at all. "The players are okay guys. She'd have been safer if she'd had a boyfriend."

"Boyfriend?" Turner leaned back in his chair. "She was sixteen. That's too young to be involved with anyone, she was asking for trouble going out with Wyatt Cooper and I told her so."

"So, how can you help me?" He looked across the desk. "They've killed again. Last night. It was another cheerleader."

"How would you know details about the murder unless you were involved?" Turner's combover dropped over a brow beading with sweat and stuck like a fly in honey. "Did you kill my daughter? Or were you involved in some way?"

"No! I didn't kill Laurie. This happened last night. Aren't you listening to me?" Unease crawled over him. "You know, I came here for help, there's no need to start interrogating me like the cops. I'm in fear for my life, man. They would kill me if they knew I'd been here."

"I know you were there." Turner glared at him. "You had to be to know the details. I can only help you if you tell me the truth."

Panic swept over him. "I was there but I didn't kill anyone."

"If you are as innocent as you claim, even if you're in fear for your life, the sheriff can't help you. You'd be charged with murder by association... for just being there and not stopping it." Turner took a folded handkerchief out of his pocket and dabbed at his face. "Now, if you want my protection, you'll have to come clean and tell me everything."

"That's all I can tell you." He went to rise but Turner raised a hand to stop him. He glared at him. "Why do you want me to stay? You've been no help at all. Now you figure I'm involved in Laurie's murder." He stared at him. "Do you figure I'd come and confess to her father, if I had? I'm not that stupid. I shouldn't have come here. I can't give the others up to the sheriff. If one of them noticed me coming in here then I'm a dead man walking. I needed your help."

"Okay. I guess if you'd been with those boys when they killed that girl last night but didn't participate, I could help you." Turner was clearly trying hard to compose himself and his mouth twitched into a grimace. "In fact, I would give you an alibi." He cleared his throat. "And maybe even one for last night as well depending on how you cooperate. You see, the sheriff has me on her list of suspects as well. The parents are always their first suspects, and I don't need her hassling me."

"Okay." He hung his head, not wanting to divulge his part in the murders, but the doctor had offered him a lifeline. "They told me last night they'd killed another girl, in a house just off Main." He lifted his head. "What they told me made me sick to my stomach, so I had to talk to someone."

"Is there anything else you remember? Everything you've said about Laurie has been in the papers. To confirm their involvement, you'd have to know something that only the killers would know. This includes the time of the murders. That information is crucial to providing an alibi."

He pushed a hand through his hair. "I'll give it some thought and get back to you."

"Good." Turner's eyes brightened. "I'll give you my number and if this happens again, you must give me the time and I'll say you were with me. I'll call you, to confirm different times you had a session with me as well or it will appear that you only came to see me when a murder took place." He looked at him. "Tell me everything you remember and I'll protect you but you must back me up. If I say you've been having counseling sessions with me at the time of the murders or at any other time I give you, you must confirm it. Are we clear?"

"Yeah, anything you say, Doc." He smiled at Turner. He had him hook, line, and sinker. He'd give him just a taste of what happened and leave out the gruesome stuff. "Yeah, they said they'd strangled them and then took one of their pompoms."

CHAPTER THIRTY-EIGHT

After waving away offers of help, Jenna delivered the paperwork to the judge for an arrest warrant for Law, and went from there to speak to the DA. She'd discovered during a brief interview with Mr. Law, that he'd been released yesterday and was out searching for his wife. He'd admitted to substance abuse. Doc Brown had dropped by and taken blood for testing. Law would be collected by the county jail and would likely remain there until his court hearing.

It was lunchtime by the time she returned to her office and she met Kane and Rio heading to the front door carrying takeout from Aunt Betty's. She smiled at them and led the way inside. "Come into my office so we can bring everyone up to speed before we leave for the autopsy."

She stared at the whiteboard, noticing Rio had updated everything since she'd left the previous day. He was an asset to have around but she missed Rowley and had checked in with him when she'd arrived earlier. It had taken little persuasion to insist he remain with his wife until she recovered. She sighed. At least all was well with Sandy but having her involved in a homicide had given the case a nasty twist. It would seem the killer or killers would stop at nothing to satisfy their cravings for murder.

"What's on your mind?" Kane pushed a bag and a to-go cup of coffee across the desk to her.

Jenna peered into the bag. She hadn't had a bagel and cream cheese for a while and gave Kane a small smile at the sight of it. He always came back from Aunt Betty's with something she enjoyed. She pulled it out and took a bite, chewing slowly as she thought through what needed to be done but first, she needed an update from Rio. "Any calls come in about the silver GMC?"

"A few, and I hunted them down." Rio leaned back in his chair. "They were owned by neighbors of people who have the same vehicle and live in Stanton but they were at home or out watching the fireworks. It's a popular truck, so we'll have tons of sightings."

Unable to remove the incident with Mr. Law earlier in the day, she stared at the file on her computer screen. "Law was released last night and has a silver GMC. He's a violent offender. How do we know he's not involved in the murders as well?"

"He hasn't come up on our radar." Kane shrugged. "And he doesn't fit the profile."

"I'm thinking outside the box here, Dave." Jenna looked at Rio. "Check him out while we're at the autopsy and hunt down the persons of interest on our list and discover their location at the time of the murder. Most are high school kids but don't forget Cory Hughes, he rates high on my list of possible suspects."

"Sure, but I'm guessing most of the kids will have been in town at the festival." He took a bite of his sandwich and washed it down with coffee. "I have traced medallions on cowboy boots. They're popular as well but one thing did wave a red flag at me: they're a feature of the cheerleading squad's boots." He put down his sandwich and accessed the files on his phone. "See in this group shot, they all have the medallions. I guess showing this to Sandy is out of the question?"

Jenna nodded. "Yeah, I don't want to cause any more stress. We'll speak to her as soon as her doctor says it's okay. Right now, they're keeping her quiet." She scanned the whiteboard again. "Cheerleaders are part of our investigation. Concentrate on Verna Hughes, she fits the profile and could be involved. Maybe include Marlene Moore as well as both are cheerleaders and fit the profile." She turned her attention to Kane. "Any info from Carter on what's happening with Stan Williams?"

"From what I understand, Carter contacted Agent Josh Martin from the Child Exploitation and Human Trafficking Task Force and forwarded the files and our reports." Kane shrugged. "You know how they work. They won't rush in and arrest him, they have a team of people who get involved and track down the entire pedophile ring. It takes time but they don't want one rat they want the entire nest."

Jenna and Kane arrived at the medical examiner's office at a little after one-thirty. After greeting Wolfe in their usual manner, she was surprised to see Kane hand Wolfe a note which he read and raised both eyebrows. Jenna looked from one to the other and followed them into his office. Without saying a word, Wolfe took a device out of his drawer and stood. "I still have some things to do before we start the autopsy. You might as well wait here. Help yourself to coffee." He handed Kane the device and left the room.

"It's like waiting to see the dentist." Kane motioned her to stand and ran the scanner over her and then held it out and showed her the reading.

Astounded to find she had a tracker implanted under her skin, Jenna pulled a sad face, took the scanner from Kane, and moved it over his shoulder. "I never minded the dentist." She handed him the reading and caught the reaction on his face. He was fuming.

"Why don't you make coffee? I could do with one right now." He took out his notebook and scribbled a note.

From the reading, only mine has audio. Go and tell Wolfe, he'll know what to do.

Jenna nodded. "You make the coffee. I need to visit the bathroom." She headed out the door and Wolfe was outside leaning against the wall. She looked at him. "Only Dave's has audio. You can't be seen to remove them. They'll know we know."

"They should have told me at least." Wolfe's brow furrowed into a frown. "Don't worry, There's a way. We destroy them first and then remove them. They won't know I'm involved."

Jenna pushed her hair from her face and sighed. "He's angry. What can you do, like today?"

"Simplest thing is a strong magnet." Wolfe rubbed the back of his neck. "It depends how sophisticated it is and it may only scramble the circuits for a few seconds." He thought for a beat. "Give me seven minutes to prepare, then come into examination room two. The autopsy will be in room three. Get him in number two without his shirt, I'll say something about having to extract metal filings from a body by using a powerful magnet. They'll expect some disturbance. It will give me time to remove his and we'll do yours next."

Jenna nodded and wrote a text to Kane explaining. She hit send. "Okay, how much is this going to hurt?"

"It depends how deep it's embedded but you'll need a couple of stitches." Wolfe inclined his head. "You're not having second thoughts, are you? You do know I can't track you from the chip, that's why I supplied everyone with a personal tracker. Your ring like the other disguised trackers are the only direct contact to the team members."

"No, I want it removed." Jenna pulled her hair back into a ponytail and secured it with a band from around her wrist. "It's not that, it's just knowing that every time I've been with Dave, someone has been listening. I know about Annie, his past life, and that makes me a liability."

"The moment you recognized him as an agent, he asked for permission to give you some details because of your clearance."

Wolfe stared into the distance over her shoulder as if considering his words with care. "You'll never know everything about his life, or his other identities. If anyone searches his birth name, they'd find an autopsy report, a death certificate, and a grave. He'd never risk you by divulging his missions or the people he worked with over that time. I'm not blind and I know you're close now but if you're planning a relationship, I'd suggest you keep it secret and avoid asking questions about his past. He won't tell you because if he did, you'd be taken out in the interests of national security."

Dismayed, Jenna swallowed hard. "So, marriage is out of the question? It would be too much of a risk for national security?"

"Not necessarily. If you applied in a different county here in Montana for a license and snuck off to a JP or retired judge." Wolfe regarded her closely. "Has he asked you to marry him?"

"No, we haven't got that far yet." Jenna's face grew hot. "But we've talked about having kids and I know he's got old school values."

"Like me." Wolfe smiled. "Well, if the time comes, I'll do what I can to help."

Jenna squeezed his arm. "That's good to know but we never had this conversation, right?"

"What conversation?" Wolfe looked at her blankly and shrugged.

Jenna chuckled and waved behind her toward Wolfe's office. "I'll leave you to get ready."

She headed back to Wolfe's office. Kane was on his feet, his jacket and T-shirt folded on Wolfe's desk. She stared at him, taking in all the scars on his body and then shook her head in dismay of what he had suffered in the line of duty. "Before he starts the autopsy, he wants to show us his new toy for extracting metal from flesh. It's some type of super magnet."

"Great." Kane headed for the door. "Let's have at it."

Jenna made idle conversation as Wolfe zapped Kane's implant and seemed to take ages to remove it. The darn thing had settled in the muscle on Kane's shoulder and took some digging to locate it. Once it was out, she destroyed it by smashing it with the hammer, Wolfe provided. A few stitches later and Kane held up a finger to his lips. He handed the scanner to Wolfe and indicated he should check him all over.

"You're good to go." Wolfe smiled at him. "Ten days for the stitches and try not to bust them open. You can shower with that dressing but I want to see it tomorrow. The device was damaged during removal and may cause a problem."

"Roger that." Kane turned to Jenna. "I'll go and collect my things and give you some privacy." He headed for the door.

Jenna pulled her T-shirt over her head and turned her back to Wolfe. "He didn't as much as flinch. Ouch!" She caught her breath as the local anesthetic needle slid into her flesh followed by a cold burst. "Thanks for the warning."

"Sorry, I'm used to working on people who don't complain." Wolfe chuckled. "But then they don't have the advantage of a local."

Not amused, Jenna glared at him over one shoulder. "That's because they're dead."

"Thanks for letting me know." Wolfe grinned. "Stand still, this won't take long."

The door slid open and Emily stood at the entrance, eyes wide. Jenna looked at her and smiled. "Hi, Em."

"What's going on?" Emily looked back down the passage. "Dave just walked past me without his shirt and now you're the same?"

"It's a cover up operation." Wolfe winked at his daughter. "Our esteemed sheriff and her deputy tangled with some thorns this morning and lost. It's all good. Go and prepare the body, I'll be starting the autopsy as soon as I'm finished here."

"Thorns, huh?" Emily wrinkled her nose and turned away. "Anything you say, Dad."

Jenna sighed. "It's hard telling lies to protect someone, isn't it?"

"Not really." Wolfe slapped a dressing on her shoulder. "It's a way of life in our business." He handed her a dish containing the small tracker. "Do you want to do the honors?" He followed her to the bench and waited for her to pulverize the device. "I'll microwave all the pieces just to be sure."

Jenna pulled on her shirt and waited for him. She led the way to join Kane in the alcove in the hallway and pulled on scrubs, masks, and gloves. She looked at Kane's bleak expression. "You good?"

"I will be when I get over the fact someone has been recording everything I say and do for the last few years." Kane's eyes flashed with anger. "I had a right to know. After years of putting my life on the line for them, it's a sobering thought to know they don't trust me."

CHAPTER THIRTY-NINE

The tension seemed to shimmer around Kane in the examination room. He needed a break, and Jenna knew just the man to do it. As Wolfe prepared the files on his preliminary examination of Becky Powell, Jenna sent a message to Ty Carter.

We're at the autopsy of latest victim. I figure Kane needs a couple of hours downtime. Can you organize something for later?

A few seconds went by before her phone signaled a message. Jenna stared at the screen.

Just us guys?

Yes, I'll stay in town and catch up with Jo.

Jo is staying over at Louan tonight. If we're having a guys' night out, Dave can bunk with me. I'll call him later. Leave it to me.

"Was that anything important?" Kane moved to her side.

Jenna didn't meet his eyes. He could read a lie in an instant. "No, Jo is heading over to Louan and staying over is all."

"Are you ready?" Wolfe peered over his mask at them. "Good. We have Becky Powell, sixteen years, Caucasian, brown eyes, and hair. She is average height and weight for her age and in good physical shape, exact details will be listed in my report. Her body was formally identified by her parents at ten this morning. Preliminary X-rays, scans, and samples are ready for examination." He pointed to an evidence bag on a bench. "I removed the black gaffer tape covering her mouth and found a pair of men's briefs stuffed inside. I also removed the tape binding her wrists behind her back. Both have been examined. From the tape all the trace I found was from Becky, so whoever was handling the tape used gloves. The DNA from the briefs isn't a match for Wyatt Cooper and Bobby Kalo is running it through the databases as we speak."

"Did you confirm the time of death as suggested last night?" Kane stepped forward to stare at the X-rays.

"Yes, from the body temperature, state of rigor, and degree of congealing in the blood from the headwound, or lack of it, I stand by my observations that this girl died within fifteen minutes of her discovery."

"The head injuries on the right appear to be less than those on the left." Kane pointed to the screen. "Yet I can only see one side of her head with any sign of injury. Would this indicate a punch?"

"This X-ray belongs to Sandy." Emily pointed to the one on the right. "We needed copies to compare as we believe two people are involved." She raised both eyebrows. "Remember the discussion on the blood spatter arc at the house?"

"I do indeed." Kane's eyes crinkled at the corners.

Jenna stared at the images. "This would indicate injury from the same type of blunt instrument used with variable force."

"Yes, and resulting in a different outcome." Wolfe pointed to spiderweb marks on Becky Powell's X-ray of her skull. "That represents massive head trauma. A skull fracture causing death. It would have taken considerable force to inflict that amount of damage. Blood has accumulated inside the cranium, so she didn't die instantly. I would estimate the killer used two blows, so not the same type of uncontrolled frenzied attack we saw in Laurie Turner's case." Wolfe moved to Sandy's X-ray. "Here we see a concussion, caused by a significant blow to the head but not resulting in a fracture. Many people consider that a concussion is nothing to worry about but it's a traumatic brain injury that affects brain function and can be delayed. This is why the doctors are keeping Sandy under observation."

Slightly confused, Jenna stared at the body of Becky Powell and the massive bruising in her neck area. "She didn't die from strangulation?"

"No." Wolfe lifted the girl's eyelids. "She has no burst capillaries in her eyes and her hyoid bone is intact. From the bruises on her body, the hip, knees, elbows, I'd say she was fighting back. The strangulation wasn't working so they hit her." He shrugged. "I'll open her up and confirm but the damage to her neck is superficial and wasn't sustained. She does have a bruise mid-spine. I would say her killer was trying unsuccessfully to gain leverage using their knee perhaps and failed."

"Any sexual contact?" Kane was scanning the body. "I can't see the usual signs of rape."

"No." Wolfe looked at Jenna. "There doesn't seem to be a motive for this murder. Apart from the fact that both victims are cheerleaders, the MO is different in each case. The only link we have is strangulation, well attempted in this case, and the men's underwear in the mouth. Without that, I'd find it difficult to believe they were connected."

Jenna thought for a beat. "They have another connection; they both got a ride with their killer. Becky's SUV was left at the library, it only has her prints on it and we found it locked, so it wasn't an abduction." She glanced at Kane. "The girls knew their killer and went willingly to their deaths. No one heard a girl screaming for help outside Rowley's old house and it's a close-knit community.

She walked in the house under her own steam. What would tempt a girl to enter someone's house at night?"

"Oh, that's pretty easy." Emily snorted with laughter. "A secret date with a hunk, maybe someone on the track team… an athlete of some kind. Most girls of that age would walk on hot coals to be seen out with a handsome jock."

"That would make sense." Kane looked at Wolfe. "The force used to kill is different from what I'd expect from say, two men. There'd be considerable bruising from restraints and it's more likely rape would be involved."

"My conclusion would be one male, one female, for that reason." Wolfe pointed to the victim's head. "From the angle of the blunt force trauma and the fact it is in two areas. I would say Becky was on her knees and the female was strangling her from behind. Becky was fighting, so the female killer was unable to restrain her, she likely ordered the male to kill her."

"Just don't forget Stan Williams." Kane peered at Jenna over his mask. "He seems to be able to lure cheerleaders into his apartment to take photographs. The FBI are watching him but don't rule him out."

"I can't see him being the killer." Wolfe narrowed his gaze. "Think about it. If he lured the girl into Rowley's house and tried to strangle her but she fought back, what would usually happen?" He looked at Kane. "A man is more likely to punch, knock her senseless, and then strangle her." He shrugged. "In my opinion, this is close to a panic kill. The first one went like clockwork, look at the comparison." He went to the computer and images filled the screen. He pointed to Laurie Turner's neck. "She was secured, likely by a seatbelt and attacked from behind in an upward fast motion. The pressure on the carotid artery would have been enough to make her black out in ten seconds. Then the killer kept the pressure going without the victim fighting. The second is a mess. I figure it's teenagers, most likely in the same age bracket as the victims."

"That would tie in with our list of suspects." Jenna turned as the doors whooshed open and Colt Webber came into the room carrying an iPad.

"I have some results." Webber handed the iPad to Wolfe. "The trace evidence we found on the bedhead is a match for the spittle we found at the Laurie Turner murder scene and the blue fabric found on the steps matches the pompoms of the high school cheerleading squad."

"Did both samples identify as spittle?" Wolfe studied the results.

"Nope." Webber pointed to a result on the screen. "The second one was sweat."

Jenna leaned against the counter, running the scenario through her mind. "They spread bleach all over the plastic cover on the mattress and slipped up again. Do you figure they tried to strangle her on the bed?"

"Just how long has it been since you were all in high school?" Emily shook her head. "We know two people are involved by the extent of the head injuries and the blood spatter. It's likely a thrill kill or perhaps a payback kill." She took a breath. "These kids have just killed again and they liked it. We know from the blood spatter they killed Becky in the middle of the room, dragged her body to the wall, and sat her up. They're young with hormones raging. They wanted her to watch them making out."

"Like a victory dance." Kane stared at Emily and shook his head. "Are kids really that irresponsible?"

"Some are but most times it's peer pressure pushing them into doing things they know isn't right." Emily sighed. "It's all about the cliques in school these days."

Jenna folded her arms and sighed. "So, this poor girl thought she was meeting her dream date and it was a trap." She allowed the faces of the kids they'd interviewed to run through her mind. Which one of them was capable of murder?

CHAPTER FORTY

Mentally drained after a hard day, Jenna dropped into her chair at the office and waited for a report from Rio. She wrapped her hands around a cup of coffee and took in all the additions to the whiteboard. She had updated Wolfe's autopsy results. As she waved Rio into a chair, Kane walked in behind him and sat down. "Okay, Zac, what have you got for me?"

"Everyone on your list of persons of interest were in town when Becky Powell was murdered." Rio waved a hand at the whiteboard. "I've listed each one and anyone who recalls seeing them at the festival. I had to break it down as before the first set of fireworks and after the last set. Mainly because with everything going on nobody could give me a specific time. I considered this logical as everyone was out enjoying the festival."

Jenna nodded. "I gathered as much. What about the library?"

"I viewed the CCTV feed from last night outside the library." Rio offered Jenna his iPad. "You can see Becky arriving, she parks, locks up, and goes inside, using the front entrance. If you fast forward, you'll notice movement at the fire door out back about five or so minutes after. An indistinguishable light-colored truck drives out, no lights and although I've magnified the frames, I see a blurred driver and no passengers."

"How long did you observe the footage?" Jenna scrolled through the feed. "Did you see Becky leave?"

"Nope and they close at ten on Tuesdays." Rio removed his hat and stroked the rim. "She didn't leave the building unless she snuck out the fire door and kept to the shadows. The truck was parked in the shadows, so if you go back, it's impossible to tell and the light is out in the stairwell, the truck's interior light was out as well."

"How convenient." Kane sorted through the pile of statements that Rio had compiled. "If this is kids, they thought of everything. Problem is we can't tie it in with a silver GMC truck or a Chrysler sedan. Both were seen at the time of the murders." He held out his hand for the iPad and scanned the screen. "I figure that is a GMC truck." He rewound and watched the feed a few times. "Send it to Bobby Kalo at the FBI. His number is on file. Ask him to enhance it. The problem is, we have two murders and two different vehicles. Maybe we can get a list of everyone who went into the library."

"I already thought of asking about that and only three people were loaned books that night." Rio smoothed his curly hair and pushed on his Stetson. "The librarian was coy about giving out personal details, so I asked if she could tell me the sex of the people. All female and then I asked if one was Becky Powell." He smiled. "Becky was there, because I saw her arrive but she didn't loan a book and if she met a guy in there, neither did he."

Jenna nodded. "Okay and what about Mr. Law? Does he have an alibi for last night?"

"Nope." Rio took the iPad from Kane and scanned through the files. "He drove from county to Black Rock Falls and was in town at the time of the murder. I have him leaving Aunt Betty's Café at eight-forty-five. He says he went home to Blackwater, has no witnesses and was arrested by you on his return."

"Again, here is a man who attacks women's faces. That's a bully, a coward. Strangulation is up close and personal. His wife was asked specifically if he'd ever tried to strangle her and she denied it. A leopard doesn't usually change his spots." Kane stood and went to the counter to pour a cup of coffee. "I can't see what motive he'd have to kill a cheerleader and I really can't see either girl getting willingly into his vehicle." His phone pinged a message and he stared at the screen. The next moment his ringtone filled the room. He glanced at the caller ID and looked at Jenna. "It's personal, I'll take it outside." He stood and went into the hallway.

Jenna turned her attention back to Rio. "Are you sure you want to move into the house? Have you had second thoughts?"

"Nope. I've spoken to the twins and they think it's cool. They're hoping for a ghost. I'm not so sure about Mrs. Jacobs, the housekeeper I've engaged." Rio met her eyes with a steady gaze. "I did wonder what security was needed and the cost of updating it. I've spoken to Jake. I've been checking in with him to make sure he doesn't need anything. He said they often left the front door key on the stoop above the door. So, I figure that's how the killers have gotten inside. This makes them locals and people who move along that road frequently to have noticed one of them taking the key from its hiding place."

Jenna sighed. "Not often, we left it there for the delivery man and for some repairmen to get inside after Jake had left. Kids walk past there on the way to school. There's a bus stop across the road, anyone might have seen them access the key." She chewed on her bottom lip. "But we will beef up security. It doesn't have an alarm system and I can arrange to have it installed. Wolfe will likely clear the house as a crime scene shortly. I'll have professional cleaners go through and make sure everything is good before you move in." She stared into the distance. "Run it past Mrs. Jacobs, the housekeeper, but she's very down to earth and no one died in her part of the building."

"Okay." Rio smiled at her. "Is there anything else I need to do, Sheriff?"

Impressed by his thoroughness, Jenna shook her head. "No. You've covered everything I've asked for." She glanced at her watch. "It was a late night for all of us, so why don't you head on home? I have the

Blackwater deputies patrolling during the festival and there's not much going on now until Saturday."

"Before I leave…" Rio stood. "Jake said he'll be back tomorrow. Sandy is staying another day at least and is doing just fine."

Jenna smiled. "That's good to know. I'll see you in the morning."

As Jenna was refilling her cup, her phone chimed. It was Wolfe. "Have you found anything?"

"Not specifically, no, but I do have something of interest regarding the unknown DNA trace we found at the crime scenes." Wolfe sounded pleased with himself. *"I've known for some time of a company which developed a very involved program in conjunction with funding from the Department of Defense. From what I've read, the Snapshot Forensic DNA Phenotyping System accurately predicts what a person looks like including eye color, hair color, and skin color."*

Fascinated, Jenna sat down at her desk. "How involved is this process?"

"It takes time and is complicated but it's worth a try. I've submitted the sample to a public genealogy database and the results will be forwarded for Snapshot's Genetic Genealogy analysis. With luck, we'll get an image of the face of the killer."

"Wow!" Jenna stared at the door as Kane walked in. "Can you get a rush on it?"

"I'll pull in a few favors and hope for the best." Wolfe cleared his throat. *"Has Dave cooled down some yet?"*

Jenna laughed. "I'll let you know later."

"Okay, copy that." Wolfe disconnected.

Jenna updated Kane and stretched. "There's nothing more we can do tonight. I think I'll grab some takeaway from Aunt Betty's and head on home."

"I'll come home and tend the horses but then I'm going for a steak at Antlers with Carter. He's booked a table for seven." Kane smiled. "It seems he doesn't like eating out alone and figured as Jo is away, we could have a guys' night out. Play cards, talk about fishing, and relax for a time." He looked at her. "I could do with some downtime. Do you mind?"

Shaking her head, Jenna smiled at him. "That's a great idea. I'll drive my cruiser home. I don't want to be stuck out at the ranch without transport. It's like tempting fate."

"Uh-huh, leaving you out there alone is tempting fate." Kane regarded her with one eyebrow raised. "It's likely I won't be back until morning. I'll bunk with Carter. He has two bedrooms in his suite at The Cattleman's Hotel." He shook his head. "Apparently the hotel upgraded him when they discovered he was FBI." He grinned. "Are you sure you'll be okay?"

Jenna sipped her coffee. "I managed just fine for the two years or so before you arrived."

"So, you'll call me if anything happens?" Kane's expression turned serious.

Jenna shook her head. "No, I'll call Rio or Rowley, they'll be home tonight. Don't worry, both men are more than capable of backing me up if needs be. Ty will be going home soon. Spend some time with him while you have the chance to do guy stuff. We spend all our downtime together and you need some male bonding." She laughed. "I'll set the alarm when you leave and keep my weapon handy, plus I'll have Duke and Pumpkin to keep me company."

"Great." Kane smiled. "Are you ready to go? Maggie will be here until Walters arrives to take over."

"Yeah, I'll just grab my keys." She stood and collected her things. Happy she'd made Kane smile again she hummed some tunes all the way to her cruiser.

CHAPTER FORTY-ONE

Thursday

The sun streaming through a crack in the drapes woke Jenna and she jumped out of bed, checking the clock. She gasped and pulled on clothes. It was six-thirty and she usually woke at five. She rubbed Pumpkin's ears. "I'll have to start setting the alarm."

Forgoing her morning coffee, she dashed out the front door and ran to the stables. Duke bounded up to her and then ran alongside, long ears flapping in the wind. She stared at the empty garage outside Kane's cottage and frowned. She'd expected him home by now but never mind, she could handle the horses just fine. After moving them to the corral, she mucked out and emptied the wheelbarrow before heading back to the house for a shower. One thing was for sure, she didn't need a workout.

Dressed and ready for work, she pushed bread into the toaster and poured coffee. The perimeter alarm sounded and she headed for the front door in time to see Kane emerging from the trees. She opened the front door and gave him a wave. The truck stopped in front of her porch and Kane slid out. She smiled at him. "Morning."

"Sorry I'm late. I was waylaid." Kane stopped at the bottom of the steps. "I'll go and do my chores and get ready for work."

Jenna walked down the steps as Duke rushed past her and did his happy dance at seeing Kane. "No need. I've tended the horses and I'm just making breakfast."

"I already ate but I'll need to clean up." He rubbed his bristled chin and stared into the distance as if he didn't want to meet her gaze.

Stifling the amusement at seeing him lost for words, she chewed on her bottom lip. He must have had an entertaining evening out with Carter. It was hard to miss the bright red lipstick kiss on one unshaven cheek or smell the stale perfume wafting from him. "Oh, yes, so I see." She turned and walked back up the steps. "You'll need to feed Duke. I'm all out of his food."

"I'll drop some by before we leave." Kane removed his Stetson and ran his fingers through his hair. "I'll see you later." He hoisted Duke into the truck and followed him.

As Kane was not a one-night stand type of guy, the lipstick and perfume didn't worry her at all. Although, he'd changed in many ways in the last six months; after finally laying the ghost of his dead wife to rest, they'd become inseparable. She sighed. Ty Carter was a man's man, a confirmed bachelor, who was enjoying life to the full, so it wouldn't surprise her in the least to imagine women had taken some part in his idea of a guys' night out.

Before she had time to finish her toast, the phone chimed. It was the 911 line. "Sheriff Alton, what is your emergency?"

"Ma'am, there's a body sitting up against a dumpster, outside the home supplies depot on Main."

Jenna grabbed a pen and notepad from the counter. "I'll need your details. Don't touch the body and keep people away."

"I drive a garbage truck, ma'am. Ian Morrison. I've blocked the alleyway and I'll wait in my truck until you arrive."

Abandoning her toast and coffee, Jenna headed for the front door. There was no time to wait for Kane and he wouldn't hear his phone in the shower. After setting the alarm, she dashed to her cruiser. "I'm on my way." She disconnected.

Turning on lights and sirens, she used the Bluetooth phone connection in her vehicle to contact Rowley and after he'd assured her Sandy was fine, she'd called Wolfe, giving them the same information. They would likely arrive before her and secure the crime scene. She accelerated onto the highway and a rush of excitement tingled through her as she harnessed the speed of her vehicle. Being a passenger for so long, she'd missed the thrill of dashing to a crime scene and into the unknown alone. The highway into town carried the normal flow of traffic but in town people had arrived early to set up for another day of the festival, which would culminate on Saturday with the crowning of the fall queen and the usual dance at the showgrounds.

With the wide blue sky and sunshine, it should have been a beautiful day but someone had spoiled it with murder. As she crawled down Main, she couldn't miss the garbage truck and parked behind it. Across the road, Rowley's SUV was sliding into the curb and Wolfe's white van had parked on the sidewalk. She made her way around the van and looked at Wolfe. "What have we got?"

"I'm not really sure." Wolfe moved to one side. "Take a look."

Jenna stared at the woman, recognizing her at once. She swallowed hard. Had she stepped into a nightmare? The dead eyes staring at her belonged to Laurie Turner's mother. She was sitting against the dumpster, naked, with a pompom in one hand.

CHAPTER FORTY-TWO

Kane had heard Jenna's cruiser tear out the front gate. He checked his phone and shrugged. No missed calls and no messages. He looked at Duke. "What's stuck in her craw?"

The dog whined and crawled into his basket. Kane smiled at him. "It looks like it's just you and me today."

He made his way into the bathroom, dumped his clothes in the laundry basket, and sighed. He'd avoided getting too close to Jenna for good reason—he smelled like a perfume store. Last evening, Carter had decided to entertain every eligible woman in town and they'd spent a good deal of their time at Antlers listening to the band. Not to be unsociable, he'd danced with the friend of the woman Carter had taken a shine to, but had drawn the line at extending the party overnight. He'd spent the night in the spare bedroom in Carter's suite but after breakfast, he'd had been obliged to give Carter's friend a ride home as Jo had taken the rental car.

Carter being Carter had slapped him on the back, collected his fishing gear, and left him with the woman before climbing into Atohi Blackhawk's truck for a day on the river. Kane took out his shaver and stared into the bathroom mirror. He touched the bright red kiss on his cheek and cringed. Carter's friend had leaned over and pecked him on the cheek when he'd given her a ride home. "Darn, Jenna must have thought I was doing the walk of shame coming home like this."

Ten minutes later, he set out for the office. When he hit Main, he slowed at the sight of Jenna and Rowley's cruisers and pulled to the curb. Crime scene tape stretched across the alleyway and Rowley was standing to one side, while Jenna observed Wolfe and his team work on the body of a woman. He went to Rowley's side. "Did you call this in?"

"Nope." Rowley gave him a puzzled stare. "The sheriff called me. She received a 911 call and called me and Wolfe." He shuffled his feet. "How come she didn't call you?"

"She left in a hurry just after I arrived home." Kane shrugged. "I had a night out with Carter and slept over at The Cattleman's Hotel." He gave Rowley a direct stare. "Jenna figured I needed a night out to do some male bonding, that I've been spending too much time with her."

"Uh-huh." Rowley grinned. "As a woman surrounded by menfolk at work, it should've been the other way around but then she does spend time with Sandy and Emily, I guess."

Kane laughed. "Don't forget Maggie, although she's not a girls' night out kind."

"Girls' night out?" Jenna looked at Kane curiously. "There's a woman lying murdered over there and you're chatting about having a girls' night out."

"Me?" Kane shook his head. "No, ma'am. The complete opposite."

"Okay." Jenna stared at her notebook. "Kane, I want you to check the apartment over the store, and Rowley talk to the bystanders and canvas the immediate area. Find out if anyone saw or heard anything last night between seven and midnight. I'll call Rio to come and assist. I want someone here until Wolfe has removed the body, so delegate. Contact Walters if you need an extra hand. When you're done here, I'll go with Kane to see Dr. Turner and inform him about his wife." She looked at Kane. "Did you remember to leave the dog food before you left this morning?"

Kane narrowed his gaze. "Yeah, of course I did. I left a bag on your porch."

"Fine. I'll see you back at the office." She walked away pulling out her phone.

"Jenna." Kane hurried after her and met her stride for stride. People had started to gather around the alleyway to see what was happening. He waved them away. "Nothing to see here folks, move along now."

"Didn't you understand your orders?" Jenna pulled open the door of her cruiser and slipped behind the wheel and stared at him.

"I understand them just fine but would like to know why you're acting so hostile this morning?" Kane removed his hat and scratched his head. His hair was still damp from the shower. "Why didn't you call me about the murder? I am the deputy sheriff."

"Dave, you'd just gotten home." Jenna wrinkled her nose. "You kinda stunk pretty bad and had lipstick on your cheek, so I figured you'd need time to get cleaned up. I'm not being hostile, I did the chores and left without as much as one sip of coffee. I'm not needed on scene at the moment, so I'm delegating responsibility. Now, I'm going to have breakfast at Aunt Betty's." She shut the door and buzzed down her window. "You know darn well, if I don't get my coffee in the mornings, I'm like a bear with a sore head. Go with the flow, Dave. I'm not the fairy princess every day—some days I'm the wicked witch and if we're going to make this thing between us work, you're gonna have to live with it."

He caught the annoyance in her eyes and swallowed the laugh bubbling up his throat. "Sure, I'm down with that."

"Good." Jenna eased out into the traffic.

Kane stared after her. He liked the way she spoke her mind to him. It had become almost a tradition between them. No lies, just honesty even if it stung a bit. He understood the mood swings. Jenna had a soft side, but on the job, she rarely let down her guard. With a male team to command, she had no other choice. No matter how close they became, she would remain aloof at work. That was Jenna and he respected her for it. He turned and headed back to the crime scene.

Observation was a massive part of detective work, comparing and mentally logging pieces of information, some so remote they don't seem to matter at the time. He avoided the body and scanned the area, moving along the alleyway keeping as close to the wall as possible. He noticed a distinct drag mark and bent to examine the turned-up dirt. The murder hadn't occurred here, the body had been dragged from somewhere else. He moved forward using his Maglite to peer into dark recesses and turned the corner into the small courtyard that led to the foot of a flight of stairs. Pulling on gloves, he moved up the steps, checking each one for evidence. The old wooden stairs creaked and groaned like most behind the old stores in town. The apartments above the stores were usually rented for extra income, the stores' owners preferring a larger home. He reached the top and found the door ajar and knocked. "Sheriff's department."

He called out several times before pushing the door wide, calling out again and stepping inside with caution. The door led to an open plan kitchen and family room. Signs of a struggle were evident, chairs tipped over, pots and pans strewn around the room as if someone had tried to use them as weapons. He pulled his Glock and checked the bedroom and bathroom. The place was empty but long strands of hair blew across the floor from the breeze coming through the door. The bed was in disarray, sheets trailed toward the door, and clothes lay scattered and torn on the threadbare rug. He holstered his weapon and went back to the family room and stared at the photographs on the mantel over the fireplace. He recognized Laurie Turner and the woman with her was the corpse in the alleyway. It didn't take him long to find Mrs. Turner's purse on a kitchen counter. The ID in the name of Jeanette Turner confirmed his suspicions.

He moved back down the stairs and went to Wolfe. "She lived upstairs. The door is open and there are signs of a struggle in the bedroom. I found drag marks in the alleyway."

"I'm assuming she was strangled." Wolfe was directing Emily and Webber to bag the woman's hands and get her into a body bag. "The contusions and scrapes appear to be post-mortem, it's different to the cheerleaders' murders but suspiciously the same, as if someone had inside information. I'll know more later. You'll need to contact her husband to come by to ID the body. I don't want to wait too long before I do the post on this one." He turned to Emily. "The apartment upstairs is the likely murder scene. We'll get her into the van and then do a sweep upstairs. Kane has been inside but I want you in coveralls and booties. I'm not planning on missing any evidence." He turned back to Kane. "I'll send Webber back with the body but I'll need two hours at least to process the scene here and upstairs. Have Mr. Turner show around noon." He sighed. "Autopsy at two as usual." He moved closer. "I'll check the dressings on your backs so arrive a little early."

Kane nodded. "Sure." He noticed Rio had arrived. "I'll go speak to the neighbors and see if anyone heard anything. Stan Williams lives right next door over the general store. Funny that, huh?"

"Maybe your hunch about him is right." Wolfe bent to heave one end of the body bag onto the gurney. "I'll see you at two." He headed for his van.

Kane walked up to Rio. "Rowley is around somewhere talking to the locals. Come with me and we'll see if Stan Williams is home."

"Not at this time of day." Rio glanced at his watch. "He'll be driving the school bus. I'd say he'll be back after ten."

Kane turned at the sound of footsteps to see Jake Rowley hurrying toward them.

"I have something." Rowley came to his side. "One of the onlookers, Dan Staple, said he was walking back to his vehicle from Aunt Betty's Café when he heard an argument last night around eight-thirty. He didn't think much of it until he saw the ME's van this morning. I asked him if he noticed any vehicles parked close by and he recalled seeing an old-style red Ford pickup. It caught his eye because it was so unusual. I showed him a photo of Laurie Turner's pickup and he identified it as the same color and model." He waved his statement book. "I have his statement and details. I've also spoken to store owners but most had closed for the night. The people aren't at home from the apartments over the stores each side. So, apart from the vehicle we've got nothing."

"Interesting. The Ford could be vital evidence." Kane rubbed his chin. "There wouldn't be any other 1950 red Ford pickups in town fitting that description. It has to be Laurie Turner's and we find her mom dead close by. I'll go check it out. The sheriff will want a media statement released as soon as possible. Zac, that's your department. You know the drill, no specifics, just asking for anyone in the vicinity between the hours of seven and ten. Jake, I'll leave you to open a case file." He looked from one to the other. "Have you eaten?"

When they both nodded, he ordered them back to the office. "I'll go and speak to Jenna. She's stopped by Aunt Betty's for breakfast."

He walked back to his truck, his mind running possible scenarios on the case. Was Dr. Bob Turner involved? It seemed too obvious for a man of intelligence to go to murder his wife driving a distinctive vehicle. Or was he trying a move to psyche them out? He smiled to himself. If this was his plan, he had no idea who he was dealing with.

CHAPTER FORTY-THREE

Over breakfast, Jenna perused her files. The tie in with the cheer-leaders' murders was obvious but why would teenagers, the most probable killers, turn on a woman in her forties? Where was the motive and how did they lure her into the alleyway? She glanced up when the chair scraped beside her. Without saying a word, Kane placed a pot of coffee and a cup on the table and then sat down. She closed her files and looked at him. "It's busy in here. If you're hungry, I suggest grabbing a slice of pie."

"The cereal I had this morning and the weak coffee didn't come close to eating toast and eggs with you." Kane checked his watch. "Maggie will have just opened the office. The deputies are hard at work. Dr. Turner will be in transit on his way to work, so we'll go see him at the school. Stan Williams is driving the school bus so we have time to spare. I ordered, pancakes, bacon, and maple syrup." He subconsciously rubbed his stomach. "Susie said she'd have them ready in no time." He poured coffee and added cream and sugar. "Have you put the witch back in her cage?"

Laughing, Jenna met his raised eyebrow and serious stare. "After two cups of coffee, yeah I think she's under control."

"Good." Kane sighed. "I need to discuss the latest case with you."

Jenna held up a hand. "Before you give me the rundown, I've been going over my notes and with everything happening so fast, we still haven't hunted down Wyatt Cooper and spoken to him about finding his DNA on the briefs found in Laurie's mouth." She ran her finger through a sprinkle of sugar on the table and frowned. "He was missing after the parade too. Is this a coincidence or is he involved in both murders?"

"Hmm, I figure we need to call his father and ask him to bring him down to the office for questioning." Kane removed his hat and placed it on the seat beside him. "As he's underage, anything he says to us without his parents' permission might be a stumbling block in the prosecution."

"Okay, I'll call Mr. Cooper when I get back to the office." Jenna leaned back in her chair. "Now what have you got for me?"

After Kane brought her up to date, Jenna stared into space and tried to process all the information. "Wolfe will do a complete forensics sweep of the apartment but if it's the kids again, they know too much about trace evidence to leave anything behind. I've been considering if Mrs. Turner's murder is a copycat. It doesn't feel like the same killer or killers." She waited for Suzie to deliver Kane's meal and more coffee. Once she had moved out of earshot, she opened her phone to scan her files again. "On the other hand, we know the killers are smart and have been trying to throw suspicion on other people by using the briefs. What if they couldn't steal another pair of briefs?"

"They'd find something else to use to shift the blame." Kane ate slowly.

Jenna leaned forward. "What if the kids got access to Laurie's pickup? We know someone disabled her truck, so they have knowledge of the vehicle. By parking it and committing another murder they're pointing the finger at Dr. Turner." She shrugged. "Just how easy is it to hotwire one of them?"

"Very easy and I could probably start one with a screwdriver but we'd have to examine the vehicle to see if it's been tampered with." Kane frowned. "I doubt we'd get a search warrant on a sighting of a vehicle parked in the vicinity late at night. It's not enough probable cause."

"We might get permission from Dr. Turner to look at the vehicle." Jenna sipped her coffee. "I'll go and speak to the people Mrs. Turner worked with in the beauty parlor. They might know if she had any enemies or threats but I doubt it. Seems to me, the only problem she had was her husband. What if he's involved?" She rubbed her temples, thinking, and looked at Kane. "Although, his hostility toward his wife, and the vehicle on scene makes his involvement too obvious, almost staged." She sighed. "And how could he possibly know details of the cheerleader murders? We've played our cards close to the vest. The causes of death haven't been divulged to anyone and we didn't tell him the details of what happened to his daughter. It seems very strange that Mrs. Turner was strangled, naked and had a pompom with her. It does point the finger to the same people who murdered the cheerleaders."

"Unless Dr. Turner believes we're pushovers." Kane nibbled on a strip of crispy bacon. "Remember he's a shrink. If he did kill his wife, making his involvement appear obvious might be a ploy. I wouldn't rule him out just yet." He shrugged. "My bet would be that the red Ford pickup will be reported stolen sometime soon."

Jenna nodded. "Yeah, if he is the killer that's the usual move but a stolen vehicle report would have had to be filed last night for me to believe it." She snorted. "I mean the pickup is a bit hard to miss, he'd notice for sure if it went missing from his driveway." She met his gaze. "I'd love you to interview him with Jo. Between the two of you, we might find out if he's involved. But first we'll inform him about his wife's murder and arrange the ID."

"We'll have to try and persuade him to give us his fingerprints." Kane finished his meal and reached for his coffee. "I'll find a way." He placed his cup back in the saucer and sighed. "I'm done here." He pulled out his wallet and dropped bills on the table. "My treat."

Jenna collected her things and stood. "Thanks." She led the way out the door, giving Susie Hartwig a wave of thanks.

After dropping her cruiser and Duke at the office, she climbed into the Beast and they headed to the high school. After speaking to the woman on the front counter, and waiting for her to call Dr. Turner, they headed down a long passageway to his office. The door was open and Dr. Turner didn't stand to greet them, just stared at them from across his desk. Jenna couldn't imagine this man was capable of counseling students, his attitude was hostile and unapproachable. She removed her hat and waited a beat to compose her words. It was better to come straight to the point without offering any reason. "I'm sorry to inform you that your wife is dead."

"Jeanette is dead?" Turner leaned back in his chair and towered his fingers as if she'd just told him it was raining outside. "Overdose?"

Jenna shook her head. "We don't have the cause of death. Would you be willing to come by and identify her around noon today at the medical examiner's office?"

"If I have to but you do have Laurie's DNA to use as a comparison. You don't really need me, do you?" Turner looked as if he'd just scored a point. "I mean you didn't need me to identify Laurie, did you?"

"I'm sorry for your loss." Kane took out a notebook, opened it to a new page, and handed it to Turner. "Would you mind listing Jeanette's next-of-kin? Do you know if she had life insurance? If so, can you give me the company name as well?"

"I'm her next-of-kin and I'll have to check my documents for the name and address of the company. I kept up the payments for Laurie's sake." Turner splayed his fingers on the notebook to keep the pages open and his eyes flickered with annoyance. "I'll have the information by noon." He closed the notebook and handed it back to Kane. "Now please leave, I have students to speak to and I don't want them to see you. They'll think I'm breaking our confidentiality."

Jenna nodded. "Sure. Do you want us to call anyone to go with you to the viewing, a clergyman perhaps?"

"No!" Turner waved them away. "Now will you please leave?"

Stunned by his reaction, Jenna turned to leave but Kane blocked the door.

"Before we go…" Kane narrowed his gaze at the doctor. "Is Laurie's red Ford pickup at home?"

"No, *my* red Ford pickup is parked right outside in the staff parking lot." Turner raised both eyebrows. "Why?"

Jenna pulled out her statement book and started to write as fast as possible. She glanced up at Turner. "Do you mind if we take a look at it? There's a loose end we'd like to tie up."

"The ME said he'd cleared the vehicle and released it? What now?" Turner pulled a key from his pocket and tossed it across the table. "You're not taking it again, are you?"

"No, not this time." Jenna handed him her statement book. "If you could sign here. I'll need your permission to search the vehicle."

To Jenna's surprise, he signed and handed it back. She collected the key using the tips of her fingernails and smiled. "We'll have this back to you in a few minutes."

"Leave it at the front counter." Turner waved them away. "I have work to do."

"Just one more thing, we have to ask, I'm sure you understand?" Kane had adopted a concerned expression. "Where were you between seven and say ten last night?"

"At home. I had a private counseling session." Turner's eyes burned with indignation.

"Okay, thank you." Jenna led the way outside and dropped the key onto the hood of Kane's truck. She pulled on gloves and opened the statement book. "Please tell me we have a few good sets of prints."

"A full hand on my notebook." Kane gloved up and took the laser fingerprint scanner from his pocket and ran it over the statement book. "Oh yeah, we have some great prints. Bag the statement book as evidence." He ran the scanner over the key and his notebook. "Yeah we have plenty to use as comparison." He pulled out an evidence bag and dropped the books inside. "I always keep a spare notebook in my pocket just in case we need to gather prints. This is the first time I've hit paydirt."

Jenna turned around and scanned the staff parking lot. "I can see Laurie's pickup. So, it wasn't stolen last night after all."

They hustled to the 1950 red Ford pickup and Jenna stood by while Kane examined the vehicle, using the scanner to capture any fingerprints, on the inside, steering wheel, doors, and seats. He locked the door and they went back to drop the key at the counter. As they walked back to the Beast, she looked at him. "You haven't said much. Did you find anything?"

"Fingerprints but no tampering." Kane removed his gloves and tossed them into the trash. "Whoever drove that vehicle last night used the key." He raised both arms in the air and dropped them. "Unless by some miracle we have another identical pickup in town, that was the same vehicle our witness spotted outside Mrs. Turner's apartment."

CHAPTER FORTY-FOUR

Once inside the Beast, Kane uploaded the prints to the files and sent copies to Wolfe, while Jenna updated her files. They had time to spare, the forensics team wouldn't be finished processing the crime scene yet and it was too early to drop by to speak to Stan Williams. He lived right next door to Jeanette Turner and if there had been an argument, there was a good chance he'd overheard something. If not, Kane wanted to know if he had an alibi for last night. His gut was telling him not to trust Williams but they would need to tread carefully as they'd be stepping on the FBI's toes if they'd already started their investigation into his penchant for cheerleaders. The files updated and evidence stowed away, he turned the truck around and headed back to Stanton. He stared out at the forest and slowed the truck to admire the view spreading out to the mountains one side and across the prairie on the other. "Just look at that, it never ceases to amaze me."

"It's a beautiful place all year around but in fall the colors are incredible and the sky goes on forever." Jenna buzzed down her window and inhaled. "The name Big Sky Country is true. Here the views are endless. It's a special place and almost timeless in parts. It's no wonder Atohi works so hard to preserve the forests, he wants everyone to know how precious they are."

Kane pressed his lips together, recalling the last time he'd seen Atohi. "I hope Carter doesn't corrupt him. They're out fishing again today."

"Corrupt Atohi?" Jenna burst out laughing. "He's pretty set in his ways. I wouldn't worry." She poked his arm with her finger. "Did he try with you, last night?"

"He tried." Kane turned and smiled at her. "But I'm pretty set in my ways too. I should've driven home. I hadn't been drinking but you know Ty. He had invited these women to his room for drinks and I had the transport." He shrugged. "I made it clear I wasn't interested and the one Ty had assigned to me decided to take a cab home. In the morning, Atohi showed and Ty just walked out and left me with his woman."

"So, you being you, gave her a ride home and she kissed you on the cheek?" Jenna squeezed his arm. "I've known you for a long time, Dave. A player you're not." She glanced at her watch. "As much as I'd love to sit here admiring the scenery, we need to talk to Williams and catch Wolfe before he leaves the crime scene, I'd like to find out what progress he's made."

Kane smiled at her. "Copy that." He headed home. "Just don't forget Williams believes I'm a friend. We don't want him to know he's under FBI surveillance."

"I might be the wicked witch some days, Dave, but my memory is just fine." Jenna laughed.

They found Stan Williams at home. His eyes widened at the mention of a murder next door and Kane stood back to allow Jenna to take the lead.

"Mr. Williams, didn't you notice the sheriff's vehicles when you left this morning for work?" Jenna's determined expression had obviously unnerved him and she played on the fact. "What time did you leave?"

"I left a little after six." Williams leaned against the doorframe and folded his arms across his chest. "As you can see, I park my truck in the courtyard, I drove out the alleyway and didn't see anyone at all. A few vehicles drove by, I don't recall any one of them in particular."

Kane exchanged a meaningful look with Jenna. Williams would have left before Jenna had received the call from the driver of the garbage truck. He took out his notebook and made a few notes, trying to look as disinterested as possible. He wanted Williams to believe he was a friend and someone who enjoyed the same interests or the FBI investigation would be over before it started. He waited for Jenna to continue the questioning and when Williams glanced at him, he rolled his eyes.

"Did you hear anything last night?" Jenna stood her ground. "Anyone arguing, a fight or anything unusual from next door?"

"Not if it was between eight and ten, no I wouldn't hear anything." Williams shrugged and turned to look inside his apartment. "I spent last evening going through the shots I've been taking and making copies for my clients. I have my earbuds in and listen to music. It helps me to concentrate. I wouldn't have heard a bomb exploding." He looked from Jenna to Kane. "I'm sorry I couldn't help you, Sheriff. I wish I could, truly."

"Okay, thank you for your time." Jenna turned to move down the stairs.

"Nice to see you again, Dave." Williams grinned. "I'll be in touch." Kane forced a smile. "Thanks." He headed down the steps.

The garbage truck had left but Wolfe's van had returned to block the alleyway and old Deputy Walters was sitting in his cruiser out front. Kane gave him a wave and went up to his window. "Need anything?"

"Nope, I'm just fine. Wolfe says he won't be more than a few more minutes and I can get back to watching TV." Walters smiled. "I always appreciate the work, Dave."

Kane nodded. "We couldn't manage without you." He headed after Jenna.

As he turned into the alleyway, Wolfe was coming down the stairs leading to Jeanette Turner's apartment. He was in a deep hushed conversation with Jenna. He moved to their side and they went into a huddle. "What did you find?"

"What you described." Wolfe looked at him. "There's been a crude attempt to cover up fingerprints but we found a variety of sets in the usual places people miss and one set are a match with Dr. Bob Turner."

"That's interesting, considering he claimed in his statement that he didn't know where his wife was living." Jenna frowned. "So, we have to assume the first time he came here was last night and as a bonus, his truck was seen outside. We have him dead to rights."

"Hold your horses." Wolfe looked from one to the other. "Just to add a little twist to the investigation. I found more than one match for Wyatt Cooper as well."

Astounded, Kane turned to Jenna. "I figure you'd better call Mr. Cooper now. I'd really like to know what Wyatt was doing in Jeanette Turner's apartment."

"Yeah, me too." Jenna pulled out her phone and made the call. She disconnected with a nod. "He can drop by at noon. He'll go and collect Wyatt from school and come see us in his break."

"I'll need to lock the apartment down and keep it as a crime scene. There's more work to do here now." Wolfe frowned. "We've completed a thorough forensics sweep but I'll need to revisit after the autopsy. I want to discover the timeline of the murder and I can't do that properly until I've examined the injuries to the victim." He smiled. "Rio filmed inside and now that we have 3D imaging software, we'll be able to see the scene from all angles in the lab as well. Having a media expert on the team is a bonus, so far his work has been exemplary."

"He is a good fit." Jenna's lips flattened into a thin line. "Although, I'm surrounded by experts, yet we have three murders and the evidence is a tangled mess. Nothing seems to fit. There are so many missing pieces in the timelines, and although my gut tells me it's two killers in one case, the evidence to date in the other two murders point to one person."

Kane looked from one to the other. "Then we have to consider we have different people responsible. A pair for sure for the Becky Powell case but maybe we have a completely different person responsible for killing Laurie and her mother."

CHAPTER FORTY-FIVE

The wind had picked up and it whistled down the alleyway in an eerie moan as if nature mourned the murder of another innocent victim. As Jenna made her way to the Beast, her boots crunched on the leaves overflowing the gutters. A beautiful nuisance, the leaves came in every shade from green to honey brown and brought back memories of her childhood, running through the piles, knee deep and kicking the leaves about to watch them settle like feathers again. She valued the leaves, and welcomed them to the small garden she rarely had time to tend. The leaves offered her rosebushes nourishment and would disintegrate come the first rain. Pushing back her memories into their safe place, she climbed into the truck and fastened her seatbelt. As they headed back to the office, she turned to Kane. "I want to drag Dr. Turner down here right now but I guess we'd better wait until he views the body."

"I figure we'll have our hands full with the Wyatt Cooper interview." Kane followed the line of traffic, mostly sightseers driving slowly to admire the town, and then turned into the parking space out front of the sheriff's department.

"I'll send Rowley over to the viewing and he can escort him back here." Jenna stared out the window thinking. "I hope Turner comes in voluntarily. He doesn't have to speak to us and I'm not sure what evidence we have is enough for an arrest warrant. The judge has been harder to convince lately."

"Tell Rowley to ask him to come in to sign some paperwork." Kane scratched his cheek. "Add that he'll need to apply to claim their bodies as well. I'll call Wolfe and make sure he gives Rowley all the documents to bring back with him. I doubt Dr. Turner will know those matters are usually handled by the ME."

Milling over the scenario, Jenna nodded. "Yeah, we'll take him down to the interview room, get him to sign the papers, and then ask the questions. I'll switch on the camera and read him his rights." She blew out her cheeks. "He'll probably walk right out the door."

"We'll see." Kane thought for a beat. "Do you think Jo would come down to sit in on the interviews with both suspects?"

Jenna lifted one shoulder. "She might be back by now, she wanted to go on a tour of the sapphire mines out at Louan yesterday. I'm not sure when she's due back. Call her and see if she can drop by."

She headed into the office and before she could stop to talk to Maggie behind the counter, Duke came flashing from her office and skidded to a halt with a half yawn, half whine. She bent to pat him but he'd spotted Kane behind her and did his usual welcome dance. She turned and laughed. "He's happy we made it back for lunch. Just how many times a day do you feed him? Most people feed their dogs once a day. He ate the entire bowl of food at my house last night."

"He's kinda stuck on three meals a day." Kane shrugged. "I don't feed him three full meals. It's become a habit since I found him. The V-E-T told me to give him small meals or he'd vomit after being starved for so long." He bent to give Duke a full body rub along both sides. "He's not overweight and I like him to be happy."

Jenna smiled and turned to Maggie. "Anything happen I need to know about?"

"Not a thing." Maggie stared at the hotline phone. "I'm expecting a few calls once the story about the murder hits the news." She waved a hand toward Rio and Rowley working at their desks. "I have help if I need it."

"Well, you'll have one of them." Jenna indicated toward Rowley. "I'm sending Rowley to do a victim identification for me at noon." She headed toward Rowley and filled him in with their plan to get Dr. Turner into an interview room. "He's prickly, so stay as friendly as possible. We need to ask him some questions and I have a strange feeling he's not going to like it."

"Copy that." Rowley leaned back in his chair and looked at her. "Thanks for giving me the time to be with Sandy. It made her settle having me there."

Jenna leaned one hip against his desk. "Family is so important and we can always manage, Jake. This is a tough job and marriages of law enforcement officers have been spoiled because of the workload. I'm going to make sure that never happens here." She glanced up as Mr. Cooper and Wyatt walked into the office. "Hmm, they're early."

She straightened and went to greet them. "Ah, thanks for coming in, can I get you anything, coffee, water?"

"No, we're fine." Mr. Cooper looked apprehensive. "What is it you need from my boy, Sheriff?"

Jenna waited for Kane to come to her side, as it was obvious he had something on his mind. She smiled at Mr. Cooper. "Just a few questions. If you'll give me a minute? I've just walked in the door. I'll have Deputy Rio take you to an interview room. It will be more comfortable." She turned to Rio. "Take Mr. Cooper and Wyatt down to interview room one for me please and wait with them." She looked at Mr. Cooper. "I won't be long. I know you have to get back to work."

She walked away with Kane. "Has something come up?"

"Nope but Jo is on her way." Kane glanced at Maggie. "Do you think Maggie would mind watching Jaime for a while?"

"I'll ask her." Jenna went to the front counter. "Jo has offered to assist with a couple of interviews but she has Jaime with her. If Rio takes over the front desk, would you be able to look after her for me? You can use my office."

"I'd love to." Maggie beamed. "She is such an agreeable child."

The door opened and Agent Jo Wells came in with her daughter, Jaime, who was cuddling a Boston Terrier. Jenna smiled at Jo. "Thank you so much for coming. Maggie will watch over Jaime for you."

"I was driving through town looking for something to do." Jo shrugged. "Jaime is tuckered out and I can't reach Carter. I wanted to ask him if he wanted to return home early." She smiled. "At last, two cases I can get my teeth into. Kane has brought me up to date. Who is first?"

Jenna led the way to the interview room. "Wyatt Cooper and his father, the subject is only sixteen and was the boyfriend of Laurie Turner before they broke up just before she was murdered."

"Yeah." Jo looked at her iPad. "I have the case files if I need them. I know I'm here as a consultant but do you want me to take the lead? I might be able to get under his guard."

Jenna nodded. "Yeah thanks, I'm getting mixed messages from this kid. I'm sure you and Dave will be able to untangle them between you. I'll take notes and observe." She scanned her card outside the interview room and they all walked inside. "Thanks, Rio. Take over the front counter. Maggie is busy." Before she took her seat, she turned on the camera and recording devices. "Mr. Cooper and Wyatt, this is Special Agent Jo Wells and you know Deputy Kane."

"The FBI? What is going on here?" Mr. Cooper's face drained of color. "Do we need a lawyer?"

"You are within your rights to have one present but it may not be necessary." Jo's face had set into a pleasant expression. "We have to divulge some information that is sensitive."

"However—" Kane leaned forward, "—I have to inform you that anything you say can be used against you in a court of law." He finished giving them their rights. "Do you understand?"

"I haven't done anything wrong." Wyatt leaned forward palms up on the table. "I've got nothing to hide. Ask away."

"Are you in agreement, Mr. Cooper?" Jo looked at the worried man.

"I guess so." Mr. Cooper shrugged.

"Do you recall missing any underwear, a pair of green briefs to be specific?" Jo stared at Wyatt.

"No, I've tons of pairs of shorts. I don't really keep track of them once they're in my laundry basket." Wyatt's cheeks pinked. "Why?"

"A pair of your briefs were found at the murder scene of Laurie Turner." Jo was watching him so intently, she didn't as much as blink. "They've been identified as belonging to you by DNA found on the garment." She leaned forward slightly. "How do you figure they got there?"

"I have no idea." Wyatt pressed a finger into the table. "Laurie was a nice girl. We didn't have sex and I've never removed my shorts in her presence. Nor did I give her a pair as a souvenir or whatever. You must be mistaken."

"No mistake." Jo made a few notes on her iPad but didn't look up. "Is there any way a person could obtain a pair of briefs you had worn?" She lifted her gaze. "Are your soiled clothes ever left in a place where someone could steal a pair?"

"I don't think so." Wyatt stared at the wall for long minutes and then snapped his fingers. "I was thinking where I've been, I figured the pool but my things are in a locker and I'd notice if my underwear was missing, but not at training or after the games. I'm usually sweaty, I strip off like most of the guys and shower. After I'm dressed, I stuff the dirty socks and underwear into a bag. I give it to my mom to wash and she replaces them in my backpack." He shrugged. "So, my things along with all the other guys are usually in a pile on the floor in the locker room during the time we take a shower." He leaned back in the chair. "No girls are allowed in the locker rooms, so how she came by them I don't know."

"How well do you know Laurie's mother?" Kane straightened the statement book and picked up a pen.

"I've met her a few times." Wyatt frowned. "Why?"

"Did you know she was once a cheerleader?" Jo smiled. "She continued on in college as well. I bet she taught Laurie a few moves."

"Yeah, that's all they would talk about as if it was the only thing on earth." Wyatt pushed an agitated hand through his hair.

"When did you last go to Mrs. Turner's apartment?" Jo's eyes bored into him. "Did you go to see her recently?"

"No. The last time would have been Independence Day. We dropped by to see her because Laurie wanted her to come see the parade. We ended up missing most of it because her ma was having one of her headaches." Wyatt rolled his eyes. "That was the last time I went to her apartment."

"Here's our problem." Kane leaned forward and eyeballed him. "We have two dead women and have evidence to prove you were at both crime scenes." He tapped his pen on the desk. "Where were you last night between seven and midnight?"

"In town with the guys. I got home before ten." Wyatt looked horrified. "I haven't killed anyone."

"What do you drive?" Jo's attention had never left his face.

"A white Ford pickup." Mr. Cooper frowned. "It's still in my name."

"Okay, Wyatt, write down who you were with last night and where you went." Kane nonchalantly slid the statement book across the table. "When you're done, sign it, and Mr. Cooper, I'll need your signature as well." He stood. "We'll be back shortly. He turned off the recording devices and led the way outside.

Jenna looked from one to the other. "Did you pick up anything?"

"I don't believe he's involved." Jo shrugged. "He kept his hands open on the table, he didn't try and come up with any excuses and appeared to be genuinely shocked." She smiled at Jenna. "We've all been fooled by a psychopath but he isn't exhibiting any of the usual smartass comebacks I'd expect. He is showing empathy. I believe him."

Jenna nodded. "That's good enough for me." She opened the door to the interview room and smiled at the Coopers. "Thank you for coming by. Once you've handed in the statement, you're free to go."

CHAPTER FORTY-SIX

Jenna leaned against the wall watching the Coopers leave the building. She held out her hand for the statement book Kane was holding and scanned the pages. "I'll get Rowley to speak to this list of kids when he gives Dr. Turner a ride back to the school. It's only general questions, we won't need their parents' permission to speak to them." She glanced up at him. "Cooper might be as innocent as he seems but he's still ticking all the boxes."

"I don't trust any of them right now." Kane slid his pen inside his pocket. "Him most of all." He indicated with his chin toward Dr. Turner moving down the hallway with Rowley.

Jenna turned her back on the visitor's arrival and walked with Kane and Jo back into the empty interview room. "We'll leave Rowley to get the paperwork sorted. Once he comes out, I'll give him the list of Wyatt's friends, it will give him time to make arrangements with the school to speak to them." She looked at Jo. "Do your thing, between the pair of you, we might get somewhere with Dr. Turner."

Her phone chimed. It was Rio from the front desk. "Is there a problem?"

"No, it's quiet so I hunted down red 1950 Ford pickups in the county. Apart from the one belonging to Turner, there's none, fitting the year, model, or description, here or in any neighboring counties." Rio cleared his throat. "They're a classic car. I found a few around the state in different colors, some are red but not as distinctive as the one owned by Laurie Turner."

Jenna nodded. "Thank you, that's good to know." She disconnected and relayed the information to Jo and Kane. "I'd like to see
how Turner explains his way out of the evidence against him." She
ran her fingers along the edge of the statement book and thought
for a beat. "I'm wondering if he's involved in Laurie's murder as well.
From her best friend's account Laurie was afraid of her father and
she has a bolt on her bedroom door. That in itself is a red flag that
something wasn't right between them."

"He is a school counselor, so he'd have access to the locker rooms
the football team uses. No one would have made mention about him
wandering inside. He could have stolen the underwear to lay blame
on Wyatt." Jo's brows furrowed. "He knows the vehicle and could
have disabled it but that doesn't account for the sighting of Laurie
getting into a Chrysler sedan the night of her death."

"We might have a witness seeing her getting into the vehicle,
but we don't know if the driver dropped her home." Kane
scratched his cheek. "Or where she died. We only have the place
she was found. Think about this scenario: Turner disables her
vehicle and not knowing about her dropping her phone, he'd
assume she'd get a ride home with her friends. When she gets
home, he strangles her in her sleep. We know she didn't struggle,
if she slept face down, he could have easily strangled her from
behind and then taken her body in his vehicle out to the mines
and left her there. The stabbing could be a ploy to make us
believe someone else was involved." He looked from one to the
other. "The bed linen was changed and everything was neat. It
all points to him."

Jenna shook her head. "The only problem here is the saliva found
at the scene matching the sweat at Rowley's house." She facepalmed
her head. "See, we have evidence but there's missing bits or things
that don't add up."

"Ma'am." Rowley poked his head around the door. "I've finished the paperwork with Dr. Turner. I told him you wanted to speak with him."

Jenna smiled and pulled open the door. "Thanks, Jake." She handed him a copy of Wyatt Cooper's statement. "While we're busy, call the school and hunt down these witnesses and see if they'll back up Cooper's alibi. See if you can talk to them after you've given Dr. Turner a ride back to the school. This is to do with Mrs. Turner's murder so there's no conflict of interest."

"Sure." Rowley smiled. "I called Sandy before and she said to thank you all for the flowers you sent to the hospital and the food." He started to back down the hallway.

"Any time." Jenna looked at his earnest face. "I'm so happy she's okay." She turned to Kane and Jo. "Let's do this."

After scanning her card and leading the way into the other interview room, Jenna switched on the cameras and once everyone had stated their names for the record and she'd read Dr. Turner his rights, she sat down. "I'm sure you're wondering why we need to speak with you, Dr. Turner. Agent Wells would like to question you about the murder of your wife."

"My wife left me six years ago, if I'd wanted to kill her, I'd have done it by now." Turner smiled at Jo. "Honestly, the FBI? My wife was a useless nobody. Why bring in the FBI?"

"You mentioned in your statement you didn't know where Jeanette lived, so I guess you've never been to her apartment?" Jo took a neutral pose.

"Why would I want to visit her?" Turner's confident twitch of the lips returned. "She left me, remember? She took all our money but she never got to keep Laurie, did she? No, I put a stop to that."

"Okay, so how did your fingerprints get all over her apartment?" Jo's eyes fixed on him. "Or why was your vehicle seen parked opposite the alleyway to where she lived?"

"I want a lawyer." Dr. Turner leaned back in his chair, looking smug. "I know my rights. Call Samuel J Cross. I won't speak to anyone unless he is present."

Jenna pushed to her feet. "As you wish." She looked at Kane. "Hold Dr. Turner for questioning of suspicion of murder and take him down to the cells. I'll see if I can locate Sam Cross." She rolled her eyes. Of all the lawyers, she and Sam Cross were usually at loggerheads. She led Jo out of the interview room and they lingered in the hallway. "I figure he's our man."

"Yeah, but he's so smug, I'm expecting him to pull a rabbit out of his hat soon." Jo stared at Turner through the one-way glass. "The evidence against him for both murders is enough for an arrest warrant but more would be better. If you could get into his office and his home to see if he's left any incriminating evidence, it might help." She shrugged. "You don't need his lawyer's permission to apply for a search warrant."

Jenna nodded. "I'll get that underway." She sighed. "We have his wife's autopsy at two. Will you be able to stick around for the interview?"

"You could hold Turner overnight for questioning." Jo pushed her iPad under one arm and stared back at the prisoner. "The autopsy findings might be crucial to further questioning. I'd wait until you return before you call in the lawyer. If Mr. Samuel J Cross informs you when he plans to arrive, I'll come back." She glanced at her watch. "I'll take Jaime back to the hotel and we'll have some lunch."

Jenna squeezed her arm. "Thanks, Jo."

The door clicked open and Jenna stood to one side to allow Kane to escort Dr. Turner from the room. The doctor said nothing when he stared at her but his face was set in a cruel smile. Jo was correct, he did have something up his sleeve.

CHAPTER FORTY-SEVEN

Nervous anxiety had given him stomach cramps all morning. The thrill of watching his girl kill again was fast becoming a nightmare. He didn't know what to do and couldn't stop her, she was like a tornado, wild and uncontrollable. She unnerved him, no she darn right terrified him. He couldn't go to the sheriff, his involvement made him as guilty as her, and he hoped Dr. Turner would supply him with an alibi. He had no choice but to go along with the final cheerleader on her list and hope it would be over. When the bells rang and students streamed out of the classrooms heading for the last class before lunch, he dragged her into an alcove. "We need to talk."

"What's up?" She gave him a slow smile and leaned in close. "We shouldn't be seen together, not until we've dealt with Vicky Perez."

Afraid someone would see him with her, he turned his back, to hide her from view. "All hell is breaking loose. They found Laurie's mom murdered this morning and now the sheriff has called in the FBI."

"The FBI?" She blinked at him. "Really?"

"Yeah, I saw them together talking up a storm. They're hard to miss in their jackets." He grabbed her by the arms. "Did you kill her?"

"Why would I want to kill Laurie Turner's mom?" She burst out laughing. "Who told you this shit?"

As if he'd divulge his clandestine meeting with Dr. Turner late last night. The doctor had found his wife murdered and asked for his help. Dr. Turner was convinced he wasn't involved and he'd gone along with his plan to move the body into the alleyway. The shock of realization that his girl was killing without him, had brought his world crashing down. He knew she was lying to him and it made him angry. He'd seen the mess in the apartment and it hadn't been easy getting Mrs. Turner's body into the alleyway, even with the doctor's help. There was no way his girl could have taken on Mrs. Turner alone. He gave her a little shake. "Stop it. It's not funny." He examined her face. "You're seeing someone else behind my back, aren't you? You went missing in town last night, just around the time Mrs. Turner was strangled."

"I went home." She blinked at him. "I wanted to hang around but when Vicky started crawling all over you like a rash, I got so mad I wanted to stab her right there." Her lips curled into a seductive smile. "It would have been too quick for her and I want to finish her in our secret place. I like that watching me kill makes you want to make out." She giggled. "You're as messed up as I am, huh?"

Am I? Guilt and sickness had overcome him after killing Becky and yet his girl seemed to thrive on murder. He chewed on the inside of his cheek. It was as if she had no feelings and the killing didn't bother her. In that moment he realized, she didn't love him at all. She wasn't capable of love and had manipulated him to live out some crazy fantasy. Now, it was obvious she'd teamed up with another guy. If he denied her now, she'd turn on him like a rattlesnake. He stared into her big guiltless eyes and ground his teeth. He'd play her game and then ask his folks to send him away to college. He'd already had offers and it was his only way to get rid of her.

"Don't look so worried. We have this." She twirled a strand of hair around a finger. "Do you know why the principal was calling students to his office? Does the sheriff figure one of us killed Laurie's mother?"

He nodded. "Yeah but don't worry, you're not on the list." He shrugged. "They're only calling guys, so if you've been seeing someone else, I guess you'd better warn him."

"It's just you and me." She stared into his eyes, her expression deadly serious. "Now the sheriff believes its someone from the school, they'll be watching everyone closely, so we haven't much time. It's got to be tonight." She leaned into him and wet her lips. "I have plans for Vicky. I'm changing up my style to confuse the cops. I'm not planning on strangling her, she's too strong." Her lips lifted into a smile. "Do you recall seeing those old bottles of chemicals in the barn?"

Dread crawled over him in a dark, cold cloak. He swallowed hard. "Yeah, acids and stuff, I think? Why?"

"I found a bottle of chloroform." She giggled. "Do you know what that does to people? It puts them to sleep. A few drops on a rag held over her mouth and she'll be out. We'll be able to tie her up and she'll be under my control. I'll be able to take my time and do whatever I want and she won't be able to do a thing. We'll need another pair of shorts. See, using different ones each time confuses the cops."

He scratched his cheek. "It's too late now and I'm not going through some guy's backpack looking for his sweaty underwear."

"Then bring a pair of yours." She cupped his cheeks. "I know what I'm doing. Having three different DNAs at a crime scene and nothing else, they'll believe someone took your shorts as well. Don't worry, no one will catch us and soon it will be over."

He pushed his hands into his pockets to stop them trembling. She was capable of anything and he wouldn't be able to watch her torture Vicky. He shook his head. "If you cut her up real bad, it will be harder to dump her. Where can we take her without being seen? The cops are all over the place right now, and they still have reinforcements from Blackwater."

"It doesn't matter where we dump her." She dropped her hands agitated. "We'll toss her out on the side of the road, somewhere remote." She picked up her backpack. "I've gotta go. I'll see you tonight at the barn. Get her there by eight. I'll be waiting inside."

He rubbed the back of his neck. "She might not come with me."

"She will, she hasn't stopped talking about you." Anger flashed in her eyes. "She makes me mad. You make sure she's there because you don't want to make me angry too, do you?"

CHAPTER FORTY-EIGHT

Exhilarated, Jenna gave Kane a high-five as she walked from seeing the judge. "Oh my gosh, I was sure he'd refuse. Although we can't read his case files, Turner will have an appointment book for sure." She grinned at Kane and waved the paperwork triumphantly. "Now when do we deliver the good news to Dr. Turner?"

"We have half an hour before the autopsy." Kane checked his watch. "Not long enough to conduct a search… and you'll want Wolfe along as well… but time enough to grab a bite at Aunt Betty's." He opened the door to his truck.

Jenna pulled open the passenger door and climbed in. "Sure, I'm hungry too."

Aunt Betty's offered a respite from the tension around a murder investigation. Jenna inhaled the smells of not a greasy spoon but a place more like Grandma's kitchen on baking days. As a child, she loved visiting her grandma and helping her bake cakes and cookies. It was part of her grandma's routine, once the family left home, with only herself and Grandpa to cook for, her grandma would cook up great pots of food each weekend and pack them into the freezer for the rest of the week. Her grandma told her it saved time and energy, doing everything on the one day. She never had to worry what was for dinner and had a choice of meals and insisted it was like eating out every night.

Refusing to think about the upcoming autopsy, Jenna went to the counter to peer at the day's specials. She ordered chunky beef pie with fries on the side and caught Kane's mouth twitching into a smile. She looked at him. "What?"

"The pie sure looks good, the pastry has so many layers it melts in your mouth." Kane ordered the same meal. "But you eat like a bird. I'm wondering if you're the same Jenna I know or you've been taken over by an alien body snatcher?"

Jenna led the way to their table in the back. "I'm hungry is all. I don't snack all day like you do and I've been too busy to fill up on coffee."

"I'm not complaining." Kane sat down and removed his Stetson and dropped it onto the seat beside him. He let out a long sigh. "What is it with festivals and crime? I'd been hoping we'd have wrapped this case up by now and made it to the fall dance on Saturday after all."

"You really wanted to go?" Jenna grinned. "You know I wouldn't step all over your toes if you took me to a place where I could just wiggle a bit to the music, we wouldn't have a problem."

"Trust me." Kane shook his head. "That ain't never gonna happen." He leaned toward her. "I like dancing with a purpose… and I'm getting used to you scuffing up my boots."

Their mood became somber the instant they walked into the morgue. The cold air was like a slap in the face and seemed to suck all the happiness out of Jenna. The too familiar odor invaded her nostrils and sent her crashing back to harsh reality. She followed Kane down the stark white hallway, the noise of his boots on the tile an irreverent echo in the silence. As they stopped in the alcove to suit up saying nothing, the tick of the clock on the wall sounded loud in the quiet. She looked at Kane. "Where is everyone?"

"Oh, that's right." He pulled the green scrubs back over his head and hung them on a peg with his jacket. "Wolfe will be in his office.

He wanted to examine our stitches before he started the autopsy. I guess Emily and Webber are getting the examination room ready." He ran the tip of one finger over the yellowing bruise under her eye. "How's the eye feeling?"

Jenna pulled off the scrubs and dropped them onto a peg alongside his. "I'm fine. It doesn't worry me at all." She headed toward Wolfe's office and knocked.

"Come in." Wolfe's muffled voice came from behind the door.

"Afternoon." Jenna walked inside. "Dave said you wanted to check our stitches?"

"Yeah, pull off your T-shirts." Wolfe took a medical kit from the bench and pulled out a few things. He snapped on gloves and removed Jenna's dressing. "Jenna, you're good to go. Leave the clean dressing on for a week and then come back and see me. It's waterproof, so you'll be fine in the shower but keep out of the hot tub." He replaced the dressing and after changing his gloves turned to Kane. "Hmm, yours is not so fine." He cleaned up the wound and went back to his field medical kit and returned with a syringe. "Show me your hip, I'm giving you a shot of antibiotics."

Jenna had her shirt over her head when the door opened. She pulled it into place and stared at Emily. "Hi, Em. Were you looking for us?"

"More prickles?" Emily raised both eyebrows. "You two are sure getting yourselves into strife this week."

"No, not more prickles." Wolfe tossed the syringe into a receptacle and removed his gloves with a snap. "I'm following up on my patients is all. Are you ready for me now?"

"Yeah." Emily leaned against the doorframe. "I've been looking over the results of all the victims and the initial examination of Mrs. Turner tells me it's a different killer. If this isn't so, I need to know what I'm missing."

"We'll work through it and see what we find." Wolfe waved her out the door. "We're on our way."

Inside the examination room, Jenna moved to the array of comparison images displayed on the screens. She liked that Wolfe had all the information on the other victims at hand, they often needed to know if the same person was responsible for a string of murders. By comparing results, a copycat stood out like a sore thumb. She scanned the images, making a mental note of the injuries to each victim. To her, ignoring the fact they all had the cheerleader involvement to link them, the injuries sustained appeared to be completely different. She glanced at Kane. "Thank God for medical examiners. Years ago, sheriffs had to make a judgment call on cases like this and from what I'm seeing here, we have two unrelated cases."

"Yeah, I'm wondering how Dr. Turner is going to slide his way out of his wife's murder." Kane shook his head. "It just seems too obvious."

"Some murders are obvious." Wolfe shrugged. "Not every murder is a mystery. The person responsible is usually a close family member. Add some marriage problems and eight out of ten times it's the spouse." He pulled the sheet from Jeanette Turner's pale body, adjusted the microphone, and looked at them over his mask. "Okay, let's begin with my initial findings."

"One thing is for sure, she didn't die in the alleyway." Kane moved closer to the body and examined the feet. "Her feet are clean, apart from the drag marks on her heels. They correspond to the marks I found in the alleyway." He turned to Wolfe. "She wasn't rolled down the steps either. I examined the bottom of the stairs for impact impressions and found nothing to indicate a fall."

"The injuries would support that but there is a mark on her left hip, a scrape that has splinters in it, no bleeding or bruising. This would indicate she was dragged over the step treads post-mortem."

Wolfe indicated to various bruises on her body. "All of these happened at the same time, all have subdermal hematomas which, indicate she was alive when they were inflicted." He moved to the victim's head. "Look at the bruises on her face, see the small cut on the cheekbone?"

A cold breeze seemed to envelope Jenna as she peered at the wound and then turned to look at the enlarged image on the screen Wolfe had flicked up. Too many times she'd seen women covered in bruises just like Jeanette Turner. "I've seen the same injury in spousal abuse. An open hand slap followed by a backhand and in this case the person responsible is wearing a ring."

"Better still." Wolfe's eyes twinkled over his mask. "I figure it may have a stone in it, if so, there's a good chance some DNA might have been snagged in the setting." He looked at Jenna. "Have you noticed if Dr. Turner wears a ring?"

Jenna shrugged. "I'm not sure."

"Yeah he does." Kane reached for his phone. "I had him place all his valuables in a bag when I took him down to the cells." He headed for the door. "And we have a search warrant. Keep going, I'll get someone to bring his belongings here."

"There's something significant we should mention at this point." Emily changed the images on the screen to X-rays. "Mrs. Turner suffered a number of broken bones in her lifetime and one is a match with what we found on Laurie. Looking back on both victims' medical files, they went to the ER with far too many injuries."

Jenna stared at the X-rays, uncomprehending. "Explain."

"The injuries to both women's arms can only be caused by someone twisting the arm." Emily's eyes reflected her anger. "If both women in the same household had the same injury it points to abuse. I'm shocked the doctors treating them at the hospital didn't put two and two together and notify the authorities."

The despair creeping around Jenna's heart was quickly followed by revulsion aimed at the man responsible for inflicting such injuries. She dug deep to find her professional demeanor, unable to allow her disgust to overshadow the investigation. "Unfortunately, until I became sheriff, many people turned a blind eye to spousal abuse. People didn't think it was their business to get involved. Things are changing now. Women know they can get help in my town and that I'll support them." She stared at Emily's distraught expression. "This doesn't only happen to women. Men can have abusive wives but many don't believe it's manly to complain and suffer in silence. I'm working on changing that view by making sure any man in that position can speak to my deputies in confidence."

"Moving right along." Wolfe nodded to Kane as he came back into the room. "The livor mortis… ah the purple discoloration in the buttocks and lower limbs is the blood settling, which indicates the victim was posed shortly after death. So, by the state of rigor and her temperature on scene, I can give you a narrow margin for the TOD. I estimate it is between eight and midnight last night, more likely between eight and ten." He indicated to the marks on Mrs. Turner's arms and thighs. "Unlike the other victims, Jeanette Turner had sexual activity prior to her death and from my examination, I don't believe it was consensual."

"No, there was no love lost between Dr. Turner and his wife." Kane shook his head. "The final domination before strangling her, do you think?"

"More likely, he strangled her during the attack." Wolfe pointed at the thumbprints on Jeanette's pale waxen throat and then turned the head to reveal impressed fingermarks on both sides of her neck. "A frontal attack, he wanted to watch her die and from the state of the apartment, she fought for her life. She didn't stand a chance, once he'd secured her hands behind her back with the cord from her robe." He lifted both bagged hands and indicated to the marks indented in her flesh. "The marks match the cord. He removed it to pose her but Turner isn't a big guy, he must have had trouble getting her down the steps." Wolfe frowned. "The stairs are steep and a dead body carried over one shoulder would be difficult, carried in the arms, impossible." He looked at Jenna. "He didn't drag her down the steps or roll her down. He must have had help."

Suspicion tingled up Jenna's spine. "Is this a copycat or do you figure the killers of Laurie and Becky were involved?"

"Copycat." Kane moved closer. "But he had some inside information, he knew about the strangling and that a pompom was involved but I figure he improvised the rest. It's Dr. Turner. He has motive and we have evidence against him. If we find DNA on his ring, we have him dead to rights."

"I have to agree." Wolfe moved away from the body. "Emily is going to conduct the internal procedure under my supervision but I don't believe we'll find anything but the obvious. Everything points to asphyxiation by strangulation as COD: the marks, broken hyoid, and hematomas in the eyes. She hadn't been drinking and I tested her for the usual drugs and found nothing although as usual a full tox screen will be conducted as routine."

Unease crawled over Jenna. Her team was like a vault. Not one of them leaked information and somehow, Turner had discovered pertinent details and tried to make his wife's murder look as if Laurie's killer had committed the crime. She ran the contents of the media releases through her mind. Laurie's had mentioned the naked body of a teenager but nothing about the strangulation or stabbing, Becky's had mentioned a scantily clad teenager and nothing else, neither had mentioned cheerleaders.

The front door buzzer made a red-light flash inside the examination room. Jenna headed for the door. "That will be the personal effects." She glanced at Kane and Wolfe. "Are we done here?"

"Yeah, Em can take it from here." Wolfe followed her out of the examination room with Kane close behind.

Jenna could see Rio waiting outside the two sets of glass doors and hurried to let him through. "How is our prisoner?"

"Screaming for his lawyer when I informed him we have a search warrant and would be seizing his belongings for forensic analysis. I gave him a copy of the warrant." Rio shrugged. "He's acting like a lunatic but I observed duty of care and gave him a meal." He handed over the envelope with Dr. Turner's name on it and a code they used to identify people's belongings. "Have you found anything to charge him?"

"Plenty." Jenna led the way back to the hallway where Kane and Wolfe waited. "If her DNA is on his ring, there's no doubt." She handed the envelope to Wolfe. "Here, unopened since Turner placed his belongings inside."

"Good." Wolfe changed his scrubs, mask, and gloves. "You can observe through the window but I don't want any evidence contaminated." He scanned his card and went inside the laboratory.

Excited, Jenna slipped inside the small observation room. Each side of her, Kane and Rio towered over her both peering intently as Wolfe set to work. A tremble of anticipation slid over her as Wolfe placed a slide into the microscope. The few seconds he took to examine the slide seemed to take a year. When he looked up and gave them the thumbs up, she gripped Kane's arm feeling the bunched muscles under her fingers and grinned at him. "He's found something."

They waited as Wolfe set up the DNA sequencer and then went back to the envelope and removed a watch with an expandable band. He examined the strap closely and pulled something out with tweezers. Jenna pressed the microphone. "What's that?"

Wolfe moved to the microscope again and fiddled around. He secured the sample inside a plastic tube, sealed it, and then pulled down the microphone.

"It's a few hairs caught in his watch strap." Wolfe looked at them over the top of his mask. "They're the right color, I'll have to run a few comparison tests to see if they are a match for Jeanette Turner. The ring held skin and blood traces. The DNA results will take up to an hour. We have Mrs. Turner's DNA on record, I'll call you as soon as I have any information."

Jenna looked at Kane. "I figure the next hour is going to be the longest in my life."

CHAPTER FORTY-NINE

Hopeful Wolfe would find DNA evidence against Dr. Turner but not taking anything for granted, Jenna and Kane headed back to the office to collect the paperwork for the search warrants. She'd taken the bunch of keys from Turner's property envelope but would need to show the search warrant at the school to gain access to his office without causing a fuss. She snorted and smiled to herself at the thought of the woman on the counter trying to stop them executing her warrant.

"What's so funny?" Kane glanced at her as they turned into Main.

Jenna shrugged. "Oh nothing, I was just thinking about raiding Turner's office at the school."

"And?" Kane gave her a puzzled look.

She giggled. "Well, if they didn't like us invading his office, who would they call to complain? The sheriff?"

"I see your point." Kane pulled into his space outside the sheriff's department offices. "That's why we do everything by the book."

They walked inside and as Jenna made her way to her office, Rowley hurried to her side. She went straight to the coffee machine. "What do you have for me, Jake?"

"All Wyatt Cooper's friends say he was with them on the night of Becky's murder but every one of them was vague about time. Apparently, they went into Aunt Betty's Café at some point but were all having a good time and didn't check their watches. Two recalled visiting the wood carving exhibition, which I checked started at eight-thirty in the city hall. So, it seems the group, all on the football team, went just about everywhere. I spoke to them all individually and kept them separate before questioning them. The principal remained in the room throughout as well as a representative of their parents. Not that it was necessary."

Jenna filled two to-go cups with coffee and added the fixings. "So, in fact none of them can verify Cooper's whereabouts between eight and ten?"

"Not exactly, no." Rowley scratched his head. "Not being able to pin any of them down on time made it difficult but they were all forthcoming."

"Hmm." Kane rested a hip on the edge of Jenna's desk. "So, if he was the killer, the defense will use that as reasonable doubt. We can't put him at the scene of the crime. He may or may not have been in the area at the time Becky was killed."

"I'm sorry I couldn't pin them down." Rowley pushed his hands into the front pockets of his jeans. "I figure checking the CCTV footage at Aunt Betty's might give us at least one point of reference."

Jenna sealed the cups and turned to him. "Get at it. Rio can hold the fort, we're going to search Dr. Turner's office and then his home, if Shane is available."

"Yes, ma'am." Rowley turned and headed down the hallway.

After handing Kane the cups, Jenna collected a copy of the search warrant and feeling something was missing, looked around the office. "Where's Duke?"

"Maggie took him out back to stretch his legs." Kane slid off the desk. "He doesn't know we're back yet."

"We don't need him on this search." Jenna folded the document and slid it into her pocket. "Maybe we could slip out without him?"

"Not a chance." Kane placed the cups on the desk at the sound of claws on the tiled floor. He turned as Duke bounded into the room. "Hey there?" He rubbed the dog's ears. "Ready to go search an office?"

Jenna rolled her eyes at Duke's bark of consent. "Maybe I should give him a badge." She led the way out of the office. "Now wouldn't that stick in Carter's craw?"

The entry into Dr. Turner's office went as smooth as silk, although the nosy woman on the front counter insisted on standing sentry to ensure they didn't breach patient-doctor confidentiality. To Jenna's surprise, the woman turned out to be a font of information. The students who came to see Turner were all issued with a number. This number was used to identify the students and was for the doctor's eyes only along with the students' case files. The filing cabinet being out of bounds, Jenna went straight for the appointment journal on the desk. The hairs on the back of her neck prickled as she flipped through the pages and found Turner took students' appointments at school and in his home. She'd assumed by the "private" sessions he'd mentioned previously as an alibi, it was part of his regular practice and was not included in the free service offered by the school. She made a mental note to ask the receptionist. Her attention moved to the night of Jeanette Turner's murder. From the notes, he was with a patient the night his wife died. *So that's how he plans to get away with murder.*

Biting her tongue to prevent speaking her thoughts to Kane, she looked at the woman watching them intently. "Is it usual for Dr. Turner to take student appointments at his home?"

"I'm not involved with any arrangement he might make outside of school hours or with the students' parents but it would be unusual. Most patients want to be anonymous and the last people they want involved is their parents, I'm sorry to say." She bristled. "Dr. Turner does have a private practice but I'm sure he deals with all the problems that arise here during class." She cast her beady eyes over Jenna like a buzzard contemplating its next meal. "He is board certified. We are lucky to have him."

"I don't understand the number system for his patients. It's not as if they would be required to discuss their problems outside this office before seeing Dr. Turner. Usually, people give their names to attend any doctor and they are seen in confidence. I can't see the reason behind this idea." Kane looked up from searching the trash basket. "Can you explain?"

"I can, yes." The woman lifted her nose. "Dr. Turner implemented the number system because students didn't trust him or anyone on the front counter not to make fun of them for asking him for assistance. So, the number system was introduced. I don't know the names of the students who come by and neither does anyone apart from the doctor."

How convenient. Jenna looked up from the diary. "What about their parents? Someone must be paying for the sessions at his home."

"I'm sure I don't know." The woman looked anxious. "It's not something I can comment on, I'm afraid."

After searching the office for any clue, note, or anything of value to the investigation, Jenna placed a notepad, the appointment book, and a few scraps of paper from the trash into an evidence bag and looked at Kane. "I'm good to go." She looked at the woman. "Thank you for your assistance." She led the way out the door.

Once back at his truck, she turned to Kane and wiggled the book. "According to this, at the time of Jeanette Turner's death, he was having a session with patient 124." She pulled out the book and flipped through the pages. "Same person when the other two murders occurred."

"No wonder he's so confident." The nerve in Kane's jaw twitched. "The law protects his patients' names and with Sam Cross as his attorney, he'll find reasons for every part of our evidence. If the DA will charge him, Cross will make sure he gets bail and he'll likely walk altogether. Unless we can find evidence to prove otherwise." He gave her a long look. "He's outsmarted us, Jenna." He opened the door for Duke and helped him into the truck and secured his harness.

Jenna shook her head. "No way." She snorted. "I never thought I'd see the day when you didn't come up with another angle to solve a problem. This mystery patient might be the key to solving this case." She slid into the passenger seat.

"That's what I'm worrying about. I'm convinced Turner needed help carrying Jeanette down the apartment stairs." Kane climbed behind the wheel and backed out the truck. "It gets back to good old grunt work. We'll be able to discover the name of patient 124 by a process of elimination."

Staring out the window but not registering anything, Jenna hugged her stomach, it was as if it had filled with acid. "If our mystery suspect is patient 124, why would he risk going to seek help from Laurie's father unless he knew how Turner mistreated his womenfolk and figured he didn't care?" She thought for a beat. "How would he get Turner on his side?"

"The first contact he had with Turner was more likely after Becky's murder." Kane stared straight ahead hands gripped to the wheel. "Laurie's murder was clean, as in strangulation from behind. I'm not discounting the post-mortem wounds but let's just think about the actual murder. Patient 124 might have witnessed the murder and assisted with the disposal of the body. His accomplice lost it and took out their rage on the corpse, but then number 124 becomes involved in Becky's murder and Sandy's assault. We know two people were involved in Becky's murder, someone tried to strangle her and

I'd bet my last dime, number 124 killed her with a blunt object. A flashlight, from Wolfe's findings, the same object that hit Sandy but maybe not the same flashlight."

As the scene unfolded in Jenna's mind, she nodded. "You don't believe number 124 killed Laurie, do you?"

"Nope, and that's why he felt secure going to see Turner, heck, he could likely pass a lie detector test if he only watched the murder. He's a follower, a subordinate who takes orders from someone he admires." Kane glanced at her. "It's a woman for sure and she couldn't finish Becky off and ordered him to kill her. He wouldn't have been able to refuse her. Now he feels sick to his stomach, guilty, and needs help. He knows Turner can't rat on him and likely played the, 'I overheard some guys talking and I'm scared for my life' ploy to make himself look innocent."

Excited, Jenna turned in her seat to look at him. "But Turner would see right through him. He'd know the person responsible for killing Becky was sitting right in front of him and he was bound by patient-doctor confidentiality."

"Then maybe it could have gone either way." Kane's mouth curled into a smile. "Turner might have threatened to expose him or maybe pretended to believe him and then offered him protection by giving 124 an alibi. He would have asked for some details of the murders to prove 124 wasn't lying and then Turner murders his wife in a copycat killing and calls in a favor. He asks number 124 to help him dispose of the body of his wife. How can he refuse?" He pulled into the curb. "Go back through the appointment book and look for first contact entries, especially when he gave his patients their numbers. Did he use the same pen for every entry? I noticed a few in a glass on his desk."

Excited, Jenna flipped through the book. "No, he used different ones." She chewed on her bottom lip as she went back through the book to the dates of the murders. Her hands trembled as she gazed up at Kane. "It looks like he used the same black pen for the appointments made at his home at the times of the murders. The notation made on the appointment at the school after Becky's murder, was when he assigned a number to his patient and is in blue ink. There is an appointment with patient 124 at the time of Laurie's murder. If this is correct how come the notes and patient number are written in a different pen and on a different day? I figure the day after Becky's murder was the first day he spoke to patient 124, and he filled in the other appointments later to cover his ass and his accomplice."

"It makes perfect sense to me." Kane pulled back out onto the road. "Now all we have to do is discover the name of patient 124 before another cheerleader is slaughtered."

CHAPTER FIFTY

After waiting for Wolfe and Webber to arrive, they searched Dr. Turner's home and found nothing of interest. It seemed all his case files were held in the locked filing cabinet at the school and in his office in his home. The appointment book on his desk, did not make any references to any local patients for the entire year, although the number 124 was added to match the appointments at the school. Apart from the appointment book, they found zip, no trophies from the murders or pompoms. In fact, the doctor had made sure no trace of his daughter or wife remained. No photographs and Laurie's bedroom was stripped bare, it was as if his wife and daughter had never existed.

As Jenna locked up the house, Wolfe's phone buzzed and she stared at him. Emily would call if the DNA sequencer had pulled up a match. Heart pounding in expectation, she moved to his side as he disconnected. "Was that Emily with the results?"

"Yeah." Wolfe turned to her with a puzzled expression. "I have good and surprising news. The DNA found on Turner's ring is a match for Jeanette, but her cause of death was from a coronary. I'll go over Emily's findings but she knows her stuff and it isn't unusual for someone fighting for their lives and suffering strangulation to have a heart attack." He rubbed his chin. "It's not unusual to find a different COD after we open them up and Em had concerns and ran a few tests. The blood samples indicate an increased level of troponin, which would back her diagnosis. It's indicative of a heart attack." He sighed. "She's sending you the files now."

Imagining the terror Jeanette Turner went through the moments before her death, Jenna nodded slowly. "I'll go straight to the DA with our evidence and get an arrest warrant for Turner. We'll officially charge him and then I guess I'd better call Sam Cross." She looked at Kane. "I can't see him getting Turner off with the evidence we have against him. The DNA is the clincher."

"I'll drop you at the office and go and speak to the DA." Kane led the way to his truck. "Unless you want me to speak to Sam Cross?"

Jenna flung open the door to the Beast. "No, I don't want him to think I'm afraid of him." She patted Duke before buckling up. "He is a damn fine lawyer, which makes us more thorough, so although he's a thorn in my side, it can't be a bad thing."

"Uh-huh." Kane gave Wolfe a wave and headed back to town. "I still figure he's an arrogant ass."

An hour later, after Samuel J Cross had breezed into her office like a tornado, she waited with Kane and Jo outside interview room one. After discussing with Jo the possibility that Turner's attitude toward women might lead to his downfall in an interview, Kane elected to remain outside. The discussion between client and lawyer had concluded and Jenna led Jo into the room. Jenna turned on the recording devices and took a seat. After introducing themselves to record who was present at the interview, Jenna took the lead. "Dr. Turner, you have been read your rights. I would like to take you back to last night. Where were you between the hours of eight and ten?"

"At home, I had a session with one of my patients." Turner leaned back in his seat with his small smug smile ever present. "It is a particularly difficult case and I needed more time, so I conducted the sessions at home."

Jenna raised an eyebrow. "Without the consent of his parents?"

"My dear, you should really understand the way of things." Turner rolled his eyes. "The parents of all the students sign a waiver that allows any student counseling if required. It's something Black Rock Falls High School offers without charge."

Although the receptionist at the school had said this was unusual, if she needed to use the evidence in court, she would follow up with the school to find out if they did actually pay for counseling outside of school hours and how frequently. Deep down, she sensed he was lying. "Okay." Jenna pushed a photograph of Laurie's 1950 red pickup across the table. "This is Laurie's vehicle, or your pickup now, I believe?"

"Yes, it looks the same." Turner frowned. "Why?"

"It's a very distinctive vehicle and after checking the MVD files we found it is the only one of its kind in these parts. Can you account for it being parked across the road to Jeanette's apartment on the night she died?"

"What proof do you have it was Dr. Turner's pickup? The town is teaming with tourists from all over." Sam Cross tipped back his Stetson. The untidy cowboy lawyer complete with ponytail was astute. "Do you have a photograph, CCTV footage, a license plate number, perhaps, or only the dubious account of someone who'd been out for a good time at the festival?"

Jenna met his gaze without hesitation. "The witness wasn't intoxicated and we have a signed statement."

"It's not worth the paper it's written on." Cross smiled at her. "Do go on."

Turning her attention back to Turner, Jenna kept her voice steady under Cross's hawk-like stare. "After the discovery of the body, the medical examiner conducted a forensics sweep of the apartment and found your fingerprints." She picked up a statement and waved it in front of him. "When we interviewed you after Laurie's murder, you stated that you'd hadn't seen your wife for over six years and you didn't know where she lived. Is that correct?"

"Yes, at the time of the statement it was correct." Turner smiled at her. "Not after the statement. I went to see my wife to comfort her after our daughter's death."

Anger rising, Jenna glared at the self-righteous man before her. "You told me you hated her for leaving you."

"That's hearsay, Sheriff and you know it." Cross leaned back in his chair. "You're two strikes down, let's go for three, huh. I'd like to be home for dinner and the judge will only hold a bail hearing before five."

Sure she could hit the home run, she took out a copy of the DNA report and slid it across the table to Sam Cross. "During Jeanette Turner's autopsy, a mark consistent to a backhanded slap from a hand wearing a ring was detected. If you'll look at the images? After executing a search warrant, Dr. Turner's ring was swabbed for DNA evidence and tissue was detected. Subsequent DNA tests revealed a match for Jeanette Turner. Our evidence puts Dr. Turner at the crime scene at the time of the murder and the victim's DNA was found on his ring. We have a strong case."

"You don't." Turner gave her a smug smile. "I hit her all the time, that's why she left me. That blood could have been there for six years. I take off the ring when I wash my hands. You have nothing. I was with a patient and it will take a court order for you to discover his name. If you do, he will confirm my whereabouts."

"I think that's strike three." Sam Cross went to rise. "The judge is waiting for us for a bail hearing but you have nothing for the DA to take this to court."

"We will be presenting more evidence as it comes to hand for his trial—and he will go to trial." Jo's voice sounded strong and confident. "DNA degrades after time and Dr. Wolfe will be able to verify if the blood sample was fresh. The DA will be more than willing to make a deal with the young person you have tried to hoodwink into protecting you. I'm sure with my report and Dr. Wolfe's evidence, the DA will proceed."

"Honestly, Sheriff, you need to come up with something better than that nonsense." Turner spread his hands wide. "Only I know the names of the people who come to my sessions and the young man in question wouldn't speak to you anyway. I'm not giving you his name and you don't have enough evidence against me to obtain a court order to open my files."

"The FBI have ways of finding people, Mr. Cross, and trust me my team doesn't fail." Jo's lips flattened. "And as smart as you believe you are, Dr. Turner, you can't fool me. Trust me many have tried but in the end I'm always right."

Nodding in agreement, Jenna stood. "We will escort the prisoner to the hearing and I will be opposing bail."

"Good luck with that." Cross chuckled. "Dr. Turner is a pillar of the community and not a flight risk, Jenna. Why do you bother when you know you can't win against me?"

Jenna forced her lips into a smile. "I don't think so. I guess we'll be letting a court decide."

CHAPTER FIFTY-ONE

Kane led the way into Jenna's office and went straight to the coffee machine and set about making a fresh pot. When Jenna came in behind him, closed the door, and slammed her paperwork from the bail hearing on the desk, he turned to look at her. "I know you're angry about Dr. Turner getting bail but the DA hasn't dropped the charges. He still believes we have enough for him to proceed to trial."

"That's if we can produce enough new evidence." Jenna dropped into her chair and stared into space. "Do you think it's too late to ask Wolfe to re-check the DNA samples?" She chewed on her bottom lip. "Lately, he gets no time at all to spend with his girls."

Turning to lean against the counter, Kane shook his head. "Nah, they're used to him being at work. When the caseload is light, he spends tons of time with them. Call him." He straightened and headed for the door. "What we need to do is to find patient 124. We know he is a student at the high school and Dr. Turner referred to him as 'the young man'."

"Yeah, he tripped up there, didn't he?" Jenna held up a hand. "Wait up. Jo is convinced Turner is as guilty as hell but for now, we'll leave the evidence finding to Wolfe. We need to concentrate on the cheerleader murders and find out the name of patient 124. I'm convinced Dr. Turner has something he's holding over him and 124 is the key to unlock the mystery of the murders. I've kept Jo and Carter in the loop and Jo is going to discuss the case with Carter and see what they can do to help."

"I'll ask Rio if he can do some overtime tonight and assist us as well. We can't ask Jake." Kane turned to face her and placed both palms on the table. "I agree with your findings, patient 124 has to be involved in the cheerleader murders and is the person who helped carry Jeanette Turner down the stairs. I figure we start looking at guys on the football team. It's more than likely it's one of them, as someone close to the team was stealing their underwear. If someone had been hanging around the locker room, I figure Wyatt Cooper would have said something. Guys notice if someone is watching them, especially in a locker room."

"We only have lists of students who were at the festival." Jenna stood and went to the counter and pulled out cups. "They were all over town at different times. What data are you planning to use?"

Kane smiled. "It's not who was there, Jenna. It's who was missing." He walked to the door and pulled it open. "Zac is like a computer and he can do things much faster than either of us because his brain works differently. You call Wolfe and I'll talk to Zac."

"Get at it." Jenna pulled out her phone.

Kane headed to the deputies sitting in their booths, both reading the autopsy results. "Hey, I need a list of the members of the high school football team. I'd like to run a comparison against our files to see if anyone was missing from the group in town on Wednesday night." He looked at Rowley. "I don't expect you to work back, Sandy is your priority right now."

"She hates the food at the hospital." Rowley frowned. "I'm guessing they'll let her come home tomorrow. I'll grab her some takeout and spend some time with her and then come back if you need me. She's happy to watch TV and sleep right now."

"I don't know how long this will take. Spend time with Sandy and I'll call you if all hell breaks loose." Kane turned to Zac. The young deputy had his own responsibilities at home as well and they'd work around them if necessary. "Are the twins okay with the housekeeper?"

"They're sixteen and yeah, Mrs. Jacobs has a tongue like a whip." Zac chuckled. "She'll make sure they're okay. They understand my hours aren't predictable. I'll call and tell them I'll be late." He smiled at Kane. "You'll have horses to tend as well."

"I'll go and tend the horses." Carter walked up behind Kane and slapped him on the back.

Kane sucked in a breath as his wound screamed in protest but he didn't react. He turned to Carter and smiled. "I thought you'd come to help with the case." He bent to pat Zorro, Carter's dog.

"I've read over what you've got so far and I do my best figuring around horses." Carter moved a toothpick across his grin. "I'd ask to take your ride but Jenna's will do as well. I'm guessing you don't have a portable device to disable your alarm system and open the gate?"

"Nope." Kane shook his head. "It would be too easy to misplace. Jenna's in her office, ask her for the keys to her cruiser." He glanced at his watch. "Grab some takeout on the way back from Aunt Betty's. It's going to be a long night. Put it on the department's tab."

"Sure. Catch you later." Carter strolled into Jenna's office. He followed Jenna out a short time later and headed for the door, whistling with Zorro walking close to his side.

"Bring your things and work in my office." Jenna turned back and sat behind her desk. "Help yourself to coffee." She looked at Kane, pulled a jar of cookies from her bottom drawer, and pushed them toward him. "I called Wolfe and he is pretty sure the skin and blood he used to extract the DNA are fresh but he is going to prepare comparison tissue samples that will hold up in court." She sighed. "He'll call back in an hour or so. He also mentioned searching for Touch DNA."

Kane poured coffee, added the fixings, and sat down. "Yeah, I've been reading about that process, now Wolfe is able to extract DNA from fingerprints on anything, including skin. I figure he'll see if he can find any trace of Dr. Turner's DNA on his wife's face. He slapped her that's for sure."

"I'm aware of Touch DNA as well." Zac poured a cup of coffee and took it to the desk. He sat down. "Everyone's skin loses cells and the new process identifies them as trace DNA, so really we're all shedding skin like dandruff and don't know it." He smiled. "In principle a person could shake hands and then take a knife and murder someone. The new process might find traces of DNA from both parties on the handle. I wonder if it's going to make DNA evidence harder to prove?"

Kane shrugged. "I'm sure the forensics team will be able to distinguish between dead skin flakes and the oil found in fingerprints or fresh blood but I guess it could make a case for reasonable doubt."

"Ah, Sheriff." Rowley stepped into the office. "I've added the names of the football team to your files and the latest team images. I've also added the images of the cheerleading squad and names as well."

"Thanks." Jenna smiled at him. "Yes, they do seem to hang out together. Thanks, Jake. It's five-thirty. You'd better head home, or to the hospital. Give Sandy my best."

"Will do." Rowley backed out the door.

Kane sent information to the printer and it whirred and chugged, spewing out documents. "I've made hard copies of the lists. It will be easier as we don't have Bobby Kalo to run them through one of his programs." He stood and went to the printer. "Who is missing from the lists?" He handed them around.

"From what I recall, everyone returned to the gym after Laurie went missing." Jenna stared at the sheets of paper. "That was a specific question. We all asked if people recalled anyone missing."

She tapped the sheets into a pile and looked at Kane. "That was a question Rowley asked each kid at the high school as well. Not all of them could remember Wyatt Cooper being with them all the time because they broke into groups and some of them had their girlfriends with them."

"Hmm, so Wyatt Cooper is a maybe?" Zac was scanning the lists back and forth and lifted his head. "If you only concentrate on the nights when the murders of Becky Powell and Jeanette Turner took place, we can condense the missing people down to a few possibilities." He pointed to the images. "The guys moved around town mainly in twos or threes and some had girls with them. We know Wyatt Cooper and Becky Powell are missing at times during both nights and moved between groups of friends. If you look at the cheerleaders, we have two girls not mentioned after the initial sightings before eight on both nights, Verna Hughes and Marlene Moore."

Kane leaned over the lists. "If Verna Hughes was in town, she'd have been there with Cory, her brother. We have two sightings of the pair of them on both nights and they seem to hang out together. Verna is a very dominant personality and has issues with the other cheerleaders. She doesn't try to hide her dislike of people." He looked up at Jenna. "They live with their mother and Cory's father left not long after they had adopted Verna. It's not a stable environment, they could slip nicely into our suspects' profiles."

"I've found one moving around as well." Jenna tapped the photograph. "Dale Collins, the quarterback. Remember him? He runs the kiosk at the gym for his aunt on cheerleader practice days." She ran her finger down the lists of people the other players remembered being with on the night of the murders. "He was there and then not mentioned. He could've slipped away, murdered Becky, and then gone back to his friends." She combed fingers through her hair. "He was chatting to Marlene Moore and Laurie at the gym if you remember."

"He's the quarterback." Rio leaned back in his chair and grinned. "If he looked like a dog, the girls would still think he's a catch. The few I've known have shared the love around. He could have been with any number of girls at the festival. He'd be very popular."

"Yes, I do remember high school." Jenna sighed. "The vehicles seen at the crime scenes or involved are all different. If we could just find a single link, we'd catch patient 124."

Kane smiled. "By process of elimination, we've cut the list down to five possible but I still don't trust Stan Williams. He would have been floating around town. He has images in his apartment taken at night during the festival."

"So, a shortlist of six." Jenna sipped her coffee. "All hearsay." She stared at Kane. "Let's keep digging. I want to know everything about these people, family, parents' occupations, and what grandma cooked for dinner last Sunday. Get at it."

CHAPTER FIFTY-TWO

A cool evening breeze drifted through the window of his truck as he slid into a space opposite Aunt Betty's Café. His heart picked up and raced at the sight of Vicky Perez sitting in the window, staring at her phone. He'd offered her supper but she'd never eat her last meal and after his girl had finished with her, Vicky would be unrecognizable. He scrubbed both hands down his face and then slapped himself. Terror and excitement mingled, like an evil twin tearing him in all directions. A voice in his head kept nagging him that watching his girl kill was wrong, but he pushed it away and embraced the insatiable hunger that roared its approval.

Becoming his girl's puppet had happened slowly and now he was trapped in her web, like a black widow's willing mate waiting to be eaten. She both scared him yet fascinated him and he craved to be with her. The murders had dragged him closer to her and excitement thrummed through him whenever she was near, but did he trust her? Would he be her final victim? He'd seen her eyes when she killed, always hungry for more. An ice-cold shiver ran down his back and chill bumps crawled up his arms. He shook his head. "No, I don't trust you."

Worried by speaking aloud she might hear him even though she was miles away making the barn ready, he looked around and then pulled out his phone. He'd been late on purpose and deep down inside wished Vicky hadn't waited for him to arrive but his girl had set the scene and he had no choice but to act it out. He stared at the cheap phone, which only contained Vicky's number. After watching the cop shows on TV, he understood how easy it was for the sheriff to obtain phone records and he'd insisted on using a burner for this part of the plan. He'd called Vicky to make a date and they'd spoken often over the last twenty-four hours. He'd explained about his stalker and the need to keep their meeting secret. He smiled. It had been so easy to convince the girls to do his bidding. They were just like his girl said they'd be, willing to go with him just to humiliate him—but they never got the chance.

He buzzed up his window and made the call, watching Vicky through Aunt Betty's window. "Hey, Vicky, sorry for not calling sooner." He let out a breath on a sigh. "My mare decided to drop her foal and I wanted to make sure she was okay. I'm outside in the red pickup but I'm not dressed for a date, being in the barn and all."

"A foal? Can I see it?" Vicky stared out the window and then waved madly. *"I see you."*

His girl had told him about Vicky's infatuation with horses and the plan had worked. He looked at her eager face and smiled. "Sure. You can admire her while I go get cleaned up."

"It's a filly?" Vicky headed for the door. *"You'll be keeping her?"*

He chuckled. "Sure. I like fillies. Hang up now, before a truck mows you down crossing the road." He disconnected, pulled out the battery, opened his door, and slid the burner into a drain.

As the door opened, he noticed her staring at the plastic sheeting covering the seats. He grinned. "I'm guessing you're wondering about the plastic? The seats were steam cleaned and are a little damp. I didn't want you getting all messed up."

"You're so thoughtful." She climbed into the passenger seat making the plastic crackle and creak. "I can't get to the seatbelt." She frowned.

He shrugged. "It's only a mile or so and most of that on backroads, you'll be fine." He gave her his best hangdog expression. "I was trying to make it nice for you. Darn carwash was busy so I used my ma's steam cleaner."

"It's okay." Vicky squeezed his arm. "Maybe we can have supper in the barn? Cookies and milk will do me just fine but remember I must be back at Aunt Betty's Café by eight-thirty or my pa will go nuts."

He nodded. "Yeah sure."

Unable to believe his luck, he headed down Main and onto the highway before turning off Stanton to follow the backroads to his family's ranch. The barn hadn't been used for years and sat solid but abandoned some ways from the house. No one but his girl and him went there, it was their secret place. He turned on the radio and hummed to the tunes. Beside him Vicky stared at him as if mesmerized. They bumped along the dirt road, rounded the corner, and his headlights picked out the barn. He pulled up outside and taking a flashlight from his jacket pocket slid from behind the wheel. "Mind your step now." He aimed the flashlight at the door and then heart pounding with anticipation, rolled it back.

"It's awful dark in there." Vicky grabbed his arm and leaned in close.

"Here, you take the flashlight." He waved her through the door. "There's a lamp just inside, I'll switch it on. Head down the back past the hayloft, the mare is down there on the left."

"Okay." Vicky's voice trembled but she moved ahead of him.

Vicky hadn't walked more than a few yards into the barn before his girl sprang out of the dark, with a scarf wrapped around her face. It happened so fast that in the next second, his girl was on Vicky's back. They fell hard onto the dust-covered floor in a tangle of limbs. Moments later his girl had a cloth pressed over the stunned girl's face. The flashlight spilled from Vicky's hands and a beam shone over them, sending huge shadows across the barn wall. A chemical smell filled the air and he covered his face and backed away. The couple rolled on the floor grunting. Vicky was fighting back but as soon as she weakened, his girl knotted the cloth around her face. It seemed to take forever before Vicky finally succumbed and fell silent.

He found the lantern inside the door and switched it on. Dust motes danced like golden rain in the pool of light. He stared at Vicky; her clothes were covered in dust and sticks of hay stuck in her hair. He dragged his gaze away and looked at his girl. "Is she out?"

"I think so." His girl pinched Vicky hard and when she didn't respond, she rifled through her pockets and came out with her phone. She stood and walked toward him. She popped open the phone, took out the battery and SIM, and dropped them into a bucket of water. "The chloroform will evaporate soon, stay outside, we have time before she wakes up."

He stared at Vicky, lying so still. "Too much will kill her."

"Not enough and she'll wake up too soon. I practiced on my dog. A few drops knocked him silly for a good five minutes." His girl removed the scarf, tied it around her waist, and leaned in close. "We'll have time to tie her up and drag her into the stall I've set up for our fun. This time I've stapled plastic sheeting all around the walls and over the ground." She gave him a satanic grin and retrieved a hunting knife from the bench. "Do you like this?"

Chill bumps crawled up his arms as he stared at the pristine knife. Flashes of his girl stabbing Laurie spun through his mind. This time there would be blood, lots of blood. He swallowed hard and tried to focus. Things were moving way too fast and he couldn't think straight. "It looks brand new."

"It could be." His girl waved it around. "I took it from a guy."

He blinked at her. "You did what? Are you crazy?"

"Nope, it was in a crowd at the festival, I just slipped it out of his belt. He'd been drinking too much to feel a thing. Neat, huh?" She turned around to look at Vicky and then pulled her T-shirt over her nose. "Help me drag her into the stall. I have everything ready." She gave him a slow grin. "Then we'll wait for her to wake up. I don't want her to miss a thing."

CHAPTER FIFTY-THREE

Jenna stood, cleared the takeout wrappers from her desk, and set up the coffee machine again. Kane and Rio had their heads bent over their laptops, and the printer was whirring and spitting out documents at an incredible rate. She heard the front door open and the sound of claws on tile and the next moment Duke came through the door, checked Kane was still where he'd left him, and then went into his basket, did his usual three turns, and flopped down. Footsteps came down the passageway and Carter came through the door with Zorro on his heels. Jenna waved a hand toward the desk. "Your laptop has been chiming, I figure you have a message."

"I hope so. I sent some information to Kalo in the hope he might find something of interest." Carter walked to his laptop and smiled. "Uh-huh."

Jenna dropped into her chair and looked at him. "What did he hunt down for us?"

"Interesting leads." Carter removed a toothpick from between his teeth and flicked it into the trash. "I had Kalo check the IRS database for missing information on two of the suspects. He discovered the current occupations of the fathers of Dale Collins and Cory Hughes. After the vague information we received from their ex-wives, I figured it might be relevant information. Mr. Collins is a car salesman and Mr. Hughes is a linesman."

"Did he work where Laurie Turner was found?" Kane looked up from his laptop.

"The very same place." Carter smiled. "How about that for a coincidence?"

"Yeah, but Al Watson was the only person working the day Laurie Turner was found." Rio leaned back in his chair. From what I know about Cory Hughes, his pa isn't living with them anymore. I don't believe it's relevant to the case."

"When we have zip, everything is relevant." Carter looked down his nose at him. "Think about it. If Cory or Verna visited their pa, he might have told them about where he'd been working and why. He could've mentioned all the old mines in the area and how isolated it is there." He tipped back his Stetson and narrowed his eyes. "How else would kids know about the mines? It's not a place they'd go for a picnic, is it?"

"I guess not." Rio stood, went to the printer, and sorted through the documents. "We seem to be avoiding Wyatt Cooper. Why is that?" He made neat piles and handed them around.

Jenna shrugged. "I'm not convinced it's him. Why place himself in the spotlight from the get-go by stuffing his shorts in Laurie's mouth? I figure we need to concentrate on the others."

"Okay." Rio ran his fingers over the documents. "These are the timelines of everyone involved based on the evidence we have to date."

"We could easily have used the split screen on our laptops." Carter stared at the paperwork with a bewildered expression.

"Sometimes old school works." Rio shrugged. "Our brains get used to the same format. Change it up and things start to pop out. Give it a try."

When Jenna's phone played Wolfe's ringtone, they all looked at her expectantly. She put her phone on speaker. "Hi, Shane, any news?"

"Yeah, the samples from the ring are fresh. I didn't have much to work with but there's no doubt, the skin sample trapped in the ring, came from the night of Mrs. Turner's murder. It seems Dr. Turner removes his ring

when he washes his hands. I found no traces of soap at all. The DNA itself hadn't broken down, that takes years so the decomposition rate of the skin sample was crucial. I've completed a comparison of the tissues found and those collected from her body. The rate of decomposition from the body and the sample taken from the ring is identical." Wolfe tapped away on his keyboard. *"I also found traces of Dr. Turner's DNA on his wife's cheek where he slapped her and on her neck around the fingerprints during the strangulation. It's conclusive evidence that Turner strangled his wife. I'll make it pretty and send it to the DA."* He cleared his throat. *"I'll send you a copy. Good work, guys, you got him."*

Jenna smiled and then her mind went to Laurie and Becky. "But unless we find patient 124, we can't tie him into the cheerleader murders. Their killer is still walking free."

"Turner is still going to try and wriggle out of murdering his wife." Kane looked at her. "There is a way a doctor can give up the name of his patients in a criminal case. It takes a court order and he has to inform the patient." He shrugged. "He'll have to go see him, won't he? Well, we have a Blackwater deputy watching his property. His vehicle hasn't left his home yet but when Shane's evidence is presented, I bet he'll make his move and then we'll find the name of patient 124."

"I've hunted down any chance of Turner being involved with the other murders but found nothing." Wolfe sighed. *"Jeanette Turner's murder was a copycat. Turner was sloppy, he left fingerprints and didn't try to disguise his presence on scene. In the other cases, the killers left little behind."*

"Have you had anything back from the Snapshot DNA Profiling System?" Kane stood, stretched out his tall frame and headed for the coffee pot.

"I should get something soon." Wolfe sounded pleased. *"The information could bust the case wide open."*

Jenna smiled. "I sure hope so. Call me as soon as you have something."

"I sure will." Wolfe disconnected.

Jenna's phone chimed again and she pulled a face. "Oh, great that's all we need, a 911 emergency." She accepted the call. "You've reached Sheriff Alton, what is your emergency?"

"This is Tony Perez. I'm concerned about my daughter, Vicky. I dropped her at Aunt Betty's Café to have supper with a friend. I told her I'd be by to collect her at eight-thirty. She's not there and she's not picking up her phone."

Jenna made swift notes and glanced up at the others. It was nine-thirty. "Did she mention going anywhere else?"

"No but I spoke to that photographer guy and he said she got a ride in a red pickup. He can't recall the time." Perez sucked in a long breath. *"Since Laurie's murder, we've been taking Vicky anywhere she needed to go and collecting her at a specified time. I set the rules, and she wasn't to go anywhere without telling us. She always answers her phone, it's never out of her hands. Something's happened to her."*

"This is Special Agent Carter FBI. Give me your daughter's phone number and I'll get someone to run it down." Carter picked up a pen and took down the details. He stood and went out into the hallway to call Bobby Kalo.

Jenna could hear the muffled conversation. "The photographer you spoke to, would that be Stan Williams?"

"Yeah, that's him. He hangs around the cheerleading squad taking their pictures all the time." Perez sucked in a deep breath. *"Look, Sheriff, my wife has called all Vicky's friends. Not one of them knows anyone apart from Laurie with a red pickup and yet Williams told me, she waved at the person and ran out to meet them. He didn't see who was inside the truck. I'm at a loss to know what to do. I've been waiting here in case she comes back. I didn't want to wait any longer before I called you. Not in Black Rock Falls with a killer on the loose."*

"You did the right thing. Could you hold the line, Mr. Perez? I need to speak with my deputies." She looked at Rio and Kane. "Run our suspects and family members through the MVD and let's see if anyone else owns a red pickup." She unmuted the phone. "Did Williams mention a make, or model?"

"Nope but he's still inside. I'll go ask him."

Jenna waited chewing on the end of her pen. The sound of computer keyboards tapping was the only sound in the room. Photographers being observant, it was likely Williams would recall the make at least. She sighed with relief when Mr. Perez came back on the line. "Yes, I'm here, Mr. Perez."

"He figures maybe a Dodge Ram."

When both Kane and Rio shook their heads, an overwhelming sense of failure swept over Jenna. "Okay, stay where you are, I'll get a search organized and send someone to your location to wait with you." She disconnected and called in old Deputy Walters, who lived close by, to head out to Aunt Betty's. She looked at the three men before her. "Rio, get a media release out, now for a missing girl, you know the drill."

"Sure." Rio stood and headed for his desk.

A phone rang and Carter took his phone from the desk. "It's Kalo." He stared at the whiteboard. "What have you got for me, Bobby?" He listened. "Uh-huh. Did you trace the number? Okay thanks." He disconnected. "The last call she received was from the same number as four previous calls in the last twenty-four hours or so. The number is from a burner and Vicky's phone is inoperative. I figure Vicky has been targeted as the next victim."

CHAPTER FIFTY-FOUR

Nauseous and giddy, Vicky forced her eyelids to open. She couldn't lift her head and something was stuffed inside her mouth. Her face hurt. Her cheek stung as if someone had slapped her repeatedly. The memory of being attacked flooded through her mind on a tidal wave of fear. She wanted to scream but remembered her father's words after Laurie was taken. He'd told her if she was ever kidnapped, to remain as calm as possible, that crazy people fed on fear. If she kept her head, there'd be a chance she'd stay alive long enough for someone to save her. It had been easy for him to say that, he wasn't tied up in a barn. Panic rose in a rush at the sensation of being tied hand and foot. She clenched her muscles but found no give against the thick black tape binding her. Against her hands, she recognized the slick feel of plastic. The dim half-light from a battery-operated lantern close by reflected in the sheets attached to the walls. Ice-cold fear wrapped around her. She'd seen enough horror movies to know they were holding her in a murder room. When the sound of people arguing in whispers drifted from outside her prison, she listened intently watching from beneath her lashes.

"I told you you'd given her too much." The muffled male voice was accompanied by footsteps as they came into the stall. "She's been here too long. We should have finished her by now. Why not just strangle her and we'll dump her somewhere in Stanton Forest?"

"After what she put me through?" A girl's voice she thought she recognized sounded angry. "I want her to pay. There's no way she's gonna sleep through her punishment. I'm going to make her feel every cut." She laughed as they walked into the stall. "See this? It's salt. I'm going to fill her cuts with it to make them unbearable." She chuckled again. "I found sulfuric acid on the shelf but that stuff stinks, so the salt will have to do." She wet her lips. "I'll let you cut her too. Did you bring a knife as well?"

"Yeah. My pa's hunting knife. He won't miss it. He never comes by the house no more." He pulled out the knife and waved it at her.

"Perfect." She stroked his cheek. "Now, try to wake her again. Slap her, she's got to come around soon. I didn't use that much chloroform."

"If I hit her any harder, I'll break her jaw." He sounded concerned. "I'll get a bucket of water and throw it over her."

"No!" The girl was obviously in charge. "Then the blood will run everywhere, we need to keep it clean in here. Slap her again. I'm going to get a bottle of water from my backpack and I want her awake by the time I get back." She flicked a zippo lighter. "I have something else to try if you can't wake her."

Heart threatening to burst with fear, Vicky remained slumped against the wall with her head on her chest. Footsteps came closer and someone wearing surgical gloves cupped her chin, and lifted it. Fighting the need to pull away, she forced her breathing in and out, in and out, slow, and even. Like when she was a kid and pretended to go to sleep. His touch was almost tender.

"Vicky, wake up now." He patted her cheek. "Please wake up, I don't want to hit you again."

He didn't want to hit her again? Did she have an ally against the raving lunatic planning to cut her? Pain sliced through her cheek and she toppled over, rolling onto the floor from an unexpected blow. Her head hit with a blinding crack and she couldn't muffle a moan. Dragged back into a sitting position, thick fingers forced her eyelid open and she stared into the face of her date but dropped her head the moment he released her. If the girl wanted her awake before she cut her, she'd play possum for as long as she could. Her pa would have discovered she was missing by now and someone would have seen her getting into his truck.

"Wake up." He shook her violently. "You're just making her mad. The longer you stay unconscious the madder she'll get and she'll take it out on you."

"Making nice with Vicky, huh?" The girl's voice was as sweet as molasses. "Now I'm jealous." She moved closer, making the plastic rustle with each step.

Her breath brushed Vicky's face and then a cold line flashed across her cheek. A rush of warmth oozed down her face and she could feel droplets hitting her bare arm. Had she cut her?

"Not so pretty now, is she?" The girl dragged back Vicky's head. "Is she?"

"I never said she was pretty." His voice was a little shaky. "I just wanted her awake so we could kill her and then make out before we dump her body." He gave a hesitant laugh. "It's only ever been you. You're my girl, the others mean nothing to me and never will."

"That isn't the plan." She kicked the bottom of Vicky's boots. "I want her awake when I cut her into pieces. I want to hear her beg for her life. She needs to know what it's like to be bullied. Now her little circle of friends are dead and when she's gone, I'll be the captain."

"You'll be the captain now anyway." His voice dropped to almost a whine. "Let's get this done before we're missed. It's getting late."

"My folks think I'm in my room and your ma thinks you're doing your chores so we have all the time I need." She giggled. "She'll wake up soon." She moved close to Vicky's ear. "Wake up so I can kill you."

Dread slammed into Vicky. Time was running out fast and no one knew she'd left the safety of Aunt Betty's Café with him. Her ally was a gutless coward. He'd insisted on secrecy and now she knew why. They'd tied her so tight, she couldn't fight back, and if they discovered she was awake they'd torture her slowly. To survive she had to outsmart them. These were the people who'd killed her friends and expected her to scream and fight but she wouldn't give them the satisfaction. Anger rose and shattered in terror. Vicky bit down hard on the cloth in her mouth in an effort to appear unconscious. She couldn't keep up the pretense forever. Her face throbbed and beneath her eyelashes she could see blood dripping onto her arm. An uncontrollable tremble rippled through her. Had they seen it? She braced herself waiting for the inevitable. *I'm going to die in a world of pain.*

CHAPTER FIFTY-FIVE

Remaining calm when the world was going to hell was part of Jenna's training and fate had given her at least two people with the same attitude. Running around in circles wouldn't help Vicky Perez. "We have four main male suspects, call them. I want to know if they're home. I'll take Wyatt Cooper, Kane, call Stan Williams, Carter, you have Dale Collins, Rio, Cory Hughes. Their home and cellphone numbers are in the files. I want to know where they are and who they're with."

Jenna called Wyatt Cooper and found him at home. After speaking to both his parents, she removed him from their list. Her deputies and Carter discovered two of the four unobtainable, their phones turned off and not at home. "So, we have Cory Hughes and Dale Collins missing. Do we know what they drive?" She stared at the evidence on the whiteboard.

"Hughes had a white pickup at the high school but that might be supplied, he could have another vehicle." Kane tapped on his computer. "Nothing else belongs to him."

"That doesn't mean a thing." Carter rubbed the back of his neck. "Kids often borrow rides. He could be driving anyone's vehicle." He waved at the whiteboard. "What about Dr. Turner, he's out on bail?"

Jenna met his gaze. "I still have the Blackwater deputies patrolling in town and keeping an eye on his home. I'll call one and ask them to go and check on him." She made the call. "He is close by. I'll hold until he has eyes on him."

She waited, for what seemed like ages before the deputy came back on the line. She nodded. "Okay, thanks. Watch him for a bit and then continue on patrol. It won't hurt for him to know we're tracking his movements." She disconnected.

"Dr. Turner is at home." Jenna stared at the men. "We have a girl out there in danger. We have to find her. Come on, Dave, where would they take a girl to murder her?"

"I'd imagine somewhere close to home. At sixteen they wouldn't risk taking her into the forest." Kane's brow furrowed in concentration. "I'll search Google Earth in their local area for abandoned ranches or businesses."

"Okay." Jenna turned to Rio. "Head down to Aunt Betty's and take a look at their CCTV feed, see if you can get a time Vicky left and maybe a look at the vehicle." She turned to Carter. "Can you check the feed on the CCTV cameras on Main? You may hit paydirt."

With a nod of their heads both men took off in a hurry. Jenna turned to stare at the board when Wolfe's ringtone filled the office. She snatched up the phone and put it on speaker. "I hope you have something for me, Shane, we have just been notified of another missing girl, Vicky Perez."

"Oh, Jesus." Wolfe paused a beat. *"I hope this will help. The Snapshot DNA Profiler came through. This is amazing technology. We have an image of a female. I'm sending it through to your phone now. Do you have anything to compare it to? Dark hair and eyes, Caucasian?"*

Astonished, Jenna stared at the image on her phone. "She looks familiar. Kane has a file with recent images of the cheerleaders. I'll get straight on it. Thanks, Shane."

"I'm at the office until late if you need backup. Call me if you get anything." He disconnected.

"I have something on the possible hideouts." Kane looked up from his laptop. "Both Hughes and Collins have outbuildings on their ranches. Hughes has what looks like an old run-down building about half a mile from the house. Collins has a similar place. Both could be old barns from when they ran stock." He tapped away again. "I have the files up for the cheerleaders, show me the image."

Jenna sat beside him as they scanned the photographs. The image Wolfe had sent was like an identikit picture, not a photograph, and she stared at all the faces. So many girls had dark hair and eyes. "What about her, Verna Hughes?"

"Yeah, it's a close enough match for us to chase down Hughes." Kane scrolled through the images. "And her. I've spoken to her. She was at the kiosk talking to Dale Collins." He stared at the whiteboard. "Marlene Moore."

Astonished two similar girls had links to two suspects, she picked up her phone and called Rio. "Get back here, we have a lead." She headed down the hallway and burst into the communications room. "Ty, we have two possible couples. We'll have to split up. Kane figures he has the most probable locations."

"Let me see." Carter ran back to her office and stared at Kane's results. "Yeah, it's secluded enough not to be heard and close enough to home the kids wouldn't be missed." He turned to look at her. "Don't call the girls. You don't want to alert them we're coming, Jenna. They might do something stupid. Give me the coordinates."

"Yeah, I agree." Kane pushed to his feet. "If I'm right and the girl is the dominant personality here, anything might happen."

Jenna nodded in agreement. "Okay, we go in silent. Wear your liquid Kevlar vests, I don't want anyone getting the jump on us."

"The day a kid gets the jump on me is the day I retire." Carter snorted. "But I'll wear the vest."

"Vicky left Aunt Betty's at eight." Rio bounded into the room. "I couldn't ID the red truck but when I called in the media report, I put out a BOLO on the vehicle as well as the girl."

Jenna nodded. "Good work. If she's been gone that long, we need to move on this now."

"What have you found?" Rio raised his eyebrows in question.

Jenna brought him up to date. "Look, I don't want these kids to die in a hail of bullets. I doubt they'll be armed and I'd like to know what's behind this killing spree."

"I hear you're a sharpshooter." Kane looked at Rio. "How good?"

"Damn good." Rio's face was deadly serious. "I don't kill unless my partner or I are in mortal danger."

"Good to hear.' Kane nodded.

"Just as a sidenote." Carter eyeballed Kane. "I can shoot a dime out of the sky. Now we've stated our creds, are we moving before this kid gets murdered or what?" He turned to Jenna. "I'll take the Hughes' ranch, Rio's SUV won't be noticed so easy."

Feeling the tension building up, Jenna took a deep breath. "Okay move out." She grabbed her phone and called Deputy Walters at Aunt Betty's to update him on her progress and then they headed out the door to Kane's truck.

As Rio's SUV weaved through the crowded festival traffic and then sped into the distance, Jenna slipped into her Kevlar vest and then strapped Duke into his harness. The bloodhound would be an asset and alert them if anyone was hiding close by. Her heart raced as she climbed into the seat and buckled up. She glanced at Kane as he pulled on his gear wearing a combat face expression. "I hope we find her."

"I figure one of us will." Kane turned the Beast onto Main and, lights flashing, maneuvered through the traffic. "Although logical thinking doesn't usually apply to psychopathic behavior but this time it's underdeveloped. If this is one of the cheerleaders, she'd just be getting started."

Jenna looked at him. "Should I run it past Jo for her opinion?"

"We don't have time." Kane turned onto Stanton Road and accelerated. "This killer is an unknown quantity, unpredictable to the max. She believes she can control people, so will try, and play the injured party. Don't let her under your guard. Going on the kills to date, especially the repeated post-mortem stabbing of Laurie Turner, we need to be on our guard. This girl will stop at nothing and she doesn't care who she hurts."

The truck hurtled into the darkness, the flashing red and blue lights making the forest look surreal. A sea of red and blue glanced over the pines as they sped past, making the dark depths of the forest flicker like a silent movie. Jenna didn't have to explain that time was against them, Kane was pushing the Beast to the limit of safety at high speed. She could never get used to the way he pointed his truck at a gap between vehicles and seemed to make it through. With her heart in her mouth, she gripped the seat as they hit the straightaway and Kane pulled out. The Beast roared its approval as if it had at last been freed from its cage. They flew down the wrong side of the highway, passing vehicles as if they were standing still, and then tucked back into the lane as they approached a sweeping bend just as an eighteen-wheeler barreled by.

When Jenna heard the voice on the GPS, she leaned forward and turned off the flashers. "About five hundred yards on the right, then take a sharp left into the road to the ranch."

"Copy that." Kane slowed the Beast. "There's an old building some ways from the house. Look out for a track on the left, from the satellite image it looks overgrown. I'll turn off the headlights and we'll be able to see our way with the parking lights. If there is someone here, we don't want to alert them."

They bounced along the tree-lined dirt road and Jenna searched for gaps that might lead to a track to the barn. A space in the trees came up and she made out a dirt road leading through the trees. "Stop. I think I can see the turnoff; we've gone past."

"Okay." Kane reversed and turned onto a trail.

Jenna leaned forward and peered ahead. "It's a well-used path, maybe this isn't the place."

"It looks about right. The barn should be about a hundred yards from the main track. We have to check this out and fast. That girl's life could be on the line." Kane pulled into the trees. "We can walk from here." He glanced out the window. "We won't need to use a Maglite; it's a full moon and I can see like a cat."

Jenna's stomach flip-flopped. Going into an unknown situation had sent her adrenalin into overdrive. She gave him a nod. "Let's go. You first. I'm not planning on walking into any spider webs."

"Sure, I just love spiders." Kane grimaced. "Stick to the path and you'll be fine."

Ahead of her Kane moved in silence, Duke heading out before him on his leash, and she followed, keeping close to the path. With trees on both sides of the track, their boughs reached out to touch each other across the divide. Moonlight speared through the branches sending zebra shadows across the ground. She moved in closer to the trees and a web caught her hair. She batted it away and then heard a muffled scream. In front of her Duke had become a rigid statue, hackles raised. Unnerved, Jenna took a step forward and tugged on Kane's shirt. She dropped her voice to a whisper. "What was that?"

CHAPTER FIFTY-SIX

The Zippo lighter clicked again and as the flame licked her bare toes, Vicky screamed, her cries muffled behind the rag inside her mouth. Unbearable pain exploded in her foot and seemed to grow more intense by the second.

"She's good and awake now." The Zippo lifted and the flame danced in the deranged eyes of Marlene Moore. "Get behind her." She discarded the lighter and lifted a knife, waving it around so it caught the glow from the lantern. "See this?" She moved closer. "Maybe I'll cut out your eyes, just one for a start. I wouldn't want you to miss any of the fun."

Terror consumed Vicky. Helpless, tied up, and at the mercy of two lunatics hell bent on killing her slowly, she tossed her head from side to side and squirmed on the plastic. Tears ran down her cheeks and she fought to breathe as her running nose threatened to block her airways. What had she ever done to Marlene to make her hate her so much?

"I heard something." Dale Collins' hands trembled as he grabbed Vicky's shoulders. "Listen."

"I don't hear anything but her whimpering." Marlene gave a satisfied smile. "But I wanna hear her make those funny noises. Shame about the gag, huh, Vicky? No one can hear you but me." She waved a hunting knife and a small kitchen knife back and forth in front of her eyes. "Which one should I use first?"

Vicky strained her ears. She'd heard something too. A dog barking but some ways away. It came again, sharp and urgent, closer this time, but Marlene had heard it too and she stood to peer around the stall door.

"It's a dog." Marlene whipped her head around to Dale. "Your dog died. Know anyone with a dog around these parts who'd be snooping on your ranch?"

"Nope." Dale's voice sounded shaky. "When the sheriff spoke to me, they had a hunting dog with them. If they've found us, what are we going to do?"

"Douse that light for a start. I'll go into the hayloft. If anyone comes in, I'll have the jump on them. They won't see me coming." Marlene ran out the door. "If it's the sheriff, she won't be expecting kids to fight back."

"Maybe we should just let her go and hightail it back to your place." Dale's voice was a husky whisper. "It's her word against ours. We can take the backroads. I'll drop you and dump the truck."

"Not a chance." Marlene sounded confident. "It might just be a dog, chasing critters in the trees. We'll wait and see."

The old steps to the hayloft groaned and Vicky could hear footsteps above her and to the right. The bark came in the distance and she rolled to one side to look up at Dale. His face, lit by a shaft of moonlight through a skylight on the roof, was set in a gray mask, lips turned down at the corners. She looked at him willing him to untie her and let her go.

"If I let you go, will you keep your mouth shut?" Dale's warm breath tickled her ear.

Jumping at the chance to get away, Vicky nodded and then the moonlight glinted over the knife in his hand as he bent over her. She held her breath. Voices loud and official broke the silence followed by footfalls and a second later, flashlight beams dazzled her.

"Sheriff's department. Drop the knife. Drop the damn knife now." A tall man emerged from the darkness.

The knife dropped onto the plastic and Dale was thrown face first against the wall and cuffed to a rail. "Who else is here?" The man had his back to Vicky. "Is Marlene Moore with you?"

Dale said nothing and just gave a shake of his head.

"Clear the area, I'll check Vicky." A woman bent and switched on the lantern on the floor and then turned to her. "It's okay, no one is going to hurt you now." She kneeled beside her.

Vicky recognized Sheriff Alton and Deputy Kane and panic gripped her. She screamed against the rag and tried to indicate to the loft with her eyes.

"Hey calm down, it's going to be okay." Sheriff Alton pulled at the tape covering Vicky's mouth. "It's over. Sit still, I'll have to cut you free."

Vicky shook her head and tried to yell the word "no" and tipped her head toward the loft. Too late, terror hit her like a tsunami. Deputy Kane was walking straight into Marlene's trap.

CHAPTER FIFTY-SEVEN

Marlene smiled to herself, how stupidly self-confident the deputy had walked through the barn. Like most men, he'd allowed a woman to make decisions for him. How easy it was to manipulate men and she'd become an expert. Yeah, she'd started with Dale but she had ambitions, to use men to get everything she wanted in life. She crouched in the shadows waiting for the deputy to search the barn, he'd turn soon and walk back, maybe head for the steps and then she'd launch herself onto him. He was big, a nice wide target and she'd aim for his neck. No one could live with a hunting knife plunged into their throat. She looked at the two sharp blades. If she missed with one, she'd strike with the other. He'd never expect her to be carrying two knives and once he was down, she'd deal with the sheriff. Watching her bleed would be exquisite.

Excitement shivered through her as she breathed slowly through her nose. This was what she lived for— the thrill of the kill. She took a look at the sheriff, still busy trying to calm Vicky who seemed to have gone crazy and was jumping around like an idiot. What a shame, she hadn't had time to watch her die. Her heart raced as the deputy turned back, checking the stalls, and moving the bales of hay to peer behind. In just a few more steps he would be in just the right position. Heart racing, she gathered her legs under her, gripped the knives, and launched from the hayloft with a triumphant scream.

It was like hitting a brick wall as she plunged the knife deep into his chest. She heard his intake of breath but instead of staggering away, his arms came around her, as if to break her fall. She lashed out, burying the second knife deep under his arm and then caught the expression on his face and the sight frightened her. His eyes were cold like those of a killer— like her own. He hadn't reacted to her attack. It was like fighting a robot, and she couldn't even slow him down. Suddenly terrified of him, she kicked out but he had her fast in his huge hands. "Get away from me."

"Next time you attack someone, don't give them a warning." He glared down at her. "Stupid little girl, pulling a stunt like that, I could have killed you."

Tossed into the stall, Marlene scrambled to her feet and backed away as Deputy Kane, with a knife protruding from his chest, stepped in and grabbed her by the arms. Satisfaction surged through her at the spray of crimson spilling down his arm. She grinned at him. "You lose, Deputy. You're bleeding."

"You really need to try harder, if you're planning to take down a guy my size." The deputy glared at her. "You're lucky I noticed you were a little girl. I don't take too kindly to people attacking me."

Marlene laughed at his stern expression. Oh, she'd cut him bad and he couldn't handle being beaten by a kid. She lifted her chin and glared right back. "Loser. I won't go to jail for jumping out at you, I'm just a kid protecting myself. Maybe they'll give me a fine is all. You were trespassing on private property."

"You'll go for murder one and likely never see the light of day again. You see, in this state you'll be prosecuted as an adult. Including an assault on a police officer with a deadly weapon." He spun her around and turned to the sheriff. "She's all yours, Jenna."

CHAPTER FIFTY-EIGHT

Shocked at the bloody sight before her, Jenna grabbed Marlene as Kane slid down the wall and slumped onto the floor. "Dave, look at me."

"I'm okay, cuff the prisoner." Blood poured down Kane's side and pooled in the straw.

Jenna gaped at him. "You *do* know you have a knife sticking out of your chest?"

"That obvious, is it? Thank God for liquid Kevlar vests." Kane grunted and pushed into a sitting position and then rested his back against the wooden panels inside the stall. He touched his side and, after examining the blood dripping from his fingers, looked at her. "It's nothing."

Terrified at seeing the color drain from Kane's face, but with a prisoner to secure, Jenna had no choice but to cuff Marlene, drag her outside the stall, and attach her to the same hitching post as Dale Collins. Immediately the prisoners started arguing.

Jenna glared at them. "Shut up, the pair of you, or I'll gaffer tape your mouths." She went back to Kane. "I'll call the paramedics."

"No, help Vicky, she's our first priority." Kane's voice came out in a gasp.

Against her better judgment, Jenna bit down hard on her bottom lip. Kane needed medical attention but their duty of care to a victim was a priority. She dropped on her knees beside Vicky. "Okay, let's get you untied. The cut on your face isn't too deep." She had the gag out of her mouth in no time but the tape was stuck hard in her hair. "That will have to wait." She cut the tape on her hands and feet. "Better?"

"Th-thanks. You g-got here just in time." Tears streamed down Vicky's cheeks as she lifted a trembling hand and pointed to Kane. "I'll be okay but he doesn't look so good."

Horrified by the blood that had pooled around Kane in the last few seconds, Jenna scrambled over to him. "You're not okay, Dave." She reached for her phone. "I'll call the paramedics."

"Not yet." Kane's voice came out on a whisper.

Heart thumping, Jenna swallowed hard, wishing she had more experience in field medicine. "Let me take a look at you."

"Don't touch the knife." Kane winced and his face turned sheet-white. "The vest took most of it but I'm light-headed. She had two knives and I figure she caught me in the gap in the vest. Left side under my arm." He took a labored breath. "Before you call the paramedics, you'll need to stop the bleeding. Find something to press against the wound and use Duke's leash to secure it tight. Then call the paramedics."

"Okay." Without, a second thought, Jenna stripped off her jacket, Kevlar vest, and T-shirt. Balling up her T-shirt, she packed it hard against the small puncture wound pouring blood. "Hold your elbow in to keep the pressure for a minute."

They'd left Duke at the barn door. "Duke, come here boy."

When the dog bounded in, Jenna grabbed his leash, looped it around Kane and pulled it tight against her T-shirt. The stream of blood eased. She sighed with relief. "That will hold it."

Duke let out a long whine, dropped to his stomach, crawled up beside Kane, and licked his hand. Jenna swallowed hard. The dog had sensed something was terribly wrong. The light caught the sheen of sweat on Kane's brow and her stomach dropped. She'd seen him badly hurt but never like this before. Grabbing her phone, she called the paramedics and discovered they were attending a multiple vehicle pileup on the highway to Blackwater. Panic gripped her, dammit, Kane needed help now. She called Carter. "We have Vicky but Kane's down. We need a medic now and the paramedics are delayed. Can you go and grab Wolfe, he's at work? Where are you?"

"Heading back to the office. We found the suspects at home. How bad is he?"

Jenna flicked a look at Kane. "Very."

"Copy that." Carter sounded concerned. *"The chopper is on the ME's roof and ready to go. I'll get Wolfe and send Rio by road. We'll need a light out there. Headlights and blinkers would do. Call Wolfe and tell him I'm on my way."* He disconnected.

Jenna made the call to Wolfe and he wanted details. "He has a stab wound to upper left of his chest. The knife is in situ. Wound to left side upper ribs, bleeding heavily. I have pressure on it."

"On my way. Don't move him and keep him awake." Wolfe disconnected.

Worry consumed her. She'd been with Kane when he'd suffered far worse injuries than this but he looked so pale. His labored, rapid breathing was becoming shallower by the minute but she tried to act as if everything was fine. "Carter is bringing Wolfe in the chopper and Zac can take the prisoners down and book them." She looked at Kane's glazed expression. "You're going to be okay. I'll go and get the truck. Carter will need the lights to find us."

"Later." Kane's fingers barely moved as he tried to pat the floor beside him. "Sit with me. There's something I need to say to you."

Anxious, Jenna dropped to her knees and took his hand. It was cold and damp. "I'm here, what is it?"

"I—" Kane's head dropped to his chest and his eyes rolled up in his head.

Oh, Jesus. Fear gripped her. "Dave, Dave come on now." She patted his face and then felt for his pulse, it was rapid and missing beats. "Dave, wake up."

She couldn't rouse him and he was slipping deeper into unconsciousness. As she searched his pockets for the keys to the truck, she could hardly hear him breathing. Not wanting to leave him, she turned to Vicky. "Look after him. Keep trying to wake him. I won't be long. We left our truck near the road."

"I'll watch over him but you don't need to go for your truck." Vicky looked at her. "Dale's pickup is just outside and he'll have the keys in his pocket."

Jenna pushed the keys to the Beast inside her jeans and ran to Collins. "Where are your keys?"

"Jacket pocket." Collins looked at her forlorn. "I didn't mean for the deputy to get hurt."

"Best you keep your mouth shut." Jenna searched his pockets and found the keys. She snatched up her jacket and a flashlight and ran outside. It didn't take long to start the engine and turn on the headlights and hazard flashers. She dropped her flashlight on the seat and pulled on her jacket. The light spilled over a few bottles of water and she collected them, sighing with relief. Dave would need water if she could wake him. Glancing at the sky, she pushed back the tears threatening to spill and jumped out the pickup. Rushing back in the stall, she handed Vicky a bottle of water and then checked Kane, but there was no change. Her T-shirt was soaked with blood and she had no option but to tighten the leash a little more. When finished, she turned to Vicky. "How did Dale get you to come here with him?"

"He asked me to have supper with him at Aunt Betty's Café and then called and lied about having a new foal." Vicky stared daggers at Collins. "He thinks he's all that but he smells like he hasn't bathed in a year."

"You smell like a pig." Marlene laughed.

"I told you to zip it." Reluctantly Jenna turned to Vicky. "Keep talking to Deputy Kane, his name is Dave. We need him awake."

"Okay." Vicky moved closer and started to tap Kane's face. "Dave. Can you hear me?"

Jenna straightened. The chopper was on its way and she could do nothing more for Kane but wanted to throw the book at these kids. They wouldn't get away with their crimes, not on her watch. She went to her prisoners and read them their rights. "As you're over sixteen you can waive your rights and answer our questions without having your parents present. You'll be taken back to the sheriff's department and held in the cells. We'll inform your parents but you won't be released and will go before a judge in the morning and likely be taken to a youth correctional facility."

"No parents." Collins looked alarmed. "I don't want my ma coming down and screaming at me and my pa won't be in the same room as her. I'll waive my rights."

"I will too." Marlene laughed. "You don't scare me."

Slightly unnerved by witnessing the bravado of an obvious psychopath in Marlene, Jenna nodded and pulled out her phone. She hit the video and held it up in one hand with her flashlight in the other. "Okay, you understand your rights and wish to waive them, is that correct?"

"Yeah." Collins blinked at the light. "I didn't do anything wrong."

"You've got no evidence we did anything." Marlene sneered at her.

"You have no idea how much trouble you're in, have you?" Exhausted, Jenna leaned against the wall but kept the camera rolling. "We have your DNA at both murders, and now we have both of you for kidnapping Vicky. In fact, I'll compile a list of charges so long to give to the DA, like my deputy said, you won't see daylight until you're an old lady." She turned to Collins. It was a bluff but she'd try it while he was off guard. "Something else, we know you've been talking to Dr. Turner. You're patient 124, right?"

"He said he wouldn't tell anyone." Collins' eyes narrowed. "He said if I helped him move his wife's body, he'd give me alibis."

"You told Dr. Turner?" Marlene pulled on the zip-tie binding her to the hitching post. "She's lying."

"Then how would I know his secret number?" Jenna wet her dry lips. She had him. "Dr. Turner wrote appointments in his diary to cover both of you but I figured he'd fold and let you take the blame for his wife's death." She shrugged. "He'll say you threatened him or something."

"I only visited him once at the school." Collins appeared shocked. "I never went to his home. He called me to go over and help him at his wife's apartment. I wore gloves and a balaclava but I dropped the body going down the stairs. She was heavier than she looked, we had to drag her into the alleyway."

"Okay." Jenna paused the video to check Kane again. The bleeding had stopped but there was no change. He was in trouble and she could do nothing to help him. She went back to her prisoners.

"We know you killed Laurie, Marlene." Jenna lifted her chin. "That was an ingenious plan to disable her pickup and then make her drop her phone."

"Yeah." Marlene seemed oblivious to the phone camera trained on her and preened at the compliment. "Once everyone was in the gym, Dale messed up her precious pickup and in the parking lot, I pushed her real hard and stamped on her phone." She grinned. "You should have seen her face."

"You shouldn't have told her." Collins looked horrified. "Now I'll be blamed for Laurie's murder and you killed her, not me."

Jenna glared at them. "Then you killed Becky Powell. We know you were involved, Dale." She held the phone high and kept filming.

She wanted all the evidence she could get. "Why Deputy Rowley's house?"

"We didn't know it was his house." Collins looked incredulous. "It was empty, is all. When Marlene saw someone leave the key over the porch, she checked it out and took one of the backdoor keys."

Jenna looked from one to the other. "So, are you claiming you didn't attack Mrs. Rowley as well?"

"I didn't touch anyone." Collins stared at Marlene. "What did you do?"

"Like I'm going to admit to hurting a deputy's wife." Marlene rolled her eyes.

Jenna swallowed hard. Her mind was on Kane and not this pair of psychopaths. She wanted to be holding his hand and making sure he was okay but she had to keep them talking. She needed the evidence. "Why leave Becky's body there? You dumped Laurie's out at the mines."

"We saw the deputy's SUV stopping outside and ran away." Collins shrugged. "We didn't have time to move her body." His brow furrowed. "I'm not going down for Laurie's murder."

Jenna turned off the video and took the light out of his eyes. "Just tell the truth and the courts will sort out who is to blame but don't allow Dr. Turner to walk free—and he will if you don't tell us everything you know about him."

"That's not going to happen—not now." Collins stared in the direction of Kane. "Why didn't your deputy stop Marlene from stabbing him? He just caught her in his arms. He could have side stepped and she'd have hit the floor." He shook his head. "Look at the size of him, he could've taken her head off with one blow."

Overwhelmed with worry about Dave, Jenna shook her head. "Deputy Kane doesn't hit women."

"Then he's a fool." Marlene laughed. "I sure taught him a lesson. He'll learn, men always do. Women rule. Isn't that right, Sheriff?"

Anger simmered and Jenna eyeballed her. "No, it isn't right. He could have broken your neck like a twig but he treated you with respect. Your attitude toward men disgusts me."

The whoop, whoop, sound of the chopper blades filled the night and Jenna ran outside with her flashlight and waved it back and forth. She jumped into the pickup and reversed to light up the wide area of open land adjacent to the barn and then got out. There would be room enough for the chopper to land. Dry grass and dirt hit the windshield as the chopper lowered to the ground and the moment it touched down, Wolfe jumped out with Emily at his side. Carter remained at the controls, the blades whipping up clouds of dirt. A gurney dropped onto the grass and Wolfe pulled it up to its full height, dumped a bag on it, and pushed it toward Jenna at speed.

Jenna led the way inside, unable to talk with the noise of the chopper. She ran into the stall. "He's been out for about ten or more minutes. I can't wake him."

"He's bleeding out." Wolfe bent over Kane and looked up at Jenna and Emily. "Grab his thighs." Wolfe eased behind Kane and with effort lifted him onto the gurney. "Em, get the plasma." He placed a tourniquet around Kane's arm. "Give me a vein, come on, Dave. Don't you dare die on me."

Legs weak, Jenna held her breath as Wolfe inserted the needle and held the plasma bag up high. She stood helpless, her body numb as he checked him and then turned to her. She looked at his worried expression and a part of her died inside. "It's bad, isn't it?"

"Yeah and I can't risk doing anything more here. Time is of the essence and I have a surgeon waiting for him at the hospital. Rio and Rowley are on their way." Wolfe squeezed her arm. "I'll take good care of him, Jenna, and I won't leave his side. He's been through worse and he's in great shape but I won't lie to you, he might not make it to the hospital."

Overcome by grief, Jenna stared at Kane's sheet-white face. The last time Kane was injured Wolfe flew him to a military hospital. "You're not taking him to Walter Reed, are you?"

"No, there's not enough time." Wolfe motioned to Emily. "Bring the girl." Without another word, they headed back to the chopper.

Desperately wanting to be with Kane, Jenna stared after them in dismay. Trembling, she watched the chopper lift off the ground and disappear above the trees. Beside her, Duke let out a howl to wake the dead but she had no words to comfort him. She looked down at Kane's blood drying on her hands. The sticky slicks appeared black in the moonlight. Unable to stop the tears overflowing, she sunk to her knees and stared at the heavens. It was as if someone had ripped out her heart. "Don't you dare take that good man away from me."

CHAPTER FIFTY-NINE

Rowley spotted the Beast on the side of the road and urged Rio on. "There. Ahead I can see lights."

The headlights of Rio's SUV picked up Jenna leaning against the barn, her head turned away from the glare. He leapt from the vehicle and ran toward her surprised when his usually cool and calm sheriff fell into his arms sobbing on his shoulder. "Hey, Jenna. It's okay, backup has arrived."

"Dave's real bad. He might not make it." Jenna looked up at him, her cheeks showing wet in the moonlight. "Stabbed twice. Lord, the knife was still in his chest." She sucked in a breath. "Have you heard anything?"

"He's critical and went straight into surgery. Wolfe is in there observing, he wouldn't leave him." Rio rounded the hood and stood hands on hips. "Carter called just before, he's at the hospital and will keep us updated but if it's good news, it's going to be hours."

"Okay." Jenna straightened, gave her head a shake and seemed to pull herself together. "These are youth offenders and must be treated as such. They're both over sixteen and will likely be charged as adults but for now we stick to protocol. We can't hold them for more than twenty-four hours so we'll be waking up a youth court judge and the DA. I have enough evidence to charge them both and we have a witness. Vicky Perez is alive, cut and burned but she'll be okay physically. I've notified her father. The poor man was still waiting with Deputy Walters at Aunt Betty's. He's heading to the hospital now."

Rowley smiled at her. "I knew you'd crack the case." He followed her inside the barn and his flashlight hit the row of pompoms on the shelf. "Did you notice the pompoms?"

"No." Jenna stared at them. "Bag them before we leave. The prisoners are through there." She indicated toward a glowing light.

Rowley winced at the pool of blood in the stall. "Is there any other evidence you need from here?"

"Not now. We'll tape the front and leave it. Wolfe will need to do a forensics sweep. The red pickup Collins used to transport the victim is outside but I've been in it and contaminated any evidence." Jenna pushed her hair from her face with bloodstained hands. "Get the prisoners loaded and give me and Duke a ride back to the Beast."

Concerned by Jenna's pale face and big wide eyes, Rowley escorted Moore and Collins out to the SUV and secured them in the back seat. After bagging the pompoms, he went to the red pickup and shut down the engine and then walked back to Jenna. "I figure I should drive the Beast. You don't look so good."

"Sure." She gave him a sideways glance. "Just don't tell Dave I allowed you to drive his baby."

Rowley laughed. "Okay." He lifted Duke into the back and patted him. "Good dog."

After he slid in beside Jenna they bounced back to the Beast and changed vehicles. He had to admit to himself the idea of driving Kane's pride and joy was daunting but he found the Beast handled better than expected and they were soon on the highway. He turned to Jenna. "I have some information to tie up a loose end in the case."

"Go on." Jenna leaned back. "I need cheering up."

"We couldn't figure out how come different vehicles were seen on the nights the victims went missing." He looked at her. "When Rio and Carter realized it had to be Dale Collins and Marlene Moore, they looked a little deeper. Dale Collins' father owns the car yard in town and Dale goes there every morning to clean the cars with a couple of other kids. But his father allows him to take any car off the lot to drive for the day. He used the vehicles to throw us a red herring and when he took them back, the vehicles went through a car wash and the interior was steam cleaned. No evidence."

"So, if we go through the inventory, we'll likely find the vehicles used in the murders." Jenna had come to life. "That's brilliant."

Rowley nodded. "Yeah and the kids were pretty smart too. They knew how to conceal evidence but I'd like to know if Collins was involved in Mrs. Turner's murder."

"Not the murder, no." Jenna sighed. "I have a confession on video. Collins admitted to being patient 124 and assisting Dr. Turner with his wife's body. The doctor is going down for his wife's murder and this evidence will seal his fate."

Rowley headed down Main. "What about Laurie, Becky, and the assault on my wife?"

"No, he claims innocence." Jenna shrugged. "Kane believed Collins was a subordinate to a dominant killer, he went along to appease a girl he loved. I'll ask Jo to interview him, he's waived his rights. She'll know the right questions to ask. I don't believe he's a psychopath. He seemed genuinely remorseful about Kane getting hurt. Marlene was the opposite." She glanced at him. "She won't break, I figure our only way to find out the truth is to hope Jo can persuade Collins to roll over on Marlene. If the DA offers a deal, he might comply but he's not going to walk. He kidnapped three girls, that's enough on its own for jail time."

Rowley pulled up outside the sheriff's department. "You'll need a statement from Vicky Perez. Do you want me to go to the hospital and see if I can speak to her?"

"Not tonight." Jenna jumped down from the truck and collected Duke. "She's traumatized. If the doctor says it's okay, we'll talk to her in the morning." She held her hands out for the keys to the truck. "Start the paperwork on the prisoners, notify the DA and the kids' parents. Maybe just call Collins' father, he doesn't want his mom involved. The prisoners can stay in the cells overnight. We'll deal with them in the morning. Call in a couple of the Blackwater deputies to stay here in shifts. I'm going to take a shower and change. I can't sit here waiting for news."

"I'll drive you to the hospital." Rio jumped out of his cruiser. "We can manage here."

"Thanks, but I'll drive the Beast." Jenna nodded. "I need to be there whatever the outcome." She looked at Rowley. "See if you can contact Atohi, he needs to know about Kane."

"I'm on it." Rowley watched her walk through the doors, head held high, Duke on her heels, and then he walked to Rio's cruiser to assist with the prisoners.

"She's one tough lady." Rio stared after her.

Rowley shook his head. "On the outside maybe but on the inside, she has a heart of gold."

EPILOGUE

Sunday

Kane woke in a world of pain and from under his lashes made out Wolfe leaning over him. He tried to speak but nothing came out of his mouth. Another face he didn't recognize peered down at him and then the pain subsided and he floated away into oblivion. It was like twilight the next time he opened his eyes. He had to be hallucinating and blinked twice before trying to focus on a blue balloon floating at the end of his bed. He moved one arm, and pain shot through him like a thousand hot blades. He gasped and scanned the room from beneath his eyelashes. The light inside the room was dim but he could make out the usual paraphernalia of a hospital room. Something was in his hand and his fingers curled around warm flesh. He turned his head to find Jenna resting in a recliner, curled up in a blanket and fast asleep. He squeezed her fingers and her eyes popped open. "Hey."

"You scared the hell out of me." Jenna reached for the call button. "The doctor will want to know you're awake."

He shook his head. "Not yet. How long have I been out?"

"It's five-thirty, Sunday morning." Jenna yawned and stretched like a cat. "Carter brought you here in the chopper and I figure Wolfe saved your life. He was pumping blood into you all the way here. You're still in town, they didn't have time to take you to Walter Reed. The doc will explain what happened but they had to work on you for hours and then they kept you sedated. The girl nicked an artery so it was a big operation and the hunting knife was embedded in your sternum, so you're going to be sore for a while." She squeezed his hand. "Do you know, Wolfe refused to leave your side? He only went home last night. He's been living in this room and we've been taking shifts."

"Thank you. I'm sure pleased to see you." Kane smiled at her. "Wolfe cares but he's also following protocol. I might have said something in a drug-induced state and he carries out orders to the letter."

"He was worried sick." Jenna pushed a hand through her hair. "He knew you were in terrible pain but you were so weak, he kept arguing with the doctor that too much morphine would kill you." She chewed on her bottom lip. "Do you remember anything at all?"

Kane took in her tousled hair and sleep filled eyes. "Yeah, Marlene Moore dropped out of the hayloft, I made the mistake of catching her, and she stabbed me. I didn't feel a thing." He sucked in a painful breath. "I figured the vest had caught the hunting knife. They're designed to solidify around a sharp blade so I wasn't too worried. The puncture wound I didn't notice until I saw the blood." He sighed. "I guess she got me under the arm. Did you find the knife?"

"Yeah, Webber and Emily went over the barn for evidence. There wasn't too much there at all." She smiled. "But they found two perfect fingerprints and they were a match for Laurie Turner. We know they murdered her there and then transported her to the mines. They used different vehicles Collins borrowed from his father's car yard and that's why we couldn't get a lead."

Astonished, Kane nodded. "So, are they in custody?"

"Yeah, they're in a youth detention facility." Jenna rested her elbows on the edge of his bed. "Collins waived his rights and Jo interviewed him, she explained his options and what would happen under the law. He decided to roll over on Marlene and Dr. Turner.

He admitted to hitting Becky twice as Marlene was strangling her and felt guilty but insisted Marlene killed Laurie. It was all Marlene's idea. He denied even knowing Sandy was in the house at the time of Becky's murder and we believe him. Sandy only heard one person. We figure Marlene attacked her before Collins arrived with Becky."

Kane swallowed but his mouth was dry. As if reading his mind, Jenna held a cup and straw to his lips. He drank and thanked her. "What conclusion did Jo come up with on the kids?"

"Collins has a dominating mother, he is useless to her and like his father, in her eyes." Jenna refilled the water and placed the cup within reach. "When his father left, he had no one to control her and it did something to him. Jo said he craved affection, so would do whatever Marlene wanted to get her approval. Like you said, typical subordinate to a dominant killer. He didn't like killing but it pleased his girlfriend so he went along with it."

"Yeah, that sums it up." Kane ran a hand over his face and winced at the stubble. "And Marlene?"

"Abused as a kid by men she trusted." Jenna's eyes narrowed. "She was probably born a psychopath and just needed a trigger. She didn't trust men, so made Collins prove he loved her by making him her partner in crime. She took trophies, we found the murdered girls' missing pompoms in the barn."

"Classic case." Kane bit back his next words as a person entered the room carrying the usual hospital breakfast and left without a word. He scanned the plate and pushed it away in disgust.

"You okay?" Jenna looked concerned. "At least drink the orange juice. You haven't eaten in days."

Kane squeezed her hand. "I'll be fine. It hurts some but I hate hospital food. I could sure go a pile of pancakes, strips of bacon and maple syrup from Aunt Betty's."

"Me too." She pulled out her phone and placed an order. "They'll have it here in no time but I should check with the doctor first."

He grinned. "There's nothing wrong with my stomach and I'd like these tubes removed but first, tell me about Dr. Turner."

"Oh, we have his case sewn up too." She smiled. "He's such an arrogant ass. You should have seen his face when we told him patient 124 had told us everything. Even Sam Cross couldn't get him out on bail this time. Turner is in county awaiting trial."

Kane yawned. "That's good and Vicky Perez?"

"She's fine. She needed plastic surgery for the cut on her face but she went home. She'll testify in court against Bonnie and Clyde." Jenna smiled at him. "Just to tie up any loose ends, Mr. Law is remaining in county to await his trial and his wife and child are safe and well. She'll remain under the protection of Her Broken Wings Foundation, until they find her work and a place to stay. You can rest easy; all the cases are closed."

Kane sighed with relief. Now he could relax. "That's great. Have Carter and Jo returned to Snakeskin Gully?"

"No, they're still in town. They didn't want to leave until they knew you were okay." Jenna smiled. "So, expect visitors soon." She leaned closer. "Do you recall, the night you were stabbed, you were trying to tell me something before you passed out. Can you remember what it was, it's been driving me nuts?"

The image of her terrified face was imprinted on his brain. He nodded. "Yeah, I remember. You looked so worried, I wanted to tell you I was okay and we'd make it through, we always do."

"And you were right. You're too darn stubborn to die." She smiled.

Kane rolled his eyes to the ceiling. "Darn, we missed the Fall Festival dance again."

"But I did bring flowers for my date." Jenna giggled.

Early morning sunlight streamed through the blinds and he took in the vase of flowers with the bright blue balloon at the end of his bed. There was a message on the balloon and it read: *It's a boy!* He chuckled. "Uh-huh."

"They'd run out of, 'Get Well Soon' balloons and it's the thought that counts, right?" Jenna laughed, and her eyes sparkled with mischief.

Kane squeezed her hand. "I'll treasure it forever."

A LETTER FROM D.K. HOOD

Dear Reader,

Thank you so much for choosing my novel and coming with me on another thrilling adventure with Kane and Alton in *Be Mine Forever*.

If you loved this book and would like to stay up to date with all of my new releases, sign up here for my mailing list. You can unsubscribe at any time and your details will never be shared.

www.bookouture.com/dk-hood

Writing this story about teenage killers opened a new dimension in my research into the criminal mind. It would seem killers come in all shapes and sizes.

If you enjoyed my story, I would be very grateful if you could leave a review and recommend my book to your friends and family. I really love hearing from readers so feel free to ask me questions at any time. You can get in touch on my Facebook page or Twitter.

Thank you so much for your support.
D.K. Hood

 @DKHood_Author

 dkhoodauthor

 www.dkhood.com

 dkhood-author.blogspot.com.au

ACKNOWLEDGMENTS

There were so many behind the scenes people to thank in creating this story.

My husband, Gary, who is my sounding post for many of the complicated scenes in this story.

Team Bookouture, you know who you are but to mention a few—Helen, my rock, who guides me along the right path; Alex, who makes sure my work is perfect; the amazing team behind the audiobooks; and my wonderful narrator Patricia Rodriguez.

Noelle Holten, who goes the extra mile for me on release days, and Kim and Sarah, who are always there to promote my books.

The promotions and advertising team, who never let me down.

The reviewers and wonderful people who host me on their blogs and last but by no means least my fantastic readers, and those who support me on social media—what an amazing group of people.

Thank you everyone.
D.K. Hood